BOUND BY DARKNESS

"Admit the truth. You want me."

His commanding words were imprisoned against his lips as she once again claimed his mouth in a kiss that demanded capitulation. He was prepared to react to her touch, but the sheer power of it caught him off guard.

God, yes. This was precisely what he'd wanted from the first minute he'd caught sight of this female stalking him.

He pressed her against the mattress, drinking in the cool enticement that was uniquely Jaelyn. And still she was not close enough. He growled deep in his throat as he reached down to grasp her top and with one tug ripped it over her head.

"You're so beautiful," he whispered in aching tones.

With a whimper, Jaelyn shifted beneath him, wrapping her legs around his hips.

"This is insanity," she muttered.

He lifted his head to meet her glittering gaze. "Do you want me to stop?"

"Stop and I'll kill you," she rasped.

"Then tell me what you want, Jaelyn."

"You." She trembled as he kissed his way over the curve of her ear. "I want you."

"Now?"

"Yes . . ."

Books by Alexandra Ivy

WHEN DARKNESS COMES

EMBRACE THE DARKNESS

DARKNESS EVERLASTING

DARKNESS REVEALED

DARKNESS UNLEASHED

BEYOND THE DARKNESS

DEVOURED BY DARKNESS

BOUND BY DARKNESS

And don't miss these Guardians of Eternity novellas

TAKEN BY DARKNESS in
YOURS FOR ETERNITY

DARKNESS ETERNAL in
SUPERNATURAL

WHERE DARKNESS LIVES in
THE REAL WEREWIVES OF
VAMPIRE COUNTY

Published by Kensington Publishing Corporation

Bound by Darkness

Guardians of Eternity

ALEXANDRA IVY

ZEBRA BOOKS
KENSINGTON PUBLISHING CORP.
http://www.kensingtonbooks.com

ZEBRA BOOKS are published by

Kensington Publishing Corp.
119 West 40th Street
New York, NY 10018

All Kensington titles, imprints, and distributed lines are available at special quantity discounts for bulk purchases for sales promotion, premiums, fund-raising, educational, or institutional use.

Special book excerpts or customized printings can also be created to fit specific needs. For details, write or phone the office of the Kensington Special Sales Manager: Attn. Special Sales Department. Kensington Publishing Corp., 119 West 40th Street, New York, NY 10018. Phone: 1-800-221-2647.

Zebra and the Z logo Reg. U.S. Pat. & TM Off.

ISBN-13: 978-1-4201-1136-1
ISBN-10: 1-4201-1136-1

First Printing: December 2011

10 9 8 7 6 5 4 3 2 1

Printed in the United States of America

Flesh of flesh, blood of blood, bound in darkness.
The alpha and omega shall be torn asunder
and through the mist reunited.
Pathways that have been hidden will be found
and the veils parted to the faithful.
The Gemini will rise and
chaos shall rule for all eternity.

—Sylvermyst Prophecy

Chapter 1

Santiago's Club
Located on the Mississippi River midway between
Chicago and St. Louis

Mother Nature never intended for vamps and Weres to live in peace. And she sure the hell never intended them to enjoy the sort of you're-my-bestest-pal bromances that were the current flavor of the month among humans. A damned good thing considering that just being in the same territory tended to send the two predatory species into a homicidal rage.

But the looming end of the world truly did make for strange bedfellows, and with the potential return of the Dark Lord from the hell dimension where he'd been banished centuries ago, both the Anasso of the Vampires and the King of the Werewolves had little option but to try and work together.

Well, the phrase "work together" might be a generous description of their uneasy truce, Styx acknowledged, leaning his six-foot-five frame against the walnut desk in his fellow vampire Santiago's office. Dressed in his usual assortment of black leather pants, shit-kicker boots, and silk shirt that stretched over his massive shoulders, he looked exactly what he was: the badass leader of the vampire clans. But it was the grim power etched into the Aztec beauty of his face and the ruthless intelligence in his dark eyes that made wise demons shudder in fear. Styx was more than an oversized bully. He was cunning and patient and capable of compromise when necessary.

Which was the only reason he was standing in the same room with a damned dog.

The tiny turquoise ornaments threaded through the braid that hung nearly to the back of his knees tinkled as he gave a rueful shake of his head, his gaze keeping careful track of his companion.

As much as he hated to admit it, Salvatore fit the elegant office—with its slate-gray carpet and the museum-quality French Impressionist paintings that were hung on the paneled walls and carefully preserved behind glass cases— far better than he did.

The bastard always managed to look every inch the king with his dark hair slicked back in a tail and his muscular body clothed in a charcoal-gray suit that no doubt cost more than the gross national income of several small countries. Like Styx, however, there was no mistaking the brutal authority in Salvatore's dark, Latin features and golden eyes.

He ruled a savage race that would quite literally rip apart and eat a weak king. It gave a whole new meaning to "Uneasy is the head that wears the crown."

The Were paused to study the bank of high-tech monitors and surveillance equipment that would give Homeland Security wet dreams, his gaze lingering on the monitor that revealed a pair of near-identical female Weres with blond hair and green eyes seated at a table several levels below them.

"You're certain that this place is safe?"

Styx snorted. The fact that he was mated to the Were sister of Salvatore's mate did nothing to ease the tension between them. Not after the bastard had done his best to kidnap Darcy from Styx.

Of course, he did have a small (very small) amount of sympathy for Salvatore's predicament. At the time his Weres were facing extinction, and in an effort to save his people he had genetically altered four Were female pups. After they were stolen the king had sworn to retrieve them. It was his bad luck that Darcy and another of the females, Regan, had both chosen to mate with vampires, although his frustrated fury had been eased when he had found a third sister, Harley, and she'd managed to bring back the ancient mating urges that had been lost to the Weres for centuries.

"Be happy that Santiago isn't around," he warned. Although the club that catered to the demons scattered around the Illinois countryside was technically owned by Viper, clan chief of Chicago, it was Santiago's pride and joy. "He would take your lack of faith in his security as a personal insult. And an unhappy vampire is never good."

"I could say the same thing about a happy vampire," Salvatore drawled, turning to flash Styx a mocking grin.

"You were the one who asked for this meeting."

The dog shrugged. "Harley misses her sister."

Styx believed him. Although it had only been three weeks since Salvatore and Harley had left Chicago for St. Louis, the two sisters had become nearly inseparable since they'd been reunited. But he was also certain that he hadn't been asked along for his sparkling personality.

"And the reunion of our mates offers the opportunity for us to speak without alerting the world to our meeting?"

Salvatore shrugged. "I prefer not to attract any pesky curiosity."

"You have information?"

"No, only questions."

"Shit." Styx grimaced. "I was afraid you were going to say that. What's your question?"

"Have your Ravens managed to track down Caine and Cassandra?"

Styx tensed at the unexpected question. It was no secret that Cassandra was the last of the missing Were sisters who'd been unexpectedly located in the caves of a demon lord. And who was now on the run with a cur who'd been magically transformed into a full-blooded Were while rescuing the female. The movement of his personal bodyguards, however, was classified information.

"What makes you think I'm looking for them?"

Salvatore arched a taunting brow. "Just because I'm beautiful it doesn't mean I'm stupid."

"It does, however, mean you're a pain in the ass."

"Jealous?"

Styx curled back his lips to reveal his massive fangs. "Increasingly hungry."

There was a prickle of danger as the power of the two alphas swirled through the air. The frigid blast of vampire slammed against the raw heat of Were, promising a violent explosion if released.

Then, with a low growl, Salvatore was leashing his wolf, the mocking smile returning to his lips.

"I know that Darcy is anxious to meet her missing sister, and since the demon world is well aware you are firmly wrapped around her finger it was a logical assumption that you would have your goons on the hunt."

Styx nodded, hoping for Salvatore's sake it had been an educated guess. He was prepared to work with the Weres to prevent the end of the world, but he'd be damned if the lice-infested bastards were going to have spies in his camp.

"Just as you have released the hounds?" he demanded.

There was a short pause before Salvatore gave a grudging nod of his head, no more happy to share intel than Styx.

"I'll admit that I sent Hess and a few of my trusted lieutenants to have a chat with Caine."

"And?"

"And they claim that he and Cassandra have vanished into thin air." The lean face hardened with annoyance. "If I didn't know they were the finest trackers in existence I would have had them skinned for either being incompetent or liars."

"And you want to know if my Ravens have had any more success?"

"Yes."

"Hess speaks the truth," Styx admitted, referring to Salvatore's right-hand man. "Jagr was able to track Caine to a lair outside Chicago, and while he couldn't enter the house past the hexes the cur has placed around the yard, all signs are that they simply disappeared."

Salvatore cursed, not bothering to pester Styx with stupid questions. Jagr was Styx's finest Raven and if he said the trail ended, it ended.

"Magic?" he instead asked.

"The trail was too cold to say for certain."

Salvatore returned to his pacing. "Dammit."

"I take it that Harley isn't going to be pleased with the news?" he taunted, pleased to be able to point out that Salvatore was equally at the mercy of his mate.

"No more pleased than Darcy." The Were shook his head, his body tense. "But it's not just being able to return Cassandra to her sisters. Or even discovering what the hell turned Caine from a mangy cur to a pureblooded Were."

"What's troubling you?"

"What isn't?" His humorless laughter echoed through the office. "Nasty creatures that we thought were gone from the world forever are crawling out of the woodwork." The Were glared at Styx as if it were entirely his fault that the streets were suddenly overrun with demons that were supposed to have been banished. Including the damned Sylvermyst (evil cousins to the fey), who made a grand entrance just a few weeks ago and promptly caused Tane's rescue of Laylah and her child to go to hell. "And it seems like every week there's a new plot to return the Dark Lord."

Styx pushed away from the desk, savage anger racing through him. "Some of them coming too damned close for comfort."

"Exactly." Salvatore waved a slander hand. "And we have the babies that supposedly fulfill some stupid mysterious prophecy."

The words of the foretelling flared through Styx's mind. He'd devoted the past weeks to discovering everything he could of the prophecy. And most importantly, trying to discover what the hell it might mean.

"Don't be so dismissive, Were," he growled. "I'm old enough to know the dangers of ignoring such potent warnings."

"Trust me, leech, I'm not dismissive." The gold eyes suddenly glowed with his inner wolf. "Not after that demon lord nearly managed to destroy my people. All the omens point to the barriers between dimensions thinning, which is precisely why I'm so concerned for Cassandra."

Styx's lips twisted, realizing Salvatore's mind had followed his own path. And that they'd both been chasing down the female Were for the same purpose.

A Were with a brain. Hell, the world truly was going insane.

"Because she's a prophet." It was a statement, not a question.

Salvatore dipped his head in agreement. "The first true prophet in centuries. Her disappearance at this time can't be a coincidence."

"No." Styx curled his hands at his side. The implication of her absence was already giving him nightmares. "She would be a priceless weapon to whoever has access to her powers."

"We need your Hunter. She's the only one with the skill to find Cassandra."

Styx hissed at the mention of the missing vampire. For all her youth, Jaelyn was the finest Hunter to have been trained in the past century. Unfortunately, she'd been kidnapped three weeks ago by Ariyal, a Sylvermyst prince.

Damn his black heart.

"Jaelyn's still missing."

"The Sylvermyst?"

"That's our guess, but we have no way of knowing for certain."

They both paused as they silently accepted that Jaelyn could be dead. Just another casualty in the increasingly dangerous war.

Salvatore stepped forward, his face hard with concern.

"Something wicked this way comes, vampire," he warned, "and we had damned well better be prepared."

Styx nodded. For the rare moment they were in perfect agreement.

"Yes."

Morgana le Fey might be dead, but her opulent palace on the isle of Avalon remained intact.

Okay, not *fully* intact.

More than one room was on the wrong side of tattered. And the grand throne room had been blown to hell, but the vast harems had escaped the majority of the damage during Morgana's last, great battle.

A damned shame.

Not just because the sprawling rooms designed with mosaic tiles, marble fountains, and domed ceilings looked like something from a cheesy *Arabian Nights* film set (although that was reason enough to burn the gaudy piece of crap to the ground) but because Ariyal had spent more centuries than he cared to remember in the harem trapped as a slave.

It had been a well-guarded secret that a handful of Sylvermyst had turned their backs on their master, the Dark Lord. They'd bargained with Morgana le Fey to keep them hidden among the mists of Avalon in return for them satisfying her insatiable lust for men and pain.

Not necessarily in that order.

Unfortunately Ariyal had been a favorite of the sadistic bitch.

She'd been fascinated by the metallic sheen of his bronzed eyes and his long chestnut hair. But it'd been the lean, chiseled muscles of his body that she'd devoted hours to exploring. And torturing.

With a low growl he shook off the unpleasant memories.

Instead he concentrated on the female who was currently enjoying the nasty surprises hidden among the velvet divans and exquisite tapestries.

Well, maybe enjoyment wasn't what she was feeling, he acknowledged in amusement, watching as she slowly came awake to discover she was chained to the wall by silver shackles.

Jaelyn, the vampire pain-in-his-ass, let loose a string of foul curses, not seeming to appreciate that he'd carefully protected her skin with leather to keep the silver from searing her flesh, or that he'd chosen one of the rooms that was specifically built to protect bloodsuckers from the small amount of sunlight that filtered through the surrounding mists.

In fact, it looked like the only thing she was in the mood to appreciate was ripping out his throat with her pearly-white fangs.

A treacherous heat raced through his body.

He told himself it was a predictable reaction.

She was stunning, even if she was a leech.

Tall and athletically slender, she was a mixture of races that combined into an exotic beauty.

Glossy black hair that spoke of the Far East was contained in a tight braid that hung down her back. The Asian influence was echoed in the shape of her eyes, although they were a dark shade of blue that revealed a European heritage. Her skin was as pale as alabaster and so perfectly smooth that he ached to brush his fingers over it.

From head to toe. And back again.

Add in the black spandex that clung to her slender curves and the sawed-off shotgun that he'd been smart enough to take off her long before they'd stepped through the portal, and she was a custom-made fantasy.

Hunter.

Lethal beauty.

Yep, there wasn't a man alive (or maybe even dead) who wouldn't give his right nut to get between those long slender legs.

But Ariyal hadn't been able to completely forget that shocking awareness that had jolted to life during his brief incarceration at the hands of this female.

Hell, her merest touch had made him go up in flames.

And it pissed him off.

Unlike most of his brethren, he didn't allow his passions to rule his life.

He ruled his passions.

A grim reminder that didn't do a damned thing to stop the heat that scorched through his blood as her indigo gaze skimmed over his lean body, which he'd left bare except for a loose pair of dojo pants.

Bloody hell.

His gut tightened and his cock hardened. From a mere glance.

What the hell would happen if he spread her across the nearby bed and . . .

The vampire stiffened, no doubt sensing his explosive desire. Then, with a visible effort, she narrowed those magnificent eyes and wrapped herself in a frigid composure.

"You." The word was coated in ice.

"Me."

She stood proudly, acting as if she didn't notice she was currently chained to the wall.

"Why did you kidnap me?"

He shrugged, not about to admit the truth.

He didn't have a goddamned clue why he'd grabbed hold of her as he escaped through the portal that had brought them from the frozen caves of Siberia to this hidden island. He only knew his reaction to the female was dark and primal and dangerously possessive.

"You held me captive," he instead drawled. "Fair is fair."

"As if a Sylvermyst would know the meaning of fair."

His smile held no apology. "Haven't you heard the old saying that 'all's fair in love and war'?" He allowed his gaze to lower to the enticing curve of her breasts, lust jolting through him at her revealing shiver. "We could no doubt add a few more activities to the list."

"Release me."

"What's wrong, poppet? Are you afraid I intend to have my evil way with you?" He deliberately paused. "Or hopeful?"

"You at least got the evil part right."

He stepped close enough to be teased by her seductive musk that was at such odds with her image of a cold, ruthless hunter.

But then, everything about this female was . . . complex.

Contrary.

"You know, there's no reason for the two of us to be enemies."

"Nothing beyond the fact that I was hired by the Oracles to capture you." Her smile was frigid. "Oh yeah, and your psycho attempts to kill two helpless children."

"Helpless?" Frustration flared through him. "Those abominations are the vessels of the Dark Lord and if Tearloch manages to use the child to resurrect the master then you can blame yourself for unleashing hell."

She ignored his warning. Just as she'd ignored it in the Siberian cave when he'd done his best to put an end to the danger.

He'd been prepared to do what was necessary, but because of the damned vampires, one of the babies had been stolen by his clan brother Tearloch, along with the mage. Now he had to pray he could track them down before they could resurrect the Dark Lord and rip open the veils that held back the hordes of hell.

"I'm not being paid to save the world. I'm being paid to hand your ass over to the Commission."

Ariyal frowned at the unwelcome reminder.

The Commission was a collection of Oracles who were the big cheeses of the demon world. It was always bad news when they decided you were worthy of their notice.

Especially if they were willing to pay the exorbitant fee to hire a vampire Hunter to collect him.

"Why?"

"Don't know. Don't care. It's just a job."

He leaned forward until they were nose to nose. "It feels a lot more personal than just a job."

For a breathless moment raw hunger flared through her eyes, making his body clench with anticipation. Oh, hell yes. Then, just as swiftly, the glimpse of emotion was gone.

"Get over yourself."

"I'd rather be over you."

"Back. Off."

Ariyal shivered at the sharp chill that suddenly blasted through the air.

Dammit. One minute the woman had him drowning in lust and the next she could give a fire pixie frostbite.

"Fine." He stepped back, his smile tight with annoyance. "I hope you're comfortable, poppet. You're here to stay."

Her wary glance skimmed around the room that was ornately decorated in shades of gold and ivory.

"Where is here?"

"Avalon."

She hissed in shock. "Impossible."

"Such a dangerous word."

"The mists are impenetrable." Her cold arrogance remained, but there was a hint of wariness in her eyes. "Unless they were destroyed by the death of Morgana le Fey?"

His lips twisted in a humorless smile. "They survived, but I didn't waste centuries as the bitch's sex slave just looking beautiful. I discovered a secret exit centuries ago."

She studied him in silence and Ariyal hid a sudden grimace. A Hunter had any number of skills. They were reputedly stronger and faster than the average vampire, as well as able to shroud themselves so deeply in shadows that they were all but invisible.

More impressive, they were walking, talking lie detectors. Supposedly no demon could deceive them.

Like he needed that kind of headache.

Christ. He should have left her in Siberia.

"If you knew how to escape the island, then why didn't you?" she demanded.

"Because I couldn't rescue my brothers without alerting the guards."

"So you stayed?"

He frowned, puzzled by her curiosity. "I wasn't leaving them behind. Does that surprise you?"

An unreadable emotion rippled over her beautiful face before it was swiftly wiped away.

"Sylvermysts aren't renowned for their generous hearts or noble natures. As Tearloch proved."

Ariyal couldn't argue.

Sylvermyst had a long, well-earned reputation for their cruel natures and hunger for violence, but he'd be damned if he allowed a cold-hearted leech to judge him.

Not after everything he'd sacrificed to save his people.

"Tearloch's frightened and . . . confused," he admitted. "Once I track him down I'll convince him of the error of his ways."

"You mean, he'll do as you want or you'll kill him?"

"Ah, you understand me so well, poppet."

"I understand that you're a bastard who is out to save your own worthless skin," she charged.

"Good. Then I don't have to convince you that I will happily leave you here to rot unless you agree to do exactly as I say."

A frigid smile curved her lips. "Don't be a moron. If I disappear the Anasso will send out a dozen warriors to search for me."

"He can send out a hundred if he wants. They'll never be able to sense you behind the mists." His gaze lingered on her lush, full lips, easily imagining the pleasure they could bring a man. With a growl, he took an instinctive step closer, ignoring the danger. "Face it, poppet, they already assume you're dead."

"Then they'll hunt you down and execute you. There's nowhere you can go they won't find you."

He grasped her chin, staring down at the eyes that had lost their ice to flash with indigo fire. His gut twisted with need.

"I spent centuries in the harem of Morgana le Fey. Leeches don't scare me."

"What does scare you?"

"This . . ."

Ignoring the fangs that could rip out his throat with one swipe, not to mention the claws that could dig through solid concrete, Ariyal leaned forward and claimed her mouth in a kiss of pure possession.

Mine . . .

Chapter 2

Jaelyn was never taken by surprise.

Never.

She was a Hunter. A vigilant, razor-sharp warrior with such superior skills that she'd been taken by the Addonexus (the vampire equivalent of black ops) mere weeks after she'd been turned.

And even with her natural skills, she'd still been trained for years before being allowed to leave the secret compound.

Tracking, weapons, martial arts, psychological warfare, and the latest tech (including being able to hack into a military-grade computer system) had been drilled into her with brutal efficiency over the past fifty years.

But this damned Sylvermyst had kept her flat-footed and constantly one step behind him.

She wanted to believe it was some mystic fey crap.

After all, a vampire's one vulnerability was magic, and since it was believed that the Sylvermyst had been banished along with their master, the Dark Lord, she'd never been taught what sort of nefarious tricks Ariyal might be hiding behind his too-pretty face.

It would explain how he'd managed to escape from an iron-lined cell after she'd captured him. And how he could catch her off guard to yank her through a portal and bring her to this godforsaken island.

And how he could claim her lips in a kiss that shut down her brain, as well as most of her higher motor skills.

His mouth was deliciously warm, demanding a response, and for a crazed moment she allowed the blinding pleasure to sear through her, the tips of her toes curling in her boots. It was only when she was actually swaying toward the hard temptation of his body that she was wrenched out of the strange spell.

Oh . . . shit.

This wasn't a spell.

It was good, old-fashioned lust that had sizzled between them since that first, jolting touch. Or perhaps it had been from the moment she'd caught his rich, earthy scent that was a combination of herbs and pure male power.

Not that the when or how mattered.

She might not have been trained to deal with dark fey magic, but she'd sure the hell been drilled in controlling her baser instincts.

Nothing like being skinned alive a few times to teach a young vampire to keep her mind on business.

With a low hiss, she jerked her head to the side, her fangs snapping toward his throat.

Ariyal cursed as he leaped backward, his stunning bronze eyes widening as he realized how easily she could have ripped open his flesh.

"Damn."

"Find someone else to play with, fairy," she warned, eying him with a proud defiance despite the fact she was currently chained to the stupid wall. And oh yeah, that she had nearly melted into a puddle of need beneath his kiss. "I bite."

"Sylvermyst," he corrected, his gaze lingering on her swollen lips. "And I bite back."

The thought of his perfect white teeth clamping onto her neck sent a dangerous thrill down her spine. Freaking fey. She clenched her hands at her sides, allowing her nails to slice into her palm. Pain was the swiftest means to regain command of her body.

"What do you intend to do with me?"

He smiled with wicked amusement at the ice edging her words.

"That depends on you."

She narrowed her gaze. "You think I'll barter for my freedom?"

He reached to run a slender finger down the curve of her neck.

"We're about to discover, aren't we?"

"Stop that," she growled, baring her fangs.

"You don't like to be touched?"

"I like it just fine." She flicked a dismissive gaze over his indecently beautiful face. "Just not by you."

"Lie," he breathed, gently mocking her own ability to read the deceptions of others.

Her lips thinned. "Tell me what you want from me."

"What I want?" The bronze eyes darkened with raw desire. "I want that hard, sculpted body spread naked on my bed so I can taste every perfect inch."

Her nails dug deeper, the blood running down her palm. "Never."

"Fine." His low voice brushed over her sensitive skin like a caress. "Then I'll be naked and you can use those lovely lips to wrap around my . . ."

"Is your bargain that I trade sex for my release?" she sharply interrupted.

His gaze briefly shifted down to the small curve of her breasts outlined by the tight spandex.

"Oh, I intend to give you release." His gaze lifted to meet her frigid stare. "But you'll have to earn your freedom."

She snorted. "Do males of all species possess a juvenile need to use sexual innuendoes rather than rational conversation when they're in the company of women?"

"Those weren't innuendoes, poppet," he drawled. "They were a promise."

She forced herself to meet his taunting gaze with a cold indifference that she could only wish was genuine. Dammit, she was a Hunter, not a wilting virgin who was terrified of a man's touch. Even if it did make her shiver with need.

Her duty was to use whatever method necessary to get free and complete her mission.

Period.

"I asked a specific question. Will you allow me to leave if I give you sex?"

He stilled, caught off guard by her blunt demand. "And if I say yes?"

"It's against the rules. But . . ."

"What rules?"

"Hunters aren't permitted to be intimate with their prey."

"Sensible, I suppose." He folded his arms over his broad chest, acting like he was more curious than excited by her proposal. Rude, conceited fairy. "What if I weren't your prey?"

"Intimacy is generally discouraged."

His unnerving gaze searched her icy expression, as if sensing the dark, punishing memories that fluttered at the edge of her mind.

"Discouraged?"

"Sex is an unnecessary distraction at best and a lethal mistake at worse."

He tilted his head to the side at her practiced words, the light from the candles glowing with a rich shade of chestnut in the loose strands of his hair. Jaelyn clenched her teeth, struck by a sharp need to run her fingers through the satin length.

His lip curled into a slow, wicked smile. "I can scent your hunger."

"Of course you can. It's been days since I fed." Her arctic dismissal salved her pride, but it did nothing to disguise her body's annoying response. "Although, I'm more likely to die of boredom than starvation if you don't release me soon. Are we going to bargain or not?"

Ariyal chuckled, not deceived for a moment. Bastard.

"We are."

"For sex?"

He shook his head, his gaze taking a slow, intimate survey of her rigid body.

"When I claim you as my lover, Jaelyn, you won't be able to hide behind the pretense that it's to fulfill some damned bargain."

His silky warning slid through her like warm honey, melting another layer of her icy defenses. Ah, it would be so easy to close her eyes and imagine his slender fingers skimming over her naked skin, his muscled body pressing her into the nearby mattress as his mouth sought those erogenous spots she tried to pretend didn't exist.

Worse, she couldn't deny the realization that she was disappointed . . . *disappointed* . . . that he didn't intend to trade the use of her body in exchange for her freedom.

Lord, she needed to get away from this man.

The sooner the better.

"Then what do you want?"

His gaze returned to clash with her icy glare. "Your skills as a Hunter."

"As a Hunter?"

He shrugged. "To be more specific, as a tracker."

She wasn't insulted.

What did she care if he was more interested in her warrior training than her female charms?

To be actually wanted as a woman . . .

That was madness.

Insanity.

Yeah. That's what it was.

"You want me to find Tearloch?" she demanded between clenched teeth.

"Yes."

"Aren't you supposed to be some kind of prince?" she mocked.

A startling hint of pain briefly flared in the bronzed eyes. "I am."

"Then shouldn't you have the skills to hunt down one of your own minions?"

With a restless shrug, Ariyal turned to pace across the mosaic tiled floor, his fluid grace a reminder that beneath his taunting manner was a lethal predator. One of the very few who could match her for strength and cunning.

He reached the priceless tapestry that covered the far wall, his gaze momentarily resting on the stitched vision of Morgana le Fey mounted on a horse as she led an army of fey into some long-forgotten war, before he turned to stab her with a frown.

"It wouldn't be a problem if it was just Tearloch I had to worry about," he muttered. "Unfortunately he's the least of my problems."

Jaelyn recalled the moments in the frozen cave before Ariyal's tribesman had made his unexpected appearance.

At the time, Laylah (a Jinn mongrel) had been busy killing Marika (the psychotic vampire who intended to become mother or perhaps it had been a creepy queen consort to the Dark Lord once he was reborn), while Marika's pet mage, Sergei, had been removing the stasis spell that had been wrapped around the child Laylah had discovered hidden between dimensions. His efforts had revealed that there wasn't one babe, but two. A boy and girl.

It was no big surprise that in the middle of the confusion

Tearloch would manage to capture the mage who had been clutching the female child and disappear with him through a portal before he could be stopped.

"You mean his companion?" she asked with a curl of her lip. She hated mages. Nasty vermin. "Vampires are incapable of sensing magic. If Sergei is hiding your tribesman I would be worse than useless in trying to track him."

Ariyal waved a dismissive hand. "If they're still together I know precisely where to find Sergei. I was with Marika long enough to become familiar with her devoted mage. He's nothing if not predictable."

Annoyance pricked her heart at the reminder that Ariyal had once offered his loyalty to the beautiful vampire who was infamous for her insatiable lust.

Had he offered anything beyond his loyalty?

And why the hell did it matter?

"Then what do you need from me?" she snapped.

"I'm a Sylvermyst."

"Yeah, I got the memo."

His brow arched at her foul temper. "Did the memo also include the fact that I'm not the most popular demon on the block?"

"I figured that out all on my own." She bared her fangs. "Did you want me to kill you and put you out of your misery?"

He prowled back toward her, halting just out of reach.

Clever fairy.

"Actually, poppet, I want you to keep me alive."

Ariyal watched as Jaelyn narrowed her eyes in genuine confusion.

"You said nothing could find us here," she reminded him, her eyes closing as she no doubt used her Hunter senses to search through the vast, broken palace and across the large island. She muttered a curse, wrenching open her eyes, and Ariyal easily guessed that the swirling mists were screwing with her powers. They were a genuine pain in the ass. "Is there an enemy on the island?"

He sucked in a deep breath, his body instantly hardening at the biting scent of female power. A shudder raced through him. What was it about this female?

She had the tongue of a viper, the temper of a pregnant harpy, and worst of all, she was a damned leech.

But there was no denying that she set him on fire.

"No, we're completely alone," he said, reluctantly shoving aside the vivid fantasies that threatened to derail his plans for the day. "But as much as I might like to stay here and play, I have to find Tearloch before he can resurrect the Dark Lord. Once I leave the mists I'm going to be the target of every damned demon who wants to mount my head on their trophy wall."

"I'm a Hunter, not a magician," she mocked. "I can't perform miracles."

He heaved a sigh. Hell, he should have bargained for the sex.

"There's only a handful of demons who would dare to try and challenge me, and most I can defeat even if I'm out-numbered."

She made a sound of disgust. "Arrogant."

"No, it's the simple truth." He met her gaze squarely. "And I'm willing to admit that I'm not invulnerable. I won't allow pride to stop me from bartering for someone to guard my back while I'm busy stopping the apocalypse."

"What makes you think I won't plant a knife in your back instead of protecting it?"

Excellent question.

Not quite as excellent as questioning why the hell he had offered the dumb-ass bargain to begin with.

Granted, he was the equivalent of Kim Jong-il among

the demon world, but he possessed the skill to travel without attracting unwanted attention. And he hadn't boasted of his power to overcome all but a rare few enemies. With any luck at all he could retrieve Tearloch and the babe before anyone realized what was happening.

The last thing he needed was to drag along a feral vampire who distracted him on a cellular level.

But the thought of leaving without her, or worse, allowing her to simply walk away, was unacceptable.

"Because the good guys are so disgustingly concerned with their honor." A self-derisive smile twisted his lips. "Once you give your word you won't be able to break it."

Her beautiful face was unreadable as she stood with that eerie stillness that only a vampire could achieve.

"You've forgotten one important point."

"And that is?"

"I've already given my word to the Oracles and more importantly, the Addonexus has already been paid for my services. They own my loyalty." The indigo eyes had frosted over, hiding the passion that burned beneath. That was fine. He knew it was there, just waiting for him. "At least until the job is done."

He shook off the warning. The reason the rulers of the demon world had contributed the money and effort to hiring a Hunter to capture him was yet another thing he wasn't going to burn any brain cells on.

If he didn't intend to get caught, then what did it matter?

"The job ended the moment I pulled you through the portal," he informed her, reaching to wrap a strand of her black hair around his finger. "I won and now you're in my power."

She jerked her head back, and Ariyal swallowed a groan at the feel of the cool silk of her hair moving against his skin. Just the thought of being naked with Jaelyn saddling his hips and that ebony mane brushing his chest was enough to make him painfully hard.

"You haven't won until I'm dead," she hissed.

"Now that would be a waste." His brooding gaze lowered to the full lips that could send a man to paradise. "Accept my bargain, Jaelyn, and make both of us happy."

If he hadn't possessed the heightened senses of a powerful fey, he wouldn't have caught the dilation of her eyes, or the faint flare of her nostrils as she reacted to the scent of his desire.

"No."

"Then you will remain my prisoner."

"You can't hold me captive forever."

He couldn't help but smile at her unmitigated arrogance. Typical leech.

No, not typical, a voice whispered in the back of his head.

Even among vampires she was . . . astonishing. Special.

"You might manage to free yourself from the chains, but you can't escape Avalon." He nodded his head to the thick mists that were visible through the heavily shaded window. "And there's something else you should know."

"What?"

"Time moves differently within the mists."

She frowned, easily sensing the truth of his warning. "How differently?"

"It's never constant," he admitted. It was his theory that the mists that Morgana had created were similar to the mists that ran between dimensions that the Jinn used to travel. It would explain why time ran differently from the outside world. "A few hours might have passed since we arrived on Avalon or it could be several weeks."

"Then why did you bring us here?" she demanded in frustration. "For all you know Sergei has already resurrected the Dark Lord."

He shuddered. This female was too young to have any memory of the Dark Lord or his loathsome hordes of minions.

Otherwise she would never speak of his return as if it were nothing more than an inconvenience.

"We would know if the gates of hell had been opened," he assured her dryly. "And it was the one place I could keep you hidden from your fellow leeches."

Too late he realized just what he'd revealed.

"You risked the end of the world just to take me hostage?"

Abruptly turning to hide his discomfort, he paced to stare out the door that opened to the attached baths. He grimaced as he realized the shallow pools were still filled with the scented waters that Morgana had demanded her sex slaves use to wash in before coming to her bed.

"I told you, I need someone to watch my back," he snapped, his voice suddenly harsh.

"Don't you have a tribe roaming around nearby?"

"They attract precisely the sort of attention I'm hoping to avoid."

"And?"

He turned to meet her disbelieving gaze. "There is no 'and.'"

The chain rattled as she took an impatient step forward, clearly sensing he was not being entirely honest.

"Yes, there is."

"Damn, that's annoying," he muttered.

"Then release me."

Not a chance in hell.

His gaze skimmed over the hard lines of her body. She was like a sleek greyhound. All muscle and grace.

And his.

He shook off the disturbing thought, concentrating on a half-truth that would satisfy her freakish, insanely annoying talent.

"I'm not entirely certain that Tearloch's madness is an isolated incident."

She was thankfully distracted. "You think it's infectious?"

"No, but the veils between the worlds are thinning, increasing the opportunity for the Dark Lord to touch the minds of others." Regret that he hadn't prevented the darkness attacking Tearloch sliced through his heart. Yeah, he was quite the prince, wasn't he? "And unfortunately it's impossible to detect his influence until too late."

A strange emotion rippled over her exquisite face before she was abruptly turning to stare at the far tapestry.

Sympathy?

Not bloody likely.

Not from his cold-hearted Hunter.

"How do you know that I'm not under some Jedi mind control?" she mocked, proving her indifference.

"Vampires are impervious to such tricks," he growled. "Not to mention the fact you're too irritatingly stubborn for the Dark Lord to bother with."

Her lips thinned. "No."

"No, you're not stubborn?"

"No, I don't accept your bargain."

He surged forward, ignoring the danger as he grasped her shoulders and forced her to meet his fierce glower.

"You're willing to remain trapped here as my prisoner?"

Her chin tilted. "Yes."

"Why?" He searched the indigo eyes. "Because I'm an evil Sylvermyst?"

"That's one of many reasons."

"And the others?"

"I refuse to stand aside while you slaughter an innocent child."

His fingers dug into her flesh before he forced himself to ease his grip. Logically he understood she was an immortal vampire who could kick his ass given a chance, but towering above her slender form, he couldn't ignore how fragile her bones felt beneath his hands.

And how screwed up was that?

"Not a child," he gritted. "A vessel created by the Dark Lord."

"That has yet to be determined."

He growled. What did he have to do to convince the demon world that the babe had one purpose and one purpose only? Let Tearloch and Sergei destroy this dimension?

"Fine," he rasped. "What if I promise merely to capture the babe and return it here where I can protect it?"

She refused to back down. Predictable.

"Even if I was foolish enough to trust you, which I'm not, I'm still bound by my contract with the Oracles."

His hands traced the line of her shoulders and down the sleek muscles of her arms. His gut clenched at the cool slide of her creamy skin beneath his palm.

"I don't believe you'll turn me over to the Commission," he said, his voice thickening.

She stiffened, but oddly she didn't pull away from his lingering touch.

"Why wouldn't I?"

"Because you couldn't bear to have me destroyed."

She made a sound of disgust. "I can't decide whether you're just arrogant or suicidal."

"Experienced." A wicked smile curved his lips at her faint tremor. "I know enough about females to recognize when one is desperate for my touch."

She took a sharp step away, her expression defiant. "Definitely suicidal."

He pulled in a deep breath that did nothing to ease his throbbing erection; then with a muttered curse, he was headed toward the door.

To hell with it.

It was obvious that Jaelyn intended to remain an uncooperative pain in the ass.

"I don't have time for this."

"Where are you going?"

His steps never faltered. "Things to do, people to see."

"When will you return?"

He headed out the door, refusing to give in to the impulse to glance over his shoulder. She would be there waiting for him when he was done with Tearloch.

"The question, poppet, is not when I'll return," he taunted, "but *whether* I'll return."

There was a rattle of chains followed by a low, wholly feminine hiss of fury.

"Damn you."

Chapter 3

London, England

Dusk shrouded the narrow streets of London as the two men halted near a high hedge.

One was a slender, impossibly beautiful man with skin the color of rich cream and long copper hair he kept tamed in a tight braid. He might have passed for human if not for the metallic shimmer to the sterling silver eyes, and thick scent of herbs that clung to his tattered robe, which blended into the green bushes behind him.

The other was equally slender, although he didn't possess the same unearthly grace, or beauty. He was of an indeterminate age with high Slavic cheekbones, and an icy blue gaze that held a cunning intelligence. And under normal circumstances he was stylishly dressed in a Gucci suit with his shoulder-length silver hair smoothed from his narrow face.

But these were far from normal circumstances.

After nearly three weeks hiding in the Florida swamps, Sergei Krakov was tired, filthy, and wishing to the gods he'd never become involved with the child he held in his arms.

Well, at least he was home now, he silently attempted to

ease his raw nerves, heaving a sigh as his gaze ran over the eighteenth-century terrace house near Green Park.

The historical society claimed the building had been designed by Robert Adam. And pedestrians often halted to gawk at the classic beauty of the aging bricks, the elegant portico, and the tall windows with carved stone swags set above them. A brave few had even attempted to catch a glimpse through the door at the carved marble staircases and grand rooms that were filled with Chippendale furniture and priceless works of art.

A mistake that often led to their deaths when Marika-the-vampire had used the house as her lair.

With a curse, Sergei shut down any thought of his previous mistress.

It wasn't because he was horrified at the memory of watching the vampire female have her head chopped off by her own niece. After four centuries of being the bitch's whipping boy, he was happy as hell to see her turned into a pile of ash.

But for all her vicious temper and addiction to causing pain, she had been a powerful partner in crime. What demon was stupid enough to cross a vampire who was teetering on the edge of insanity? She was definitely a "kill first and ask questions later" kind of gal.

Now he was without her protection, which might have been fine if he'd been allowed to escape the Russian caves without having to barter for his safe passage with yet another lunatic, this time a crazed Sylvermyst, and a child who had been created by the most evil of all evils.

Perfect.

On cue, Tearloch poked him with the tip of the massive sword he was never without. Not even in his sleep.

Which was the only reason that Sergei hadn't tried to strangle the bastard before now.

Or turned him into a frog.

"What is this place?" the dark fey demanded.

"Civilization." Sergei breathed in the damp air. Summer had arrived, but the fog remained. *Ah, good ol' London.* "You're welcome to skulk around in the filthy swamps, but I've had enough. I want a bath and a bed with satin sheets."

"Pampered human," Tearloch sneered, his gaze roaming over the line of tidy houses. "These walls make you weak."

"Mage, not human," Sergei corrected in cold tones, allowing the air to fill with a hint of his magic. "And I don't need to live like an animal to prove my powers." He deliberately paused. "Do I?"

The fey snorted, although he made no effort to prove his superiority.

At the moment the two men were precariously balanced between hate and need. One misstep and they would erupt into violence that might very well leave them both dead.

"Does Ariyal know of this lair?" he instead demanded.

"What does it matter?" Sergei shrugged. "The vamps are obviously holding him hostage or he would already have tracked us down."

The silver eyes narrowed. "Don't be so certain. There could be any number of reasons he has not yet come in pursuit."

At last convinced that the house was empty and that no enemies lurked among the shadows, Sergei tucked the motionless child beneath his ragged jacket and crossed the street.

"If you're scared of the traitor then feel free to return to the muck," he muttered.

Predictably Tearloch was directly on his heels.

"I'm not leaving without the child."

"Then it would seem we're at a stalemate."

Sergei climbed the steps and muttered words of magic beneath his breath. There was a faint click before the door swung open. He stepped into the black-and-white-tiled foyer, reluctantly waiting for Tearloch to join him before he shut the door and reset the spell of warding.

Nothing would be able to enter the house without alerting him.

Then, climbing the curved marble staircase, he headed directly for a back nursery that was dusty from disuse. Crossing the Aubusson carpet that matched the pale yellow and lavender upholstery, he set the child in the hand-carved cradle. The babe didn't stir, her eyes remaining firmly shut.

So far as Sergei could tell the child was still under the stasis spell that had kept her and her twin brother unchanged and impervious to the world for centuries.

Tearloch glanced down at the child, but he was wise enough not to try and touch her.

Sergei had wrapped the babe in a blanket that held a powerful curse. A Sylvermyst, or any fairy for that matter, foolish enough to try and steal the child would suffer excruciating pain.

"When do you intend to perform the ceremony?" the fey demanded.

Sergei grimaced.

Never sounded good to him.

A damned shame that he was caught between the proverbial rock and hard place.

Once upon a time he'd been stupid enough to believe he was destined for greatness, but after years of being exposed to Marika's cruelty he'd realized that infesting the world with a horde of creatures that made her look like a Girl Scout wasn't exactly a future to covet.

But while Tearloch hadn't tried to take the child from him, Sergei hadn't lived so long by being a moron. He knew that he was only alive because the Sylvermyst was depending on him to cast the spell that would resurrect the Dark Lord's soul into the child. If he refused . . .

Well, he didn't intend to discover what would happen.

"I told you, I need to wait for the signs to align so I will be at my greatest strength," he said, desperate to put off the inevitable.

Tearloch eyed him with blatant suspicion. "I begin to suspect that these mysterious signs are no more than an attempt to avoid fulfilling your duty."

"Do you truly want to take the chance of ruining your best shot at returning your master—"

"*Our* master."

"Because I'm not at the pinnacle of my power?" Sergei continued, ignoring the harsh correction.

Tearloch muttered a foreign word of power that made the air stir with a prickle of warning.

"You have until the full moon."

"Is that a threat?" Sergei demanded at his most imperious.

In the less of the blink of an eye the tip of the massive sword was digging into Sergei's throat, the Sylvermyst leaning forward until they were nose to nose.

"Yes."

Sergei heard the sizzle as the strange blade absorbed the drop of blood from the pinprick wound in his throat. Then the fey was spinning away and heading out the door.

"Crazy bastard," Sergei muttered.

It took Jaelyn nearly an hour and several layers of skin to at last wrestle out of the chains that held her captive. Once free, she gingerly inched her way out of the harems, her senses on full alert.

Damn, but the place was a disaster.

Shattered glass, crumbling stone walls, and missing dome ceilings that allowed the swirling mist to creep through the vast spiderweb of chambers.

She shuddered to imagine the power necessary to create such damage, even as she cursed Ariyal for having abandoned her on the godforsaken island.

Not only was she forced to constantly retrace her steps to avoid the seemingly perpetual sunlight that pierced the mists at unexpected junctures, but the endless series of corridors seemed to lead from one dead end to another.

Was it true?

Was it possible that she was trapped on Avalon?

Halting before an arched door with odd carvings that blocked her current path, she was debating the best means of destroying the heavy iron lock when she felt the air pressure shift behind her.

"I would not stray too far, Hunter," a low female voice warned. "Morgana le Fay had a nasty habit of leaving traps for the unwary."

"Holy . . ." Spinning on her heel, Jaelyn flashed her fangs at the intruder. Expecting a massive demon who would match the crushing flare of energy that filled the dark corridor, she was caught off guard by the tiny female, who was no larger than a child, with a heart-shaped face and long silver hair that was pulled into a braid that hung nearly to the tiled floor. She frowned. The black almond eyes and razor-sharp teeth appeared remarkably similar to those of the spirit whom Ariyal had summoned to hold Jaelyn captive in the Russian caves, as did the long white robe. But this female appeared older. Oh yeah, and not a spirit. "Yannah?"

The female stepped forward, her hands folded neatly at her waist.

"No, I am Siljar." She paused. "An Oracle."

Ah. Of course. An Oracle would explain the deluge of power that battered against her.

Jaelyn hastily fell to her knees, her head bowed. Although she hadn't been personally approached by the Commission when she was hired to track down Ariyal, she'd been schooled in the proper etiquette.

It was the same etiquette that a person used when

confronted by any lethal predator who could kill you with a thought.

"Forgive me." Jaelyn kept her head lowered. "You startled me."

"Yes, you did appear to be preoccupied."

Wondering how long the female had been watching, Jaelyn carefully glanced upward.

"I was attempting to escape."

"Hmm." The female tilted her head to one side. "I fear there is no means of escaping Avalon without fey blood."

"You're fey?"

She instantly regretted the impulsive question as Siljar wrinkled her nose in visible disgust.

"Certainly not." Her brief annoyance was replaced by a sudden smile as she gave a wave of her hand, indicating that Jaelyn could rise. "But I am impervious to Morgana's magic, which means I can come and go as I please. A fact that used to infuriate the woman."

Jaelyn cautiously straightened, not foolish enough to believe that the danger had passed.

Oracles didn't drop by for idle chitchat.

"You were acquainted with Morgana le Fay?" She politely kept the conversation ball rolling.

The smile widened to emphasize the razor-sharp teeth. "I had the pleasure of reminding her that she was not above the laws of the Commission."

"From what I've heard the Queen of Bitches thought she should be ruling the world. I can't imagine she was happy to be reminded she had to obey the laws."

"It's true our little visits tended to sour her mood." The woman heaved a small sigh. "A pity she did not heed my warnings."

Jaelyn glanced toward the crumbling walls. There had been endless rumors concerning Morgana's last battle, but no one seemed willing to reveal what had actually happened to the woman.

"Is she dead?"

"Worse."

"What—" Jaelyn abruptly bit off her question. "No, I don't want to know."

"A wise choice." The Oracle's black, unblinking gaze held a hint of warning. "I have discovered that curiosity does indeed kill the cat."

Yow. Jaelyn squashed her lingering questions, fiercely reminding herself that for once she wasn't the baddest, scariest thing in the room.

Not the happiest thought when she had to accept there was only one reason that an Oracle would seek her out.

She cleared her throat, forcing herself to stand with her spine straight and her shoulders squared.

"Ariyal mentioned that time passes differently here."

"It does."

"What's the date?"

Siljar immediately understood her question.

"Three weeks have passed since you entered the mists."

"Damn." She'd missed her deadline. It didn't matter that she'd been jerked onto an island wrapped in mystical mists that altered time. Or that there was a looming apocalypse. She'd been given three months by the Addonexus to track down Ariyal. And the head honchos of vampire hunters didn't accept excuses. "I have failed to fulfill our contract."

"The Sylvermyst is proving to be surprisingly resourceful," Siljar agreed.

Resourceful?

"He's a pain in the ass," she muttered.

"A male is allowed to be a pain in the ass when he is so wondrously gorgeous," Siljar murmured, shocking Jaelyn. "It's a pity I'm not a few millennia younger."

Jaelyn wisely kept her thoughts to herself. She had all the troubles she needed, thank you very much.

"Do you want me to return to the Addonexus?"

Siljar paused, as if puzzled by the question. "Why would I want such a thing?"

"The Ruah will send another Hunter to complete the contract," she explained, referring to the traditional leader of the council.

"So you can be executed?"

Jaelyn shrugged. "My fate is irrelevant."

"I must disagree." Pressing her palms together, Siljar stepped forward, her unrelenting stare starting to make Jaelyn twitch with unease. "Your fate has become of utmost importance. As has Ariyal's."

Jaelyn knew she should be grateful that Siljar wasn't in a hurry to have her executed. No matter what her training, she wasn't anxious to take one for the team. But her spidey senses were tingling, warning her that she wasn't going to like where this conversation was going.

"I don't understand."

"Neither do I," the Oracle bluntly admitted. "The threads are shifting."

Jaelyn wasn't sure what bothered her the most.

The fact that the Oracle was baffled, or that she seemed to be implying that Jaelyn was a part of her confusion.

"Threads?"

Siljar gave a wave of her hand. "I am not a true seer, but I am capable of occasional visions, and more importantly I can detect those individuals who are to be woven into destiny to fulfill those visions."

Jaelyn took a hasty step backward. "You can't mean . . ."

"You, Jaelyn." She paused. *Dramatic effect, anyone?* "And Ariyal."

Shit, shit, shit.

"That's impossible."

"Ah, the cold logic of a vampire." Siljar smiled, but there was no missing the warning in the dark eyes. She didn't like Jaelyn arguing. "But denying your fate will not alter it."

"You can see my future?"

"No, as I said, I am not a seer," Siljar reminded her, "but I do know that you are a thread."

Jaelyn clenched her hands at her sides. "Is that why the Commission hired me to track down Ariyal?"

"No, when you were requested to bring the Sylvermyst before the Commission it was to question his intentions in remaining in this dimension rather than joining his brethren with their master." A punishing energy swirled through the air as the demon's eyes glowed with a sudden silver light before returning to black pools of mystery. "But the fabric of the future is changing and your destiny has been irrevocably entwined with Ariyal."

Shaken by the glimpse of power contained within the tiny demon, Jaelyn chose her words with care.

"How can the future change?"

There was a long silence. As if the Oracle was debating the wisdom of sharing insider info. Then she gave a small shrug.

"There is always a certain measure of fluidity in matters of time, but it is more chaotic than usual."

"Do I want to know why, or is that one of those 'curiosity kills the cat' things?"

"It indicates that there will soon be a powerful flux in the universe."

Jaelyn grimaced, wishing that she hadn't asked. Or that the demon hadn't answered.

Or . . .

Hell. She scrubbed a hand over her weary face. She was tired, hungry, and wishing she could get a hold of Ariyal and kick his ass. This might not be entirely his responsibility, but she was willing to blame him.

"The return of the Dark Lord?" she hazarded.

Siljar considered before giving a shrug. "It is impossible to say."

Yeah, sooooo not helping.

She shifted her concern from the looming end of the world to her own looming end.

"Well, if the future is in flux then maybe my elevation to being some mystical thread is nothing more than a cosmic glitch that will soon be forgotten."

Siljar cocked her head to the side, her expression curious.

"I thought Hunters were fearless?"

Jaelyn snorted. "Facing death is one thing; knowing I'm a part of destiny is quite another."

"Is it destiny that troubles you?" She flashed her pointed teeth. "Or Ariyal?"

Was the woman *trying* to piss her off?

"It would seem they're one and the same," she muttered.

"Very true," the demon agreed with a shrug of indifference. Then she gave a lift of her tiny hands. "Well, I must go."

"Go?" Jaelyn took a hasty step forward. "Wait."

"Yes?"

"Do you intend to leave me here?"

Siljar slowly blinked, like a lizard.

"Oh, did I not say?"

"Say what?"

"The terms of our contract have been altered."

Oh . . . crap.

Why did she suspect that the alteration didn't include a one-way ticket to Maui to hunt fire pixies?

"You no longer want me to capture the Sylvermyst?" she asked, ever the optimist.

Or maybe it was sheer desperation.

"No."

"Oh." She didn't bother to hide her relief. "Thank the gods."

"I want you to remain with him and keep the Commission informed of his movements."

Remain with him? Her brief moment of hope was crushed beneath a tidal wave of horrified disbelief.

It was bad enough to hunt down the damned Sylvermyst and haul him to the Commission. But to become Hutch to his Starsky?

Oh hell, no.

"Why?"

Pinpricks of pain stabbed deep into Jaelyn's flesh, effective reminders that nasty rumors whispered about the Oracles were well earned.

"I have no need to explain."

"Forgive me. I will, of course, do everything in my power to fulfill our contract." She returned to her knees, bowing her head as she waited for the brutal pain to dissipate. "How much of a head start does he have on me?"

"Three days."

Jaelyn grimaced. For her it had only been two hours since Ariyal had disappeared.

Damned mists.

"Do you know . . ." She swallowed her question, and almost her tongue, as there was a loud *pop* and a small demon who looked nearly identical to Siljar made a sudden appearance, standing at the side of the older woman. "Holy crap!"

Siljar motioned to the familiar woman with the heart-shaped face and long gold hair that was pulled into a braid.

"This is Yannah, my daughter."

"Yeah, we've met." Jaelyn returned to her feet, her gaze never leaving the tiny demon who had helped Ariyal hold

Jaelyn captive while they were in the Russian caves. "But at the time I thought she was a spirit that Ariyal conjured."

"Such a yummy fairy." Yannah heaved a dreamy sigh. "How could I resist?"

Jaelyn blinked. *Good . . . God.*

Did Ariyal have this sort of effect on every female he met? No wonder he was such an arrogant SOB.

"Yes, she can be quite naughty," Siljar gently chided. "But she will be able to assist you."

Naughty? That wasn't the word Jaelyn would have used. But then again, she'd already pissed off Siljar more than was healthy. She wasn't about to insult her daughter.

"I welcome any assistance she can offer," she instead muttered.

Yep. Just call her Queen of Diplomats.

"She will take you to Ariyal," Siljar informed her. "She will also be the one who will be responsible for contacting you to retrieve the information you have gathered."

Jaelyn made one last bid for escape. "There are others who are trained in the arts of espionage. . . ."

"You have been chosen, Jaelyn," Siljar pronounced, her expression unyielding.

If Jaelyn could have sighed, she would have. Instead she gave a grudging nod.

"So, I'm to spy on Ariyal and report my findings to Yannah?"

"It is more than keeping track of his movements," Siljar corrected.

"More?"

"We must know the contents of his heart."

Jaelyn frowned. "I can sense the souls of humans, but I'm not an empath who is capable of reading demons."

Siljar shrugged. "Remain close enough and you'll be capable of detecting the taint of the Dark Lord."

For no logical reason, Jaelyn found herself annoyed by the Oracle's words.

"I don't like the bastard, but I can assure you that he hasn't been infected," she growled. "He's determined to sacrifice the missing child rather than allow his evil master to be reborn."

"That is his plan for the moment," Siljar agreed. "It is vital that he is not swayed into . . ."

"Switching teams," Yannah finished for her.

Siljar smiled and patted her daughter on the head. As if she'd just performed a remarkable trick.

"Yes. Switching teams."

Jaelyn understood their concern. Ariyal had admitted that he feared the Sylvermyst might be susceptible to the Dark Lord's influence. And obviously Tearloch had already fallen victim to the madness.

But that didn't make her the best choice to fulfill the contract.

In fact, she was fairly certain she was the last person who should be taking on the delicate task.

She wasn't subtle, or sneaky, and she sure the hell wasn't tactful.

She was a Hunter who knew how to track and kill.

End of story.

"There's no guarantee that he'll let me stay with him," she warned.

For some reason her muttered words made Siljar chuckle. "I'm confident in your ability to convince him, my dear," she assured her, turning her attention to the tiny demon at her side. "Are you ready, Yannah?"

The younger demon appeared far from happy. "If I must."

Siljar folded her arms over her chest, her expression one of universal parental warning.

"And do try to behave yourself, child."

"Fine."

Yannah wrinkled her nose, giving a wave of her small hand. Instantly the air shimmered next to Jaelyn. As a vampire she couldn't sense magic, but she knew a portal when she saw one.

"Wait," she hissed, attempting to back away. She had feet for a reason. There was no need to be zapping from one place to another.

She had barely taken a step, however, when Yannah was behind her, planting her hands on Jaelyn's ass and giving her a rough shove forward.

"In you go."

It shouldn't be possible for the tiny female to manhandle a vampire, but Jaelyn found herself tumbling into the shimmering air before she could regain her balance.

"No . . . dammit."

Blackness surrounded her and Jaelyn knew that she was being magically transported to another location, but she could sense nothing. And that was worse than if she was being tortured by a horde of Copaka demons.

At last she was jerked from the strange nothingness and, falling forward, she barely got her hands stretched out before she did a face-plant.

She felt the skin being ripped off her palms as she hit the damp pavement, but as she rose to her feet she was far more concerned with the knowledge that she'd just been dumped into the middle of London. And that she wasn't alone.

Baring her fangs she whirled to study the narrow street that was shrouded in shadows.

It was just past midnight, she easily determined, and most of the humans were safely tucked in the expensive townhouses that lined the road. In the distance she could sense a park with dew fairies dancing among the trees, and a handful of hellhounds sniffing along the Thames River, but it was the thick scent of herbs that had her bracing herself for the slender male form that barreled from behind a hedge to knock her back to the ground.

Unable to rip out his heart or suck him dry, Jaelyn was forced to allow the damned Sylvermyst to cover her with his hard body, a large silver dagger pressed to her throat.

At least that's what she told her battered pride.

Perched above her, Ariyal's bronzed eyes widened in shock. Then a wicked amusement suddenly shimmered in the streetlights.

"Jaelyn?"

"This job is really starting to piss me off."

Chapter 4

Ariyal didn't believe in Santa Claus.

If a fat man in a red suit snuck into his lair he would slice off the bastard's head.

But he had to assume there was some magic involved in beautiful vampires appearing out of thin air.

Especially when it was this particular beautiful vampire.

That was a gift any man could appreciate.

For a crazed moment, he simply savored the sensation of her slim body pressed beneath him. God, it had been so long since he'd felt genuine desire.

Not since Morgana le Bitch had taken him into her harem.

Now his body was determined to make up for lost time.

Still, for all his rampaging desire, he wasn't so lost to reason that he didn't recall this female posed an extreme danger to him.

"How the hell did you get here?" he growled, keeping the knife poised near her throat even as he made certain it didn't mar the perfection of her alabaster skin.

Her hands pressed against his chest, but she made no attempt to kill him.

Progress.

"Get off me, you ass," she hissed.

"Not until I'm certain you don't intend to alert all of London to our presence."

Something that might have been embarrassment at her less than graceful entrance rippled over her starkly beautiful face before she was glaring at him in outrage.

"Don't blame me. It was your little spirit who dumped me here."

"Spirit?"

"Yannah."

He scowled. He had occasionally conjured a spirit who went by the name of Yannah, but she wouldn't be able to enter Avalon. And certainly she couldn't have brought Jaelyn to London.

"Spirits are incapable of forming portals."

"Spooks are your specialty, not mine," she muttered, her expression abruptly shuttered. "All I know is that she made an unexpected appearance in Avalon and shoved me through a portal. Next thing I knew I was making a face-first landing in London."

She was lying.

He was certain of that much.

The question was whether anything she told him was the truth.

"I sensed there was something different about Yannah when I summoned her from the underworld," he at last admitted.

"Obviously you should be more careful when you're inviting in creatures from hell," she taunted.

Yeah, he wasn't going to argue with her logic.

"I was distracted at the time, if you'll recall. And it was you who allowed her to escape before I could properly banish her."

"Whatever." She refused to meet his gaze. "Now will you get off of me?"

Damn. What the hell was she hiding from him?

"Spirit or not, why would Yannah follow us to Avalon and then conveniently be around to help you escape?"

There was a barely perceptible pause. "She owed me for releasing her from your bondage. I called in my debt."

"I don't believe you."

She struggled, the sensation of her hard muscles squirming against him nearly sending him up in flames. Holy shit. If only he could turn all that pent-up aggression to passion she'd be naked and riding him like a bucking bronco.

The image burned into his brain, making him so hard and ready he feared he might explode.

"Tough," she growled.

He ground his teeth. Dammit, he wouldn't let himself be distracted.

At least, not without the promise of satisfaction.

"Why did you follow me here?"

"You know why."

He smiled without humor, pressing his aching arousal against her hip.

"Tempting, but I'm afraid you'll have to wait to have your wicked way with my body," he mocked. "At least until I've halted Armageddon."

Her eyes flashed with indigo fire, her struggles becoming serious.

"My only interest in your body is hauling it to the Commission."

He pressed the knife against her throat, refusing to regret the smell of burning flesh.

If she tried to take him to the Commission then he'd have to do a hell of a lot worse than singe a bit of skin.

"Wrong answer."

"Shit, that burns."

"Hold still and you won't be hurt," he informed her, lifting his free hand to form a portal.

Instantly the familiar shimmer floated beside him. No other fairy could match his speed in forming a portal. Or his tolerance to iron.

Which were only two of many reasons he'd been chosen to lead his people.

Jaelyn froze, her gaze trained on the magical opening that hung near her head.

"What are you doing?"

"Returning you to Avalon." His gaze narrowed. "And this time I will make certain no one will be coming to your rescue."

She cursed, grudgingly turning her head to meet his ruthless gaze.

"Wait."

"Why should I?"

"We . . ." She looked like she'd swallowed a lemon. ". . . might be able to negotiate."

Instinctively he lifted the dagger from her neck, absently watching her skin heal the small burn.

He should return her to Avalon. No ifs, ands, or freaking buts. The odds were that she was either there to haul his ass to the Commission.

Or kill him.

Neither possibility was particularly pleasant.

Still, he hesitated.

Wasn't there some human saying about keeping your friends close and your enemies closer?

It was surely wiser to have her in sight until he discovered how she truly had escaped from Avalon?

Dubious logic, but he was going with it.

"Another bargain, poppet?"

"Something like that."

His gaze lowered to the small breasts perfectly outlined by the black spandex.

"What do you intend to offer?"

She growled, but amazingly she made no effort to sink her pearly fangs into his arm. In fact, her mouth curled into what he assumed was intended to be a smile, although it was remarkably closer to the onset of rigor mortis.

"I'm willing to give you a few days to track down Tearloch," she managed to choke out. "If you swear you will only capture the child and not sacrifice her."

Curiouser and curiouser.

"Why?"

"I won't help you kill an innocent."

He pressed the blade back to her neck. "Don't play stupid."

She snapped her fangs, barely missing his fingers. "Careful, fey."

"Earlier you refused to even discuss my need to stop Tearloch and Sergei," he reminded her. "What changed?"

She shifted until the blade was no longer burning her skin, her raven braid spilling across the damp pavement.

"I'm no more anxious than you for the world to end. Especially if it means becoming enslaved by the minions of hell."

Ariyal shook his head. "You really are a terrible liar, poppet."

She made a sound of impatience. "Look, I've offered to give you the time you need to track down your tribesman. What does it matter why?"

"Because I don't trust you."

She met him glare for glare. "Believe me, the feeling is entirely mutual."

"I should return you to Avalon."

Something that might have been panic flared through her eyes before she was crushing it beneath a layer of ice.

"I'll only escape again," she warned in frigid tones. "And the next time I won't hesitate to haul your ass to the Commission."

Ariyal silently cursed.

He was an idiot.

His tribe had suffered untold pain and humiliation to be rid of their ties to the Dark Lord. He couldn't afford to be distracted now that there was a chance the brutal bastard might be returned to this world.

The sensible solution would be to kill the perilously tempting vampire. Or at the very least to return her to Avalon and lock her in the lower harems where *nothing* could escape.

Instead, he was going to keep her with him.

What choice did he have? There wasn't any place he could put her, not even in her grave, where she wouldn't be nagging at his thoughts.

"You swear not to interfere?" he rasped.

"Not unless you try to kill the child."

"Bloody hell, I know I'm going to regret this," he muttered, rising to his feet, although he kept the dagger handy.

Jaelyn was upright and angrily tossing back her long braid in less than a heartbeat.

"You and me both."

Still fully aroused from the feel of her body beneath him and furious with his odd compulsion to have her near, Ariyal grasped her upper arm and jerked her across the road.

"Let's go."

"Go?" She scowled, but allowed herself to be led toward the back of the looming townhouses. "Where?"

"If you insist on hanging around then you can at least make yourself useful."

Her lips parted to offer a scathing comment, only to snap shut as they came to a halt near a servants' entrance.

"The mage," she said, her hand instinctively reaching for the shotgun that she usually carried strapped to her side. She glared at him when she came up empty. "And he's brewing something."

He nodded, catching the sweet scent drifting through the air.

"Yes."

"It smells . . ." She blinked in surprise. ". . . good."

"Fey."

"What?"

Ariyal breathed in deeply. "The plants he's using are grown only by the fey."

Her surprise hardened to suspicion. "Do you know what he's concocting?"

He shrugged. "I would guess it's a potion used to keep him from aging. Mages are humans and must use magical herbs to make them immortal."

The suspicion remained.

No big surprise.

"You're sure it's not a spell he's about to cast?"

"He's a dark mage."

"Yeah, I got that," she snapped impatiently. "All the more likely he's about to create some nasty potion, right?"

He studied her pale, perfect face. It was impossible to determine a vampire's age. Jaelyn could be a few decades old or several millennia. But he suspected that she was barely out of her foundling years, despite her skills as a Hunter. There were too many gaps in her knowledge for her to be an ancient.

"His power comes from blood." He wrinkled his nose in disgust. Blood magic was a perverted form of true magic. "Either his own or that of a sacrifice."

Her gaze weighed his open revulsion toward Sergei. "And your power?" she demanded.

"A gift from nature."

It was the truth, and yet Jaelyn's gaze narrowed as she sensed he was keeping something hidden.

"There's more."

He hesitated. He preferred to keep a few of his lesser-known skills . . . lesser known. It was, after all, his secret tolerance to iron that had allowed him to escape from Jaelyn just days ago.

Who the hell knew when he might need another surprise or two?

But her expression warned that she wasn't going to stop nagging until she was satisfied with his answer.

Dammit.

"When necessary I can draw on the powers of others," he admitted between clenched teeth.

She stiffened. "How exactly does that work?"

"Relax, poppet," he assured her dryly. "It'll be a cold day in hell when I need power from a leech."

She studied him, not entirely convinced. "Hmmm."

He made a sound of impatience, pointed toward the nearby townhouse.

"Can you sense the child?"

Her lips thinned, as if she was annoyed to have to be reminded of why they were lingering in the foggy night.

"No," she muttered, "but I think the spell that guards the baby prevents me from being able to scent it." She tilted back her head, allowing her acute senses to absorb her surroundings. She abruptly turned to regard him with a hint of bewilderment. "The Sylvermyst is missing."

He nodded. "Tearloch left just before your dramatic arrival."

"He left? Do you know where he was headed?"

His lips twisted. "South."

Her annoyance intensified. "You know what I mean. I find it hard to believe he would willingly leave behind the baby after he went postal trying to track it down."

Ariyal had been equally startled when he'd caught sight of Tearloch's slender form hurrying away from the townhouse. He had even taken a step to follow him, when he realized that the Sylvermyst was alone.

He'd melted back into the shadows, forcing himself to recall that he was there to steal the baby, not confront his tribesman.

"If it was me, I would be seeking allies," he shared his assumption. "Tearloch's crazy, not stupid, and he has to know that we'll be coming after him. And once word gets out he's in London with the child . . ."

She shuddered. "Yeah, every nasty demon with delusions of grandeur is going to be trying to get their hands on the kid."

"Which is why we're going to be first in line."

"We?"

He met her mocking smile with a lift of his brow. "You're the one who followed me, remember?"

"Unfortunately."

His gaze drifted down her slender body. "Then we're in this together."

"Fine." She snapped her fingers before his face until he returned his attention to her frustrated glare. "What's your plan?"

Plan?

Hell, he hadn't had a plan since following his former prince into the mists of Avalon.

Look how that had turned out.

Now he preferred to stumble from one disaster to another.

"Is the mage alone?"

She again allowed her powers to search through the darkness. "I don't sense anyone else."

"Then let's do this." He moved to stand directly before the door, holding out a hand as Jaelyn stepped to stand at his side. "Wait."

"A spell?"

"Yes."

The sharp chill of her frustration filled the air. "I hate mages."

He ran his hand over the door, testing the magic that kept it sealed shut.

"It's one of defense, not offense."

"Are you certain?"

"It's either an alarm system or a curse. Difficult to say." He stepped back, flashing a taunting smile toward his companion. "Ladies first."

"That's not funny."

Pulling her away from the door, he led them toward the back garden.

"Trust me, poppet, I don't intend to let anything happen to you," he murmured, flashing a wicked smile. "At least not until I've had my fill."

She bared her fangs. "Are you *trying* to make me kill you?"

A hot, urgent need hardened his cock. Shit, what was wrong with him?

For all he knew Jaelyn was just waiting for the opportunity to force him back to the Commission.

Or to rip out his throat.

But beneath her prickling aggression he could smell the sweet tang of her matching arousal, and the need to press her against the wet bricks and plunge deep into her body until they were both screaming with satisfaction was becoming an overwhelming compulsion.

"I just can't seem to resist," he confessed with a stark honesty that scared the hell out of him.

Caine's private lair outside Chicago

Santiago stood outside the brick farmhouse with a grim expression.

He was an impressive sight with his black jeans that

clung to a tight butt and long muscular legs and a black T-shirt that was stretched over his broad chest. His face was narrow with high cheekbones and his eyes the deep brown of his Spanish ancestors. He was exquisitely handsome with long, raven hair that was left to fall in a perfect curtain down his back.

But it took only a glance to know precisely what he was.

A trained vampire warrior who would kill without mercy.

Which might have explained why the coven of witches who'd been bustling about the cur's lair for the past two nights had been torn between sexual fascination and abject terror when he strolled past.

That and the big-ass sword he had strapped to his back.

Santiago barely noticed the females as they chanted and brewed and lit their candles.

Like all vampires he detested magic.

Unfortunately, Styx had commanded that Santiago find his mate's missing sister.

And when the Anasso commanded, a wise vampire obeyed.

Even if it meant calling upon the local coven to break through the layers of hexes, curses, and other nasty magical traps that had been laid around the farmhouse.

Of course, he hadn't expected it to take the witches so long to breach the protective layers around the house, he acknowledged with a flare of impatience.

He'd been told the cur was paranoid. Hardly surprising considering the fact he'd made a deal with a zombie Were with ties to a demon lord. And now he had Cassandra to protect.

A true prophet.

The rarest creature to walk the earth.

It was a task he wouldn't wish on his worst enemy.

Still, Santiago was damned tired of waiting for the witches to do their mumbo-jumbo crap and get him inside.

As if on cue a tall, silver-haired woman dressed in a neat

black skirt and white shirt warily approached him. She looked as if she should be handing out loans in a bank, not brewing potions as she waved her heavily jeweled hand toward the house.

"We've cleared a path to the door."

Santiago studied the double line of candles that led from the hedges to the front door. Despite the late-summer breeze that stirred the night air the flames stood at stiff attention, not so much as flickering.

He grimaced.

Madre Dios. He hated magic.

"You're certain it's safe?"

"It should be so long as you remain between the candles."

"And the house?"

She patted her neatly coiffed hair. "There's nothing we can detect inside, but I can't make any guarantees."

Santiago pulled the sword from the leather sheath. "Fan-fucking-tastic."

The woman paled, taking a hasty step backward. As if the shiny sword was more dangerous than his massive fangs, or his claws that could rip through steel.

"You should also know that the barrier we've formed will only last until the candles burn down," she said in a trembling voice. "You won't have more than an hour."

"Magic," he muttered.

Ignoring the females who scurried out of his way, Santiago forced his reluctant feet to carry him past the hedge and onto the narrow pathway. He refused to hesitate as he moved forward, climbing the steps to the wraparound porch and pulling open the heavy oak door.

If he was going to be skewered by some nasty spell, tiptoeing around wasn't going to help.

Of course, it wasn't until he had the door shut and he was standing inside the large living room with white plaster walls and open beamed ceiling that he managed to loosen his death grip on the sword.

He didn't fear death in battle. But the thought of being struck down by some unnatural force was enough to give any vampire nightmares.

With a disgusted shake of his head, Santiago turned his attention to his surroundings.

He had no interest in the rustic furniture upholstered in blue-and-white-checked linen, or the hand-carved banister that led to the second floor. Instead he moved directly to the heavy rolltop desk to sort through the various drawers.

Most of the papers were indecipherable scratchings, reminding Santiago that Caine had been a notable chemist before his transformation. A fact that was reinforced by the leather-bound books that lined the towering bookshelves. Only a scientist could appreciate *Stratospheric Sink for Chlorofluoromethane* or *Introduction to Quantum Mechanics*.

Finding nothing that might hint at where he could find the missing Weres, and more importantly, discovering no sign of any intruders, Santiago made his way through the spotless kitchen and up the staircase. Although the scent of the couple was spread throughout the house, his senses were acute enough to pick out their last trail.

He cautiously moved down the hallway to a large bedroom with a heavy, walnut bed that had been carved by wood sprites and walls painted a soft shade of ivory. He halted in the center of the hardwood floor.

Here.

In this precise spot the two had disappeared.

Santiago crouched down to inspect the floor, searching for any indications of a struggle. His fingers had barely touched the wood when he felt a burst of frigid power and he was surging to his feet.

Vampire.

And close.

Spinning around with a low growl, he had his sword poised for a death blow, only to hesitate at the sight of the female framed in the doorway.

Dios.

She was . . . magnificent.

Despite working in a vampire club that was renowned for offering the world's most beautiful demons as entertainment, he was struck speechless.

She was tall and lithe, with dark hair that fell to her waist. Her face was a perfect, pale oval with eyes as dark as ebony and elegantly carved features. Her lips were full and tinted the color of cherries, and just looking at them made Santiago as hard as granite.

His bemused gaze skimmed lower, taking in the dark robes that draped over her full breasts and the ancient gold medallion that was hung around her neck. Farther down, the folds of the silk hinted at long legs and offered a glimpse of her dainty feet encased in silk slippers.

She should have looked matronly in the outfit, like a staid old professor.

Instead she looked . . . hot as hell.

A damned shame there was a good chance he was going to have to kill her.

Seemingly unaware of the danger shimmering in the air, the female strolled forward, studying Santiago with an unreadable expression.

"They are not here."

Her voice was low and throaty, flowing over Santiago with a startling power.

"*Mierda*," he breathed, an unfamiliar unease trickling down his spine. "Who are you and how the hell did you get in here?"

She tilted her head to the side. "I presume you are here to find the seer?"

"I asked you a question," he snapped.

She stiffened and Santiago smothered a curse as a crushing pressure surrounded him, warning him that he was right to be unnerved by her presence.

She had enough power to rival Styx.

Something he would have claimed impossible of any vampire only a few seconds ago.

"Take care, Santiago," she purred.

He wisely shifted backward, lowering the sword that was all but useless against a vampire of her strength.

"How do you know my name?" he demanded.

There was a short pause, as if she was considering whether or not to answer his question. Then she gave a faint shrug.

"I am well acquainted with your sire."

Santiago hissed. No one knew of his sire. It was something he refused to discuss with anyone.

Including Viper, who was his clan chief and closest friend.

"Impossible." He glared at the vampire with a savage suspicion. "Gaius went beyond the Veil centuries ago."

She offered a slow nod. "He is a most welcome member of our small clan. Indeed, he sits upon the Grand Council."

Santiago took another step backward as realization slammed into him with painful force.

"You're an Immortal One," he rasped.

"I am."

His gaze lowered to the medallion hung about her neck. "Nefri."

"Yes."

Well, it all made a revolting sense now.

The female's ability to make a sudden appearance. Her outrageous power. Her knowledge of his sire. Her formal pattern of speech.

Immortal Ones were vampires who had left the world centuries ago to create a clan within another dimension where they were allowed to exist without the primitive passions that plagued this world.

No hunger, no thirst, no lust.

Just endless days of tedious peace they devoted to studying in their vast libraries and meditating in their supposedly endless gardens.

Most of the bastards had the mistaken idea they were somehow superior to their more "barbaric" brothers.

And this woman was one of them.

No, not just one.

The one.

The big kahuna. The CEO and founding member.

It was Nefri's medallion that allowed her to travel through the Veil. And it was her powers that kept her people safe from those demons who attempted to break through the misty barrier that surrounded their world.

Ironically most vampires would be fascinated to meet one of the Immortals.

They were a source of myth and mystery and only a rare few vampires could ever claim to having encountered one. *Like freaking leprechauns*, Santiago acknowledged with a wry smile.

He, on the other hand, had barely been out of his foundling years when his sire had grimly informed him that he could not bear this world after the loss of his mate and was leaving to join those beyond the Veil.

The memory of his rejection was like a raw wound that had never fully healed for Santiago.

"I thought your . . . clan had turned their backs on the mortal world," he accused between clenched teeth. "What are you doing here?"

"The disruptions that are thinning the barriers between dimensions are affecting us as well."

"Ah." He regarded her with an acid gaze, even as his body continued to react as if it had never seen a woman before. *Madre Dios.* If he didn't leash his instincts he'd have her tumbled on the nearby bed and showing her just what she'd been missing all those long, lonely years. Maybe she would even discover a new appreciation for a mere barbarian. *Or maybe she would rip out your heart and feed it to the wolves*, a voice whispered in the back of his mind. For some reason the thought only intensified his smoldering anger. "So you were willing to remain in your little slice of paradise while the rest of us went to hell, but now that you're being threatened you're ready to take notice of the danger?"

Her dark gaze held a piercing intelligence that warned she could see far more than he wanted to share.

"So bitter," she murmured softly. "You cared very deeply for Gaius."

He squared his shoulders, refusing to allow the memory of his sire to rise to mind.

"I care about the family who didn't abandon me," he growled, "which is why I would do anything to protect them."

"I am here to offer assistance, not harm."

"Easy enough to claim."

"True," she readily agreed. "What will it take to convince you?"

Oh, he could think of several possibilities.

Erotic images flashed through his mind, most of them focused on having those cherry lips wrapped around a specific body part.

With a growl he was crushing the dangerous thoughts. How often had he used his own potent sexual attraction to defeat his enemies?

He wasn't going to be led around by his cock.

"It's no coincidence you are in this precise spot at this precise moment," he accused.

With an elegant motion Nefri moved toward the window overlooking the backyard, her hair rippling like liquid ebony in the moonlight.

"No, it is no coincidence," she admitted. "Like you I am searching for the prophet."

Santiago curled his fingers, ignoring the itch to run them through those satin strands of hair.

"Why?"

She turned back to meet his wary gaze. "It was our hope to protect her from the Dark Lord by taking her beyond the Veil." She waved a hand toward the empty room. "I fear we were too late."

Yeah. He knew the feeling.

"How did you even know of Cassandra?"

A Mona Lisa smile curved her lips. "We are not utterly isolated."

"So you've been spying on us?"

"There are those who travel between worlds," she said without apology. "And when it became known that there were rumors of a seer I began to investigate. She is . . ."

He frowned as she hesitated. "What?"

Nefri reached into the pocket of her robes to pull out a thin book no larger than the palm of her hand.

"She is vital to the future of all our worlds."

He studied the book, sensing its age. "What is that?"

She stroked loving fingers over the battered red cover. "A book of prophecies that I took beyond the Veil when the Dark Lord began to destroy them."

His brows lifted. Books of prophecies were as rare as actual prophets.

"And?"

"Most of them are gibberish, I fear."

Santiago snorted. "Typical."

"But, there is one that speaks of the birth of the Alpha and the Omega."

The Alpha and the Omega . . .

Santiago stiffened. They were the same words spoken by the Sylvermyst who warned that the child Laylah had protected for so long was destined to return the Dark Lord to this world.

It couldn't be a coincidence.

"What does it say?" he rasped.

"It warns that the 'harbinger of truth' must not be silenced," she said without hesitation.

"That's it?"

"Yes."

He clenched his teeth. Why the hell couldn't prophets just spit out the future in words a person could understand?

"Still gibberish."

"No." Nefri shook her head. "A warning that I intend to heed."

She lifted her hand to grasp the medallion around her neck. The gold metal inscribed with some ancient hieroglyphs began to glow, filling the room with a strange heat.

Santiago instinctively lifted his sword. "What the hell are you doing?"

"I am going to search for the female."

Despite his hatred toward the Immortals, and the very real possibility she might fry him if he tried to interfere in her dramatic departure, Santiago stepped forward, grasping the woman's arm.

"Not without me, you're not."

She went rigid beneath the firm grip of his hand, her dark gaze studying his fierce expression.

"I had forgotten," she whispered.

His fangs throbbed at the exotic scent of jasmine and pure female.

"Forgotten what?"

"How aggressive males tend to be in this world."

He leaned forward, allowing their lips to brush as he spoke his low warning.

"*Querida*, you haven't seen aggressive yet."

Chapter 5

Jaelyn perched on the steeply slanted roof, her eyes narrowed as Ariyal easily tugged open the unlocked skylight.

She shook her head, her unease intensifying as she shifted to crouch beside the Sylvermyst.

"It must be a trap."

"No one ever thinks an attack will be coming from above. Especially vampires." Ariyal shot her a taunting smile. "Not surprising considering the fact they spend the majority of their lives in the dank ground."

Jaelyn clenched her hands, silently condemning Siljar and the rest of the Oracles to the nearest hell.

It had been bad enough to be stuck with the unpleasant duty of tracking down Ariyal and hauling him to the Commission. But now . . .

She was a Hunter, not a babysitter for an aggravating, pain-in-the-ass Sylvermyst.

"We aren't dealing with a vampire," she said between clenched teeth.

He shrugged. "No, but this lair was built for one and Sergei spent most of his life in the company of a leech."

She allowed her frigid power to swirl through the air. "You're pressing your luck, *fairy*."

He flashed a wicked smile before he was shifting to drop through the skylight with a liquid grace. He landed without a sound and tilted back his head to meet her jaundiced gaze.

"Are you coming?" he softly demanded.

"As if I have a choice," she muttered beneath her breath, refusing to acknowledge his astonishing beauty as a stray beam of moonlight played over his pale, perfect features and the fascinating shimmer of his bronze eyes. Instead she pushed forward and landed next to the fey in the narrow hallway, her senses sweeping through the townhouse. "The mage is below us."

"Yes." He paused, turning his head toward a closed door just down the hall that was paneled in a dark, glossy wood with gilt-framed paintings gathering dust. "But there's a spell of protection through there."

She frowned. "The babe?"

"Only one way to find out."

"Don't forget your promise," she warned, muttering a curse as he ignored her to shove open the door and disappear into the room beyond. She was swiftly following behind him, stepping into the obvious nursery to find the annoying man standing near a wooden cradle. "Ariyal, did you hear me?"

"Perhaps you should let me concentrate, poppet," he commanded, his gaze focused on the crib, where she could see a tiny bundle she presumed was the child. "We're surrounded by a spell."

She froze, glaring at her companion in smoldering frustration.

Dammit. She hated taking orders almost as much as she hated magic.

A double reason to feel the urge to rip off someone's head.

"I told you this was a trap," she hissed.

"It's not a trap." He held up his slender hands, waving

them above the crib as if trying to sense some unseen force field. "There's a magical web to protect the child."

"Can you get rid of it?"

His brow furrowed as he concentrated on the magic he could apparently sense beneath his hands.

"Yes, but not without alerting the mage."

"Too late," a voice drawled from the doorway.

Jaelyn whirled around, prepared to pounce as she caught sight of a man standing in the doorway wearing nothing more than a burgundy robe with his silver hair hanging about his thin face.

Vaguely she recognized him as Sergei, the mage from the Russian caves, although his gaunt, unshaven face and his shadowed eyes suggested the past weeks hadn't treated him kindly. Still, whatever his troubles, his magic was obviously working just fine as he managed to cloak his scent and approach them without warning.

He flinched at the flash of her fangs, his hand shaking as he held up a small glass vial filled with an amber liquid.

"Stay back, vamp," Sergei warned. "I spent several centuries concocting the perfect spell to kill a vampire as slowly and painfully as possible."

"Do you think you can cast it before I put an arrow through your heart?" Ariyal stepped beside her, stretching out his arm to clench and unclench his fingers. There was a shimmer in the air and suddenly an ash bow complete with a wooden arrow was in his hand. With a smooth motion he had it cocked and ready to fire.

Jaelyn grimaced. She might fully approve of the mage becoming a human pincushion, but the knowledge that Ariyal could make the bow and arrows appear from thin air creeped her out.

She had a definite allergy to wooden arrows.

Sergei paled, no doubt recalling his one-time ally had an itchy trigger finger.

"Relax, Ariyal," the mage attempted to soothe. "There's no need for any of us to be hasty."

Ariyal remained poised for battle. "Put away the vial."

"You're the trespasser." Sergei nervously licked his lips. "You put away your weapon."

Jaelyn shifted. The two clearly had issues that had nothing to do with her and she had no intention of getting caught in the cross fire.

Not when the damned mage had a spell specifically designed to harm a vampire.

"A stalemate," Ariyal mocked.

Sergei took a cautious step forward, his gaze darting toward the crib.

"If you've come for the child then you're wasting your time," he said. "You'll die if you touch him."

Ariyal made a sound of disgust. "You think that I can't break through your magic?"

Sergei made a visible effort to gather his shaken courage. "I don't doubt that you could shatter the protective shields around the cradle, but the spell I've placed on the child is specifically cast to harm those with fey blood." He gave a tilt of his chin, covertly shifting another step into the room. "It was the only way to keep your friend Tearloch from taking off with my prize."

Jaelyn scented the mage's sour desperation, and she shifted to block his path to the baby, a cold smile curving her lips.

"Don't even think about it."

He halted, his pale eyes narrowing with a barely concealed hatred.

No love for vampires there.

"Stay back, leech," he hissed, holding the vial over his head.

"You can't win this game, mage," Ariyal warned in lethal tones.

"You think I don't know that?" the man snapped. "I'm no longer playing to win, merely to survive."

"An unlikely outcome," Ariyal drawled, deliberately drawing back the bowstring another fraction of an inch.

"Wait," the man breathed, sweat blooming on his forehead.

"Why?" Ariyal demanded. "If you die the spell dies with you."

"Along with the child," the mage blurted out.

Jaelyn moved to place her hand on her companion's arm. "Ariyal."

"You would, of course, claim that you've bound the child to you," Ariyal mocked, not bothering to glance in her direction. "I'm familiar with your habit of telling the truth only when it's convenient."

The pale eyes darkened with fear. "Do you want to risk killing the brat on the slim chance I'm lying?"

"Yes."

"No," Jaelyn interrupted, rolling her eyes at the typical male need to huff and puff at one another. Why actually communicate when it was so much more fun to bang on their chests? She turned to study to the mage, sensing that his terror went way beyond their own arrival in the townhouse. "What do you mean you're merely trying to survive?"

Sergei gave a restless shrug. "I'm not a lunatic. Marika convinced me that resurrecting the Dark Lord would bring us both the power we craved, but I've discovered that such powers come at a price I'm no longer willing to pay."

"Convenient," Ariyal taunted.

"Actually it couldn't be more inconvenient," the mage snapped.

Ariyal didn't hesitate. "Then give me the child and you won't have to worry about the Dark Lord."

"Right. And how long do you think I would survive without the child as protection? If you didn't kill me then Tearloch most certainly would."

"We could keep you alive," Jaelyn smoothly offered, not at all surprised when Ariyal sent her a smoldering glare.

"Speak for yourself," he rasped. "I have no reason to keep this spineless coward from his long-overdue grave. In fact, I've waited a long time to rid the world of his infection."

"Ariyal . . . shit." Jaelyn moved with blinding speed toward the windows that overlooked the damp street, her senses on full alert. A swift glance was enough to discover the shadows that were moving through the front gate toward the portico. "It looks like your tribesman found reinforcements."

Ariyal cursed. "How many?"

"I count six—no wait, seven Sylvermysts including Tear-loch. And . . ." Jaelyn gave a shake of her head as the shadows disappeared from view as they entered the townhouse.

Even out of sight her Hunter instincts could detect the heat of their bodies as they silently moved through the bottom floors, clearly searching for intruders. She could smell the distinct scent of herbs that revealed they were Sylvermysts and the hormones that marked them as male. But there was a strange . . . emptiness, was the only way she could explain it, that was swiftly traveling in their direction.

"What?" Ariyal prompted.

She turned back to the Sylvermyst, her hand reaching for her shotgun only to come up empty. Dammit. She was getting a new weapon and hell would freeze over before Ariyal would take it away again.

"I don't know what it is," she admitted through clenched teeth.

Ariyal paused, allowing his own powers to search the house. "Tearloch." His face was grim as he met Jaelyn's wary gaze. "He's called a spirit."

"Can it hurt us?"

"Tearloch has a talent for raising the most powerful souls."

"I'll take that as a yes," she muttered, glancing back toward the window. "We need to get out of here."

"Not without the child."

"For God's sake." She turned back, not surprised to find his beautiful features set in stubborn lines. "Have you ever heard the phrase 'live to fight another day'?"

"Have you ever heard of 'not putting off 'til tomorrow what you can do today'?" he countered, giving a tiny wave of the bow. "Get the child, Sergei."

The mage shook his head, backing until he hit a cherry-wood armoire set in the corner of the nursery.

"No, I can't."

Ariyal shrugged. "Then I'll kill you."

"Better an arrow through the heart than what the Dark Lord's minions will do," Sergei choked out.

Ariyal hid a wry smile as he watched Jaelyn's struggle against her desire to rip out his throat.

Or maybe it was his heart.

Whichever, she somehow managed to overcome her bloodlust. The question was . . . why?

He was powerful, but if she truly wanted him dead, or even captured and hauled to the Oracles, there wasn't much he could do to stop her.

Which only made him all the more curious what the hell she was doing there. And what she intended to do with him when she grew tired of her game.

Worries for another day, he was forced to accept as a dark mist floated through the wall and moved to hover next to the crib.

Lowering the bow that would be useless against the spirit, he watched as the mist solidified into the shape of a tall, sparse man with gaunt features and shaved head who appeared to be covered in a satin robe with a heavy silver pendant hung about his neck.

The spirit reached a thin hand toward the sleeping child. "Ah, the anointed one."

His voice rumbled through the air, bringing with it the foul scent of the netherworld.

Ariyal stepped forward, but he was abruptly distracted as the mage moved at the same time, his thin face hard with revulsion.

"Rafael." He breathed the name as if it was a curse.

The spirit slowly lifted his head, glancing toward the mage. Amusement seemed to flutter over the gaunt features before his lips twisted into a sneer.

"It is Master Rafael to you, mage."

"No wizard is my master," Sergei hissed.

Ariyal shifted to keep an eye on the two magical buffoons as well as Jaelyn, who was clearly unnerved by the sight of the spirit.

"You two acquainted?" he drawled.

"Our paths have crossed," Sergei spat out, his gaze never leaving Rafael. "But while I am a true magic-user, he has given his soul to the Dark Lord."

Ariyal arched a brow. "And you?"

The spirit released a low laugh that sent a shudder down Ariyal's spine. Working with spirits had never been his talent and he rarely used his powers to draw the ghosts from the netherworld. Especially not one with the strength that he could sense pulsing about the dead wizard.

"He pledges his loyalty to the highest bidder," Rafael said, his hollow voice echoing eerily through the room. "A magical hack."

"Rafael." The soft whisper came directly beside him and with a low curse he turned his head to discover Jaelyn regarding the spirit with a sudden suspicion. Holy shit. He hadn't seen her move. "I recognize the name," she said, shifting her head to meet his startled gaze.

"You know this spirit?"

She shook her head. "No, but the Chicago vampire clan battled a dark wizard who was attempting to sacrifice the Chalice and open a pathway through the dimensions a few months ago." She shuddered, her attention returning to the wizard. "They killed him."

Rafael pressed a hand to his pendant, his features twisting with fury.

"I was surrounded by incompetent fools." His gaze lowered to the babe who remained unnaturally still. "On this occasion I will have the means to restore my prince to his rightful place."

Ariyal glanced toward Jaelyn. "Prince?"

She curled her lips in disgust. "A few of the more dedicated disciples have elevated themselves to the position of deities and the Dark Lord to their personal prince."

"I would have thought the deity theory might be reconsidered after he actually died," he pointed out, allowing his words to carry toward the arrogant wizard. Spirit or not he was a nasty piece of goods. "That's not very godlike."

"I knew it was only a matter of time before my master rescued me from the pits of hell," the wizard snarled, a crazed light shimmering in his eyes. "Death has no hold over me."

"Obviously neither does sanity," Jaelyn muttered.

About to agree, Ariyal felt the familiar stir of air before a portal formed next to the wizard and Tearloch stepped into the room.

Wearing traditional leather leggings and tunic with his copper hair pulled into a braid, the Sylvermyst looked painfully familiar.

It was only when Ariyal met the fevered glitter in the silver eyes that he was forced to accept that this was no longer the friend and confidant whom he had depended upon for centuries.

"Ariyal, I'm glad you're here, my brother," Tearloch said with a faint bow.

Ariyal deliberately glanced toward the shimmering opening his tribesman had left open. Among Sylvermyst it was an insult to maintain a portal when in the company of friends. It implied a lack of trust.

"Are you?"

The slender fey glanced toward the nearby spirit before at last returning his attention to Ariyal.

"It's not too late to join me," he said, a hint of pleading in his voice. "Together we shall restore the Sylvermyst to their former glory."

Ariyal frowned, disturbed by Tearloch's odd hesitation. It was almost as if he had been seeking approval from the spirit.

"What former glory?" he demanded, keeping his voice soft, unthreatening. "There is nothing glorious about slavery."

Remembered pain flared over Tearloch's thin face. "We were slaves to that bitch. The Dark Lord will set us free."

Ariyal spread his arms. "We are free, Tearloch. Just look around."

"No." He shook his head in sharp denial. "Without the power of the master we will be at the mercy of the heathens who infest this world."

"Listen to me, my brother." Ariyal took a cautious step forward. "That is the voice of madness whispering in your ear."

"Do not heed him." The spirit abruptly spoke, shifting until he could place a gaunt hand on Tearloch's shoulder. "Clearly he now intends to sacrifice you and your brothers to the vampires, just as he sacrificed you to Morgana le Fey."

A ball of sick dread lodged in the pit of Ariyal's stomach. Bloody hell. What had Tearloch done?

"You know he speaks lies," he said, concentrating on the spirit who regarded him with a smug arrogance.

"Do I?" the wizard mocked, maintaining his possessive

grip on Tearloch. "You stand there with a vampire who is your obvious companion." He glanced toward the silent Jaelyn. "Or is she your lover?"

Instinctively he shifted to stand directly in front of Jaelyn, hiding her from the spirit's dangerous gaze. For all her power, a vampire was always vulnerable to magic.

Not that he knew why the hell he would bother. She was as likely to stab him in the back as to appreciate his efforts.

For now, however, he was far more intent on his friend who was in obvious trouble.

"Tearloch, look at me," he commanded, the authority in his voice rippling the air and making his tribesman jerk in reaction.

"Do not," the wizard hissed, leaning down to whisper directly into Tearloch's ear. "He is jealous of your powers and he knows you shall be rewarded above him once our master is returned." His malevolent power swirled through the room with far too much force for a mere spirit, battering against Ariyal with a dangerous strength. "Why else would he be so eager to destroy the child and halt your efforts to resurrect your lord?"

Ariyal lifted his hand, muttering a word of command in the harsh Sylvermyst language.

A smile curved his lips as the wizard attempted to speak, his face twisting with fury when he realized that Ariyal had managed to silence him.

"Much better," Ariyal taunted.

Something perilously close to fear tightened Tearloch's expression.

"What have you done?"

"Brought a welcome end to the poison he is spewing."

Tearloch shifted in agitation. "Release him."

"Not until you have listened to sense."

Tearloch shook his head, moving closer to the spirit, who glared at Ariyal with a baleful intensity.

"I listened to you once before," the younger man breathed, "and see where that got us."

Ariyal flinched. Although it had been the previous prince's decision to accept Morgana's bargain, he'd offered his full support, which had swayed more than a few into agreeing to break ties with the Dark Lord.

"You would prefer to have been banished with the others?" he asked.

The younger Sylvermyst glanced toward the spirit, almost as if seeking the answer to Ariyal's question.

"We should have remained pure," he at last muttered.

Ariyal forced himself to crush the angry accusations that trembled on his lips. Tearloch was clinging to sanity by a thread.

He didn't intend to snap it.

"Tearloch," he said, his tone low and soothing, "when did you first call this particular spirit?"

Tearloch blinked in bewilderment. "I don't remember. What does it matter?"

"You better than anyone understand the dangers of calling upon the same spirit too often," Ariyal pointed out. Every Sylvermyst was taught to limit their contact with spirits. Not only was there a danger of becoming emotionally attached to the ghost, but there was always the nasty possibility that the spirit might manage to twist the relationship so that they became the master rather than the servant. "Especially such a powerful spirit."

"No, you're just trying to deceive me."

"I'm not the one trying to deceive you, brother," Ariyal murmured softly, inching closer. "But together we can make this right."

Tearloch blinked, his silver eyes focusing on his friend. "Ariyal?"

"Yes, old friend, we have fought side by side. You know you can trust me."

"Yes . . ." For a split second Ariyal thought he might actually have gotten through the fog that was obviously clouding his friend's mind. The copper-haired Sylvermyst even took a half step toward him. Then the damned wizard squeezed his shoulder and Tearloch was once again under the sway of the bastard. With a faltering shake of his head, he came to an abrupt halt. "I mean no."

Ariyal leashed his frustration. As much as he might want to grab his friend and beat some sense into him, he knew it would be a waste of time so long as he was in the power of the spirit.

And worse, he couldn't return the wizard to the hell, where he belonged. He might be able to manipulate Rafael on a small scale, but only the actual summoner could dismiss him.

He would have to somehow convince Tearloch to do the deed.

Lifting a hand in a gesture of peace, Ariyal took a step back, feeling Jaelyn punch him in the ribs as he stepped on her toe.

"Fine, I'll stay here, and we can just talk."

"There's nothing to discuss." Tearloch flicked a glance toward the hovering spirit, who reached into the crib and scooped the child into his arms. "I intend to resurrect the Dark Lord."

"Of course." Sergei abruptly thrust his way into the conversation, licking his thin lips as he realized that he was about to be cut out of the deal. "We can begin preparing for the ceremony this very moment, if you wish."

Tearloch jerked his gaze toward the mage, his face hardening with disgust.

"You had your opportunity, mage. I no longer trust your . . . enthusiasm for returning our master."

Sergei stretched out his hands as he edged toward the cradle, ignoring the spirit of Rafael, who was furiously attempting to speak, no doubt hoping to cast a spell against his nemesis.

"Don't be a fool, Tearloch," he chastised. "I have prepared for years for this moment. There is no other mage who could possible match my skills or my powers."

"You are the fool," Tearloch snapped. "And now you will suffer for your lack of commitment." His gaze shifted back to Ariyal. "You will all suffer."

Ariyal's attention never shifted from the mage. He easily sensed Sergei's rising desperation at the knowledge he was no longer needed by Tearloch. It wasn't going to take much for him to do something stupid.

Almost on cue, the idiot gave a muttered curse and rushed forward.

"Stay back," Ariyal commanded, not at all surprised when the mage continued his terrified charge. "Dammit, mage. What the hell are you doing?"

"I'm dead without that child," Sergei hissed. "No one's taking it away from me."

Ariyal watched the disaster unfold, already accepting there was no way he was going to halt Tearloch as the Sylvermyst pulled the spirit who still clutched the child in his arms into the waiting portal.

The air shimmered as the portal began to close. Sergei screeched in frustrated horror, his hands lifting toward the disappearing Tearloch.

At first, Ariyal assumed the mage was trying to reach the portal so he could enter before it closed. It wasn't until he heard the low chanting that he realized the stupid bastard was intending to lob a spell at the opening.

Gods, was he a complete moron?

Even a thick-skulled troll knew better than to point magic directly at a portal.

Spinning on his heel, he turned toward Jaelyn, who was watching the spectacle with a disgusted frown.

"Get down," he snapped.

She blinked, then instinctively backed away as he surged forward.

"What?"

With no time to explain, Ariyal tackled her to the ground and covered her with his larger body. He ignored the fangs she flashed and her foul words of warning. Instead he braced himself for the inevitable explosion of magic.

There was the hissing sound of the spell hitting the portal, destabilizing the massive amount of magic needed to rip a hole through space. The predictable chain reaction was less than a heartbeat behind, and Ariyal cried out as the blast of shattered magic slammed into him with painful force.

Shit.

He was at last on top of his beautiful, aggravating vampire and he was going to die before he could get her naked.

Chapter 6

Jaelyn was knocked unconscious briefly by the invisible wall of power that had crashed over them with terrifying force.

Groggily, she managed to shake off the clinging darkness. What the hell?

Had there had been some sort of magical tsunami?

A nuclear explosion?

The end of the world?

No, surely not the end of the world, she tried to reassure herself.

Fate couldn't be so cruel as to condemn her to an eternity being squashed beneath an infuriating Sylvermyst. Could it?

Pretending that the earthy scent of herbs wasn't teasing at her senses and that the hard, male body wasn't cloaking her in welcome warmth, she pressed her hands against his chest.

"Get off me," she muttered, giving a shove to roll him off her aching body.

Ariyal landed on his back with an awkward flop and Jaelyn belatedly realized the explosion had knocked him well and truly out. With a startled curse, she rose to her knees, swiftly scanning the room as she prepared for the next attack.

An attack that thankfully never came.

A glance was enough to discover the Sylvermyst and his pet spirit had disappeared along with Sergei. Thank-freaking-God. It was bad enough to be surrounded by magic-users without adding in a weird-ass spirit who would give anyone nightmares.

She allowed her senses to filter through the house, assuring her there was nothing lurking in the shadows before she returned her attention to the man who lay unnervingly still beside her.

He wasn't dead. She could hear the steady pump of his heart and the soft rasp of his breathing, but it was obvious the magical blast had injured him.

"Stupid show-off. Like I need you to play He-Man," she muttered, annoyed by the vivid memory of him jumping on top of her, shielding her from the massive explosion.

When was the last time someone had tried to protect her?

Never.

That was when.

And the fact that this man had done so should have annoyed her, not made something warm and mushy bloom in a secret part of her unbeating heart.

Infuriated with her peculiar behavior, with the Sylvermyst who was making her freaking nuts and the situation that she couldn't control, she leaned over her unconscious companion and laid a hand against his throat, allowing the steady beat of his pulse to reassure her nagging concern.

"Ariyal," she hissed. "Dammit, wake up."

Nothing.

Not so much as a twitch.

"Now look what you've done." Her fingers moved to

trace over his starkly beautiful features, something perilously close to fear churning through her stomach as she wondered just how badly he was injured. "I should leave your sorry ass to rot here."

Even as the words left her lips, Jaelyn was scooping her arms beneath the Sylvermyst. She didn't know where she was going, but she couldn't linger at the townhouse.

Not when the Three Stooges might decide to make a sudden reappearance.

She rose to her feet with a fluid motion. Ariyal was heavy, but her innate strength gave her the ability to sling him over her shoulder as she headed out of the room and down the curved staircase. Unfortunately, he had a good eight inches on her, and considerably more bulk, which was going to make toting him around London more than a little awkward.

Reaching the bottom of the steps, Jaelyn paused as she caught the unmistakable scent of granite coming through the front gate.

Gargoyle?

It wouldn't be that uncommon in London. There was a large Guild in the city. But they didn't usually stroll up to the door, did they?

Hastily Jaelyn cloaked herself as well as Ariyal in the thick shadows only a Hunter could create. So long as she didn't move there was no demon who could detect her presence.

Prepared for a lumbering monster, Jaelyn froze at the sight of the tiny demon who stepped across the threshold.

Well, she'd gotten the gargoyle part right, she wryly conceded. There was no mistaking the gray, grotesque features and stunted horns. Or the long tail that was lovingly polished. But she wasn't sure the Guild would claim this three-foot version with large, gossamer wings in shades of crimson and blue.

Levet.

The last time that Jaelyn had seen the miniature gargoyle had been in Russia where he'd helped Tane rescue her from the cave where Ariyal had left her tied and guarded by Yannah while he went to destroy the babe.

Perhaps sensing that he was being watched, the gargoyle halted in the center of the foyer, his tail twitching as he peered through the gloom.

"Hello?" he called softly, his voice laced with a French accent. "*Ma cherie?* Where are you, you tiresome demon?"

Jaelyn lifted her brows at the realization that it wasn't co-incidence that had brought the gargoyle to this particular house.

"Searching for someone, Levet?" she demanded, allowing the shadows to dissipate.

"Eek!" With a tiny jump, the demon turned to study her with wide gray eyes. "Oh! Jaelyn."

"Who were you expecting?"

He wrinkled his tiny snout. "I thought I smelled . . ."

"Smelled?" she prompted.

"Yannah. Her scent is lingering on you."

She grimaced, still annoyed with Yannah and her powerful mother.

"Sorry, I haven't seen her since she shoved me through a portal and I landed face-first in the gutter."

Levet cleared his throat, looking oddly uneasy as he rubbed one of his horns.

"She . . . um . . . she did not happen to mention where she was headed, did she?"

"At a guess, I'd say the pits of the nearest hell," Jaelyn muttered.

"Oh." His brow furrowed. "Do you have directions?"

Jaelyn blinked. Was he serious?

"No, but I'm miserably certain she'll be tracking me down in the next few days."

"Truly?"

"Truly."

He heaved a dramatic sigh, pacing the foyer as he considered her words.

"I suppose I have no choice but to wait with you then. I have been attempting to find her since she left Russia." His wings fluttered in frustration. "She is annoyingly elusive."

"You've been following her for the past three weeks?"

"Oui."

"Why?"

"Why?" The gargoyle blinked, seemingly astonished by the question. "Because she kissed me."

"That's it?" Jaelyn had a brief memory of Yannah grabbing the tiny gargoyle and kissing him before she'd planted her fist into his face, knocking him across the cave. "She kissed you."

"What can I say?" He lifted his hands in a helpless motion. "I am French."

Jaelyn abruptly laughed.

There was something oddly endearing about the small gargoyle.

"Well, you're certainly tenacious," she said.

The gray gaze shifted toward the unconscious Sylvermyst draped over her shoulder.

"I could say the same of you."

Jaelyn's lips flattened. "Not by choice."

Levet wagged his heavy brows. *"Non?"*

Jaelyn frowned. Did the silly creature think that she'd knocked Ariyal unconscious to drag him off like she was some sort of cavewoman?

Not a wholly repulsive thought, a treacherous voice whispered in the back of her mind.

Perhaps if she had him alone in her lair for a few nights she could rid herself of the raw, pulsing awareness that he stirred deep inside her.

Just for an instant the vivid image of Ariyal's lean body spread across her black satin sheets seared through her mind. Would his eyes shimmer with a pure bronze as she slowly explored him from his head to the tips of his toes? Or perhaps she would tie him to the hand-carved headboard and ride him until they both collapsed in sated exhaustion.

It was the aroused ache of her fangs that recalled Jaelyn to her surroundings and the fact the gargoyle was watching her with a knowing gaze.

Dammit.

What the hell was wrong with her? Sexual need was a weakness that was brutally beaten out of Hunters.

Or at least that's what she'd always believed.

Of course, Ariyal was also the only man capable of smashing through her icy control and igniting the temper she had never realized she possessed.

She hastily thrust aside the disturbing thought.

"No," she snapped with more force than necessary. "This is a job, nothing more."

"Hmmm." The fragile wings twitched as Levet stepped toward her, his gaze locked on the unconscious Ariyal. "Is he dead?"

"Of course not. He was hit by a spell." As the explanation tumbled from her lips she felt a sudden surge of hope. Gargoyles were creatures of magic, weren't they? "I don't suppose you could wake him up?"

Levet waddled forward, sniffing at Ariyal's feet, which nearly brushed the floor.

"It will soon wear off," he assured her.

"Damn." She adjusted him on her shoulder. "He weighs a ton."

Levet tilted his head to the side. "You are taking him to the Oracles?"

"Eventually," she offered vaguely, her gaze traveling

toward the open door. Despite the darkness she could feel the relentless approach of dawn. "For now I need shelter."

The gargoyle blinked in bewilderment. "Surely you must sense that there are tunnels beneath this house?"

She gave a sharp shake of her head. "The mage and the Sylvermyst have vanished for the moment, but I can't risk lingering here."

"Ah." The gargoyle tapped a claw to his chin as he considered their options. "Victor has a lair not far from London."

"Victor?"

"The clan chief of London," Levet explained with a smug smile. "He is a close and personal friend of mine. I do not doubt he would be pleased to offer us shelter if I were to approach him."

A close, personal friend? Jaelyn hid a smile. She was fairly certain that Victor would give a different story if asked.

Not that she intended to cross paths with the powerful clan chief.

"Actually, I prefer something more . . ." She chose her words with care. "Discreet."

Genuine concern touched his ugly little face. "Are you in trouble?"

She shrugged, glancing toward the Sylvermyst draped over her shoulder.

"I just don't want to answer unnecessary questions."

"I . . . see."

"Do you know a place where I can disappear for a few hours?"

Levet hesitated before heaving a reluctant sigh. "There used to be a blood pit near Fleet Street, but I do not suggest it."

She ignored his warning. Granted the usual blood pits were filthy, underground clubs where demons could buy whatever they desired: sex, drugs, and of course, willing blood hosts. But, they also rented rooms with the strict policy of don't ask, don't tell.

"It sounds perfect," she assured him.

"It is not really a suitable place for such a beautiful woman."

"I'm not a woman, I'm a Hunter."

Levet's eyes widened even as a mysterious smile curved his lips.

"You may call yourself whatever you please, *ma enfant*, but I can assure you that you are very much a woman."

She snorted, refusing to recall that since meeting Ariyal she'd *felt* like a woman for the first time in decades.

Surely she had enough disasters looming on the horizon without adding yet another?

"Can you lead me to the blood pit or not?"

Still, the gargoyle hesitated. "There's bound to be an assortment of unpleasant creatures staying there."

"Trust me, I can take care of myself."

"Very well." Levet's wings drooped, but turning on his heel he led Jaelyn out of the house and down the path to the front gate. Once they reached the street, he turned east. "This way."

Jaelyn was on full alert as they walked through the neighborhoods still slumbering in the pre-dawn hours. Most creepy-crawlies were too intelligent to attack a vampire, but she was still edgy from their earlier encounter and the thought of the dead wizard popping out of thin air did nothing for her nerves.

Neither did the covert glances from the tiny gargoyle waddling at her side.

At last she turned her head to meet his searching gaze. "Do I have something on my face?"

Levet shook his head, his expression one of blatant curiosity.

"I am merely wondering why such a lovely female would become a Hunter."

She resumed scanning their passing surroundings, skimming over Nelson's Column, which stretched toward the heavens, and the flanking fountains as they cut through Trafalgar Square.

"It wasn't by choice," she muttered, quickening her step in the hopes her companion would take the hint and drop the subject.

She might as well have hoped for a night with Robert Pattinson or world peace, she wryly acknowledged as the gargoyle churned his tiny legs to keep pace beside her.

"You were forced?" he persisted.

"After I was turned, it was discovered I had the height-ened senses required for a Hunter," she said, stripping her voice of emotion. It was a night she'd done her best to forget. "The Addonexus arrived at my lair and informed me I was about to become their newest recruit."

She felt his gaze searching her profile.

"Whether you wished to be recruited or not?" he asked softly.

"Vampires have never embraced democracy. Not even with Styx as the Anasso."

"Might makes right, eh?"

She shrugged. "Something like that."

"So typical of that overgrown Aztec," he muttered, abruptly turning on a dark street and leading her past the small, historic churches nestled among the taverns. "Were you held as a prisoner?"

Her brows lifted. How the hell had the gargoyle become acquainted with the most powerful vampires in the world?

A story for another day.

"Not a prisoner," she said, "but I was . . . encouraged to complete my training."

"I can imagine the encouragement," he muttered.

"No, you really can't."

A silence descended as her words sliced through the air

with a bleak edge. Then, sensing the gargoyle was slowing his pace, Jaelyn turned to meet his sympathetic gaze.

"But now your training is complete?" he asked.

"Yep." Her lips twisted. "I'm a card-carrying, full-fledged Hunter."

"There are cards?"

She couldn't halt her abrupt laugh. "If I told you I'd have to kill you."

An answering smile curved his lips. "I never thought I would ever meet such a charming vampire," her companion murmured. "You are truly unique."

"I might agree with unique," she said dryly, "but I've rarely been called charming."

"I doubt you have much opportunity to reveal your softer side in your current profession."

Softer?

Had she ever had a softer side?

"No."

"Can you quit?"

She blinked at the unexpected question. "Quit being a Hunter?"

"Oui."

"It's a position of great honor among vampires," she mouthed the well-rehearsed words. It was true enough that most vampires envied those chosen by the elite Addonexus. They saw only the power and wary respect offered to the members, without ever understanding the cost. "Why would anyone wish to leave?"

He narrowed his eyes. "I can think of a few hundred."

She came to a halt, the hair on the back of her neck rising at the unmistakable stench that filled the air.

"I smell trolls."

The gargoyle gave a delicate shudder. "I did warn you that it was a low-class establishment."

"So you did." With a smooth motion, Jaelyn was bending

to lay Ariyal on the hard pavement, sliding her hand over his hard body until she found one of the numerous daggers he had hidden. Gripping the ivory handle, she straightened and pointed toward the gargoyle. "Remain here with the Sylvermyst. I will return as soon as I can."

"Where are you going?"

"To negotiate for a room."

She had already turned to make her way down the steps that led to the cellar beneath the silent pub when Levet reached to grasp her free hand.

"Be careful, *ma enfant*," he pleaded softly.

She glanced back in surprise. First Ariyal tried to protect her and now this creature was looking at her as if he was truly concerned.

It was . . . unnerving.

"Don't worry about me," she said gruffly.

A faint smile curved his lips, lifting his hands in a helpless gesture.

"It is what I do."

With a scowl she ignored the tiny flare of warmth as she vaulted to the bottom of the steps and shoved open the heavy oak door that was hidden from humans by a spell of concealment.

Dammit.

She was supposed to be terrifying others with her mad skills, not encouraging them to treat her as if she were some helpless female in need of coddling.

Thankfully she had no trouble slipping back into her I-want-to-kill-something mode as she stepped into the large room with wood-plank floors and a low, open beamed ceiling.

Her gaze skimmed over the nearly empty booths that lined the walls, where a handful of weary humans sprawled, their eyes glazed with drugs and their thin bodies barely covered. She grimaced. Even at a distance she could see the bite marks where vampires had fed on their tainted blood.

She crossed toward the bar at the back, allowing her senses to flow through the building. The fighting pits were beyond the bar as well as the cubbies for those demons who preferred a bit of privacy for their sex. Beneath them she could sense several locked cells where a troll, two ogres, and at least three curs were sleeping off their numerous injuries.

Her attention, however, was trained on the male imp behind the bar. With his long golden hair pulled from his narrow face and slender body encased in skin-tight leather, he should have been handsome, but there was a hard cunning in his green eyes and an unpleasant curl to his thin lips.

Reaching the bar, she stiffened as a half-breed troll stepped out of a cubby, his rough features almost human if one didn't look too closely at the beady eyes that glowed red in the overhead lights or the double row of teeth that were razor sharp.

"Vampire," the creature growled, hitching up his filthy pants that matched his too tight T-shirt. "Tasty."

She returned her gaze to the imp even as she felt the disgusting mongrel move to stand at her side.

"I need a room," she said.

Predictably the mongrel troll leaned close enough to gag her with his putrid breath.

"You can share mine, pretty bloodsucker." He grabbed her hand, pulling it toward his crotch. "So long as you suck on—"

His words broke off on a high-pitched scream as she allowed her fingers to wrap around his aroused cock, squeezing until she threatened to make him a eunuch.

"Touch me again and I'll fillet this tiny dick and serve it to you for breakfast," she drawled in sweet tones. "Got it?"

"Got it," he squeaked, his round face flushed as he danced on his tiptoes.

For a minute she considered simply carving out the bastard's black heart. Trolls, even those of the mongrel variety, possessed an insatiable appetite for rape and she didn't doubt he would have thrown her to the floor and forced himself on her if she hadn't fought back.

Then, with a disgusted hiss, she shoved him away, barely noting his glare of hatred before he was scurrying toward the door.

The imp flashed a mocking smile. "That time of month?"

Jaelyn narrowed her gaze. "You next?"

"Here." The man slapped a key on the counter before pointing toward a narrow door carved into the paneling. "Vamp rooms are down the stairs, last door on the left."

"How much?"

"One hundred pounds for the room and another hundred for a host." He nodded toward the pathetic humans. "Top of the line."

She rolled her eyes. "More like scraping the gutter."

The imp shrugged. "Take it or leave it."

Jaelyn reached beneath the neckline of her spandex top, pulling out a folded bill.

"Fifty American bucks for the room." She dropped the money on the bar. "I brought my own host."

The green eyes glittered with a sly greed. "Seventy-five and I don't let every demon in the place know there's a female in the basement."

Jaelyn smiled as she moved with a blinding speed, pressing the edge of the dagger against the imp's throat before he could blink.

"Twenty-five and I don't cut off your head."

"Deal."

An abandoned church west of Chicago

The neglected ruins on the outskirts of the ghost town only hinted at the once-proud beauty of the Victorian church. Now the stained-glass windows were shattered and the hand-carved pews empty, while the attached graveyard was a pitiful shell of tumbled crypts and tenacious weeds.

Beneath the piles of stone and forgotten corpses, however, the vast catacombs had been tended to with scrupulous care.

Or at least the majority of the tunnels, Tearloch acknowledged.

Weeks ago the lower chambers had been nearly destroyed by a series of violent explosions that had had collapsed tunnels and filled caverns with rubble.

Making his way through the unnaturally smooth passageway, Tearloch grimaced. It wasn't just the evil the pulsed through the air, or thick silence that made him twitchy as hell.

No, it was the sensation he was once again trapped against his will that made his skin crawl.

With an effort he leashed his instinctive urge to charge out of the claustrophobic catacombs and instead forced his feet to carry him to the large cavern where the spirit of Rafael hovered in the center of the stone floor.

He shuddered at the sensation of icy power prickling over him as he stepped past the barrier that the wizard had conjured to protect them from intruders.

If his mind hadn't been clouded by his growing madness he would've been horrified by the spirit's increasing strength. It was always a delicate balance between a summoner and the summoned, and Sylvermyst were taught from the cradle to keep a careful leash on their spirits.

Otherwise the master could all too easily become the slave.

As it was, he felt more annoyance than anger as Rafael drifted toward him, his skeleton-thin fingers caressing the pendant hung around his neck.

"The mage?" he questioned softly.

Tearloch's lips flattened. He'd just wasted the past two hours searching the tunnels for Sergei Krakov. It was more than a little irritating that the bastard managed to elude him.

"He's managed to cloak his presence," he snapped.

"You are certain he went through the portal with you?" Rafael demanded.

Tearloch scowled. "Of course I'm certain. Do you think I could mistake hauling a grown man through a portal from London to Chicago?"

"Then he no doubt has used his powers to escape." The wizard dismissed his rival with a sneer. "He always was a coward."

Tearloch hissed at the arrogant claim. He agreed that Sergei was a spineless fool, but that didn't mean he didn't need the mage. His gaze stole toward the bundle of blankets that hid the child in the corner of the cavern.

"He might be a coward, but he told the truth when he claimed that he was the best equipped to resurrect the Dark Lord." His gaze shifted back to the spirit. "He has prepared far longer than you have."

Rafael tilted his chin to a haughty angle. "He is unworthy to perform such a holy ceremony. I have warned you from the beginning that—"

"I think you're forgetting who makes the decisions, wizard," Tearloch interrupted the increasingly familiar complaint.

Rafael had been whispering that they had no need of Sergei since Tearloch had managed to capture the child along with the mage. It was blatantly obvious he wanted Tearloch to get rid of his magical rival, just as he had wanted him to turn his back on his tribesmen.

He's isolating you. . . .

Easily sensing he'd pushed too far, the spirit was offering a deep bow of apology.

"No, Master."

"Don't call me that," Tearloch snarled.

Rafael bent until his hairless head scraped the floor. "As you wish."

With a growl, Tearloch twirled away from the wizard, shoving his fingers through his hair.

"These tunnels are suffocating me," he rasped. "I need fresh air."

"You cannot leave the caves. Do not forget you are being hunted."

Tearloch jerked back toward the wizard with a fierce glare. At the moment he was hot, frustrated, and in the mood to blame the damned wizard for all his troubles.

"I'm not likely to forget. Not when I'm being buried alive like I'm a damned rock troll." He shuddered. "Why did you insist we come here?"

"These caves were my home for centuries." Rafael's own expression was . . . loving, as he glanced around the smoothly carved room. Of course, he'd spent the past months in hell. Anything was bound to seem like the Ritz. "My power is greatest here as well as my ability to protect you."

"It reeks of blood."

"You know as well as I that the Dark Lord demands a sacrifice for his gifts."

Tearloch gave another shudder, ancient memories threatening to sear through the fog clouding his mind.

"Yes."

"Do not waver now, Tearloch." Without warning, the spirit was standing at Tearloch's side, his clammy hand touching his shoulder. "Not when we are so close."

Tearloch shook off his hand, a strange ache pulsing behind his eyes.

"You say we are close and yet you offer more delays," he growled, struck by a sudden urge to find a place to lie down. He was tired. So tired. "I'm beginning to wonder if there's a conspiracy among magic-users to prevent the resurrection."

The wizard allowed a hint of anger to touch his gaunt face. "If you wish to assign blame then you may point your finger at the damnable Weres. It was their battle with the demon lord that destroyed my altar and closed the conduit I had opened to my prince." His fingers grasped the heavy pendant. "It will take time to restore all that I have lost."

Tearloch backed away.

He didn't give a damn about Weres or demon lords or any other pathetic excuses.

The Dark Lord had reached beyond his prison to touch Tearloch with a searing demand to be set free.

Until he'd managed to resurrect his master there would be no peace.

"You have a week," he snapped, heading toward the opening of the cavern. "Fail me, wizard, and I'll banish you back to hell."

Chapter 7

Jaelyn walked through the long, steel-lined corridor, knowing on some level she was dreaming.

Not that it didn't feel real.

Terrifyingly real.

She shivered at the sensation of the white silk robe that covered her from neck to toe brushing against her skin. At the familiar hum of the florescent lights. At the cool air that stirred her hair, which spilled down her back.

She was back in the private compound owned by the Addonexus.

There was no mistaking the military perfection of the steel passageways that were carved beneath the Tibetan mountain, or the ventilated air that remained a monotonous sixty-five degrees.

Nor was there any mistaking where she was headed.

This wasn't the first occasion she'd been locked in this particular nightmare. But like every other time, Jaelyn was powerless to halt the unfolding drama that clenched her stomach with dread.

Trapped, Jaelyn continued down the corridor until she reached the heavy metal door at the end. Without hesitation she pushed it open and stepped into the dark room beyond.

Too late she sensed the waiting vampire as he uncloaked directly beside her.

"Samuel?" She turned her head to regard the pale-haired vampire with more surprise than alarm. "What are you doing here?"

"Waiting for you." A disarming grin spread across the handsome face, the blue eyes twinkling.

Jaelyn wasn't fooled by the boyish charm. She knew the cunning predator who lurked just beneath the golden good looks. Still, she wasn't prepared for the man to dart forward, snapping a thick, silver collar around her throat.

She hissed in pain, her hands lifting to tug at the collar that was searing into her skin.

"What the hell?"

Samuel's smile widened. "Surprised?"

She warily backed into the center of the room, futilely attempting to remove the collar even as her senses spread through the sparsely furnished office to make certain there weren't any other attackers looming in the shadows.

Better late than never, right?

"I was summoned by Kostas," she said. "He's not going to be pleased when he finds out you've been screwing around in his office."

Samuel clicked his tongue, his expression mocking. "I've warned you that you should never take anything at face value, sweetie. Your weakness has always been your habit of trusting others."

Damn.

She dropped her hands, a cold dread forming in the pit of her stomach.

She'd been brought to the compound only a few years after Samuel. For thirty years they'd trained side by side, sometimes as partners and sometimes as opponents. And for thirty years he'd tried to lure her into his bed.

But in this moment she wasn't feeling the whole BFF vibe.

In fact, there was an ugly glint in the blue eyes that made her inner alarms clang.

"You sent the message?" she demanded, inching back until her butt hit the edge of the walnut desk.

She wasn't trying to escape. At least not yet. Instead she was judging the precise measurements of the room. Six feet from the door to the two wing chairs beside the bookcase. Three feet to the file cabinets in the corner. Two feet from the desk to the wall.

During a fight it was vital to be familiar with her surroundings.

Tripping over a piece of furniture could mean the difference between life and death.

Samuel smiled with cocky confidence as he strolled toward her, his muscular body shown to advantage in the black running shorts that were all that covered him.

"You should have made sure the note was genuine before you left your rooms."

Yeah. Master of the Obvious.

"I'm assuming that Kostas isn't going to be making an appearance?"

"No, we're all alone."

She licked her dry lips. "What do you want?"

His gaze traveled down her body. "You know, my dear, there was a time when I might have been satisfied having you in my bed."

She didn't bother to disguise her grimace. "Never."

"There's no need to rub it in," he chided. "You've made your lack of interest painfully clear."

"So now you think you can force me?"

"Jaelyn." Genuine indignation darkened the blue eyes. "I would never rape a woman. Surely you know me better than that?"

She refused to react as he allowed his powers to fill the air. A Hunter never revealed weakness. Not even when her skin beneath the silver collar was being scorched to a crisp and a frigid pressure threatened to crack a rib.

"Actually, I don't think I know you at all, Samuel," she said, her voice carefully devoid of emotion. No use provoking the crazy vampire. "If you don't want sex, then what do you want?"

He shrugged. "I'm not an animal, but I am ambitious."

"Big shocker," she muttered.

Since her arrival at the compound she'd been aware of Samuel's insatiable obsession with gaining the approval of the Ruah. She truly thought he would get on his knees and kiss Kostas's ass if it would earn him brownie points.

"So long as you're around I'm always going to come in second place."

"Second place?" She frowned at the bitterness in his voice. "Are we in a competition I didn't know about?"

"We've been competing since we were brought here, sweetie." He reached to grasp her chin in a crushing grip. "Of all the recruits the two of us have emerged the strongest. Why else do you think the Ruah have pitted us against one another over and over?"

She made no effort to escape his hold, still hoping to bring an end to the madness without violence.

"I thought we were supposed to be a team?"

"There's only room for one at the top." His smile faded to reveal the cold, empty hunger that burned deep in his eyes. "And since I'm honest enough to admit that I can't win in a fair fight, I've decided to get rid of you with less than honorable means."

Okay.

Any hope of ending this with a smile and a handshake died a painful death.

"This is crazy, Samuel," she breathed. "I'm not your enemy."

"But you are." He tightened his grip, her jaw cracking beneath the strain. "So long as you exist you will always be the golden child of the Addonexus."

She hissed at the pain flooding through her body. "What the hell does that mean?"

"You'll always be given the best assignments, along with the glory."

"What glory? We work in secret."

He shook his head, refusing to acknowledge the truth of her accusation.

"No. I won't live in your shadow."

"Samuel . . ."

She slumped forward, as if overcome by the silver poisoning her body and sapping her strength. Instinctively he reached to catch her, which was all the opening Jaelyn needed. Using his forward momentum to her advantage, she grasped his arms and flipped him over her hip.

He cursed, landing on his feet at an awkward angle. He swiftly recovered. He was, after all, blessed with the same gifts that she was. But it gave her just enough room to leap over the desk, covertly snatching the letter opener out of its stand on the way.

Samuel straightened, his eyes glittering with a hate he'd kept hidden for years.

"You'll pay for that, bitch."

Jaelyn didn't bother to respond, her concentration narrowed to the smooth pearl handle of the letter knife that was clutched in her fingers and the distance to her opponent's heart. Samuel's problem had always been his love for the dramatic.

Jaelyn was a killer. Cold, clean, efficient.

Samuel was a braggart.

"Nothing to say before you die?" he taunted, reaching

behind his back to pull out the handgun he'd tucked in the waistband of his shorts. "No pleas for mercy? Or perhaps you'd rather barter? Are you ready to spread your legs now, my dear?"

She balanced her weight, her gaze never wavering from the center of his chest.

The silver was draining her strength at a dangerous pace. She would have one chance to strike.

She intended to make it a killing blow.

"Fine, I'll make up some cool shit for you when I describe your death scene for the poor, grieving Ruah."

She sensed the moment his finger squeezed the trigger, and with one fluid motion she was leaping through the air. The bullet sliced through her lower calf, but she ignored the pain as she landed directly before him. She would have a fraction of a second before he could shoot again.

All the time she needed.

With blinding speed she was stabbing the knife directly into Samuel's heart, watching as the blue eyes widened in agonized shock.

"No . . ."

Allowing his panic to overcome his training, Samuel dropped the gun and grasped her wrist, attempting to yank the weapon from his heart. Jaelyn, however, was already slicing through his chest, ruthlessly ignoring his hoarse cry.

The crimson blood spilled down the ivory skin of his chest, filling the room with the scent of death.

Distantly Jaelyn was aware of the door being pushed open and the cold rush of power that warned a vampire was entering the room, but she didn't allow her concentration to waver.

Samuel was weakening, but so was she.

Driving him backward, she pinned his flailing body against the wall. Then, with the clinical detachment that had been drilled into her over the past three decades, she used the knife to cut off his head.

It was a slow, messy business, but she never wavered. Not until Samuel's head rolled across the floor, halting at the heavily booted feet of the large vampire standing near the door.

Feeling oddly hollow, Jaelyn allowed her gaze to travel from the lifeless eyes of Samuel up the well-honed body covered in black fatigues to the square face that was all too familiar.

"Kostas," she breathed, dropping the bloody knife.

The leader's soulless black gaze skimmed over her and Jaelyn prepared for his punishment. It didn't matter that she had been lured from her rooms by Samuel. Or that he'd tried to kill her.

If the head of the Addonexus decided she'd broken the rules, then he'd make certain she lived to regret her mistake.

Instead he pointed toward the silver collar around her neck.

"The release is in the back."

She lifted her hands to search the smooth metal, painful minutes passing until she at last located the hidden lever. There was a faint click before the heavy silver parted and she was tossing aside the torture device with a grimace.

"Are you permanently injured?"

She returned her wary attention to the elder vampire, already feeling the charred flesh of her neck beginning to heal.

Kostas looked like a Roman general with his large, muscular body, his finely hewed features, and black hair he kept slicked back into a short tail at his nape. But it wasn't his physical strength that made him dangerous. Or even his considerable powers as a vampire.

It was the utter lack of conscience.

He was the perfect psychopath.

"I'll be fine," she muttered, her gaze dropping to the head that was swiftly turning to ash at his feet. "Samuel is dead."

"So I see. A pity."

He didn't sound like it was a pity.

Actually he sounded . . . satisfied.

Jaelyn wrapped her arms around her chilled body, desperately longing to strip off the soiled robe and spend the next few hours in a hot bath.

"I don't know what happened to him. He . . ." She struggled to keep the horror from her voice. "He attacked me. I had no choice but kill him."

"Yes." With the air of a teacher examining the work of a student, Kostas bent to study the disintegrating head.

"A clean cut despite the dullness of your weapon," he at last concluded, straightening to meet her startled gaze. "Well done."

"Well done?"

His lips stretched into the semblance of a smile. "Actually, I suppose I should say congratulations."

"I don't understand."

"You have passed the last of your tests." He offered a faint nod. "Tomorrow evening you will walk as an equal among the Addonexus."

She tensed.

Did he just say what she thought he said?

"This was a test?" she rasped, the empty sense of shock being swiftly replaced with a white-hot fury.

"It was obvious from the beginning that you possessed all the skills necessary to become one of our finest Hunters. Indeed, it has been centuries since we have found a recruit with your potential." His black gaze was without apology. "But there was concern that your tender heart might make you vulnerable. I am pleased to see that your instinct to survive is capable of overcoming any ridiculous attachment to another."

"You sacrificed Samuel just to see if I would protect myself?"

"You misunderstand." He arched a brow, as if puzzled by her smoldering disbelief. "We sensed the envy that ate at Samuel and we knew it was only a matter of time before he attempted to be rid of you, but we did nothing to encourage his attack."

Was that supposed to make her feel better?

Holy shit.

If she'd been a half a step slower. Or if she'd hesitated for even one second . . .

"And it never occurred to you to warn me?" she hissed.

"Of course not." A hint of annoyance touched his arrogant face. "This was a lesson you needed to learn."

"Damn you." She stumbled backward, disgust toward the Addonexus, toward Samuel, and most of all, toward herself flowing like acid through her veins. "Damn all of you."

It had been several centuries since Ariyal had woken in a strange bedroom with a thick head and queasy stomach.

In fact, the last occasion had been after a two-year-long bender with a Lamia demon who had taught him the meaning of "party 'til you drop."

Now he opened his eyes with a wary caution, not entirely surprised to find himself sprawled on the floor of a cramped chamber that smelled of old blood and sex. None of it his, thank the gods.

What he didn't expect was the unmistakable scent of vampire.

Momentarily disoriented, Ariyal flowed to his feet, instinctively reaching for the dagger he kept at his lower back. Why the hell would he be in the room with a leech . . . ?

Memories crashed through him with the force of a sledgehammer as he glanced toward the narrow bed to discover a female so beautiful she made his heart hurt.

Jaelyn.

They had been together at the mage's townhouse along with Tearloch and his spooky spook. And then Sergei had lobbed a spell at the portal, causing a massive explosion of magic. Dumb-ass.

That's all he remembered until waking in this nasty hellhole.

So the question was, had Jaelyn carried him away from the townhouse to protect him? Or was this just a brief layover before she handed him to the Oracles?

He forgot to care as she stirred on the narrow mattress, her hoarse cry of pain echoing through the room.

"Jaelyn," he called softly. "Jaelyn, can you hear me?"

She continued to thrash about and he moved to perch on the edge of the bed. He wasn't stupid enough to reach out and shake her awake. Poking a sleeping vampire was about as smart as pointing a loaded gun to his head. Instead he sucked in a deep breath; then with one smooth motion he stretched on top of her, grasping her wrists in his hands to tug her arms above her head. Then, using his superior weight, he pinned her lower body to the bed.

He told himself it was the only way to wake her before she attracted unwanted attention, but as he settled against the firm curves he couldn't deny a low groan of approval from rumbling in his chest.

Oh . . . hell. She felt so good pressed against him, her dangerous scent stirring his senses and the cool brush of her power teasing his overheated skin.

He could spend the next several years in this precise position.

Almost as if sensing his treacherous thought, Jaelyn's blue eyes snapped open, dark with a bleak agony that stole the breath from Ariyal's lungs. Seconds later she realized where she was and who was perched on top of her and those magnificent eyes narrowed with a sudden fury.

"Get off me," she hissed, her knee jerking upward with the intention of making him a eunuch.

Blocking the blow with his leg, he smiled down at her frustrated expression.

He far preferred Jaelyn hissing and spitting. The wounded creature he'd briefly glimpsed when she first woke reminded him far too much of himself.

"Careful, poppet," he teased. "I have high hopes of needing that later."

Her lips thinned, but he didn't miss the tiny shiver that raced through her body.

Yeah, she wanted him.

She didn't want to want him. But she wanted him.

"What the hell are you doing?" she muttered.

"You were having a nightmare."

She abruptly averted her gaze, perhaps realizing she'd revealed far more than she desired.

"So you thought you would crawl in bed with me?"

"I was trying to keep you from waking the entire building." His gaze slid over her profile, a moan escaping him at the sharp urge to nuzzle along the vulnerable line of her throat. "I assume you didn't want someone coming to see if you needed help."

"Fine," she snapped. "I'm awake now."

"What were you dreaming about?"

"A damned Sylvermyst who wouldn't get his ass off me," she snarled, turning back to stab him with a fierce glare. "It would make any woman howl in fear."

With a low chuckle he gave into temptation.

"Oh, I could make you howl," he breathed, leaning down to nibble along her lower lip.

"Like I haven't heard that before," she growled even as she arched against him in blatant invitation.

His body reacted with a savage speed, his cock hard and aching to be of service.

"Are you challenging me, poppet?" he murmured, giving her lip a sharp nip before exploring the sensitive curve of her neck.

"Ariyal."

"Mmmm?"

"I told you to get off me."

"Yes, I heard you the first time."

"Then why . . ." She gave a small shriek as he gently bit the flesh at the base of her neck. "Shit."

"More?" he demanded, running his tongue along the line of her tender vein. "How about here?" He gave her another bite just below her jaw.

She squirmed in obvious pleasure. "You did that on purpose," she breathed.

He laughed at her accusing tone. "I wouldn't be much of a lover if I did it by accident."

"You're not my lover."

He pulled back to meet her guarded gaze. "Do you object to the concept or the term?"

"Both."

His gaze dipped down to where her tightly budded nipples pressed against the spandex material of her top.

"Liar."

Her eyes flashed indigo fire. "You're so damned arrogant."

"Confident," he corrected, lowering his head. "If you don't want this then tell me no."

He moved slowly. Slowly enough that she would have ample opportunity to refuse him, despite the fact she could have knocked him across the cramped room from the moment she woke.

He didn't want her later claiming he'd forced her into anything.

Feeling her tense he paused just over her lips, waiting for her to push him away.

Deep inside, a cowardly part of him almost hoped she would call an end to the madness. This addictive craving for a female who might very well prove to be his enemy was a weakness he couldn't afford. Not if he was to bring an end to the threat of the Dark Lord.

That part, thankfully, was buried beneath a jolt of white-hot pleasure when she lifted her head off the pillow to close the shallow space between their lips.

The taste of her was like the finest brandy. Smooth, silky, with a burn he could feel to the tips of his toes. Oh . . . bloody hell. Over the past centuries he'd forgotten the explosive excitement of mutual passion. He'd trained himself to use sex as a weapon for the survival of his people. It had become an unfortunate necessity.

And then Jaelyn had crashed into his life.

A beautiful, lethal predator in spandex who had managed to kick-start his lust into hyperdrive and reminded him in vivid detail the pleasure of being a fully functioning male.

The wonder of touching and being touched. Of feeling her tempting body soften in welcome. Of being consumed by the tidal wave of desire.

"Tell me that you want me, poppet," he murmured against her lips. "I need to hear the words."

"You talk too much," she growled, allowing her fangs to press against his lower lip.

The feel of those lethal fangs should have jerked him out of his sensual haze. The female could drain him in a heart-beat. But instead of fear a raw sense of anticipation seared through him.

It was . . . intoxicating.

"Admit the truth. You want me."

His commanding words were imprisoned against his lips as she once again claimed his mouth in a kiss that demanded capitulation. He was prepared to react to her touch, but the sheer power of it caught him off guard.

God, yes. This was precisely what he'd wanted from the first minute he'd caught sight of this female stalking him.

He pressed her against the mattress, drinking in the cool enticement that was uniquely Jaelyn. And still she was not close enough. He growled deep in his throat as he reached down to grasp her top and with one tug ripped it over her head to reveal the smooth perfection of her alabaster breasts tipped with pale rose nipples.

"You're so beautiful," he whispered in aching tones, his head dipping down to capture the tip of her beaded nipple between his lips.

With a whimper, Jaelyn shifted beneath him, wrapping her legs around his hips.

"This is insanity," she muttered.

He lifted his head to meet her glittering gaze. "Do you want me to stop?"

"Stop and I'll kill you," she rasped, wrenching her arms from his confining grasp to reach for his T-shirt. With one motion she was wrestling it off him with obvious impatience.

Ariyal had imagined the sensation of her hands running over his skin a hundred times, but nothing could prepare him for the actual reality. He shuddered beneath her exploring touch, his erection straining against the zipper of his jeans.

"Then tell me what you want, Jaelyn."

"You." She trembled as he kissed his way over the curve of her ear. "I want you."

"Now?"

"Yes."

His hands trailed up her bare arms, savoring the cool silk of her skin.

"No regrets." He gave a small nip at the lobe of her ear, smiling as she jerked beneath him.

"Did I mention you talk too much?"

He gave her another nip. "Yes."

"I . . ."

Her sharp retort was lost as his hands shifted to cup her breasts, his thumbs circling her straining nipples.

"Yes?" he prompted.

"I don't remember."

He softly chuckled as his lips drifted over her cheek before nuzzling the edge of her mouth.

"I want you naked," he murmured as he forced his reluctant hands to leave the delicious temptation of her breasts to skim down her slender hips, pushing off the spandex pants before jerking off the rest of his own clothes. Then, urging her legs to wrap back around his hips, he settled until his arousal was pressed directly against her point of pleasure. "Perfect."

Jaelyn shuddered at the feel of his hard erection rubbing against her. Holy shit. She'd always been in control on the rare occasions she'd taken a lover.

She found it oddly erotic to be in bed with a man who could equal her in strength.

And stubborn determination.

His power was as heady as the rarest aphrodisiac.

"Jaelyn, look at me."

She shivered at his soft command; then at last she lifted her gaze. Any lingering hesitation was seared away by the smoldering heat that filled his bronzed eyes.

"Satisfied?" she murmured.

"Not nearly." A slow, wicked smile curved his lips. "Touch me, beautiful Jaelyn."

Jaelyn's head tilted back as she eagerly allowed her hands to explore the hard plane of his back.

She wasn't beautiful. She was too skinny. Her muscles too hard. Her breasts too small.

But beneath his predatory gaze she felt desired.

Growling deep in his throat Ariyal lowered his head, his lips kissing a hungry path down her throat to her collarbone. He pressed hard enough for Jaelyn to feel the blunt edge of his teeth, but she made no effort to pull away.

She shifted her hands to his chest in a restless path, reveling in the satin heat of his skin. It was a fascinating contrast to the vampire lovers she'd taken in the past.

Intrigued with exploring his body, Jaelyn barely noticed when Ariyal lowered his head. Not until he captured a nipple between his lips.

She sighed in approval as his tongue swirled over the sensitized tip, teasing it until her back was arched in delight. Oh, he was good. So amazingly good.

Now if only he would stop tormenting her with the hard brush of his cock and actually enter her.

"Are you going to finish this or not?" she moaned, shivering as his lips traced the curve between the mounds of her breasts before moving to taste her neglected nipple.

"Patience, poppet."

She hissed, her fingers tugging at the clasp holding back his hair to allow the chestnut strands to spill over her skin, heightening the pleasure that pulsed through her body.

Don't bite, she fiercely reminded herself, as his hands branded a path down the curve of her hips and over her thighs. Things were complicated enough without taking his vein.

It was a compulsion that was becoming increasingly difficult to resist as Ariyal eased his hand between her legs and sought the aching cleft between them. Her hands shifted to his shoulders, her fingers unwittingly digging into his flesh to draw a pinprick of blood.

The potent scent of herbs filled the air even as his finger stroked over the sweet spot of her pleasure. She was falling into a maelstrom of sensations that were almost overwhelming.

"Ariyal."

Perhaps sensing her battle against her twin hungers, Ariyal lifted his head to stroke his lips over her mouth.

"Let go, Jaelyn," he softly urged.

"I can't," she rasped.

"What do you fear?"

She moaned as her hips instinctively lifted to press more firmly to his caressing finger.

"Losing control."

He lifted onto his elbow and peered deep into her wary eyes. "I've got you, sweetheart."

For a long moment she studied his starkly elegant face.

His beauty wasn't the same as the frigid perfection of a vampire. He was mist and hot enchantment and dark magic.

Don't be a fool, Jaelyn, a warning voice whispered in the back of her mind.

She'd been taught a brutal lesson in trusting others.

One she didn't intend to repeat.

But even as her mind warned of caution, her hands were framing his face so she could kiss him with the pent-up passion that thundered through her.

He groaned, his hand shifting to spear his finger into her body. He swallowed her cry of pleasure as her hips left the mattress, his tongue stroking a dangerous path over her fully extended fangs.

She was being consumed by flames, drowning in the heat of his touch and the blaze of his unrestrained need.

Opening her mouth to his thrusting tongue, she skimmed her hand down his chest. She didn't mind sharing control, but she wasn't a passive lover.

Ariyal sucked in a startled breath as she brushed her fingertips over the rippled muscles of his stomach and then clutched his cock in a firm grip.

"Shit," he hissed between clenched teeth. "I can't play games tonight."

She knew the feeling.

She was close. So very close.

"Then finish this."

"Yes."

Holding her gaze as she positioned him, Ariyal gave her one last stroke of his finger before sinking his erection deep inside her.

They groaned in unison, holding absolutely still as they absorbed the sensation of being so intimately connected. Then, feeling the hunger once again threatening to overwhelm her, Jaelyn dug her fingers into the tight muscles of his ass.

"Ariyal."

"I know," he muttered against her mouth, his hips slowly pulling back before shoving forward with a blissful force. "Hold on tight."

She pressed her face into the curve of his neck as he set a fierce pace, her fangs aching and the bed shaking beneath the impact of his thrusts.

"Please," she moaned, the building pressure narrowing to a shimmering promise that hovered just out of reach. "More. I need . . ."

"That's it, poppet," he breathed into her ear, his hand slipping between them to caress the tiny nub of pleasure. "Trust me and let go."

"Yes."

Her entire body clenched and hovered for a timeless moment; then with shocking force she shattered into a million, joyous pieces.

Chapter 8

A part of Ariyal cringed at the realization he'd just made fierce, passionate love to this beautiful female in surroundings that weren't fit for a hellhound.

No matter how desperately he wanted Jaelyn, he should have been capable of waiting until he could offer her at least the illusion of comfort.

But a larger part of him was indifferent to the hard, narrow bed and grimy cell. Or even the distant stench of demons entering a large room overhead.

He had just experienced the most shockingly blissful climax of his long, long life. The last emotion he could stir up was regret.

Actually, he wasn't sure what the hell he was feeling as he snuggled the silent vampire against his chest, his fingers running through the cool silk of her hair.

"Tell me about your nightmare," he commanded before he could halt the words.

Not surprisingly she stiffened, her reluctance to discuss her past a tangible force in the air.

"Give it a rest, fairy," she growled.

"No."

She pulled back to stab him with a steely glare. "Do you want to talk about your years with Morgana le Fey?"

His jaw clenched. Of course he didn't want to discuss that crazy-ass bitch. If he had his choice the name of Morgana le Fey would be scrubbed from the history of the world.

But for reasons that should no doubt be making him wail in fear, he wanted to know what haunted her when she slept.

No, not wanted. *Needed.*

"What do you want to know?"

She frowned, caught off guard by his abrupt capitulation. Had she been bluffing? Then he felt the slight easing of her muscles as she nestled against him and a genuine curiosity melted the frost on the indigo eyes.

"Were you her lover?"

"I was her slave, not her lover."

She gave a slow nod. Did she understand the soul-numbing difference between the two?

"Did she hurt you?"

"She took pleasure in causing pain."

"She tortured you?"

"In the beginning." His arms tightened around her as he was battered by the memories he struggled so hard to keep buried. "Eventually she discovered that it caused me far greater distress to see my brothers hurt."

She paused, clearly sensing his injuries ran far deeper than a few scars.

"Did she use her magic?"

"Sometimes." His voice was thick as he choked on the vivid image of blood. So much blood. "Usually she preferred to carve them with her knife." He shuddered. "She called it her living art."

She stroked a tentative hand over his chest. As if unfamiliar with offering comfort.

"She made you watch?"

"Yes."

"Bitch."

Oddly her simple condemnation was more soothing than any amount of fancy words of sympathy.

"That was the general consensus," he agreed dryly.

She paused, studying him with an unwavering gaze. "Was it worth the sacrifice?"

He shrugged.

It was a question that was never far from his mind.

It didn't seem possible that anything could be worth enduring such pain and loss. But then he had only to recall the brutal days beneath the rule of the Dark Lord to be reminded of why they were willing to sacrifice everything to be free.

"It will be if I can prevent the return of the Dark Lord," he said, tugging a strand of her raven hair. "Which is why I'll do whatever I have to to keep him imprisoned."

She ignored his warning. "What will you do if you succeed?"

"Live in peace with my tribe."

"With you as their prince?"

He shrugged. He'd never asked to become prince.

"Until they choose a new leader."

"Do you get a throne and a crown?"

His brows lifted. Was she actually teasing him?

The thought was unexpectedly erotic.

Okay, every thought that included Jaelyn was erotic, he wryly conceded, rolling on top of her slender frame with a low groan of satisfaction.

"No, but I do get my choice of consorts," he murmured.

"Really?" Her lips tightened. Ah, feminine disapproval. It spanned the species. "I suppose you have them all picked out?"

He shifted until he could press his hardening erection against her inner thigh.

"One, at least."

A dark emotion flared through her eyes before it was being ruthlessly crushed.

Had it been . . . yearning?

No, impossible.

"Don't look my way, fairy. Even if I didn't want to constantly punch you in the face, I'm not consort material."

"I'm a patient man," he assured her, bending down to whisper against her lips, still swollen from his kisses. "I'm willing to train you."

She rammed her fingers into his hair, but she made no effort to push him away.

Thank the gods.

"For a fairy who claims he wants to live in peace you play a dangerous game."

He traced her bottom lip with the tip of his tongue. "Your turn to share."

She shivered, the scent of her arousal spicing the air. "I think I've shared more than enough."

"Tell me, Jaelyn."

"Tell you what?"

"Why do you have nightmares?"

She cursed, abruptly pressing her hands against his chest. "Levet."

He lifted his head with a frown. "The gargoyle?"

"Yes."

Ariyal had a vague recollection of the miniature demon who had been traveling with the vampire Tane.

Aggravating pest.

"Well, he would certainly give anyone nightmares, but I'm not sure what he has to do with our conversation," he muttered.

"He's approaching."

"Now?"

"Yes."

"Damn."

With a pang of regret, he rolled off the bed and yanked on the jeans that had replaced his dojo pants before he left Avalon. Then, holding out his hand, he muttered the harsh words of magic that called his bow and arrows.

Behind him he heard Jaelyn pulling on her bits of spandex before she moved to stand at his side.

"What are you doing?"

"His arrival can't be a coincidence." Ariyal concentrated on the door, prepared to shoot the moment it opened. "The creature has obviously followed us here."

"Not us," Jaelyn corrected. "He's looking for your charming spirit."

"Who?"

"Yannah. He has some sort of gargoyle crush on her."

He turned to watch her efficiently pull her hair into a smooth braid.

"Is this a joke?"

She crushed his brief hope with a decisive shake of her head. "No. He scented Yannah on me when I arrived in London and decided to join us."

"And you let him?" he snarled in disbelief.

"Hey, he helped me rescue your ass, so just . . ."

"Just what?"

"Chill."

The King of Were's lair in St. Louis

Santiago shuddered as the mists at last cleared.
Mierda.
He hadn't signed up for this when Styx had sent him in search of Cassandra.

He was prepared to battle demons, Sylvermyst, and even a mage if necessary.

He wasn't prepared to be hauled around in a strange,

choking mist by an exquisite female who had turned her back on the world centuries ago.

Or to abruptly find himself in an unfamiliar room miles from where he'd started.

Swiftly he took stock of his surroundings.

A dirt floor. Cement walls that were lined with towering shelves that held hundreds of dusty bottles. A collection of aged-wood barrels in the center of the room. And at the far end a series of arched doorways where Santiago could catch the low hum of refrigerators.

A wine cellar?

"Where the hell did you bring me?" he muttered in confusion.

"I am not entirely certain." Nefri shrugged, not looking nearly as troubled at having dumped them in this strange cellar as she should. Not even when an unmistakable stench filled the air.

Santiago yanked the dagger from the sheath hidden at his lower back.

"Dogs," he hissed.

"Bloodsucker," a mocking voice retorted as one of the shelves slid aside to allow a pureblooded Were and a cur to step out of a hidden tunnel.

Santiago lifted his brows at the sight of Salvatore and his faithful sidekick Hess.

As always, the King of Weres was dressed in a hand-tailored designer suit. This one was an Italian wool in a pale charcoal with a white shirt and a burgundy tie. With his dark hair pulled into a neat tail and his lean face freshly shaved, he looked more like a mobster than a Were. His companion, on the other hand, looked like a hired thug with his six-foot-six, heavily muscled body and shaved head.

"Ah, not just a dog, but the King of Mutts," he taunted, grimacing as Salvatore snapped his impressive teeth in his direction. "Shouldn't royalty be house-trained?"

Pointing a gun that was loaded with silver bullets directly at Santiago's heart, Salvatore nodded toward Hess, who swiftly moved to stand behind Nefri. The cur's indecent bulk and the brutal glint in his eye made the slender female appear dangerously vulnerable, but no one in the room was stupid enough to doubt that she could kill any of them in a blink of an eye.

Her power pulsed about her in terrifying waves.

"Santiago." Salvatore placed himself so he could keep an eye on both intruders. "Clearly I need to have a word with Styx. The arrogant bastard doesn't seem to understand the concept of barriers."

"Styx had nothing to do with our . . ." Santiago considered his words. Vampires and Weres were natural-born enemies. And both species relished their mutual desire to exterminate the other. But for the past few months Salvatore and Styx had called an uneasy truce as they were forced to work together to halt the greater evil. The Anasso would skin Santiago alive if he screwed up the temporary treaty. "Unexpected arrival."

Salvatore narrowed his gaze. "You expect me to believe you managed to sneak past my guards without assistance?"

Santiago deliberately glanced toward the silent Nefri. "Our arrival was unconventional, to say the least."

The King of Weres turned to study the dark-haired vampire, giving a whistle as he took stock of her delicate beauty.

"Cristo." He returned his gaze to Santiago. "She's way out of your league, *amico*. Did she lose a bet or are you holding her hostage?"

Santiago scowled. Out of his league? Was he supposed to be insulted? Nefri was out of everyone's league.

Not only was the female heart-meltingly beautiful with the sort of regal grace that made a man itch to tumble her on her back and kiss away that aloof perfection, but she was also proving to be intelligent, cultured, and surprisingly resourceful.

And oh yeah, there was a very real possibility that she was the most powerful creature walking the face of the earth.

Besides, even if he was idiotic enough to long for the exquisite, unattainable Nefri (which he most certainly was not) she was a member of a clan who thought they were superior to the common vampires.

Arrogant snobs.

"She's an Immortal One," he said, his voice carefully bland.

"Really?" Salvatore blinked in genuine shock. "I thought they were a myth."

Santiago met Nefri's dark gaze, childishly annoyed by her serene composure. Did nothing rattle her?

"Unfortunately they're very real."

"Unfortunately?" Salvatore shot him a glance filled with pure male disapproval. "Have you gone blind?"

"He is somewhat prejudiced," Nefri explained, a mysterious smile curving her lips.

Salvatore moved toward the bewitching female, leaning close enough to draw in her exotic jasmine scent.

"Interesting," he murmured.

Santiago didn't even know he was moving until he was suddenly standing at Nefri's side, his fangs bared in warning.

To hell with the treaty.

If Salvatore touched Nefri he was a dead dog.

"Stay back."

The golden eyes briefly glowed as the wolf sensed a direct challenge; then with a sudden laugh the Were stepped back.

"Feeling a little possessive, are you, Santiago?" he mocked.

Possessive? Of course he wasn't possessive. He adored women. All women. And they adored him. But he was a firm believer in the more the merrier.

It was just . . .

Mierda, he didn't know what it was, but he did know that Salvatore was annoying the crap out of him.

"I doubt your mate would be pleased to know you spend your days sniffing other women."

Salvatore's smile widened, as if sensing Santiago's strange reaction.

"And you're concerned for my marriage? How thoughtful."

Nefri smoothly stepped between the two bristling men, giving a small dip of her head.

"I offer my apologies, Your Majesty," she said. "It was not my intent to trespass upon your territory."

Salvatore's gaze remained trained on Santiago. "A leech with manners? Isn't that an oxymoron?"

"Such a big word for such a mangy dog," Santiago said.

With a lethal swiftness, all sense of amusement was wiped from Salvatore's handsome face to reveal the true predator beneath.

"How did you get here?" he demanded.

Seemingly realizing that playtime was over, Nefri reached to brush her fingers over the medallion hung around her neck.

"I have the power to travel between worlds."

"Like a Jinn?"

"It is similar, although my powers come from the medallion and not my innate abilities."

Salvatore's eyes narrowed, clearly not comforted by her explanation.

"A nice trick," he growled. "Perfect for an ambush."

"I do try not to abuse the skill," Nefri assured him.

"If you didn't abuse the skill then you wouldn't be in my very private wine cellar, would you?"

"Watch your tone, Salvatore," Santiago snapped.

Nefri waved her slender hand. "He has a right to answers."

"More than a right," Salvatore corrected, his inner beast prowling close to the surface. "In fact, let's pretend your lives depend on your explanation."

"As you are perhaps aware, Santiago is searching for the seer," Nefri answered before Santiago could tell the King of Mutts exactly where he could shove his threats. "I have come in search for Cassandra as well."

"And you think I have her hidden in my wine cellar?"

"Do you?" Santiago asked. "It would certainly explain . . ."

"Gentlemen, please," Nefri gently protested.

"Gentlemen?" Salvatore snorted. "He's a cold-blooded bastard who will kill on a whim."

"And you're a mangy prick who likes to play Dr. Frankenstein."

Nefri's power swirled through the air with just enough force to make both men shudder at the promise of pain.

"I am beginning to think the term 'children' would be more appropriate," she said in dry tones.

The men grimaced in unison before Salvatore gave a wave of his hand.

"Continue."

"We entered your clansman's lair. . . ."

"Clansman?" the Were interrupted with a frown.

"Caine," Santiago clarified.

Salvatore gave a sound of disgust. The King of Weres still blamed the one-time cur for being a pawn of the demon lord intent on destroying the werewolves. Caine's transformation to a pureblood hadn't dimmed Salvatore's desire to eat him for breakfast.

Literally.

"Did you find any trace of them?" Salvatore demanded.

"No, they had disappeared," Nefri explained.

"And it didn't occur to you to follow?"

"There was no means to track them."

"A pity," Salvatore retorted, "but I'm still not hearing what brings you to my humble abode."

Nefri shrugged. "If I cannot follow her trail forward, then I must follow it backward."

"Backward? Is that some sort of vampire logic?"

"If we can retrace their steps then we can speak with those who saw them last." Without warning, the female vampire drifted toward the nearby shelves, her beautiful face distracted. "It might tell us if they were traveling to a particular destination or if they feared they were being followed. If nothing else they might have mentioned if they were to meet anyone in Chicago."

Seemingly impressed by Nefri's logic, Salvatore slid a glance in Santiago's direction.

"Intelligent as well as beautiful—you're in trouble, *amico mio.*"

Santiago wisely ignored the taunt, suddenly realizing why Nefri had brought them to these particular cellars.

She had followed Cassandra's scent to this location.

"You failed to mention that Cassandra paid you a visit," he said in cold accusation.

Salvatore scowled. "That's because she didn't."

"Are you certain?" Santiago demanded, shifting so he could keep an eye on Nefri as she ran a hand over a wooden shelf.

The golden eyes glowed with an eerie power. "No one calls me a liar and survives."

"Keep your fur on," he snarled. "Maybe she visited your mate while you were out."

Salvatore looked at him as if he'd lost his mind. "Harley has been desperate to be reunited with her sister. If Cassandra had dropped by, then I would have heard every detail, no matter how insignificant, of their reunion."

"Maybe Cassandra asked her to keep the meeting a secret."

"Obviously you've never been mated," Salvatore muttered. "She wasn't here."

"She was." Nefri intruded into the argument, giving a sharp shove of the shelves.

There was the sound of creaking wood; then the shelves swung to the side, revealing a cement-lined room the size of a walk-in closet. The perfect size for a prison cell. At the moment it was empty, but clutching the medallion in her hand, Nefri briefly closed her eyes and muttered a low word. The air stirred and Santiago stiffened in shock at the unmistakable scent of a female pureblood.

"Cassandra."

"Her scent was masked by a spell," Nefri explained.

For the first time since their entrance, Hess moved, reminding Santiago that he was more than a lump of muscle.

"And Caine the Traitor," he rasped, his eyes glowing the red of a cur on the point of shifting.

Salvatore sent his lieutenant a warning glare before brushing past Nefri to enter the cement cell. He smoothly crouched down to study the dried blood on the floor.

"Can you tell us how long ago?" he demanded of Nefri.

"Two, maybe three weeks."

Santiago moved to stand next to the Were, still not entirely certain the mangy beast was as baffled as he pretended to be by the revelation of Cassandra and Caine's presence in the wine cellars.

"Why would they sneak into your lair?"

Salvatore straightened with unnerving speed, standing nose to nose with Santiago.

"Careful, bloodsucker."

With a click of her tongue Nefri shooed them away from the blood stains, still clutching the medallion in her hand. As she whispered a low word there was another shift in the air, revealing a tangle of scents that had been hidden by illusion.

Santiago muttered a curse, glancing at the stain. "It's Caine's blood. He must have been trying to protect Cassandra."

"Si." Salvatore absently agreed, his head tilted back as he breathed deeply of the stale air. "I smell vamp." He stabbed Santiago with a suspicious glare. "Do you recognize the scent?"

"No."

"What do you mean, no?"

"It's . . ." Santiago struggled to explain. "Missing. I can sense it was a vampire, but there's a void around him."

The Were scowled. "An amulet?"

"No." Santiago shook his head, as confused as the Were. "The vampire isn't hidden, it's more like he, or she, has been stripped of his identity."

"Impossible."

"Then you explain what the hell it is."

The dark eyes glowed a dangerous gold. "At first guess, I would say it's a trick."

Santiago ran a finger down the edge of his blade. "It's not just a vampire. There was also a cur."

"Two curs," Nefri murmured, a troubled expression marring her Madonna calm. "And a witch."

Salvatore arched his brows in surprise. "The witch would explain the magic to cover their presence here. But what the hell were they doing with Cassandra and Caine?"

Her dark, magnificent eyes skimmed the stark cement cell.

"They lured them here."

Santiago moved to stand at her side, shivering as her cool energy wrapped around him, licking over his skin and stirring his hair. *Santa madre*, that much power roused him like the finest aphrodisiac.

"Why?"

Her dark eyes held an ancient sadness. "They intended to capture them."

Santiago grimaced. "Traitors."

She dipped her head in reluctant agreement. "Traitors."

Chapter 9

Jaelyn stumbled out of the portal and into the large meadow with the grace of a drunken harpy.

Recovering her balance, she whirled around, fully prepared to punish anyone stupid enough to be laughing at her. Luckily for them, her companions were struggling with their own exits.

Levet landed on his head, his horns stuck in the soft dirt. And right behind him, Ariyal fell to his knees, his long braid falling over his shoulder as he bent forward, struggling to catch his breath.

Obviously the effort of creating a portal to take three demons from England to America, not to mention bending time to make sure they arrived precisely at nightfall to keep Jaelyn from being turned into ash, had taken its toll.

"Bloody hell," the Sylvermyst panted, casting an evil glare at the gargoyle, who had managed to free himself and was busy knocking the mud from his horns. "That's the last time I haul your stony ass halfway around the world."

The gargoyle squeaked in horror, his wings flapping as he turned in a circle, attempting to peer over his shoulder.

"Are you implying that I'm fat?" He halted to turn a pleading glance toward Jaelyn. "*Ma enfant*, am I fat?"

"Of course not," she assured the tiny demon.

"There, you see?" He sent a raspberry toward Ariyal, patting his backside. "I have buns of steel."

The Sylvermyst growled a harsh obscenity while Jaelyn struggled to hide her smile.

She'd convinced Ariyal they couldn't leave the gargoyle behind. He was too intimately acquainted with their quest to track down the child of the Dark Lord to risk him falling into the hands of their enemies.

How much torture would the tiny creature endure before he was blabbing everything he knew?

Battle tactics demanded they keep him close at hand.

But she couldn't deny the fact that Levet irritated Ariyal on an epic scale was a decided bonus.

"You're a lump of granite who should have been left in the sewers of London," Ariyal snapped, rising to his feet with a fluid grace that tugged at something deep inside Jaelyn.

She shifted uneasily, her gaze tracing the elegant male profile.

Dammit. This was why she was trained to avoid sexual relationships.

It would be bad enough to take him as her lover if he was still her target, but at least then she could have turned him over to the Commission after the deed was done. Or better yet, killed him.

Now she had no choice but to follow him when he claimed he could use his tribal connection with Tearloch to track him down.

A breeze stirred the air, bringing with it the rich scent of herbs. Ariyal's scent.

Her fangs lengthened, her hunger rising as her gaze instinctively slid to the strong column of his neck. She swallowed a groan, sharply turning away.

She needed to feed.

This brutal urgency had nothing to do with Ariyal's blood in particular.

Nothing, nothing, nothing.

"I'll leave you two to your male bonding," she muttered, heading down the path as she sought to get her bearings.

Although they were currently surrounded by open meadows on one side and cornfields on the other, she easily sensed the press of humanity that marked Chicago. It also included a large clan of vampires she hoped to avoid.

Thankfully closer at hand was a decent-sized town that should offer a meal as well as a much-desired shower.

Intent on her escape, Jaelyn clenched her hands in frustration as Ariyal abruptly appeared before her, his face tight with suspicion.

"Where are you going?"

Her brows snapped together at his possessive tone. "Does it matter?"

His eyes shimmered with a pure bronze in the moonlight. "Yes, it damned well matters."

"Why?"

"I don't intend to be stuck with that miniature pain in the ass." He pointed toward Levet, who was busy sniffing a bush. "Besides, how do I know you're not going for reinforcements to force me to the Oracles?"

She snorted. "As if I need reinforcements."

"Then tell me where you're going."

She folded her arms over her chest. "My errand has nothing to do with you."

"Shit, Jaelyn," he growled. "Does everything have to be a fight?"

Her lips thinned as she squashed the urge to continue with their petty squabbling.

"Fine. I must feed," she grudgingly confessed. "Satisfied?"

Expecting the aggravating fairy to step aside, Jaelyn

wasn't prepared when he instead reached out to grab her upper arms and yanked her hard against his body.

"No, I'm not satisfied."

She glared at him in astonishment. Had he lost his mind? Nobody manhandled a vampire.

Not unless they had a death wish.

"Well, that's too bad," she hissed, telling herself it was only her duty to the Addonexus that kept her from ripping out Ariyal's throat.

Instead she planted her hands against his chest and shoved just hard enough to give her the necessary space to continue down the pathway.

"Wait." He was once again standing in front of her, his expression set in stubborn lines.

"What?"

"Use me."

"You?"

"I have blood." He deliberately angled his head to expose the tempting length of his throat. "Drink."

A piercing yearning shot through her, the vivid image of her fangs buried deep in his throat as he held her pressed tight against his body searing through her mind.

Oh . . . hell.

She was in trouble.

The sort of trouble that could get her killed if she wasn't careful.

"No," she muttered, wrenching her gaze from his neck to meet the fierce glitter in his eyes. "No."

"Why not?"

"It's not the kind I need."

"Liar." His hand cupped her cheek, his thumb teasing at her lower lip. "Vampires find Sylvermyst blood intoxicating. I've had to kill more than one to keep them off my neck."

She shuddered, her fangs aching.

"Hunters have a specific nutritional need."

There was enough truth in her words to make him scowl in frustration.

"And where do you expect to find these nutritional needs?"

"There's a town not far from here."

"Will you hunt?"

She studied him in confusion. She'd been so shocked by her barbaric reaction to his offer of a vein that she hadn't considered why the arrogant, highly distrustful fey would share his royal blood.

Now she studied him in confusion. "What are you asking?"

"Will you sink your fangs into another man's vein?"

She blinked. Holy shit. Was he jealous?

"That's none of your . . ."

"I made it my business when I took you as my lover," he snapped, his head swooping down like a bird of prey.

She braced herself as his mouth branded her lips in a kiss that she felt to the tips of her toes.

For a crazed minute she simply savored the intoxicating pleasure that threatened to consume her. There was no logical explanation for why this man's touch could overcome decades of brutal training, but the urge to rip off her clothes and beg for him to ease her throbbing desire was undeniable.

And why shouldn't I?

A quickie in the cornfield might take the edge off and allow her to regain the icy control that was annoyingly elusive.

"No." She shook her head, ruthlessly crushing the wicked temptation. She was in this stupid mess because she'd been weak. It wouldn't happen again. "Last night . . . it was . . ."

The heat of his fey magic filled the air, as enticing as it was lethal.

"Try to claim that it was a mistake and I'll prove you wrong, regardless of our audience," he snarled, his expression warning that he wasn't bluffing.

"Barbarian," she accused, even as a deep, primitive part of her wanted him to make good on his threat.

To simply toss her on the ground and have his evil way with her.

Over and over and over.

"You'd better believe it, poppet," he agreed without apology.

Appalled by her arousal, which was scenting the air, she yanked free of his arms and pointed a finger in his too-handsome face.

"Don't ever make the mistake of thinking you own me."

Her warning delivered, she shrouded herself in shadows and moved with lightning speed down the pathway.

There was no way she was going to risk being stopped again. Not when she couldn't be trusted not to take the blood she so desperately craved.

She skirted several farmhouses where the humans were nestled in front of their televisions or finishing up the last of their chores. Not one would ever suspect how closely death had brushed past them.

Maintaining the thick shadows that kept her hidden from even the most perceptive demons, Jaelyn angled through a field of soybeans and then slowed her pace as she reached the outskirts of town.

It was set up in the typical Midwest style.

A few brick, colonial-style homes discreetly hidden behind massive oak trees that eventually gave way to the convenience stores and local hotels. Along the main street was a line of small shops that were shuttered for the night, and farther down a cluster of chain restaurants that glowed with neon invitation to the residents.

The side streets led to tidy, well-manicured neighbor-hoods where the humans covertly kept track of their neigh-bors while attempting to hide their own naughty secrets. And of course, on the fringes were a few of the more shabby neighborhoods where the residents were too busy surviving to give a crap what anyone else was doing.

Jaelyn ignored both as she instead crossed the parking lot that was shared between the junior college and the small hospital. She slipped through a side door, choosing the back staircase despite the fact she could have easily moved down the brightly lit hallways without attracting the attention of the medical staff.

Why tempt fate?

Bounding up the steps five at a time, she reached the upper floor in a matter of seconds and was shoving open the door to the closed lab. Just as quickly she was searching the refrigerator units that lined the back wall, pulling out three bags of blood and taking them to the high-powered microscopes that were set on the long table in the center of the room.

She hadn't lied to Ariyal when she told him that Hunters had specific dietary requirements.

Although vampires tried to keep the knowledge a deep, dark secret, their greatest vulnerability was through the blood they had to drink to survive.

With the proper skills and the willingness to risk certain death if they failed, a demon could inject just enough silver into their bloodstream so a vampire could not scent the danger until too late. Of course, they would have to be impervious to silver themselves and then convince a vampire to drink enough of their blood to poison them.

Not as easy as one might think.

And then there was the danger from their primary food source . . . humans.

When a vampire consumed the blood of an addict there was a danger they could become addicted themselves. Slowly and inevitably they would be driven insane as their brains rotted from the contaminated blood.

She'd been trained never to put anything in her fangs that hadn't been tested.

A task made considerably easier by technology, she conceded, taking a small drop of blood from each bag and studying it beneath the high-powered microscopes. Her senses were extremely acute, but they could be deceived.

Science was absolute.

Once assured the blood was hygienic, she swiftly emptied the bags, telling herself that it didn't matter that it tasted flat. Food was for sustenance, wasn't it? She fed because it was a necessity. Only idiots combined passion with their dinner.

And if her hunger for a certain herb-scented blood continued to plague her . . . well, too bad.

Cursing the day, or rather night, she'd crossed paths with Ariyal, the pain-in-the-ass Prince of Sylvermyst, Jaelyn took time for a thorough shower in the employees' private bathroom before heading out of the hospital and back to the main avenue. Once there she found the nearest clothing store and pulled on a pair of black stretchy workout pants that hugged her from her hips to just below her knees as well as a matching crop top that covered her breasts and not much else.

She didn't bother to consider what she looked like in the outfit. She chose the clothing because it didn't impede her movements and would blend into the night. Her feminine vanity had been the first thing to be taken from her by the Ruah.

On her way out the store, her attention was captured by a rack of men's clothing. A slow, wicked smile curved her lips as she yanked one of the shirts from the hanger, then for good measure moved to collect a pair of faded jeans from the sale bin before heading out of the door.

With her foul mood abruptly lightened, Jaelyn tucked

the clothes in a bag. Then, leaving the store, she made one more stop before heading out of town.

Ariyal had never understood the claim that someone was "fit to be tied."

Not unless it included a beautiful female, a length of satin rope, and a soft bed.

Forty-five minutes after Jaelyn had disappeared he was learning the painful meaning of being "fit to be tied."

Pacing through the meadow, he absently gathered handfuls of blackberries that were just ripening as well a few of the more tender leaves that he dipped in fresh honey. Like most Sylvermyst, he was a vegetarian who preferred his meal directly from nature, although his brute strength came from the blood of his enemies.

But satisfying his physical hunger did nothing to ease his frustration.

It was insane.

After centuries of being enslaved by a vicious bitch, the last thing he should want was to be at the mercy of another female. Especially one who couldn't seem to decide if she wanted to lick him to paradise or rip out his throat.

Psycho women should be on his list of things to kill not on his list of those to get in his bed with all possible speed.

So why wasn't he getting on with his business? He knew better than anyone that as long as the child remained with Tearloch there was the danger that the Dark Lord would be returned. The clock was ticking, and he couldn't afford to waste a second.

Instead, he was pacing the meadow and imagining a dozen different scenarios, all of which included Jaelyn injured or captured or . . .

A frigid chill swept through the air, sending a flood of sharp relief through his body, closely followed by a ready male response to the potent womanly scent that filled his senses.

Precisely the two reactions he didn't want, dammit.

He turned to watch as she stepped into the meadow, his heart squeezing at the mere sight of her.

Gods, but she was beautiful.

She'd showered while she was gone. Her silken hair was still damp and it glowed as glossy as a raven's wing in the moonlight despite being wrenched into a tight braid. She'd also changed, although the stretchy bits of black cloth did nothing to lower his blood pressure. To top it off she'd matched the sexy ensemble with a brand-spanking-new sawed-off shotgun, which she'd strapped to her slender waist with a belt lined with cartridges.

Holy . . . shit.

Beautiful didn't come close to capturing the sight of her drenched in moonlight.

She halted next to Levet, who was perched in the low branches of a tree, and with one smooth motion she tossed a sack into his stubby arms.

"Food?" The miniature beast sighed in pleasure. "Ah, you are an angel."

Ariyal snorted. "You just consumed an entire deer."

"There is always room for cake."

He was distracted from the smirking gargoyle as Jaelyn turned to toss him a second sack.

"What's this?"

"Clean clothes."

He lifted his brows, sensing her hidden anticipation. He was almost afraid to check and see what she'd brought for him. Then his enjoyment at her unexpected playfulness was destroyed as he noticed the faint color that stained her cheeks.

She'd obviously fed. And the mere thought of her fangs buried in some stranger's throat was enough to send a raw burst of fury through him.

"Did you enjoy your dinner?"

She stiffened, futilely attempting to scurry behind the icy dignity that he detested. Thankfully his ability to annoy her overcame her brutal training and she moved forward to punch him in the center of the chest.

He would take a broken rib to her clamping down her emotions any day of the week.

"Oh for God's sake," she hissed. "I went to the nearest hospital and raided their blood supply. Can we move on to something more interesting than my dietary habits?"

He grasped her wrist, using her blow to tug her off balance.

"Come with me," he urged as she tumbled against his chest, his arms automatically wrapping around her slender body.

"Where?"

"There's a stream hidden by the trees." His gaze dipped toward her full lips, his feral satisfaction at the knowledge she hadn't taken another man's vein pounding through his blood. "You can wash my back."

The scent of her desire spiked the air before she was roughly shoving him away.

"I just showered."

He smiled, breathing deeply of her enticing arousal. "What's your point?"

With a deliberate motion she allowed her fingers to caress the hilt of her shotgun.

"You can wash your own damn back."

Ariyal reached to brush his thumb along her lower lip. "So cruel."

"Be happy I haven't stuck a dagger in it yet," she muttered, turning to stomp away.

Resisting the suicidal urge to toss her over his shoulder and haul her to the privacy of the woods, Ariyal contented himself with the absolute certainty that she wanted him as he headed to the stream. The Addonexus might have done their best to mold her into ruthless executioner without thought or feeling, but they hadn't succeeded.

At least not completely.

Below the ice was a passionate female just aching to break free of her restraints.

And he was just the man to help her discover her suppressed needs.

Entering the woods that lined the edge of the meadow, Ariyal briefly halted as he caught the unmistakable stench of cur.

It wasn't unusual for dogs to be sniffing around such prime hunting grounds, but he kept his senses on full alert as he stripped off his clothes and waded into the hip-deep water of the creek.

Once clean, he slid on the jeans he found in the bag that Jaelyn had tossed at him, tucking a dagger into the waistband at his lower back and strapping another to his ankle. Then after braiding back his wet hair, he reached back into the bag to pull out the shirt.

A brief glance was all that was necessary for him to comprehend Jaelyn's earlier amusement. Good . . . gods. The silk Hawaiian shirt painted with gaudy yellow and red flowers was an affront to fashion.

Clutching the offensive garment in one hand, and his sword and scabbard in the other, he marched out of the woods and across the meadow, finding Jaelyn and Levet resting beneath the large oak tree.

"I suppose you think this is funny?" he demanded, dangling the shirt in front of her nose.

Beside her the annoying gargoyle doubled over as his laughter echoed across the countryside.

"*Oui*. I think it is *très* amusing."

Ariyal glared at the pest in warning. "I thought I caught the scent of cur near the creek. Why don't you go investigate?"

"Why me?"

"Because if you stay there's a good chance I'm going to skewer you to the nearest tree."

"Are you always so surly?" Levet asked. Then, as he met Ariyal's dark glare, he gave a frustrated flutter of his wings and headed across the meadow. "I thought fey were supposed to be shiny, happy people?" he called over his shoulder.

Jaelyn rose to her feet. "He's right," she accused. "You are surly."

He was.

And it didn't have a damned thing to do with butt-ugly shirts, he acknowledged as his gaze ran a hungry path down her body.

"I'm frustrated."

She put her hands on her hips at his blunt explanation. She was obviously as frustrated as he was. But was she willing to admit the truth? Oh no, she rolled her eyes with a faux female annoyance.

"Men."

"Women," he mocked in return, waving the shirt like a flag. "And you chose this deliberately."

She shrugged. "It's clean, isn't it?"

"It's hideous."

"Fine. Next time I won't bother."

He stepped close, shivering at the delicious feel of cool power washing over the bare skin of his upper body.

"Which begs the question why you bothered this time," he pointed out. "Can't get me out of your mind even when we're apart, eh, poppet?"

"I wanted to annoy you."

"Sure you did."

She growled deep in her throat.

"In case you haven't noticed, time is a-wasting," she snapped. "Aren't you supposed to be hunting your friend and his freaky wizard?"

Ariyal grimaced, tossing aside the shirt and strapping

the sword over his bare skin. She was right. They had more
pressing problems than the state of his wardrobe.

He had managed to follow Tearloch's portal to this spot,
but once he'd landed in the meadow he'd realized that his
connection to his tribesman was muted, making it impossible to pinpoint his exact location.

"I can sense he's near, but there's some sort of spell of
protection surrounding him."

Predictably the vampire glared at him with a seething
impatience, making it clear she held him entirely to blame
for being stuck in the middle of nowhere with no immedi-
ate enemies to suck dry.

"So you intend to sit here and wait for him to stroll past?"

He clenched his teeth. Aggravating female.

"I'm waiting for midnight."

"Why?"

"That's when the spirits are easiest to raise."

"What do you need with spirits?"

"The wizard that Tearloch called from the grave possesses an abnormal amount of magic." He grimaced, more
deeply disturbed by Rafael's power than he wanted to admit.
"I have no intention of walking into a trap when I can use
spirits to track him down and tell us of any dangers."

She shuddered in distaste. "Does it have to be spooks?"

He arched a brow. Was it possible the fearless Hunter
was unnerved by a harmless ghost?

Of course, Rafael had proved they weren't all harmless,
a voice whispered in the back of his mind.

"Don't worry. They dislike vampires." He smiled at her
sour expression. "If you leave them alone, they'll leave you
alone."

"Isn't there another way?"

He shook his head. "It will be the most efficient—" A
sharp shriek pierced the air, and smoothly pulling his sword
free, he turned toward the sound. "Bloody hell."

Jaelyn was flowing to his side, her gaze trained toward the woods. "Was that Levet?"

"Unfortunately."

On cue the tiny demon charged across the meadow, his wings flapping and his short legs churning as he attempted to outrun the dark shapes that were following behind him.

"Something's coming!" the gargoyle bellowed. "Something dead!"

The stench hit Ariyal at the same time Levet charged past them and headed down the dirt road. Shit. His gut twisted at the sight of the creatures who shambled forward with jerky motions.

Zombies.

At least a dozen of them.

The abominations were recently deceased mortals who had been reanimated by magic. They were nothing but mindless shells, which was why he hadn't sensed them the moment they'd been called from their graves.

Unfortunately, they were also impervious to pain and nothing could stop them but fire or killing the magician who was controlling them.

He heard Jaelyn's hiss of shock as she belatedly realized what was approaching.

"Friends of yours?" she muttered.

"I don't have friends."

Chapter 10

Jaelyn ignored Ariyal's revealing words as she surveyed the nightmares that shuffled toward them.

Even in the world of demons the zombies were . . . gross.

The moonlight starkly revealed their rotting flesh and the dirt that clung to the patches of the clothing that survived the climb out of their graves. Worse were their odd, jerky movements. As if they were ghastly marionettes being pulled by invisible strings.

"Where did they come from?" she rasped.

Ariyal shifted at her side, the sword held ready for battle.

"How would I know?"

"It's your people who go around raising the dead."

He snorted, his gaze never wavering from the approaching horde (or whatever it was you called a group of ambling zombies).

"I believe there are many who would claim your people are the grave robbers, vampire."

She didn't bother to dignify his accusation with a response. Mostly because he was right.

"Did Tearloch make those"—she grimaced, waving a hand toward the zombies—"creatures or not?"

He shook his head. "Sylvermyst can call upon the souls of those in the underworld. They don't raise the dead."

"And the difference?"

"Zombies are recently deceased bodies that have been animated by the magic of a necromancer." His profile was hard with disgust as he swung his sword at the nearest attacker, slicing off its head with one smooth stroke. The body never faltered as it continued forward, the hands held out as it sought to grasp Ariyal. "They're mindless weapons that have been forbidden since the beginning of time."

Jaelyn took an instinctive step backward, firing her shotgun at a gray-haired grandma who clutched a shovel in her hands. The creature reeled backward but was swiftly replaced by another who lunged forward.

She danced backward, scowling as the hideous things began to circle them.

"So they can't think for themselves?"

"No." He kicked the nearest zombie, sending it flying halfway across the meadow. Not that it helped matters. Without hesitation, the creature was on its feet and shuffling back toward them with a stoic determination. One alone would be easy to chop into tiny pieces. But there were too many and with no visible means of actually killing them, the horde would eventually overwhelm their prey. Even if that prey did happen to be a powerful Sylvermyst and vampire. "They're directed by the witch or wizard who animated them."

She swiftly shot two more of the demons. "Sergei?"

"Doubtful." Ariyal muttered a curse as a zombie darted from the side to hit him on the temple with a large rock. Blood ran down the side of his face as he turned to slice off the bastard's head and kicked away the body. "The mage is an immoral snake, but his black magic is minor league. Only a true disciple of the Dark Lord could raise zombies."

Her mind coldly clicked through their various options even as she reloaded her gun.

"Rafael?" she pressed, needing all the information she could gather.

"It should be impossible." Ariyal ducked the clumsy fist directed at his chin. "But then I would have said a lot of things were impossible just a few weeks ago."

Yeah, no crap.

She shuddered, the rancid odor of the zombies nearly overwhelming as they closed in.

"Can you keep them distracted?"

He shot her a suspicious frown. "Why?"

"I'm going on a witch hunt."

"Dammit, Jaelyn . . ."

Ignoring his protest, Jaelyn shoved the shotgun back in the holster and grasped the nearest zombie and used it as a battering ram to clear a path through the hands that reached out to try and halt her.

Once clear of the encroaching circle, she tossed aside the nasty corpse and flew with blinding speed across the meadow. Reaching the woods, she climbed up the nearest tree and used the spreading branches to silently make her way deeper into the shadows.

At last she halted, wrapping herself in shadows and sending out her senses to search for the magic-user.

She filtered out the mundane scent of the native wildlife that scampered in the underbrush and even the approaching scent of gargoyle. Her sole focus was finding the person responsible for controlling the zombies before they managed to rip Ariyal into bloody shreds.

Which would explain why she nearly jumped out of her skin when there was a flutter of gossamer wings and Levet abruptly landed on the branch beside her.

"What are we hunting?" he whispered directly in her ear.

Jaelyn nearly fell out of the tree.

And wouldn't that be the cherry topper on her humiliation?

A highly trained Hunter not only allowing a miniscule demon to see through her shadows, but to alert every creature in the area to her presence by taking a tumble from the tree like a five-year-old human.

"Holy shit." She released her powers, turning to glare at her companion. "How did you know I was here?"

He smiled at her furious disbelief. "I possess nutty skills."

"Nutty?" It took a second to decipher his words. "You mean mad skills?"

He waved a hand. *"Oui."*

"And your skills allow you to see me even when I'm cloaked?"

"Oui. I can see through most illusions when I make the effort. Vampire, fey, and even witches' spells."

"Do all gargoyles possess the same skill?"

Something that might have been pain rippled over the ugly little face before the gargoyle was hiding it behind his smile.

"Some are better than others."

She tucked away the vital bit of information to share with the Ruah, concentrating on her companion.

"Are you the best?" she asked, her voice softening.

He grimaced with rueful resignation. "When you are my size you must learn to recognize approaching danger no matter how well camouflaged."

"Yeah." She gave a slow nod, reaching to pat his head between the stunted horns. "I get that."

They stiffened at the same time, turning their attention to the bulky form that was weaving through the trees.

"Cur," Levet breathed.

Jaelyn scowled at the unwelcome intruder. He was a young man who appeared to be thirty in human years with blond hair that was buzzed in military fashion and a square face that might have been handsome if you liked the "all brawn and no brain" sort.

At the moment his head was bent over a mirror he clutched in his hands, indifferent to the danger that lurked just above him.

"Damn," she whispered.

Levet pressed close to her side. "What is it?"

"I'm searching for the witch who is controlling the zombies, not a damned dog."

The gargoyle sniffed the air. "The magic is coming from the cur."

She hissed in shock. "You're certain?"

"*Ma enfant*, did I not just prove my skills?"

Jaelyn didn't truly doubt him. It was growingly obvious the tiny gargoyle harbored unknown depths. But . . . hell. This was a complication she didn't need.

"I've never heard of a dog being a magic-user," she muttered.

"It is rare," Levet conceded. "They must be a powerful mage or witch before they are turned or their skills are lost during the transformation. And since most curs are terrified of magic they usually do their best to avoid them. Certainly they would never deliberately try to attack a magic-user." He leaned forward to study the man below them. "I would guess this particular mage sought out a cur to transform him on purpose."

"Why?"

Levet gave a lift of his hands. "It could be a desire for greater physical strength, or a longer life span, or perhaps he is mated with a cur."

Jaelyn regretfully glanced down at the shotgun she'd stolen in town. It was a fine gun, but it was made for humans and they had no need for silver bullets.

"It looks like we're doing this the old-fashioned way."

"Do not fear." Levet squared his shoulders. "I have powerful magic of my own."

"No." Jaelyn grabbed the gargoyle's arm as he pointed it

toward the cur. "I think it would be better if I take care of the mage."

"You doubt my abilities?" Levet asked, his wings drooping in a visible pout.

"Of course not, but I was trained to kill in silence," she smoothly assured him. "We don't want to attract any unnecessary attention. You keep an eye open for his companions."

The gray eyes widened. "Companions?"

"Curs always travel in packs."

Levet made a sound of disgust, but even as Jaelyn judged the precise distance to the cur, he lightly touched her shoulder.

"Be careful, *ma enfant*."

She stiffened at his soft words.

Dammit. Why did he keep doing that?

Surely by now the tiny gargoyle realized that demons weren't supposed to offer her concern. She was a Hunter. An unfeeling weapon who had been taught that emotions were nothing more than a weakness that others could use to manipulate her.

All this fussing around over her and her safety was . . . unnerving.

Levet lifted his heavy brows. "Did I say something wrong?"

"No." With an effort she pulled her crap together. For God's sake. Now wasn't the time to get all sappy. "Nothing's wrong."

Before she could make a fool of herself, Jaelyn leaped through the air, landing on the cur with a lethal silence. The dog howled in pain as her fangs sliced through his neck, barely missing his jugular as he tumbled backward.

Jaelyn cursed at having missed the killing blow, although she had at least made him drop the mirror he'd been holding. She assumed he used the thing to control the zombies, which meant that Ariyal, at least, should be safe.

Which was more than she could say for herself.

Possessing the strength of a cur and the magic of a witch, the man beneath her managed to toss her aside with a disturbing ease.

They both rose to their feet, circling one another with the wary caution of trained warriors.

"Who are you?" Jaelyn demanded, knowing it couldn't have been sheer coincidence that brought the cur to this particular place at this particular time.

The cur eyeballed her in annoyance, clearly more outraged at being taken by surprise than upset at the fact he was facing a pissed-off vampire.

Of course, there was the very real possibility that he was too stupid to comprehend his danger.

"Do you know how long it took me to prepare that spell, you stupid cunt?" he growled. "You're going to pay for every minute."

Cunt?

Oh, he didn't just go there, did he?

She smiled, running a tongue along her razor-sharp fang. "I was going to ask you if you wanted to do this the easy way. Now there's only one way."

"And what's that?"

"The hard way."

"Oh yeah? You and what army?"

With a smirk, he reached toward the glowing crystal hung around his neck as he whispered words of magic.

No doubt he was conjuring a nasty spell, depending on his magical skills to protect him. Unfortunately for him, he'd never encountered a Hunter's speed and before he could finish his chanting, Jaelyn was moving forward to jerk his tongue from his mouth.

The cur stood in frozen shock, his eyes shifting to the bloody length of flesh she held in her hands. Then with a mangled scream of horror he was spinning on his heels and attempting to flee. Jaelyn allowed him a few seconds of hope that he might actually escape before she slammed her foot into his retreating back and sent him flying into the nearest tree.

He slid face-first to the ground, his arms and legs churning in a combination of pain and panic.

She crouched at his side, her arms loosely wrapped around her bent knees.

"I did warn you it would be the hard way," she taunted, dropping his tongue near his head. Eventually he would heal, but for now his wounds had to be near unbearable. "Listen very carefully, I'm going to ask you a series of questions. You will nod your head for yes and shake it for no. All very simple. Oh—" She leaned down far enough he couldn't miss her deadly fangs. "And for every lie I will rip off another body part. Got it?"

He flattened himself against the underbrush, as if wishing he could sink through the hard ground. But his hasty nod assured her that he was ready to play nice.

"Were you responsible for the zombies?" There was a faint hesitation before the cur was nodding. She patted his head. "Good boy. Are the rest of your pack nearby?" Another hesitation and another nod. "Are they all curs?" she demanded, certain she was sensing a presence at the edge of the woods, but unable to determine exactly what it was.

Something that bothered her almost as much as a magic-using cur.

Mysteries in the demon world were never good things.

He started to shake his head, but before she could probe into the members of his crew, a gunshot echoed through the air.

With a speed that defied physics, Jaelyn was able to dodge the projectile that was aimed at the center of her chest. Still, it managed to graze her shoulder with a searing pain that warned the bullet was made of silver.

Shit.

She could catch the scent of a nearby cur, no doubt the shooter, and moving closer was that oddly muted scent.

For a second she debated taking the wounded cur as a hostage. She didn't doubt with the proper encouragement, and perhaps a few more missing body parts, she could get all the information she needed out of him.

Unfortunately, she couldn't be certain what was lurking in the dark. It could be a mere witch with an amulet, or something recently coughed out of the bowels of hell. And with Ariyal possibly injured . . . well, she couldn't take the risk.

Time to get the hell outta Dodge.

Tearloch felt the prickle of magic before he entered the cavern to discover Rafael standing over a shallow pool of water in the center of the floor.

"Fools," the spirit was muttering in disgust. "Why must they always call upon zombies?"

Tearloch crossed to peer suspiciously at the images reflected in the water. So the wizard possessed enough power to scry. A handy trick, but one a mere spirit shouldn't be able to manage.

"What the hell is going on?" he rasped.

Rafael pointed a skeletal finger toward the floor. "We have been followed."

Putting aside his unease at Rafael's powers, Tearloch leaned forward to study the scene that was unfolding in the water like a soggy movie.

"Ariyal," he muttered, easily recognizing his prince, as well as the fact that he was currently standing less than five miles from the entrance to the hidden caves.

"Yes," Rafael hissed. "Your prince is annoyingly persistent."

Tearloch abruptly leaned closer to the water, realizing

that Ariyal wasn't battling a group of humans as he'd first assumed. Or at least they weren't human any longer.

With a shudder he stepped away from the water, glaring at the spirit, who was watching the fight with a faint sneer.

"Zombies are forbidden."

"Surely you must realize that we are now above the tedious laws of this world?" Rafael questioned before giving a dismissive wave of his hand. "Still, I do agree that such abominations are regrettable. They are far too unpredictable and attract precisely the sort of attention we had hoped to avoid."

"Then why did you call them?"

"This is not of my doing."

Tearloch clenched his teeth. Was it possible for the spirit to lie to him?

Just a few days ago he would have laughed at the mere possibility. A spirit was bound by the will of the summoner and utterly at his mercy.

Now he wasn't nearly so convinced.

"They didn't crawl out of their graves by themselves," he accused in harsh tones.

The spirit's smug expression faltered as he belatedly sensed Tearloch's annoyance.

"No, this is the work of your new allies."

"Allies?" Tearloch growled in outrage. "What allies?"

"Our master comprehends how truly important the child is to his future." Rafael spoke slowly, as if considering his words with care. "He has called his followers to assist us in protecting the babe."

Tearloch felt his throat tighten and his head throb at the smooth explanation. Was it possible the Dark Lord now talked directly to the wizard? Or was this a trick?

Either possibility was enough to make his stomach cramp with dread.

"And so you plotted behind my back?"

Rafael attempted to appear properly shocked at the allegation. "Certainly not."

"Then how did you know of these so-called allies while I was left in the dark?"

"His Lordship finds it easier to communicate with those of us who have a direct connection to the underworld. He assured me that he would call upon his disciples to offer us whatever we might need to succeed."

Tearloch pressed his palms to his aching temples, pacing across the cavern.

The fog in his mind made it difficult to think, but he knew he didn't like the threat of unknown demons becoming involved in his business.

Disciples of the Dark Lord were by nature untrustworthy creatures who had traded their souls to evil. They would betray and destroy Tearloch at the first opportunity.

He turned back to glare at Rafael. "And you didn't think it was necessary to share that information with me?"

"There seemed no purpose in bothering you with the small details."

Tearloch lifted his hand, pointing it toward the spirit. Plainly, Rafael needed a reminder of who was in charge.

"No purpose?"

"You have more important matters to occupy your mind." A smarmy smile curved the wizard's lips. "It is best that you allow me to—"

Tearloch clenched his hand and jerked it downward, the motion helping him focus on his intangible connection to the spirit.

On cue Rafael was jerked to his knees, a satisfying fear twisting his too-thin face.

"I will decide what's best," he snarled. "Or have you forgotten who is in command here, Rafael?"

"No, Master."

He gave another twist of his hand, and the arrogant ass was pressing his forehead against the stone floor.

"I think maybe you have. Which would be a lethal mistake."

"I merely wish to be of service."

Tearloch hissed in disgust. Gods, he hated the wizard. Almost as much as he hated the knowledge that he couldn't return the sleazy worm back to hell where he belonged, no matter how much he might want to.

Why had he ever started this madness?

"You're an arrogant prick who would betray me in a heartbeat if I was stupid enough to give you the opportunity," he said between gritted teeth. "Which I thankfully am not."

Rafael's fingers dug into the stone floor, but he was not stupid enough to make the move for an open revolt.

At least not yet.

"What do you want of me?"

"Tell me of our new allies."

"I can show you."

Tearloch childishly continued to squash Rafael's face into the floor. The spirit couldn't be physically hurt, but he could be humiliated. Something far worse for a man with Rafael's swollen pride.

At last he unclenched his hand and stepped back. "Fine. Show me."

The wizard rose to his feet, his fingers twitching as if he was barely restraining the urge to launch a spell in Tearloch's direction. Instead he wisely smoothed his rumpled robes and with rigid composure moved back to the shallow pool of water.

He waved his hand, murmuring soft words. Then, lifting his head, he gestured for Tearloch to join him.

"Our allies, as you commanded, Master."

Tearloch moved to peer in the water, not at all comforted

by the vision of a tall, slender man with short black hair slicked from his lean face. Dressed in a designer suit and glossy wingtip shoes, he might have been a banker.

But Tearloch didn't miss the pale, too-perfect features and the dull, emptiness in the black eyes.

Dead eyes.

"A vampire?" he hissed.

"Not only a vampire, but one that possesses skills beyond most," Rafael corrected, as if the leech's extra mojo would make him less offensive to Tearloch.

"What does that mean?"

"He is an Immortal One."

"I thought they were all immortal?"

"There are a few vampires who left this world to form their own clan," the wizard explained in overly patient tones. "They developed very unique talents that I believe will be of use to you."

"The talent to create zombies?"

"No, he has two curs as companions, as well as a witch," Rafael grudgingly confessed. "One of the curs is a magic-user."

A vampire with juiced powers, two curs (one of them a magic-user), and an extra witch tossed into the bargain?

That was enough firepower to easily overwhelm his handful of Sylvermyst.

"Damn you, this is a trap."

Rafael held up a soothing hand. "No, I swear."

"As if I would trust you."

"They were sent by our beloved master."

"I only have your word for that." Tearloch gave a shake of his head, wishing the painful fog would clear. "I should have listened to Sergei."

Rafael cautiously moved forward, waving his hand as if casting a spell.

"There is no need to upset yourself."

Tearloch swayed, the fog briefly clouding his mind to the point he could barely remember why he was standing in the cavern.

Then, with a curse, he forced back the numbing cloud of confusion.

"Can you communicate with the leech?" he rasped.

Rafael's thin lips nearly disappeared, but he gave a ready nod of his head.

"I can."

"Then you warn him that if he or his trio of misfits attempts to enter these caves I will not only allow my Sylvermysts to slice and dice them into pieces so small their mothers won't be able to recognize them, but you will be returned to the underworld and your name cursed so that you will never again be allowed to pass beyond the boundaries of Hell."

Tiny flames smoldered in the depths of the spirit's eyes. "The master will not be pleased."

"Perhaps for now you should concern yourself with making certain I'm pleased," Tearloch warned, turning to head for the entrance to the cavern.

Gods. He needed air.

Fresh air.

"Yes . . . for now," whispered Rafael behind him.

Chapter 11

Ariyal stumbled backward in revulsion as the zombies began to literally drop like flies around him.

Not that he objected to their stop, drop, and return-to-dead routine.

A pile of rotting corpses was considerably better than a ravaging horde of rotting corpses. And more importantly, the sight of them assured him that Jaelyn had managed to overcome whoever was responsible for calling the abominations from their grave.

Relief surged through him, along with a wry flare of humor.

He didn't know why he worried.

Jaelyn was a female who could take care of herself. Hell, he'd bet good money that the powerful Hunter was in better shape than he was.

Leaning against a tree, Ariyal glanced down at the numerous wounds that continued to seep blood. The zombies had been relentless in their single-minded devotion in ripping him to shreds and it had taken all his skill just to keep the damage to a minimum.

Thankfully, none of the injuries were life threatening, but

still they were sapping his energy. And worse, they hurt like a bitch.

Cursing zombies and witches and every other minion of the Dark Lord who was probably lurking in the shadows, Ariyal lifted his head as the cool wash of power filled the air, watching as Jaelyn flowed toward him with a mesmerizing beauty.

A slender, enticing female who was as gloriously lethal as she was beautiful.

His entire body clenched in . . . what?

Recognition, he at last decided.

There was simply no other word for it.

But recognition of what?

Desire? Need?

Fate?

The question went unanswered as she halted at his side, her hand reaching out to touch his bare chest before she was yanking it back as if she thought he might contaminate her.

"How badly are you injured?" she asked, her voice cold.

His lips twisted. No one could claim the female was at the mercy of her emotions. But then, what had he expected?

Horrified dismay that he'd been hurt? A tender need to nurture him back to health?

Yeah, she was more likely to sprout wings and fly.

"Nothing that won't heal."

"How long?"

He frowned, sensing there was more to her question than mere impatience.

"Two, maybe three hours."

She glanced over her shoulder. "We don't have that long."

"Are you in a hurry to get somewhere?"

"It's too exposed out here."

Absolutely more than impatience. Biting back his groan of pain, Ariyal pushed away from the tree and scanned the seemingly empty meadow.

"Exposed to what?"

"The mage escaped."

"The one controlling the zombies?" He reached down to grasp the sword he'd dropped at his feet.

"Yes." She grimaced. "And it gets worse."

There was something worse than zombies?

Fantastic.

"I'm listening."

"The magic-user was a cur."

Ariyal abruptly recalled the scent of cur that he'd noticed earlier. Obviously he should have paid more attention.

But then again, who had ever heard of a cur/mage?

Or was it mage/cur?

"I didn't know that was possible," he muttered.

"Not only possible, but a pain in the ass."

He hid his smile at her peeved tone. Jaelyn was accustomed to being the winner. No matter who or what her opponent might be.

Now she was clearly irked that the cur had escaped, although the blood on her hand revealed she'd done serious injury to the dog.

"Is there more?" he prompted.

"He's not alone."

He snorted. It just got better and better.

"Tearloch?"

She shook her head. "No, at least one other cur and a human witch." She absently stroked the handle of her shotgun. Ariyal suspected it was an unconscious gesture that offered her comfort. He suppressed a groan, easily imaging those slender fingers stroking something far more interesting. "There's also a creature who is capable of masking his scent," she confessed, unaware of his erotic fantasies.

He grimly forced his thoughts away from his distracting urge to press her against the tree and ease the need that pulsed just below the surface whenever she was near. His life was in enough danger without adding sex with a feral vampire.

Not that he wouldn't. . . .

He hissed in frustration, crushing the thought before it could form.

"Another magic-user?" he rasped.

She shrugged. "My guess would be a demon, perhaps even a vampire."

"A Hunter?"

"I don't know." Concern flickered in the indigo eyes. "That's what troubles me."

Ariyal tilted back his head to draw in a deep breath, sorting through the various scents that filled the meadow.

A family of sprites that was scurrying out of a nearby cavern and through the cornfields in obvious panic. A pack of hellhounds hunting a deer.

And more distant, the stench of curs as well as the strangely muted scent that was troubling Jaelyn.

All rushing away to leave them alone and isolated in the meadow.

Alone?

His eyes snapped open in surprise.

"Where's the gargoyle?"

She glanced back at the line of trees, a frown marring her brow.

"He insisted on following the trail of the cur while I returned here."

Ariyal snorted, not sharing his companion's regret at Levet's absence.

"It's about time he made himself useful."

"Don't underestimate him. He has . . ." She paused, considering her words, turning back with a faint smile. "Unexpected talents."

"His talent is to drive a rational man over the edge."

"No doubt it's all that testosterone." Her smile widened

as she shifted to place an arm around his waist and tugged his free arm over her shoulders. "It rots the brain."

Ariyal stiffened as his body reacted to her touch with predictable eagerness, even as his pride violently rebelled at her imitation of a vampire crutch.

It was one thing to offer him sympathy for his injuries.

It was quite another to treat him as if he was a damned invalid.

Not after Morgana le Fey had taken such gruesome delight in tormenting him when he was injured and at his most vulnerable.

"As much as I want to be in your arms, poppet, I hardly think this is the time or the place," he drawled.

She made a sound of impatience. "We have to find shelter until you can heal."

He pulled from her grasp, ignoring the weakness that was only growing worse as his injuries continued to bleed.

"No."

"No?"

"I'm not going to have you carrying me around like I'm some sort of feeble dew fairy."

She slapped her hands on her hips. "Because I'm a woman and you're a big, tough, virile man?"

"Because I will never be at the mercy of anyone. Not again."

His stark words rang through the meadow, and just for a second Jaelyn's expression softened with understanding. This female knew precisely how it felt to be helpless and abused.

"Fine." She gave in without an argument. A rare and wonderful occurrence. "Then what's your plan?"

Plan? He swallowed his urge to laugh. It was a little late in the day for a plan.

What they needed was a fast means of getting him back to fighting strength.

"I want your blood," he bluntly admitted.

She took a sharp step backward, her face rigid with shock. "For what?"

He arched a brow. Her outrage seemed a little hypocritical considering she was a damned leech.

"To help me heal."

"Is this a joke?"

"No." He lifted his sword, the moonlight dancing over the silver metal. "I can draw power from my blade."

"How?"

"Our people have many weapons, but our true Sylvermyst blades were forged before the banishment of the Dark Lord," he slowly admitted.

Her eyes narrowed. "Which means?"

"The metal was smelted in the pits of hell with silver and the heart of a Lamsung demon."

Her gaze shot to the sword. "Soul stealers," she muttered.

He nodded. Lamsungs were rare demons who survived by sucking the life from their enemies.

"The blade absorbs the power of my enemies."

She turned to meet his gaze, her own expression guarded. "And gives you strength."

"Precisely."

A short, oddly tense silence settled between them before Jaelyn took another step backward.

"Stay here."

He reached out to grab her arm. "Where are you going?"

"To get you blood." She jerked her head toward the woods. "There's a pack of hellhounds less than a mile away."

He regarded her in confusion. "I can use yours. I don't need much."

She jerked away, licking her lips. Almost as if she was nervous.

"No."

"Why not?"

"I . . ." There was another lick of her lips. "I can't."

No, not *can't*.

Won't.

The vampire had already made it clear she wouldn't lower herself to feed from a nasty Sylvermyst. Now she was making it equally clear that she wasn't going to lower herself to offering her precious blood to restore his powers.

He squared his shoulders, hiding his shredded pride behind a mocking smile as he swept past her rigid body.

"Right. See ya around, poppet."

"Ariyal, what are you doing?"

"I'll do my own damn hunting, thank you very much."

Jaelyn cursed her stupidity as she watched Ariyal march away, his back stiff with wounded pride and his steps not nearly as steady as he would no doubt wish them to be.

She'd blown it.

In spectacular fashion.

She smacked her palm to her forehead. For god's sake, all she had to do was keep an eye on one Sylvermyst.

A job she should be able to do in her sleep.

But over and over she'd managed to screw up her assignment.

Now she was stuck watching him walk away, furious with her weakness but smart enough to know that for the moment she had no choice.

She couldn't allow him to take her blood.

Not when she didn't fully comprehend the ramifications.

Yeah, it was more than likely that the blade would absorb her blood and it would do nothing more than give Ariyal the strength he needed to heal.

Then again . . .

She shivered, turning to gaze over the silent cornfields.

What if the blood reacted as if he'd taken it straight from her vein?

The consequences could be nothing short of cata- clysmic.

"He's getting away, you know."

The disembodied voice sliced through the air a mere second before there was a whiff of brimstone and Yannah suddenly appeared directly in front of her.

Jaelyn yelped as she grabbed her shotgun and pointed it at the intruder. Her finger was ready to squeeze the trigger when she belatedly recognized the heart-shaped face and black eyes that shimmered like chips of ebony in the moon- light.

"Dammit." Jaelyn shoved the gun back into its holster, glaring at the creature, who calmly stroked her hands down the white silk robe. "You scared the bejeezus out of me."

"Did I?" Yannah blinked with exaggerated innocence. "I thought Hunters were trained to never be caught off guard?"

"I wouldn't be caught off guard if you walked around like a normal demon," Jaelyn protested in cold tones, hiding her embarrassment behind a layer of ice. It wasn't her fault she'd allowed herself to be dangerously distracted, was it? If Ariyal would stop being a pain in the ass then she could concentrate on the important stuff. And he wasn't the only one to blame. Yannah and her mother Siljar certainly had their share of guilt. "You should wear a bell or some- thing. It's not polite to just pop in front of people like that."

Yannah arched her brows. "Well, aren't you the fussy one?"

"You would be fussy if you were forced to play baby- sitter to that . . ." Jaelyn snapped her lips together, words failing her.

"To that delectable, gorgeous, completely edible . . ."

The words returned in a rush. "Temperamental, stub- born, egotistical Sylvermyst."

"He's a man." Yannah shrugged. "They're all a pain in the backside."

Well, wasn't that the freaking truth?

"Some more than others," she muttered.

"I suppose so." Yannah appeared to consider the various flaws of the male sex before heaving a deep sigh. "Still, it's a pity."

"What is?"

"You cost me one thousand latinum."

Jaelyn frowned. Had the demon had made an appearance just to mock her?

"Which might make sense if this was *Star Trek* and we were both Ferengi."

"I made a bet with my neighbor, but Mother won't allow me to wager with real money." She wrinkled her tiny nose. "Besides, Jinns are touchy about their treasures."

Jinn? Holy crap. Just what neighborhood did this female live in?

She dismissed the inane thought as she concentrated instead on the suspicion she was being led into a trap.

"What were the details of this bet?"

"I said you would have the Sylvermyst leashed and properly house-trained by the end of the week. Maric said you would kill him before you could ever reach the baby." She pointed a finger at Jaelyn. "Neither of us thought a mighty Hunter would simply throw in the towel. It's a grave disappointment, I must say."

Jaelyn narrowed her gaze. *Yep. Definitely a trap.*

"Do you have a specific reason for . . . popping in?" she demanded, refusing to rise to the bait.

"Have you forgotten you're supposed to be reporting to me?"

"No, I haven't forgotten, but for now there's nothing to report."

"Nothing?" There was a short, dramatic pause before Yannah smiled with wicked enjoyment. "Nothing at all?"

For the first time in decades, Jaelyn was relieved she couldn't blush. Did the female know she'd committed the ultimate sin and had sex with her mark?

"Ariyal is still searching for the child," she said, her words clipped. "We were attacked by zombies. Tearloch's summoned a crazy-ass spirit wizard from the depths of the underworld, and Sergei might or might not be with them." She absently stroked the wood stock of her shotgun, not above her own dramatic pause. "Oh, and there's a gargoyle named Levet who has been following me around like a lost puppy because he's searching for you."

The creature's smile only widened to emphasize the sharply pointed teeth.

"The sweet thing."

Jaelyn waved an absent hand. "He's that way if you want to put him out of his misery."

"No." She gave a rueful click of her tongue. "Not yet."

"Fine." Jaelyn shifted with a growing impatience. "Now you're all up to date. Was there anything else you needed?"

Yannah drifted closer, her power a tangible force in the air. "I do have a question."

Jaelyn shivered. "What is it?"

The black eyes surveyed her with an unwavering curiosity. "Shall I tell Mother that you've decided to break your contract?"

Jaelyn jerked at the dangerous suggestion. Hunters who failed in their missions didn't get second chances.

And who the hell knew what happened to anyone stupid enough to fail a contract authorized by the Oracles?

"Of course not."

"Then you intend to go after the Sylvermyst?"

As if she had a choice?

"Eventually," she grudgingly promised.

"That seems dangerously vague."

Not missing the warning in the low voice, Jaelyn lifted her hands in defeat.

"I'm going, I'm going," she growled, stepping around the tiny demon to stomp across the meadow.

She ignored the sensation of Yannah watching her stiff retreat, instead concentrating on the man who was swiftly becoming the bane of her existence.

Not that she had to use her considerable Hunter skills to follow in Ariyal's trail.

She could have shut down her senses entirely and been able to find him.

And that, of course, was what scared the hell out of her.

"Christ, why won't someone just shoot me?" she muttered, picking up her pace as she skirted past the trees and crossed the stream, where she caught the scent of a wounded hellhound.

Obviously Ariyal had managed to find the blood he needed to restore his strength. But instead of returning to her, he was moving even farther away.

At a pace that assured her he wasn't just pouting.

He was truly trying to leave her behind.

Annoying fairy.

Jumping over a fence that marked the edge of a cow pasture, she at last caught sight of Ariyal as he crossed through the overgrown yard of a farmhouse.

She briefly surveyed the white, two-story home with black shutters and peeling paint before shifting her attention to the nearby chicken coop that lurched to a drunken angle and the more distant sheds and a tin-roofed barn that held the lingering scent of hay.

The place was deserted of humans, although the stale stench of beer cans warned they occasionally used the isolated property to party in private. And she couldn't detect any nearby demons.

This seemed as good a spot as any to confront the angry Sylvermyst.

With a graceful motion, Jaelyn was leaping on top of the screened-in porch attached to the house and then dropping directly in front of Ariyal.

The Sylvermyst came to a grudging halt, his unbearably beautiful face set in lines of leashed fury.

He was so different from the male vampires who had sought to become her lover, she recognized.

There was no cold calculation. No aloof expertise that offered a clinical pleasure without the messy involvement of emotions.

No.

Ariyal was fierce and temperamental and so passionate he nearly set the air on fire with the force of his emotions.

He was dominating, but he was no bully.

And while he had more than his fair share of male arrogance, there was an inner vulnerability to him that touched her in places she didn't know she could be touched.

He was exactly what she didn't need, at exactly the wrong time.

The bronze eyes blazed with breathtaking power. "Get out of my path, vamp."

She ignored the sudden heat that swirled through the air. She was relatively safe. At least until he called for that damned wooden bow and arrows he could conjure from thin air.

Then things might get dicey.

"Where the hell are you going?"

"I don't discuss my plans with my foes."

"Are you pouting because I wouldn't share my blood?"

"You're the one who insists on treating me like the enemy," he snarled. "So either do whatever it is you were sent here to do, or get out of the way."

Foe? Enemy?

Ah, if only.

That she understood.

This messy, confused muddle that plagued her . . .

"You need me," she said abruptly.

He snorted, folding his arms over his chest. The picture of a male at his most stubborn.

"And you call me arrogant?"

She tilted her chin. "Do you know where the babe is?"

"I will."

"And you can battle your tribesmen as well as the spirit on steroids without me?"

The muscle in his jaw knotted, his pride once again threatened.

"Yes."

"What about Sergei?"

He shrugged. "What about him?"

"Enough," she hissed in exasperation. "I'm not going to let you waltz into a trap just because you're pissed off at me."

He arched a mocking brow. "And just how do you intend to stop me, Hunter?"

Later Jaelyn would question whether she was overly stressed—it had, after all, been a crazy few days and any vampire was bound to feel a little on edge—or whether it had been temporary insanity.

In that moment, however, there was no thought.

Just mindless, primitive instinct.

Grasping his face in her hands, she leaned forward to kiss him with all the raw hunger that refused to leave her in peace.

"Like this."

Chapter 12

Ariyal reeled beneath the impact of Jaelyn's sudden kiss.

He couldn't have been more shocked if she'd pulled out her gun and shot him directly in the heart.

What else could you expect from a cold-blooded leech? Death and mayhem were her specialty.

But this . . .

This was white-hot, all-consuming pleasure that bypassed his brain and sent his body up in flames.

Without giving himself time to question what the hell she was playing at, he grasped her around the waist and with one motion had her tossed over his shoulder. Ignoring her startled squeak, he headed directly toward the nearby house, entering through the screened-in porch.

A few long strides led him into the kitchen with its worn linoleum and white-painted cabinets. There was a forgotten china cabinet pushed against one wall and a matching table in the center of the floor.

A nice, sturdy walnut table.

With a flare of anticipation he kicked aside the chair blocking his path; then, leaning forward, he rolled Jaelyn off his shoulder and seated her on the edge of the table, tugging her legs apart so he could step between them.

His hands remained on her slender hips as he at last allowed his gaze to shift to the pale beauty of her face.

He'd half expected to find her fangs exposed and her eyes flashing with the cold promise of death.

Jaelyn was not the sort of woman a man went all caveman on.

Not if he wanted to keep his heart beating in his chest.

But while her expression was cold and diamond hard, she couldn't disguise the hunger that smoldered in the depths of her indigo eyes.

He might not know why she insisted on being near him, but he did know she wanted him.

Even if the stubborn female would rather slice out her own tongue rather than admit it.

As if to prove his point she gave a toss of her head, placing her hands flat on the table so she could lean back to meet his heated gaze with a pretense of indifference.

"Do you feel better now you got to play macho man?" she demanded.

A slow, wicked smile curved his lips as he reached to grasp the stretchy fabric of her barely there top. With one ruthless tug he had it over her head and lying on the floor.

"Not yet, but I intend to feel much, much better."

"Careful, fairy," she hissed, her fangs suddenly visible. "I've killed men for less."

He didn't doubt the threat, but he was filled with a strange sense of reckless need.

In the distance he knew that Tearloch waited along with who knew how many of the Dark Lord's minions to protect the child. There seemed a damned good chance he was going to die before the night was over.

For now he wanted to drown in his aching need for this woman.

"You started this, poppet," he reminded her, his voice

thick as his gaze lowered to the proud thrust of her breasts. "Are you just a tease or do you have the balls to finish it?"

Her expression became wary although her fangs remained fully extended. Insanely the sight of them was hot as hell.

"I didn't start anything. I kissed you to try and keep you from storming off in a huff."

His gaze narrowed. No. Hell no. She wasn't going to hide behind a pretense of duty.

Not this time.

"What do you care if I storm off in a huff, Jaelyn?" He trailed a finger down the curve of her throat.

She shivered, her eyes darkening with the same craving the pulsed deep inside him.

"I don't care."

"I think you do." His finger continued downward, tracing the curve of her breast. "Why else would you follow me? It's obvious you can't bear to be away from me."

Ariyal watched the emotions that flitted over Jaelyn's delicate features. Outrage, wariness, and . . . fear?

Her tongue darted out to touch her lower lip, sending a shock wave of need through Ariyal and making him forget her odd reaction.

He had walked away from Jaelyn in the meadow, determined to leave her behind. Didn't he have enough troubles without adding a beautiful female who made a sport of trampling his manhood?

Now any desire to be alone with his seething anger was seared away by the intoxicating scent of woman and cool, satin skin beneath his searching finger.

"You arrogant . . ." She hissed as his fingers found the tip of her breast, tugging the nipple to a hard peak.

"You like that?" He growled deep in his throat as he continued to torment her nipple. He was already fully aroused, his erection pressing painfully against the zip of his jeans. "Tell me, Jaelyn. Tell me what you want."

Her lips parted as she tilted back her head to meet his hooded gaze.

"Sanity," she muttered. "Unfortunately it seems in short supply."

She was right.

There were a thousand perfectly rational reasons why this was all kinds of a bad idea. But as he moved forward, pressing the hard width of his cock to the juncture of her spread legs, he couldn't think of a damned one.

"Sanity is highly overrated," he assured her, his head lowering to tongue the tip of her hard nipple. "Shall we drown in madness together, Jaelyn?"

Her lashes drifted downward as she shifted to clutch at his shoulders, her legs wrapping around his hips in silent invitation.

"Ariyal."

"Tell me." He blazed a path of kisses over her breast, lingering in the small valley before seeking out the tender bud on the other side. "Say the words."

She moaned softly. "What words?"

"That you want me."

"I . . ." With an obvious effort she tilted back her head to regard him with a smoldering gaze.

"The truth, poppet," he commanded softly.

She shivered against his tense muscles, her eyes raw with a stark need that slammed into him with brutal force.

"Yes, dammit," she growled. "I want you."

A fierce satisfaction jolted through him at her unwilling confession.

"Thank the gods," he muttered.

"Not that I'm happy about it," she continued.

He gave a short, humorless laugh. "Join the club. Do you

think I want to be distracted by an arrogant leech? Especially one who happens to be bipolar?"

She frowned. "What's that supposed to mean?"

"You swing from hot to cold so fast you give me whiplash," he rasped. "I have better things to be doing with my time."

He swallowed a laugh as she narrowed her eyes. She looked offended by the thought that he might not be any more anxious than she was to be tormented by this ruthless craving.

Then, as if unable to resist his deliberate challenge, a small, tantalizing smile curved her lips, her body deliberately arching to press her soft breasts against the hard planes of his chest.

"Bipolar, eh?"

"Yes."

Her legs tightened around his hips, rubbing against his cock with a promise that nearly sent him to his knees.

"And yet you're desperate for me."

He grunted, feeling as if he had just been kicked in the gut.

Yeah. Desperate just about covered it.

He had barely touched her and yet he was ready to explode.

It was downright embarrassing for a man who was known to make sex last hours, if not days.

"Careful, Jaelyn. Don't start something you're not prepared to finish," he warned.

In answer, she reached to tug at the button of his jeans. "You are wearing too many clothes, fairy."

His heart slammed against his chest as she tugged down the zipper, her fingers circling his straining erection.

A groan was wrenched from his throat at the sheer bliss of her touch.

His gaze skimmed over her pale, beautiful face and down the elegant curve of her neck to the small mounds of her breasts. A part of him admired her sleek lines and well-defined muscles. There was no mistaking the fact that she was honed to be a lethal weapon. But a greater part was busy savoring the perfect ivory skin drenched in the moonlight that was peeking through the kitchen window and the contrast of her rosy nipples.

"Gods, Jaelyn, you're killing me."

Without warning she leaned forward, circling his nipple with the tip of her tongue.

"Hmmm, warm skin . . ." She nibbled a path to the center of his chest, lightly scraping his skin with the tips of her fangs. "A pounding heart." She pulled back with a taunting smile. "You still have some life left in you."

Their gazes locked and held as a tangible, branding awareness scorched the air between them.

Despite their bickering and sniping, there was a potent force binding them together that was bigger than both of them.

Destiny had entwined their fates for its own mysterious reasons.

And he didn't have the sense to give a damn.

"Let's find out just how much life," he muttered, shifting to sweep a soft kiss over her lips, wisely taking the precaution of removing her holstered shotgun and tossing it onto the floor. One less weapon seemed like a good idea if things went to hell. "What do you say, poppet?"

"Yes."

He deepened the kiss, sweeping his tongue between her dangerous fangs, his fingers tugging at her hard nipples with increasing urgency.

For a heartbeat Jaelyn stiffened beneath his onslaught of raw hunger, her fingers digging into the muscles of his chest. Ariyal groaned, but before he could leash the savage need pounding through his body, she was tangling her tongue with his, meeting his every thrust with a ready fervor.

Any hope of restraint was shattered by her response.

He groaned, drinking deeply of her lips as his hands ran an impatient path down her back until he reached the edge of her pants.

Still it wasn't enough.

He needed more.

Slipping his hands beneath the waistband of her pants, Ariyal peeled them off her legs and tossed them aside, pausing only long enough to kick aside his own jeans before he slowly sank to his knees.

Jaelyn made a faint sound of surprise, but Ariyal was too enthralled by the sight of her spread before him to notice.

She was exquisite.

Perfect.

And, unable to resist temptation, he leaned forward to worship the very heart of her femininity with his tongue and teeth.

He wrapped his arms around her slender thighs, urging them farther apart as he relished the slick satin beneath his tongue. She tasted of cool shadows and stormy nights.

A heady combination that could easily become addictive.

Her faint moan whispered on the air, and Ariyal glanced upward to catch a glimpse of her as she gripped the edge of the table, her back bowed and her head tossed back in blatant pleasure.

Yes.

This was what drove men to conquer empires and destroy civilizations. It made reasonable men commit murder.

This exquisite, wondrous madness.

And he was lost, he inwardly accepted, capturing her clitoris between his teeth. She gave a keening cry as he tormented her tiny knot of pleasure. The sound echoed deep within Ariyal, stirring that primitive, possessive part of him that he wanted to ignore.

Mine . . .

The potent word echoed through his mind, branding across his heart.

With a low growl he forced away the dangerous thought, concentrating on Jaelyn's pleasure. He wasn't going to ruin the moment.

Not when he couldn't be certain it would ever come again.

As if to reward his dedication to his current task, Jaelyn moaned, her fingers plunging into his hair to pull it free of the braid. He gave her a last, lingering lick before he was off his knees and standing between her legs.

Grabbing her hips, he scattered heated kisses across her cheek.

"Are you ready for me, Jaelyn?" he breathed.

Her hands skimmed downward, grasping his cock and angling it toward her waiting body.

"I'm ready," she said with an edge of desperation in her voice, her fingers stroking him from the tip of his erection to the thick base. "Please, Ariyal."

Ariyal hissed as he battled back the looming orgasm. He wasn't ready to lose himself in oblivion.

"Tell me, Jaelyn. Tell me you want me," he commanded as he watched her eyes glaze with need.

"I already told you," she rasped.

"I need to make sure it's crystal clear between us," he breathed, leaning down to brush his lips over hers. "I won't be accused of forcing you."

Her arms lifted to encircle his neck, her eyes glittering like jewels in the moonlight.

"No man could force me."

"Then say the words."

She cursed, but, tilting back her head, she met his stubborn gaze.

"I. Want. You."

"Ariyal."

"Ariyal." Her nails raked down his back. "Happy?"

"I intend to be," he muttered.

Sliding his hands over her breasts, he molded the firm mounds, lowering his head to taste the puckered tip. She quivered, her legs circling his hips as she urged him to put an end to their torment.

"Ariyal . . . dammit."

He chuckled, smugly proud of his ability to reduce her to begging. Then her fingers tightened around his cock and his laughter became a low groan of need.

Bloody hell. He was close.

Too close to continue his teasing.

"You win," he muttered, his hands smoothing down the curve of her waist before slipping between her legs, his fingers closing over hers to guide his aching cock to her welcoming entrance.

"Always," she breathed, her determination to have the last word ruined as she gasped in pleasure as he stroked deep into her body.

He gripped her hips, his features tight with retrained need.

"Hold on, Jaelyn," he said. "This might be a bumpy ride."

She flashed her fangs, moving her hands over his chest as she tightened her muscles to clamp around his cock, which was buried to the hilt.

"Bring it on, fairy."

Barely recalling how to breathe, Ariyal claimed her lips in a possessive kiss, pulling out until he was once again poised at her entrance. Jaelyn muttered low words of protest, reaching down to grab his ass.

His soft laughter echoed through the empty house. "Slower is sweeter, Jaelyn."

Sucking his lower lip into her mouth, she dug her nails into his flesh.

"Do you want me to beg?"

He eased back inside her, a thin sheen of sweat coating his body as he buried himself to the hilt.

"I want you to scream," he commanded.

"Make me," she whispered, her legs tightening around his hips.

He nibbled a path of kisses of her neck so he could whisper directly in her ear.

"A challenge?"

"Are you up for . . . oh!"

Her words were forgotten as he pulled out and then rocked his hips upward, nearly lifting her off the table with the force of his thrust.

They cried out in unison, Jaelyn burying her face in his neck as he held on to her hips and briefly absorbed the sensation of his erection sheathed in her tight channel. Then, as she trembled against him, he repeated the forceful surge, keeping his pace just as slow and sweet as he promised.

Or at least that was the plan.

With every thrust Jaelyn lifted her hips upward, possessing the strength to meet his thrusts with an explosive impact. He'd never had such a powerful lover. At least not one who could meet him stroke for stroke with pleasure instead of pain.

It was . . . intoxicating.

And unnervingly intimate.

It was as if they were being fused together. Not just physically, but in the passion that bound them.

In this moment they were one.

Her lips trailed down his throat, creating tiny jolts of electric excitement as he felt the sharp tip of her fangs brush his skin.

He grimly crushed the insane desire to feel those fangs sinking into his flesh, concentrating on the building tension that clenched the muscles of his groin.

"Are you with me, Jaelyn?"

Her nails dug into his skin, her head angling back to stab him warning glare.

"Don't stop," she growled. "Don't you dare stop."

He grinned with wicked enjoyment at her demands. "I told you I was going to make you scream, Jaelyn," he reminded her, his hands shifting to pull her legs higher on his waist, angling her upward so he could plunge even deeper.

With swift, relentless strokes he urged her toward that perilous edge, his breath rasping through the air. Her eyes squeezed closed, her body clenched so tight around his cock that he was certain he would combust before giving her satisfaction.

Over and over he plunged deep inside her. Then just when he was certain he was going to embarrass himself, he gave one last surge and she gave a shout of release.

He claimed her lips in a branding kiss as he pressed her shuddering body tight against him and shattered beneath the maelstrom of exploding bliss.

Holy . . . shit.

Still holding her in his arms, he spread tiny kisses over her face, continuing to pump into her as he sought to regain his composure.

Or his sanity.

Whichever came first.

Rocked by the tiny aftershocks of pleasure, Jaelyn had no choice but to hang on to Ariyal.

Or at least that was the excuse she used as her hands smoothed down the satin skin of his back and her face remained pressed into the curve of his neck as she wallowed in his warm, addictive scent.

Alarms buzzed in the back of her mind. Yeah, as if she needed to be reminded of the complete lunacy of giving in to her passions. But it wasn't until the persistent ache of her

fangs penetrated her fuzzy glow that she abruptly stiffened
in his arms.

Not all her hungers had been satisfied.

And the violent urge to sink her fangs into his neck was
all but irresistible.

With a hiss, she placed her hands against his chest, yanking her head back to meet his brooding gaze.

"Don't," he warned.

She scowled at his commanding tone. "Don't what?"

"Try to squirm away from me."

"Are you always such a bossy lover?"

"Yes," he admitted without apology. *Typical.* "Are you
always so eager to leave your lover's arms?"

Jaelyn shivered. *Lovers.*

Grimly she forced herself to ignore the possessive glow
in his bronze eyes and the delicious sensation of his warm
flesh still buried deep inside her.

She wouldn't compound her stupidity by wishing that
things could be different.

Even if he weren't her current assignment, her position
as a Hunter meant she couldn't take a long-term lover. And
certainly she could never have a mate. . . .

She slammed the door before the dangerous thought
could fully form. She *soooo* wasn't going there.

"Vampires don't do cuddling," she said, coating her
voice in ice. "Sorry."

Anger tightened his exquisite features, but while he
slowly pulled out of her body, his arms remained wrapped
around her.

"It's more than an allergy to cuddling," he accused.
"You treat me like I carry the plague." A mocking smile
curved his lips. "At least when I'm not making you scream
in pleasure."

She forced herself to meet his gaze, desperate to divert him.

"I had an itch and you scratched it." She shrugged. "What do you want? A trophy?"

She'd intended her cutting words to bring an end to his questions. Didn't men want their sexual encounters to be a no muss, no fuss deal? She was offering it to him on a platter.

But of course, Ariyal refused to behave as he should.

Aggravating ass.

"I want the truth," he growled. "Something that seems a foreign concept to you most of the time."

"I just told you. . . ."

His hands moved to grasp her face, his expression grim. "Dammit, Jaelyn, enough games."

The scent of herbs filled the air as his power seared over her skin, but it wasn't fear that shivered down her spine.

She pressed her hands against his chest. "This isn't a game."

"No, it isn't. So stop jerking me around and give me a straight answer." He resisted her halfhearted efforts to push him away. "Does it disgust you that I'm an evil Sylvermyst?"

Disgust?

Was the man mental?

She'd just literally begged him to take her on a dusty table in an abandoned farmhouse in the middle of freaking nowhere.

Did that seem like the actions of a woman who was disgusted by him?

She gave a sharp shake of her head, careful to keep her expression guarded.

"You aren't evil."

"That wasn't what you said when I announced my intention to sacrifice the child before it could be used to resurrect the Dark Lord."

"I have no intention of allowing you to harm the babe, but wanting to protect your people isn't evil." She grimaced. "Believe me, I've seen the difference."

He scowled down at her. "Then why did you refuse to share your blood when I needed it?"

Dammit, was he still on that? Why wouldn't he let it be?

"We have more important things to discuss," she muttered.

His hands tightened on her face as she tried to glance away.

"No, I'm not going to be distracted," he warned. "Tell me."

They glared at one another in silence. Then with gritted teeth Jaelyn at last lifted her hands to grasp his wrists and pulled his hands away from her face.

"I was afraid what might happen," she snapped, accepting that the stubborn Sylvermyst wouldn't give up until he'd managed to drag the humiliating truth out of her.

Predictably the annoying man didn't appear at all pleased with her confession.

"You didn't trust me," he said in flat tones.

"I didn't trust *me*," she huffed. "Satisfied?"

"No, I'm damn well not satisfied," he snapped. "I don't speak cryptic. What the hell are you talking about?"

She studied the perfectly chiseled lines of his face, her heart squeezing as if it had been put in a vise.

The Addonexus had done everything in their power to destroy her emotions. She was supposed to be a weapon, not a woman.

And she'd assumed they had succeeded.

Until this man.

This beautiful, powerful, truly aggravating man.

She didn't know how or why, but he'd smashed through her defenses and threatened her in a way she didn't fully understand but was smart enough to fear.

"I couldn't take the risk that the blade would bind us together," she forced herself to admit.

He glanced toward the sword that had been tossed on a wooden stool near the refrigerator.

"The blade merely absorbs your energy, it doesn't actually steal your soul, regardless of the rumors."

"Don't be dense. I mean . . ." She battled against a wave of embarrassment. Dammit. He was making her feel like an idiot. "Bind us. Forever."

"Obviously I am dense. How could a few drops of your blood on my blade bind us together?"

"Because the blade transfers the blood to you."

"And?"

"And it might very well be the same as if you took it directly from my vein."

"I've never heard that taking the blood of a vampire is binding. Not unless . . ." He froze, the bronze eyes narrowing with disbelief. "Not unless they're mates."

Ding, ding. Give the fairy a gold star.

A vampire needed blood to survive. And it wasn't unusual to take the vein of a lover during sex.

But the exchanges were about body functions. Food and pleasure.

Nothing that a wise vampire couldn't walk away from without a backward glance.

But for the rare few who found their true mate, the exchange of blood would entwine their souls.

They would be irrevocably connected.

Forever and ever and ever . . .

Unable to bear his piercing scrutiny, she gave him a sharp shove backward, slipping off the table before he could regain his balance.

"We should be deciding what we intend to do next," she reminded him in clipped tones, pulling on her clothes and belting her holster around her hips. "If you've healed I think we should concentrate on finding Tearloch and the child. We can worry about the cur who raised the zombies and his mystery friends later."

Without warning he grabbed her upper arm and swung her around to confront his probing gaze.

"You're babbling."

She stiffened, sternly ignoring his gloriously naked body. Now was not the time to be thinking of how good it felt to have him between her legs, his heat seeping deep inside her as he plunged. . . .

No.

She gave a sharp shake of her head.

"I do not babble," she informed him, frost coating her words. "I was sharing a reasonable argument for a possible course of action."

"You were avoiding the subject."

"Because I don't want to discuss it. That should be obvious even to a stubborn, pigheaded Sylvermyst."

"Too bad."

Jaelyn hissed in shock as he abruptly scooped her off her feet and carried her across the room to the door leading to a small cellar dug beneath the house.

"What the hell are you doing?"

Lowering her to her feet, Ariyal slammed shut the the door and leaned against it, trapping them in the dark, musty space that was lined with shelves holding hundreds of glass jars coated in dust.

Obviously the previous housewife had been dedicated to canning and juicing and pickling everything that came out of her garden.

Ariyal folded his arms over his chest, his expression brooding.

"One of us is always walking out just when the conversation is getting interesting."

She snorted. "You and I clearly have different definitions of interesting."

"You don't think it's mildly interesting that I happen to be your mate?"

The cramped space seemed to shrink even further.

Talk about awkward moments.

"You're not my mate."

The bronze eyes blazed at her denial. Almost as if he was bothered by her stubborn refusal to admit their growing bond.

"That's not what you implied a few minutes ago."

She shrugged. "What I said was . . ."

"Yes?"

She glanced toward the shelf of pickled ochre. Yeah, time to split hairs.

"I said I didn't want to take the risk. You might drive me nuts, but I feel . . ." What was the word? "Aware of you. Like we're connected on some level I don't even understand."

"And you think ignoring the connection will make it go away."

Bingo.

"That's exactly what I think."

"And I don't have any say in the future of our relationship?"

She turned back to meet his scorching gaze, fiercely determined to hold her ground.

It wasn't like she had a choice in any of this, did she?

"There is no relationship."

"That's not how it felt when you were begging me not to stop."

She shifted, just the memory of being wrapped around this beautiful Sylvermyst sending a heat swirling through her chilled body.

"Sex," she muttered, ignoring the fact that she would happily beg again given the opportunity.

"No." He shook his head. "It was more than sex."

"It can't be."

"Why not?"

She hissed in frustration. Weren't men supposed to want a female who didn't expect "happily ever after"?

Ariyal acted as if he wanted her to claim him as her mate. As if . . .

No. She shook off the mere thought.

What was the point?

"Because I'm a Hunter."

"And?"

"And we're not allowed to mate."

He studied her with a grim expression. "Never?"

"Never."

"What happens?" He sharply pushed away from the door, moving to tower over her. "You get voted off the island?"

"No." She tilted back her head, her expression equally grim. "There's only one way out of the Addonexus."

The bronzed eyes darkened with swift comprehension. "Death."

"Death."

Chapter 13

Santiago shuddered as the King of Weres' power blasted through the air. The mangy mutt wasn't pleased that a pack of traitors had managed to waltz through his wine cellars without his knowledge.

Dios.

He'd known Salvatore was the top dog, but he hadn't realized just what that meant until this moment.

It wasn't an entirely pleasant revelation.

Barely aware he was moving, Santiago positioned himself between the Were and Nefri. As if the insanely strong vampire needed his protection.

And why the hell would he protect her anyway?

It was a puzzle he easily dismissed as the Were gestured for his overgrown guard to step forward.

"Hess, question the guards," he commanded. "I want to know if anyone noticed anything out of the ordinary over the past two weeks. I don't care how meaningless it might have seemed at the time."

The cur fell to his knees, his bald head pressed to the floor.

"Yes, sire."

"And bring each of them down here." A scowl marred

the Were's brow. "It might be that someone will recognize one of the scents."

"At once."

Scrambling with surprising haste considering his bulk, the cur was on his feet and darting toward the stairs leading to the mansion above.

"Does he fetch and roll over on command?" Santiago mocked.

Glowing golden eyes turned in his direction. "No, but he does kill unwanted intruders when I whistle. Do you want a demonstration?"

Santiago didn't need one.

He was absolutely certain the cur killed on command.

Not that he was particularly concerned.

"He's welcome to try," he said with a shrug.

With that tiny sound of impatience that all women made when men were having fun, Nefri stepped around him to speak directly with Salvatore.

"Is there any way in or out of this room beyond this entrance?"

"No." He lifted his hand as they both regarded him with suspicion. "I swear."

Santiago wasn't entirely convinced, but he turned his attention to the beautiful vampire, who was busy pacing from one end of the cellar to the other, her movements as graceful as a water sprite.

"What is it?" he at last demanded.

"I can sense the path of the prophet and her Were," she explained, returning to stand at the entrance of the cell even as she waved a hand toward the hidden doorway where Salvatore and his goon had made their appearance. "They entered the basement through the tunnels. But I can find no indication of where their attackers came from."

"They couldn't have appeared out of thin air," Santiago pointed out.

Salvatore snorted. "You did."

Abruptly reminded that Nefri had indeed managed to bring them to the cellars out of thin air, Santiago grasped the female vampire's arm and tugged her toward the center of the wine cellar.

He wasn't stupid enough to think he could have a private conversation with a pureblood Were standing a few feet away, but he wanted to make clear that this was vampire business, and opinions from the Lassie-section weren't welcome.

"Nefri?" he prompted as she stood lost in thought.

"Hmmm?"

His jaw clenched. "It's obvious the mystery vampire has rare abilities."

She shrugged. "I have no knowledge of a vampire capable of disguising his scent so thoroughly."

"And what of a vampire capable of arriving in this cellar without leaving a trail?"

She didn't need him to spell out the fact that curs and witches were incapable of popping from one place to another. Or that the only vampire capable of entering the cellar was one who possessed her own skills.

Her pale, exquisite features smoothed to an unreadable mask.

"It is a possibility I need to explore."

"Explore?" Santiago tightened his grip on her arm, suddenly sensing he wasn't going to like where this conversation was going. "Explore where?"

The dark, fathomless eyes gave nothing away.

"I must seek the Council of my Elders."

Yep. He was right.

He didn't like it. In fact, the mere thought of this woman disappearing to a place he couldn't follow pissed him off.

"You're returning behind the Veil?" he snapped.

"For now."

"Do you think the vampire was a member of your clan?"

Her slender fingers reached to touch the medallion hung about her neck, her perfect calm only adding to his annoyance.

"It is only one of many possibilities."

"I thought your precious people had evolved beyond the failings of us mere savages?"

There was a muffled cough before Salvatore was stepping to stand beside Nefri.

"This is beginning to feel like a party for two and I have more important things to do," he murmured.

Santiago happily shared his annoyance with the Were. There was, after all, plenty to go around.

"What better things?" he demanded in suspicion.

The king's suffocating power rushed through the room. "Not that I answer to you, bloodsucker, but I intend to take my pregnant mate to a more secure location."

Santiago grimaced. Whatever his enjoyment in taunting the Were, he was as devoted as his Anasso to the precious babies that Harley carried.

Not only because she was the sister to his queen, but because children were a rare and wonderful gift among all demons, and most especially among the pureblooded Weres.

"She is always welcome with Styx and Darcy," he offered. "There are few places more secure."

Salvatore nodded. "That is no doubt where she will demand to be taken. I would prefer to return her to my lair in Italy, but Harley has a mind of her own."

Santiago slid a covert glance toward the silent vampire at his side. "It used to be a woman knew her place."

Salvatore gave a sharp laugh. "Yeah, and pigs used to fly," he mocked, his own gaze shifting to Nefri. "When I've settled my mate, I want answers. Understood?"

She dipped her head in agreement despite Santiago's suspicion that she could rip the Were into tiny pieces with terrifying ease.

With his point made, Salvatore turned to follow the cur's exit path up the stairs, closing and locking the door above with an audible snap.

"Arrogant dog," Santiago growled.

"I believe there is a saying about a pot calling a kettle black," Nefri said in smooth tones, stepping away from his grasp with a determined motion.

She was going to try and escape without him.

Unacceptable.

But why?

Disliking the tiny voice that whispered he didn't want to dig too deeply into his reasons, Santiago told himself that it was his distrust of those who vanished from this world that made him uneasy at allowing her to escape.

What if the vampire responsible for taking Cassandra was hiding behind the Veil? They would never find him. And they could hardly trust this woman to rat him out.

Everyone knew the Immortal Ones were a closed society that protected each other with fanatical dedication.

Yeah.

Only a fool would allow her to disappear.

"I'm not a dog and we haven't finished our conversation," he warned, barely resisting the urge to reach out and yank her into his arms.

"I was not aware we were having a conversation," she countered, her low voice holding an edge of censure. "As I recall you were venting your disdain for those of us who chose to leave this world and I was ignoring you. A conversation is an exchange of ideas and information between individuals who respect one another."

Santiago frowned. No one had dared lecture him since he'd been a foundling.

"You can't just leave."

"Actually I can."

"We must share what we've discovered with Styx." He

latched on to the convenient excuse. "He has to be warned that there's at least one vampire who has turned traitor."

"You can do that without my presence."

"He'll have questions for you."

Her brows lifted at his persistence. "I have no more answers than you do. If I do learn any new information then I will send word."

"No."

Her brows lifted at his persistence. "I beg your pardon?"

Santiago shrugged. "My king commanded that I find Cassandra and right now you're my best hope. I won't fail him."

She paused, studying him with a searching gaze. "He means so much to you?"

He did.

After Santiago had been abandoned by his maker, he had become a slave to those vampires more powerful than himself. There had been days when he truly thought he was living out his personal hell until Styx had found him and trained him to become one of Viper's guards.

That had changed everything.

Suddenly he was no longer fair game for sex or sport or any other brutal pleasure that might amuse his latest master. He was treated with a dignity that had transformed him into a warrior who was never again at the mercy of another.

Santiago would never forget.

Never.

"Loyalty means that much to me," he said, unwilling to share his deep connection to his Anasso. He liked his reputation as an unfeeling bastard. It had taken him years to earn. "It's not something I offer only when it's convenient."

"Very noble." There was a knowing glimmer in her dark eyes, as if she saw far more than he wanted. "I admire your devotion, but I must return to my brethren and ensure that we have not been betrayed."

"Then I go with you."

She looked as startled as he felt.

"Beyond the Veil?"

His resolve briefly faltered.

Of all the gin joints in all the world . . .

Then his gaze skimmed over her pale, impossibly lovely face and he squared his shoulders.

Once she disappeared there would be no means to trace her.

"You can take me, can't you?"

The dark eyes narrowed with undisguised suspicion. "I could."

He forced a smile. "Then let's do this thing."

"Why should I?"

He shrugged. "Why shouldn't you?"

"You have not bothered to hide your contempt for my people." A hint of ice coated her words. "I will not allow you to disturb their peace."

"Despite being a barbarian I was taught a few manners."

"Were you?" She blinked in blatant disbelief. "Astonishing."

"Do you want me to swear in blood I'll behave myself?"

Her gaze never wavered, studying him as if he was a strange specimen that she might or might not keep for further study.

Then a slow smile curved her lips.

"Actually that will not be necessary."

Santiago felt his instincts stir. There was something about that beautiful smile.

Something dangerous.

"It won't?"

"No." The smile widened. "I am perfectly capable of making sure you behave."

"Are you certain . . ."

His words were ripped from his lips as she grasped his

arm at the same moment that she squeezed the medallion. This time, however, the world didn't dissolve with the creepy impression of simply melting away. Instead he felt as if he were being roughly jerked through a curtain of lightning.

Mierda.

Darkness surrounded them, the electricity dancing over his skin and his hair floating despite the lack of a breeze. His teeth snapped together to muffle his scream, his only reality the feel of Nefri's slender fingers still gripping his arm.

What the hell had he gotten himself into now?

Tearloch knew he should be sleeping.

At the moment his loyal tribesmen were finishing their task of clearing the rubble that blocked the altar they needed to complete the ceremony. And the wizard continued to hold his spell of protection that surrounded the caves.

What better opportunity to give his weary body time to recover?

Instead he stood at the upper level of the caverns, glancing with a heartsick longing at the overgrown fields and the star-spattered sky he could glimpse beyond the opening.

The darkness called to him to run free as his people were meant to do . . .

Being locked within the spiderweb of stark, unnaturally smooth passageways was like being buried alive.

There was a faint stir of air as Rafael entered the large cave. Tearloch didn't bother to glance in his direction. The annoying spirit was no doubt there to remind Tearloch that he dared not venture out of the range of his damned spells.

Typically Rafael ignored Tearloch's obvious wish to be left in peace.

The wizard more and more often forgot he was a slave to Tearloch's will.

"Master," the spirit murmured.

"What do you want?"

"I believe there is something you should see."

Tearloch turned a reluctant gaze toward the gaunt face that hovered in the shadows, a shiver of loathing inching down his spine.

"More surprises?"

"Please, if you would come with me?"

Words of denial hovered on his lips.

He was tired and his head ached.

Could he not have an hour without having to sort out some new disaster?

Then, knowing Rafael would remain hovering behind him like some sinister wraith of doom, he heaved a resigned sigh.

Who knew being the leader was such a pain in the ass?

Ariyal always made it look so easy.

Well, maybe not easy, he conceded, vaguely recalling the hours of endless abuse at the hands of Morgana le Fey.

But he had never complained.

"Fine." He turned to meet the sunken eyes that flickered with crimson fire in the shadows. "What is it?"

The spirit gestured him to follow him back through the dark corridors, returning to the cavern where they'd spoken earlier. Once there he crossed directly toward the shallow pool in the floor, pointing a skeletal hand at the images that hovered on the surface of the water.

"Look."

Tearloch was already prepared for the sight of the Sylvermyst who was standing in what looked like the middle of a barnyard.

"Ariyal." Regret stabbed through his heart before he was hardening himself against the sight of his brother. "I already knew he was near."

"But not alone."

Rafael gave a wave of his hand. The image scanned back

to include a beautiful, raven-haired woman who paced through a human kitchen, her fingers stroking the butt of the shotgun holstered on her hip.

"The vampire," he breathed.

"His lover. Such a pity," the spirit crooned, his words dripping like poison. "She has obviously clouded his mind. They are plotting to come and kill the child."

Tearloch scowled. The treacherous wizard wasn't fit to speak Ariyal's name.

"What does it matter? You said your powers would prevent us from being followed."

Rafael grimaced. "His ability to sense you is greater than I suspected. He should never have been able to follow us from London."

"I warned you of his power."

The spirit shrugged. "He couldn't know your precise location or he would already have attacked."

"Then why are you bothering me?"

"Because of this."

There was another wave of his hand and the scene changed, revealing the graveyard overhead. It took a second for Tearloch to notice the misty shadow that drifted toward the entrance of the caves.

"A spirit," he said, tensing in surprise.

It wasn't a full-blown apparition. Merely a ghost that was easily called and easily dismissed. Which meant that it had been conjured to gather information rather than to perform a specific task. Ghosts were incapable of taking solid form.

"One of yours?" Rafael murmured.

"No."

"Can you get rid of it?"

"Yes, but the moment I do then Ariyal will know that I'm here." Tearloch pressed a hand to his aching head. "Damn. We have to leave."

"Wait." Something in the wizard's voice suddenly eased

Tearloch's panicked urge to flee. "Do not be so hasty. I believe we can use this to our advantage."

"How?"

"The ghost is clearly approaching us as a spy."

"I'm not stupid," Tearloch snapped. "I know why Ariyal conjured the ghost."

Rafael pressed his hands to the pendant hung about his neck, a faint smirk curving his thin lips.

"Then why don't we allow him to see what we want him to see?"

"And what's that?"

"The babe."

"That's your plan?" Tearloch's sharp burst of laughter bounced against the polished wall of the cavern. "To lead the most powerful of all Sylvermyst and a vampire directly to the child we have risked everything to keep hidden?"

Rafael smiled with an eerie anticipation.

Gods. The Cheshire Cat from hell.

"The child will merely be the bait."

"Bait for what?"

"To lure the two of them to a very special section of the caverns that was specifically designed for my enemies," the wizard explained.

Tearloch swallowed a resigned sigh. Of course there were caverns devised to capture, and no doubt torture, the wizard's enemies. He suspected that Rafael had been even more of a paranoid, ruthlessly brutal bastard when he'd been alive than he was dead.

"A trap?" he demanded.

"Precisely."

Tearloch hesitated, revolted by the thought of deliberately luring Ariyal into Rafael's trap.

It went against everything he believed.

But what choice did he have?

Ariyal had lost sight of the true path during their time on

Avalon. Now it was Tearloch's holy duty to restore the Sylvermyst to their former glory.

Of course, he didn't have to like it.

"This had better work, wizard," he warned. "Or we're both on our way to hell."

Chapter 14

Jaelyn paced from one end of the kitchen to the other, refusing to glance out the window where Ariyal stood in conversation with a blob of mist that hung in the air.

It was just . . . wrong.

Who used a ghost to do recon?

It would give any sensible demon the shivers.

Which was why she was hiding in the kitchen instead of questioning the creature herself.

Wasn't it?

Reaching the wooden table she came to an abrupt halt, heat blasting through her at the memory of being perched on the edge with her legs wrapped around Ariyal's thrusting hips.

She had told herself that she didn't want to be around the creepy blob of mist, but if she was entirely honest with herself she would admit that she'd needed a few minutes away from Ariyal to try and patch back together her shattered defenses.

Yeah, like that was going to happen anytime soon.

She wrapped her arms around her chilled body, unable to ignore the tug of awareness nestled deep inside her.

Dammit, she didn't want to dwell on her connection to Ariyal.

Even if she wanted to mate with a Sylvermyst who was as annoying as he was gorgeous, it was never going to be in the cards.

Not only would the completion of the binding mean that Ariyal would have to commit fully to becoming her mate and exchange blood with her, but she would have to convince the Addonexus to release their best Hunter when the potential end of the world hung over them all like Damocles's sword.

Accepting that being alone wasn't doing a damned thing to help, Jaelyn was relieved when Ariyal's voice cut through her dark broodings.

"You can come out now."

She moved to the door, scanning the darkness. "It's gone? I mean gone, gone?"

Ariyal's lips twitched, but the smile didn't reach his eyes. Those remained guarded, unreadable.

"Yes, he's been returned to the underworld."

"Good."

"I can't believe a vampire could be squeamish about a spirit," he said, folding his arms over his chest as he watched her descend the wooden steps and cross the yard to join him.

She shrugged. "The dead should be allowed to rest in peace."

"Moving on to the afterlife doesn't guarantee peace, poppet. It's a rare spirit who rests easy in their grave."

Well, wasn't he a bundle of joy?

"Have you considered the possibility that they might be perfectly content until you start messing with them?" she asked wryly. "Anyone would be cranky at being jerked out of the underworld and forced to become a slave to a fairy."

There was a fleeting heat in the bronzed gaze as it skimmed down her body.

"There are some who are positively giddy to be my slave. I have that effect on women," he murmured, as if she needed a reminder of his potent sexuality. Hell, he literally screamed sex. "And a surprising number of men."

"Conceited ass."

"Confident," he corrected, a fleeting heat flaring through his bronzed eyes before he lowered his head to kiss her with a harsh frustration.

For a crazed moment Jaelyn returned his ferocious kiss, her hands grasping his shoulders as she went on tiptoe to arch against the addictive heat of his bare chest.

Then reality slammed back into her and she was pushing him away with a low, pained growl.

"No, Ariyal."

He stiffly stepped backward, his expression once again indecipherable.

"We should go."

"Did you discover what you needed?"

"The spirit was able to locate Tearloch and the babe."

"Where?"

He tilted his head toward the north, his hands fisted at his side.

"A series of caverns less than three miles north of here."

So close?

For no reason at all a chill inched down her spine.

"Why do I sense this is a good-news/bad-news kind of deal?" she asked.

"The good news is the child is currently alone in one of the caves."

"And the bad news?"

"Besides Tearloch there are half-dozen Sylvermyst as well as the wizard."

She frowned, studying the arrogant perfection of his

face. She could sense the emotions that churned beneath that careful mask, and she hated the knowledge he wanted to keep them hidden from her.

"That was more or less what you expected, wasn't it?"

"Yes."

"Then what's the problem?"

He silently debated her question before he at last heaved a sigh.

"I don't know."

She arched a brow. "Maybe you can be a little more vague?"

"I think you should stay. . . ."

"No."

His eyes blazed with a bronzed fury. "Dammit, Jaelyn, there's a very good possibility that this is a trap."

"All the more reason you need me to go with you."

"You were trained better than that, Hunter," he rasped. "If I don't return then you must alert your Oracles that I have failed and that Tearloch will soon use the child to resurrect the Dark Lord."

He was right.

If her current task was to retrieve the child and save the world from the Dark Lord, then she would have to concede that it was preferable for one of them to sneak into the caverns while the other waited to determine if it was a trap.

But she had been charged with staying near Ariyal and keeping track of his movements.

Which in this moment suited her just fine.

"They aren't *my* Oracles," she denied.

"We aren't going to argue about this." He slashed a hand through the air, looking every inch a prince. "The only sensible plan is for me to try and rescue the child while you find a sun-proof location to wait out the approaching day."

She shook her head. "I can't."

"Can't? Don't you mean won't?"

The air smoldered with the force of his barely restrained power.

Jaelyn stood her ground. "No, I mean I can't."

"Why?"

"I have to remain with you." She met his gaze squarely. "That's all I can say."

She braced herself for Ariyal's explosion of anger. Even a threat to lock her in the cellar and leave her to rot.

Instead he held on to his grim control, taking a deliberate step backward.

Not that he needed to.

Jaelyn could feel the mental barriers he was erecting between them without the physical demonstration.

"And you accuse me of being vague."

She wanted to . . . what? Plead for his understanding? Demand to know if he thought this was fun and games for her?

She hadn't asked to become a pawn for the Oracles, had she? Or to become entangled with the one male in the entire world who treated her as if she was something more than a killing machine.

And she certainly hadn't asked for her emotions to be stripped bare after decades of believing they had been efficiently destroyed.

"I don't have a choice," she ineffectively muttered.

"Of course not." A humorless smile curved his lips. "Tell me, poppet, if I weren't your current duty would you already have taken off?"

Well, he certainly wanted his pound of flesh.

She fingered her shotgun, shifting beneath his bleak gaze. She'd rather be skinned alive than to continue this agonizing conversation.

"Being a Hunter means I must go where I am commanded to go."

"And that truly does put me in my place, doesn't it?"

With liquid grace Ariyal turned on his heel and headed

across the barnyard, his spine stiff and his head held at a proud angle.

"Shit."

A brutal pain seared through Jaelyn as she forced herself to watch him walk away.

As much as she might ache to follow, she forced herself to remain standing alone in the darkness.

She didn't know jack squat about men, but she did know that you didn't poke at a lethal predator when he was licking his wounds.

Even if they were just superficial.

Ariyal wasn't a vampire, after all.

And she doubted that Sylvermyst mated for life.

In a day or two she would be a bad memory that he could tuck away with those of Morgana le Fey.

Telling herself that was exactly what she wanted, Jaelyn stood immobile, feeling as if the slight summer breeze might shatter her into a million pieces.

She lost track of time as she stood there; then the distant scent of blood abruptly destroyed her full-blown bout of self-pity.

What the hell?

She was flowing past the outbuildings to a small pond at the bottom of the hill before she realized that the blood she smelled wasn't Ariyal's but that of a feral pig that Ariyal had obviously sacrificed to increase the power of his blade.

Her panic eased, but not her need to seek out Ariyal and make certain he was unharmed.

It was a compulsion that refused any logic.

Vaulting over the sagging barbed-wire fence, Jaelyn continued forward, not halting until she was kneeling beside the Sylvermyst, who was crouched next to the water, washing the blood off his hands.

He didn't turn his head. In fact, he stubbornly refused to acknowledge her arrival at all as he shook the water off his hands. Then, rising to his feet, he grasped his sword over his head, the blade glowing with a white-hot magic.

"What are you doing?" she stupidly asked.

Anything to break the awful silence.

His gaze remained locked on the sword as he sliced it through the air in a slow, practiced pattern.

"Preparing for battle."

She watched his graceful dance as he performed the ancient Sylvermyst ritual, her heart clenching at his sheer beauty.

His hair shimmered with colors of autumn, his delicately crafted features set in lines of a warrior, and his body honed to an elegant weapon.

Only when he was finished did she straighten, squaring her shoulders for yet another clash of wills.

During her wild run down the hill she'd come to a decision, and now she wasn't going to be denied. Even if it was destined to drive a greater wedge between them.

"There's no need for battle," she said.

He sheathed his sword. "That's the hope, but we both know our luck isn't that good."

"I could improve our luck."

He turned to meet her stubborn gaze, his face carefully devoid of expression.

"How?"

She crushed her pang of regret. This was how it had to be.

Strictly professional.

"I have the ability to travel in and out of the caves without being sensed," she reminded him. "Once I'm wrapped in shadows no one will be able to track my movements, not even the wizard. It only makes sense that I go after the child."

He was shaking his head before she even finished. "No."

Her brows snapped together. "Have you forgotten there's a spell on the child that will prevent you from even being able to touch it?"

"I'll figure out something."

"But . . ."

"I said no."

Her hands landed on her hips as she glared at him. "Why are you being so stubborn?"

"It's too dangerous."

"Dammit." She stepped forward, poking a finger into the center of his bare chest. Okay, so much for being strictly professional. She was suddenly so mad her fangs throbbed. "I'm sorry if it offends your male pride that I'm not a helpless woman who needs a big, strong man to take care of me, but this is who I am. I'm a Hunter, and that means I'm stronger and I'm faster and I'm better trained than ninety-nine percent . . ."

He was moving before she could react, grabbing her upper arms in a punishing grip.

"This has nothing to do with my pride," he growled.

She made a sound of disbelief. "Really?"

"Really." His glare seared over her pale face. "Okay, I'm male enough to occasionally want to flex my muscles just to prove I have them, but I would never want you to be less."

She stilled, savoring the feel of his warm hands against her skin. It didn't matter that he held her in anger. She was so hungry for his touch she would take whatever she could get.

Pathetic.

"What does that mean?" she demanded.

"It's your power and your beauty and your stubborn independence that make you who you are," he said, as if the words were being yanked from him. "I would never change that. Not ever."

His words touched the vulnerable place deep inside her, but Jaelyn fiercely refused to be distracted.

In this moment all that mattered was that she keep Ariyal from walking into such an obvious trap.

"Then is this because you don't trust me with the child?" she accused.

His jaw clenched so tight she could hear his teeth grinding together.

"No, it damn well has nothing to do with trust."

"Then what?"

"Because if you are hurt or worse . . ." He struggled against a fierce tide of emotion. "I'm not sure I will survive."

Stunned by his raw confession she lifted her hands to frame his face.

"Ariyal . . ."

She didn't know what she was going to say. Nothing that would have improved the god-awful situation. And Ariyal thankfully didn't give her time to flounder in her helpless yearning.

"So don't expect me to be happy when you put yourself in danger."

She held his smoldering gaze with a wistful smile. "I don't expect you to be happy, but I need you to understand why I can't deny my true nature as Hunter. I'll never be the sort of female to wait in the corner for her man to return."

"Dammit." With a shake of his head he conceded defeat. "Let's go."

"Ariyal . . ."

With a foul curse he was jerking away from her touch and running north at a speed that made sure there would be no opportunity for further conversation.

They arrived at the abandoned church with less than an hour left until dawn.

Ariyal ruthlessly ignored the whispers of panic that Jaelyn needed to be tucked in a nice, sun-proof crypt. She'd made it brutally clear that she didn't want or need his concern, hadn't she?

After all, she was the big, bad Hunter. And he was just the poor slob who happened to be her current job.

If not for her mysterious contract with the Oracles she would be long gone.

He kept the warning in the front of his mind as he halted at the entrance to the cavern and once again described the exact route through the tunnels to where the baby was being kept.

Thanks to the efforts of his friendly ghost he possessed a complete map of the sprawling caverns burned into his brain. As well as the members of Tearloch's motley crew.

And while he wasn't willing to assume that no one had noticed his approach, they would be expecting a Sylvermyst to try and make a grab for the child. There was no way they could prepare for a vampire who could make herself practically invisible.

With the least amount of luck Jaelyn should be able to slip in and out before anyone realized the baby was missing.

His pretense of aloof indifference briefly faltered as he felt the prickles of ice filling the air. She was preparing to call on her powers.

"Jaelyn," he said in urgent tones, reaching to grasp her forearm. "Wait."

"I got it." Her smile was rueful. "Be careful. Get in and get out. Don't stop for anything or anyone. I am trained, you know."

He heaved a frustrated sigh. "I don't like this."

"And you think I do?" Her eyes narrowed. "There's no need for a distraction."

Ariyal shrugged. He'd waited until they had reached the caverns before he announced his intention to enter the tunnels. He claimed he wanted to create a distraction to make sure no one noticed the missing child until she was clear. It was true enough. He would make one hell of a distraction.

But he had his own agenda. One he didn't intend to share with Jaelyn.

"We'll only have one opportunity to grab the child," he said with undeniable logic. "I intend to give us the best possible chance."

She held his gaze. "And you swear you aren't going to try and go after Tearloch?"

He held up a hand. "I swear."

"Fine." A dangerous warning glittered in the indigo eyes. "But if something happens to you . . ."

His hand skimmed up her arm, craving the feel of the cool silk of her skin.

It didn't matter how furious he might be; if he didn't make it out of the caves then he wanted his last thought to be of this female.

"What?" he prompted.

"I'm going to be pissed."

Her warning delivered, Jaelyn spoke a low word and the chill in the air became a frigid blast of ice. At the same moment her slender frame simply seemed to disappear, no doubt already headed through the caves.

"So romantic," he muttered, reaching out his hand to clench and then spread his fingers.

There was a stir of air before a smooth ash bow abruptly appeared.

Not as good as Jaelyn's stealth act, but it would have to do, he wryly acknowledged, grasping the smooth wood in a loose grip as he silently slid into the entrance of the cavern.

He paused a moment to examine his surroundings.

There was no sense of Jaelyn, of course, but with an effort he could catch the scent of his fellow tribesmen despite the wizard's dampening spell.

It was impossible to make out individual scents, but he had what he needed.

Moving as swiftly as he dared considering he was surrounded by enemies, Ariyal headed deep into the earth, barely noticing the too-smooth surface of the tunnels or the growing stench of evil that tainted the musty air.

He had only a few minutes to accomplish what he'd come to do and try to make a clean getaway.

In and out.

No problem.

He chanted the words beneath his breath as he used the images the ghost had shared to find his way through the confusion of passageways and abandoned caverns. The scent of Sylvermyst thickened, but instead of following the rich aroma of herbs, he darted into a narrow cave directly above them.

The ghost had been commendably thorough in his investigation of the caverns. Which was why Ariyal knew that half a dozen Sylvermyst were frantically working to clear a tunnel.

The question he wanted answered was . . . why?

Tearloch might have tumbled into madness, but the wizard remained coldly cunning. He wouldn't waste that sort of man power unless it was essential to returning the Dark Lord.

Which meant that Ariyal needed to halt whatever they were doing just in case Jaelyn failed.

He crushed the surge of fear that threatened to distract him, kneeling on the floor next to the large crack that ran the length of the cave. Whatever had destroyed the tunnel beneath him had left this floor split nearly in two. A wrong step and it would collapse.

As he hoped, he could easily hear the sound of his tribesmen as they struggled to remove the rocks that blocked their path.

For several excruciating minutes there was nothing but
the sound of stone scraping against stone. He wasn't concerned about the fact his presence was already seeping
through the passageways. He wanted to attract attention so
they didn't realize the baby was missing. But he wasn't any
closer to discovering why his tribesmen were burrowing
through the rubble.

Then, as if some kindly deity had decided to have mercy
on his black soul, the sound of voices at last drifted through
the air.

"Why aren't you working?" a male voice roughly demanded.

"I'm a soldier not a damned mole," another male responded, his tone edged with disgust. "If the wizard wants
to clear out the tunnel then why doesn't he do it himself?"

Ariyal easily recognized the two Sylvermyst as Elwin and
Toras. Not surprising. Both had lost their females to Morgana's jealousy. They had never hidden their bitterness, or the
fact they held Ariyal to blame for the death of their mates.

"Keep your voice down," Elwin rasped.

"Or what?"

Ariyal could sense the man's shudder. "I don't think
either of us wants to find out."

Toras gave a growl of frustration. "When Tearloch promised the return of the Dark Lord he didn't mention the fact
we would have to dig out an altar that was buried beneath
a ton of rocks. Or that we'd have to take our orders from a
specter who should have been left to rot in hell."

Ariyal's lips twisted.

There was a mutiny brewing.

Did Tearloch know how close he was to losing his few
tribesmen?

"The sooner we uncover the altar the sooner the wizard
can complete the resurrection and the sooner he can be
banished," Elwin muttered.

"Always assuming that Tearloch hasn't lost complete control," Toras pointed out with a bleak resignation.

"Shit. Just get back to work."

The voices faded and Ariyal sat back on his heels.

Altar?

It made sense.

Those who worshiped the Dark Lord often used altars to make their sacrifices. The blood was a conduit that allowed them to thin the walls that separated them from their evil master.

Obviously Rafael needed his altar to complete the ceremony.

That was all the information Ariyal needed.

Tossing aside his bow, he shoved his fingers into the crack. The rock scraped off his skin, but he ignored the blood that threatened to make his grip slippery and yanked with all his strength.

He wasn't a troll who could tunnel through rock with his brute strength, but the floor was already unstable and the exact pressure in the weakest spot was enough to make the stone buckle beneath his feet.

Snatching up his bow, Ariyal darted toward the outer tunnel, leaping across the gaping chasm that abruptly appeared as the collapse picked up speed at an alarming rate. Bloody hell. He had expected a minor cave-in, not a landslide.

He sent up a brief prayer that his brothers would manage to find safety. Whatever their sins, he hoped that they could eventually put the past behind them and be reunited as a tribe. There were too few of them to allow petty resentments to separate them.

Then all thoughts of his brothers were forgotten as he at last reached solid ground and sought a passageway that would lead him up and out of the caverns.

Following the faint scent of fresh air, he was desperate to leave behind the choking cloud of dust that billowed through the tunnels. Obviously too desperate, since he was unprepared when Tearloch abruptly darted from a side tunnel to block his path.

"Tearloch," he growled, skidding to a reluctant halt at the sight of his tribesman.

Good . . . gods.

The younger Sylvermyst looked like shit.

His hair was tangled and hung limply down his back, his skin was a strange, grayish hue, and there were bruises beneath his eyes that revealed he hadn't slept in far too long.

Obviously the effort to keep control of Rafael was taking its toll on him.

Or was it the damned spirit draining Tearloch's power?

Either way, it was a dangerous situation that might very well kill the Sylvermyst if something wasn't done.

Soon.

A pity he wasn't about to let Ariyal help him.

Not if the hectic glow in the silver of his eyes and the big-ass sword he was currently pointing at Ariyal's heart were any indication.

"I should have suspected that you would manage to cause trouble no matter how clever our plans," Tearloch growled.

Ariyal forced a stiff smile to his lips. He had wanted to be a distraction, hadn't he?

It looked as if he was roaring success.

Yippee ki yay.

"You know me, I can't resist crashing a party." He glanced down at the dust covering him from head to toe. "Sometimes literally."

Tearloch's jaw locked even as he tried to look as if he was indifferent to the considerable damage.

"It's annoying, but nothing that can't be repaired."

Ariyal smiled. "In time."

The silver eyes narrowed. "So you sacrificed yourself just to delay the inevitable?"

"But it isn't inevitable, Tearloch." Ariyal held his companion's gaze. "Your mind has been twisted by those who only want to use you for their own glory."

"No." Tearloch shook his head with more force than necessary. "It's your mind that has been twisted. That vampire has seduced you and stolen you from those who have always offered you their loyalty."

Ariyal grimly refused to allow his thoughts to stray to Jaelyn. This wasn't the time for distractions.

"But your loyalty wasn't unwavering, was it?" he reminded his one-time friend. "You betrayed me."

The bastard managed to look offended. "I didn't betray you. I was only trying to protect our tribe."

"Were you?" Ariyal gave a lift of his shoulder, knowing that he couldn't force the man to accept blame for his treachery. "A pity then that they no longer trust you."

Tearloch's fingers tightened on the sword. "That's a lie."

"I heard them complaining only a few minutes ago. They fear you're now the slave of your spirit instead of the master. And who could blame them? You obviously take your orders from the creature."

"That's ridiculous."

"Is it?" Ariyal folded his arms over his chest. "Then banish him."

"I . . ." Tearloch licked his lips, his eyes nervously darting over Ariyal's shoulder as if fearing the spirit might be hovering just out of sight. "I can't."

Ariyal swallowed a curse.

It was revolting to witness one of his people in thrall of a spirit.

"You see?"

"I need him to cast the spell to resurrect the Dark Lord."

"There are other magic-users who could do the task just as well, if not better."

"No." Tearloch pressed a hand to his forehead. "We're too close."

Ariyal took a stealthy step forward. Tearloch was weary. Unfocused.

If he could just get close enough, he could strike.

"What happened to Sergei?" he asked, hoping to keep Tearloch off balance.

"I don't know."

"You could no doubt track him down and let him perform the ceremony."

"Haven't you heard me?" Tearloch lowered his hand, his face flushed. "It's too late."

"No, it's not." Ariyal took another step forward. "Let me help you."

"You should really listen to your brother," a voice mocked from behind him.

"Wizard," Ariyal hissed, spinning around to fire two arrows directly in the center of Rafael's chest. Predictably, the arrows passed directly through the bastard, but Ariyal noticed that the spirit briefly flickered, as if he'd been injured.

Something to remember.

"Don't be hasty, Sylvermyst," Rafael drawled.

"Hasty?" Ariyal curled his lips in disgust. "I should have destroyed you the moment I realized your power over Tearloch."

Flames smoldered in his sunken eyes. "Ah, but I have something you want."

Ariyal snorted. "You have nothing . . ."

His words died on his lips as the wizard gave a wave of his skeleton hand and pointed toward the wall of the tunnel. There was an odd glow; then a strange mist formed on the rock, revealing the image of a beautiful vampire in black spandex trapped in a small cave.

It was almost like watching her on a television with fuzzy reception, but there was no mistaking her identity or the fact that she was currently trapped in the cave where he'd told her the child was located.

"Jaelyn," he breathed, his gut clenching with a sick dread as he watched her trying to claw her way out of the trap.

"I will say you have excellent taste," Rafael taunted. "She is exquisite."

"Damn you," he rasped. "Release her."

"If you insist."

The wizard's sinister laugh was like something out of a cheesy horror flick, but Ariyal wasn't amused. Not when the bastard gave another wave of his hand and he watched in helpless horror as Jaelyn abruptly glanced upward, her eyes wide as the rock above her slowly parted and the early morning sunlight poured through the cave.

"No."

Pulling his sword from the leather scabbard, he launched himself at the wizard. Not that he truly believed he could hurt the spirit. As long as Tearloch allowed him to draw so deeply on his powers he was all but indestructible.

But any lingering sanity that he might have once claimed had been savagely stripped away as he watched Jaelyn being exposed to the dawn, and his black rage had no room for logical thinking.

Swinging his sword over his head, he was preparing to ram it through the wizard's dead heart when Rafael muttered a harsh word of power and the magic slammed into Ariyal with shattering force.

One moment he was screaming for blood and the next a wave of darkness had swallowed him whole.

Chapter 15

Ariyal had always known he had a one-way ticket to Hell when he died. After all, it wasn't as if he'd done anything to earn his way into a more luxurious afterlife.

But he hadn't expected Hell to include a throbbing head and the sensation of sharp rocks digging into his back.

And he sure the crap hadn't expected to be tormented by a stunted gargoyle who was leaning over him and smacking him in the face.

"Hello," the damned demon screeched in his ear, slapping his cheek. "Are you in there?"

Hell or no Hell, Ariyal wasn't going to endure being pummeled by Levet. At least not lying down.

Surging to his feet, he grasped the pest by his horn and dangled him high enough to meet his furious glare.

"Are you out of your mind?" he roared. "You hit me again and I'll turn you into a bowling ball."

"Sacrebleu." With a flap of his wings, Levet broke free of Ariyal's grip and was floating to land on the stony ground. "I thought you were going to sleep away the entire night."

"Night?" Ariyal scowled as he glanced around the dark, barren cavern. "It was dawn. . . ." The sudden memory of dawn and what that meant to him drove Ariyal to his knees as the weight of his grief threatened to crush him. "Shit."

Levet moved to his side. "What is wrong?"

"Jaelyn," he rasped in raw pain, pressing his hand to the center of his chest where he could still feel her presence.

Seemingly oblivious to his pain, Levet gave a small shrug.

"She's not in the caves. Trust me, I searched everywhere. She seems to just have disappeared."

He shuddered. "Not disappeared."

At last sensing Ariyal's distress, Levet gave a sharp shake of his head.

"*Non*. Impossible."

Ariyal lifted his head at the gargoyle's absolute certainty, a dangerous flare of hope flickering deep in his heart.

"I watched as the wizard opened a trap door to expose her to the dawn," he said, rubbing that spot in his chest that whispered his beautiful vampire still lived.

The demon remained stoically unconvinced. "You were there?"

"No." Ariyal gave a slow shake of his head. "He showed me a vision."

"And you believed him? *Imbecile*."

"Careful, Levet."

"Do you not see? It had to be a trick."

A trick?

But the vision had appeared all too real, the voice of common sense whispered in the back of his mind. And the gargoyle had admitted himself he hadn't been able to find the Hunter.

Still . . . the wizard was capable of all sorts of nasty deceptions.

How hard would it be to conjure a vision revealing what he wanted Ariyal to believe?

Yes, of course.

That had to be it.

Ariyal eagerly shoved aside the knowledge that he was grasping at straws.

No matter how illogical, he desperately needed to cling to the gargoyle's assurance that Jaelyn had survived.

Because if he truly accepted that Jaelyn was dead, then he might as well curl in the nearest corner and wait for his own death.

He had no choice but to believe in miracles.

Yep, he truly was an *imbecile.*

"How did you get in here?" he demanded, fiercely forcing himself to concentrate on the one thing he could control for the moment.

Escaping from the cavern.

Slowly, like a man coming out of a nightmare, he straightened, his hand instinctively reaching to make certain his sword was still strapped to his back.

When he felt the familiar hilt that had been crafted specifically for his hand, he didn't know whether to be relieved to have his weapon or insulted that Tearloch assumed he could be so easily defeated.

"Ah." Levet's expression brightened as he gave a flap of his gossamer wings. "It is truly quite an amazing story. I have had such adventures."

Ariyal held up a silencing hand. "Just the facts, gargoyle."

The tiny demon responded with a raspberry. "And I thought vampires were rude."

"Don't press me."

"Fine." His tail twitched in outrage. "If you will recall I was in pursuit of the curs who attacked Jaelyn."

"Not really."

Ariyal shrugged, crossing the floor to run his hands over the smooth stone of the cavern.

Only to flinch back in pain.

Shit. Behind the thin layer of stone was a wall of pure lead that was sucking his power with a ruthless speed.

"Well, I was," Levet continued, predictably indifferent to Ariyal's discomfort. "And at considerable risk to myself, I might add. One of those curs was a mage."

Turning, Ariyal studied his companion with a lift of his brows. "I notice you appear unharmed so it couldn't have been that dangerous."

"I happen to be a master of stealth," Levet assured him with a sniff. "It is only one of my many skills."

"You're a master of annoyance. Do you have a point?"

"I followed them until they met up with a witch and vampire on the outskirts of Chicago."

He narrowed his gaze.

So Jaelyn had been right to be concerned there was a mysterious leech involved.

"Vampire? You're certain?"

"*Oui.* One I did not recognize."

Ariyal waited for the gargoyle to continue. He already suspected he hadn't heard the worse.

"And?" he at last prompted.

"And they disappeared."

Ariyal frowned. "What do you mean, disappeared?"

"I mean poof." Levet waved his hands. "Gone."

"Magic?"

There was another wave of his tiny hands. "*Je ne sais pas.* They were there one minute and the next they had vanished into thin air."

"Damn." Ariyal scrubbed his face with his hands, frustration bubbling through him. "Just what I don't need. Something else to worry about." Reluctantly he returned his attention to his companion. "What happened next?"

"I had no means to follow the curs so I returned to the meadow and managed to track Jaelyn to these caves." The gargoyle grimaced. "I was leaving when that ghastly wizard hit me with a spell that knocked me unconscious. *Cochon.*"

"For once we're in perfect agreement," Ariyal muttered. "Have you searched the cave for a way out?"

Levet stepped back, his ugly face rigid with outrage. "What do you imagine I have been doing for the past hour? Admiring your Sleeping Beauty impersonation?"

"Someday . . ." Ariyal growled.

The gargoyle waved aside the warning. "Can you not make a portal?"

Ariyal shook his head. "There's too much lead embedded behind the stone for even me to overcome."

"Ah, so it falls upon my shoulders to release us. Very well." With a dramatic motion, Levet moved to the center of the room and lifted his hands. "Stand aside."

"Hold on," Ariyal commanded. "What are you doing?"

"We need an escape tunnel." Levet pointed toward the far wall. "*Violà.* I shall create one."

"No." Ariyal shuddered at the mere thought of being trapped in the enclosed space while Levet created havoc.

"Just because you are impotent does not mean that I am," the gargoyle informed him with a sly smile. "Indeed, my magic is *formidable*."

"What you are is a walking disaster and I don't want you collapsing a ton of rocks on my head," Ariyal snapped.

On cue a large rock tumbled from the ceiling, forcing the two of them to leap back or be smashed in the head.

"Hey!" Levet yelped.

"Dammit, gargoyle."

"That was not me."

Ariyal glared at his companion as another rock crashed onto the floor.

"Levet, I'm warning you . . ."

Levet lifted his hands. "I swear."

The words had barely left his lips when a male voice echoed through the air.

"Stand back, you fools."

Ariyal hissed. He recognized that voice.

"Sergei?" He glanced around the gloomy cavern. "Where the hell are you?"

"I'm in a cave just above you," the mage spoke through the hole he'd made in the floor. "I have a spell that will provide a large enough opening for you and the gargoyle to escape."

Ariyal had promised himself that the next time he crossed paths with the mage he would fulfill his fantasy of slicing off the bastard's head and using it to decorate his lair.

It didn't improve his foul temper that he had to put his pledge on the back burner.

"Then do it."

"Not until you've agreed to my price for your freedom."

Ariyal rolled his eyes. He hadn't expected the damned magic-user to actually free them.

This had to be yet another trap.

"Price?"

"You don't think I'm going to rescue you out of the goodness of my heart, do you, Sylvermyst?" Sergei mocked.

"What if I promise not to rip out your intestines and use them as fertilizer?" he offered, ignoring Levet's glare.

Did the tiny pest think that they could convince the mage to release them with sweet words and flattery?

"Charming," Sergei snapped. "Did you learn your bartering skills from Morgana le Fay?"

Ariyal clenched his fists at the deliberate taunt. Oh yes. That head was absolutely going to be mounted over his fireplace.

"Just get us the hell out of here."

"Only after you swear you will take us out of these cursed caves with a portal."

"Dammit, how many times do I have to say this? There's too much lead. . . ."

"Only in this section of the caverns," the mage interrupted. "This particular cave was obviously built to hold fey as prisoners."

"Obviously," Ariyal said dryly, wondering what game the mage was playing. "Lead, however, doesn't keep a wizard from escaping if he wanted. Why do you need me?"

"Mage," Sergei corrected, his voice thick with anger at the apparent insult. "And it isn't lead that is keeping me here."

"Then what is?"

There was a tense silence, as if Sergei was considering how much to reveal.

"When I got sucked through Tearloch's portal I was dropped not far from here," he finally rasped, a tiny shower of rocks warning his control over his magic wasn't entirely perfect. "I've managed to keep myself hidden, but I'm not stupid. I know the moment I try to escape my presence will be noticed. I won't make it out without help."

"And you're willing to leave behind the babe?" he demanded in suspicion. "I thought you were dead without it to offer you protection?"

"I have no choice."

Ariyal's humorless laugh bounced off the walls of the cavern.

"That didn't stop you before. You nearly killed us all with your idiotic attempt to keep Tearloch from escaping from London. Tell me why you're willing to risk leaving it behind now."

The mage swore in Russian before reluctantly giving into Ariyal's demands.

"Fine, I've used most of my powers just to keep myself hidden. Until I manage to rest and eat a decent meal I'm as helpless as a baby."

Ariyal paused.

He didn't possess Jaelyn's ability to sense lies, but he could hear the throb of fear in Sergei's voice.

A man didn't fake that.

Not a man with Sergei's enormous pride.

"I agree to your bargain."

There was another pause. Clearly Ariyal wasn't the only one with trust issues.

"Do I have your word?"

"For what it's worth."

"Actually I think it will be worth a great deal." The mage struggled to bolster his flagging arrogance, perhaps sensing he'd revealed more than he intended. "I just happen to have information about a certain vampire that I will be willing to share once we're safely clear of these caves."

"Jaelyn?" His power blasted through the room as he glared at the ceiling of the cavern. Was this yet another trick? "Dammit. Tell me what you know."

"Now, now, Ariyal," the bastard drawled. "You give me what I want and I'll give you what you want. Fair trade."

"Someday very, very soon I'm going to kill that son of a bitch," Ariyal swore.

Chapter 16

The dreams came again.

But this time Jaelyn wasn't in the Addonexus training facility.

Not that the dungeons of the slave-auction house on the outskirts of Chicago were any better.

She stood in the middle of a barren cell, the air thick with the stench of trolls and her skin still scorched from the silver manacles that had been removed while she'd been unconscious. But despite her discomfort, she felt a stab of satisfaction as she paced toward the silver bars and glanced down the narrow path that ran past the numerous cells to the thick door at the far end of the cavernous room.

This was her first job as a full-fledged Hunter and she'd been anxious to prove she was worthy of her Ruah's trust.

Of course she hadn't expected to be asked to play the role of a vampire whore in the hopes of discovering what idiot possessed the cojones to kidnap vampires in the middle of a crowded brothel. Or for it to take nearly three weeks of prowling the local demon dives before she'd at last hit pay dirt.

She'd been ready to chuck in her dog-collar necklace, her see-through top, and three-inch fuck-me pumps that were an open invitation for any and every demon to put their hands on her ass before she at last had been approached by an imp who had lured her to a seedy backroom and slapped the silver cuffs on her. Then, with equal speed she found herself being shoved into a tiny silver box that had sucked the energy from her at an alarming rate.

Now she could only hope that this slave-auction house would give her the information she needed.

With no option but to remain in her self-imposed role while she waited to see what would happen, Jaelyn turned back to investigate her cramped cell, cautiously reaching for the cheap goblet that had been left on a wooden table in the center of the floor.

"I wouldn't if I were you," a soft voice whispered from the adjoining cell.

Jaelyn had already sensed the young nymph, as well as the harpy who was slumbering in the cell farther down the dungeon.

"Wouldn't what?" she asked, glancing toward the golden-haired female, who had been stripped of her clothes to reveal her lush, perfect curves.

Nymphs were always beautiful; this one was drop-dead gorgeous.

"Drink the blood," she clarified.

"Why not?"

"It's laced with a drug that keeps a vampire unconscious. Sometimes for hours."

Jaelyn set aside the goblet, her gaze never shifting from the female's wide blue eyes.

She couldn't detect any deception in the nymph, but that didn't mean the young demon wasn't an unwitting dupe to the villains who ran the nasty slave business.

"How long have you been here?"

"I'm not sure." The female abruptly shuddered. "At least a couple of weeks."

Jaelyn's suspicions deepened. "You weren't brought here for the auction?"

"I was."

"Then why haven't you been sold?"

The nymph abruptly wrapped her arms around her waist, as if she were cold.

"The guards prefer to keep me here for their entertainment. I suppose they'll eventually tire of me and I'll be taken upstairs."

Jaelyn grimaced, attacked by an unfamiliar stab of pity. The wretched creature had obviously suffered at the hands of her captors, even if she didn't have the physical scars to show.

"I'm sorry."

"Yeah, so am I." The nymph struggled to hide her misery behind a determined smile. "Oh, I'm Valla, by the way."

A part of Jaelyn told her to turn away and ignore the chatty demon. She had a very specific agenda that didn't include becoming BFFs with her fellow inmates. But her training warned that she couldn't ignore such a potential source of information.

"I'm Jaelyn."

"That's pretty." Valla tilted her head to the side, her glorious mane of hair tumbling over her shoulder. "Did you get to choose your own name?"

"No." Jaelyn absently rubbed the raw skin of her wrists. She would need to feed before she could fully heal. "It was given to me by my maker."

The nymph moved closer to the bars. "Are you injured?"

Jaelyn instantly dropped her hands. A Hunter never revealed weakness.

"I'll recover."

"If you need a drink I'll share." The female held her arm through the bars. "I'm not on drugs or anything."

Jaelyn frowned, once again searching for some sign of

deceit. Why would this female be so kind? For God's sake, she was offering her vein to a complete stranger.

Surely there had to be an ulterior motive?

But no matter how deep Jaelyn searched she could find nothing but purity in the nymph's soul.

Oddly disturbed, Jaelyn abruptly paced back toward the door of the cell to peer at the distant door.

"Are they all trolls?"

"Who?"

"The guards."

"No." The sharp scent of Valla's fear filled the air. "There's at least two imps and a pack of hellhounds who guard the exits. There's no way out if that's what you're thinking. And if you try . . . they'll hurt you."

"There's always a way out."

The nymph was momentarily speechless at Jaelyn's cold confidence; then she gave a forced laugh.

"Yes well, I suppose a woman like you would think that way."

Jaelyn turned to meet the faintly envious blue gaze. "A woman like me?"

Valla shrugged. "A warrior."

"All women are warriors."

Valla's lips twisted. "Nice to think so."

Jaelyn swallowed the urge to point out that the mere fact Valla had managed to survive two weeks in the dungeons of a slaver proved she was as tough as any soldier.

Focus, Jaelyn, focus.

"Who runs the place?"

"There's a half-breed troll who is in charge of the auctions."

"And?" Jaelyn prompted.

"There's something . . ." She wrinkled her nose in disgust. "Else."

Something else?

That covered a lot of territory.

"What?"

Valla lowered her voice until it was barely a whisper. "A monster."

Jaelyn moved closer to her new friend, sensing that she was coming close to discovering precisely what was making vampires disappear.

"A demon?" she pressed.

"I don't know exactly what it is, but whenever they bring in a vampire it comes out of the cellars and drags them down there."

Jaelyn followed the direction of Valla's pointed finger, noticing the faint outline of a hidden door on the back wall of the cell.

"You don't know what species it is?"

The nymph shrugged. "It's something I've never seen before. . . ." Her eyes abruptly widened as the stench of old leather suddenly filled the air. "Oh no. That's it."

"Sssh."

Motioning for the nymph to return to her narrow cot on the far side of her cell, Jaelyn moved to overturn the table, allowing the goblet and its nasty contents to drain into the dirt floor. Then, lowering herself to the floor, she stretched out as if she'd been struck unconscious, careful to make sure she could see the hidden door.

She had barely arranged herself to her satisfaction when the door slowly swung inward and a large form squeezed through the opening to step into the cell.

Peeping beneath her lowered lashes, Jaelyn barely repressed a shudder of disgust.

A vicious cross between a gargoyle and an ogre, the creature had dark, armor-like skin and a ridge of spines that ran from the base of its large, misshapen head down between its leathery wings to the tip of his long tail. Its short arms ended with clawed hands, as did his powerful legs, and when it turned toward Jaelyn she shuddered as she caught sight of its face.

Even by demon standards the thing was butt-ugly.

It had the grotesque features of gargoyles with beady crimson eyes and a snout with flaps over its nostrils. It also had a mouthful of razor-sharp teeth it proudly displayed.

But Jaelyn wasn't fooled by the loutish cruelty etched into the face. There was an unmistakable intelligence shimmering in his eyes that was more dangerous than all his brute strength.

Remaining motionless, Jaelyn watched as the mongrel sniffed the air before it cautiously began to shuffle in her direction.

She didn't so much as twitch a muscle as it halted near her feet, reaching out to poke her calf with a claw that was at least three inches long. She would bet good money that the creature was like most ogres, who preferred their meals to be alive and struggling.

The thing no doubt intended to drag her down to its private lair and wait for her to wake before it tried to eat her.

There was another poke; then the mongrel grabbed her around the ankle and began to drag her toward the back of the cell.

Knowing she'd only have one shot at catching the creature off guard, she remained limp until his head turned to glance toward the opening. His brief distraction was all she needed and, jerking her ankle free of his claws, she used the motion to rise to her feet and slammed her hand into his snout as he turned in shock.

She felt bone and cartilage shatter beneath her blow, but while the creature bellowed in pain, he remained upright and seriously pissed off.

Moving with surprising speed considering his heavy bulk, the thing grasped Jaelyn around the neck, ignoring the spikes of her dog collar, which bit into his thick hide, and lifting her to meet his glowing crimson gaze.

"Bitch," he hissed, the word barely distinguishable between the sharp teeth.

Jaelyn smiled with cold anticipation, already knowing exactly where she would strike the killing blow.

"You've been a very naughty boy," she mocked, hanging loosely in his grasp. "You should have known the vampires would come searching for you. We don't like being prey."

The thing wheezed out what she assumed was a laugh. "Tasty leeches. Yum, yum."

He leaned forward to lick a rough tongue over her cheek.

A revolting mistake that Jaelyn made him pay for . . . with interest.

While he was occupied with his pre-dinner snack, Jaelyn was swinging her leg forward, landing a perfect blow to his manly bits, which were swollen with arousal.

As expected, the brute lost his grip on her as he doubled over in pain, but Jaelyn didn't take time to appreciate her handiwork. Instead she used his contorted position to her advantage as she wrenched off her shoe and with one smooth motion had the three-inch heel stuck in the bastard's eye.

With another bellow, the creature reeled backward, struggling to remove the shoe as the blood poured down his naked chest. Jaelyn smiled as she deliberately removed her other shoe and stalked forward. The heels were made from a combination of lead and silver since they hadn't known exactly what sort of creature she'd be facing.

As luck would have it, a perfect blend to destroy the mongrel.

Hurray for her.

Sensing her approach, the demon lifted his head, swinging a clawed hand at her head. Jaelyn easily ducked the clumsy blow, and without the least amount of regret, she lifted the shoe and punched it into his other eye.

Screaming in pain the creature flailed forward, his arms swinging and his wings flapping as the metal in the heels allowed him to swiftly bleed to death.

Jaelyn stepped back and waited for nature to take its course, deeply relieved she didn't have to actually drain the nasty thing to kill it.

On the downside, it seemed to take forever for the beast to collapse to the floor as the last of his life drained into the dirt.

"Jaelyn, the guards are coming," the voice of Valla warned.

"Shit."

Too well trained to leave a mark before she was certain it was dead, Jaelyn bent over the mongrel and allowed her senses to search some sign of his life force. Only when she was convinced that the beast was dead did she tug off the dog collar and remove the key that was enchanted to fit in any lock.

A handy little item.

Careful not to touch the silver bars, Jaelyn swiftly unlocked the cell door and allowed it to swing open. She had just stepped into the pathway when Valla reached out of her cell to brush her fingers over Jaelyn's shoulder.

"Help me."

Jaelyn stiffened, desperately refusing to glance at the vulnerable young female.

She was here on a mission. Which meant she didn't have the luxury of caring what happened to the nymph. After all, if she dared to help Valla escape then the Addonexus would only hunt her down and kill her. Just to teach Jaelyn a lesson.

"I can't."

"Please," the female begged. "Please, don't leave me."

"I . . ." Jaelyn struggled against her screaming instinct to unlock the damned cell and release the pleading female. For all she knew this was another test of her training. "I don't have a choice."

"Of course you do. Just open the door." Valla's choked sob stabbed Jaelyn directly in the heart. "I swear, I won't slow you down."

"You're not part of the job."

"Job? What job?"

"I have to go." Jaelyn took off for the door, desperately trying to shut out the female's scent of absolute terror.

"Wait," the nymph cried out. "At least put me out of my misery."

"No."

"Jaelyn, I beg of you."

The screams followed her as she escaped from the dungeons and then the auction house.

They followed her back to her lair with the Addonexus, haunting her. . . .

Always haunting her.

Jaelyn woke with a low curse, rising to her feet to glance around the abandoned church.

She told herself the dream was a result of her near-death experience.

After all, if she hadn't been a Hunter with the ability to shroud herself in shadows so thick she could bear the sunlight for short periods of time she would even now be a tiny pile of ash in the nearby caves.

As it was, she'd barely managed to climb out of the cave and dart to this church before she'd passed out from exhaustion.

Was it any wonder that in her weakened state she would be plagued with a nightmare she'd struggled so hard to banish?

Yeah, a convenient excuse.

A pity she didn't believe it for a minute.

Not when she knew the sensations of guilt and nearly overwhelming regret that she had felt walking away from Valla that night had been stirred by Ariyal.

She had never forgiven herself for leaving the nymph behind, no matter what punishment the Addonexus would have doled out.

How could she survive if she abandoned the man destined to be her mate?

With a shiver she stepped over the rubble that littered the floor of the nave and made her way to the nearest window, which boasted a few tenacious shards from the once magnificent stained-glass window.

Now was not the time to brood on her complicated relationship with Ariyal.

Not until she was certain he'd escaped from the caves unharmed.

And oh yeah, stopped the end of the world.

Ignoring her lingering weakness and growing hunger, Jaelyn cautiously made her way out of the church and crossed the graveyard. Halfway through the moss-covered headstones she came to an abrupt halt, her senses on full alert.

Ariyal.

Or at least it had been Ariyal. Along with the granite scent of Levet and . . .

Sergei?

Shaking her head in confusion, Jaelyn bent down, running her fingers of the faintly singed grass. A portal had briefly opened and then closed here.

Dammit. Had Ariyal been captured by the mage and forced to use his powers to leave this place? And if so, where the hell had they gone?

She lingered in the spot long after she was forced to accept that Ariyal wasn't coming back. As if his fading scent could give her some sort of clue to where the mage had forced him to go.

Or perhaps she desperately needed to cling to the tangible assurance that he was still alive.

At last she forced herself to straighten and consider her options. Although her sense of duty had been beaten into her with brutal force, she knew what she had to do.

What Ariyal would want her to do.

And if that meant she was punished by the Addonexus and the Oracles . . . so be it.

A smile curved her lips as she abruptly stiffened her spine and squared her shoulders. Hell, before she was done this small transgression would be the least of her concerns.

Wrapping herself in shadows, Jaelyn headed directly toward the glowing lights of Chicago.

She didn't slow as she hit the suburban outskirts, knowing that her destination would be in the seedier part of the city. Not that there wasn't plenty of evil lurking behind the perfectly manicured homes. But she needed to find a specific place.

It took nearly an hour of searching, but at last she managed to track down the Viper Pit. Predictably, the most exclusive club in the entire city of Chicago was also the most difficult to find.

Not only was the entire building hidden behind a magical glamour, but there hadn't been a single demon willing to reveal the location.

If she hadn't been a Hunter she wasn't sure she'd ever have stumbled across the hidden entrance.

Once inside, she hurried past the marble pillars and glittering fountains. She had no interest in the demons who were busy indulging in the various vices on offer, from gambling to orgies to cage fighting that made the MMA look like a fun game of slap and tickle.

If she was running the joint, she'd have an office on the second floor where she could keep an eye on the entire club.

Reaching a back hallway, she had just caught sight of a

narrow staircase when her path was abruptly blocked by an Andrax demon.

At least a foot taller than her, the demon had taken the shape of a human with a brutish face and bulging muscles that were covered with scarlet tattoos. His head was shaved and his ears were lined with gold studs, but it was the teeny-tiny loincloth that attracted her attention.

A loincloth? Really?

Oblivious to her flare of amusement, the demon flexed his muscles before pulling back to lips to reveal his massive fangs.

Andrax demons didn't drink blood, but they did eat raw flesh. Usually while it was still attached to the person.

"Going somewhere, beautiful?" he demanded.

She rolled her eyes. Did males always have to be so predictable?

"Step aside."

"Hmmm . . ." He skimmed a hungry gaze down her body. "A mouthy one. I could change that." He stepped close enough to nearly overwhelm her with the stench of his sour sweat. "All you need is a little training."

She bared her fangs in warning. "All I need is for you to move your ugly ass before I forget how much I hate Andrax blood."

"Bitch."

"I'm not telling you again. Move."

"Yum." He licked his lips. "I'm going to enjoy teaching you a lesson. By the end of the night you'll be begging for it."

She snorted. "Begging for what?"

He grabbed the bulge beneath the loincloth. "Some of this, baby."

"Ah." She tapped her tongue against the end of her fang. "That nasty piece of shrunken flesh that I'm going to bite off and shove down your throat?"

"Big talk for such a tiny thing . . ."

His taunting words ended in a scream that would have made a banshee proud as Jaelyn leaped over the Andrax's head and then, pressing herself against his back, wrapped her arms around his body, her hands grabbing the tender bits of manhood he'd been so proud to point out to her.

It made it so much easier to know where to hurt him.

"Now tell me again what you're going to do, demon," she murmured, her claws digging through the loincloth as her other hand wrapped around his beefy neck, threatening to crush his windpipe. "Nothing to say?"

"I'm . . ."

"Yes?"

"Sorry."

Her claws dug a bit deeper. "Try it again."

"I'm sorry," he moaned.

"Sorry that you tried to rape me? Or sorry that I'm about to castrate you so you can't force yourself on some other woman?"

"No. Please, no . . ."

The Andrax stiffened at the sound of approaching footsteps. Always cautious, Jaelyn kept her grip on the demon as she shifted to watch the two males making their way down the staircase.

No, not men.

Vampires.

Those too-perfect features and elegantly muscular bodies could never belong to humans.

She briefly ran her gaze over the nearest, a vampire with dark, spiky hair and crystal-clear green eyes who was dressed like a badass in black leather with a large dagger casually held in one hand. Dangerous. But it was his companion who sent a chill of alarm through Jaelyn.

This one was taller with lean muscles beneath the ruffled

white shirt that was worn beneath a gold velvet jacket and black satin pants. He should have appeared ridiculous, but with his long hair the pale silver of moonlight and his eyes the startling darkness of midnight he was hauntingly beautiful.

A fallen angel.

Already suspecting the identity of the powerful vampire, the Andrax took away all doubt as he held out a pleading hand.

"Thank god, Viper. You have to help me."

Ignoring the whining demon, Viper regarded Jaelyn with a piercing intelligence.

"Hunter," he at last murmured, offering a formal bow of his head.

She returned the gesture. "Clan chief."

The dark gaze briefly dipped to the struggling demon, his beautiful features unreadable.

"I see you've met Lector."

She shrugged. "He introduced himself."

"Viper, do something," Lector gasped.

A smile of anticipation curved Viper's lips. "Oh, I intend to."

Jaelyn tightened her grip. She was the one who had been insulted and threatened by the overly aggressive bully.

"I'm not finished playing yet."

"I understand your desire for blood, my dear, I truly do," Viper drawled with seeming regret.

"But?"

"But I fear that I have first claim on torturing our friend." The dark eyes glittered with a frigid fury that made Jaelyn shudder in relief that it wasn't directed at her. "I really must make him an example for my other fighters who think they can flout my rules."

"My lord . . ." Dropping to his hands and knees as Jaelyn abruptly released her hold, Lector crawled over the marble floor, desperately kissing Viper's glossy leather shoes. "Please."

With a casual ease, Viper kicked the Andrax in the face, sending him flying across the hallway to land in a bloody heap.

"Stop groveling, you pathetic worm," he growled. "I did warn you what would happen if I caught you out of the pens."

"Forgive me. . . ." Lector gave a choked groan as Viper's power filled the hallway.

"And now you've attacked one of my guests."

The Andrax warily returned to his feet, wiping away the blood draining from his broken nose.

"I didn't lay a hand on her," he protested. "She attacked me."

Viper appeared unimpressed by his defense. "Spike, would you escort Lector to the dungeons?"

The young vampire at his side made a sound of protest. "I told you not to call me that."

Viper arched a brow. "Will you do the honors or not?"

"With pleasure." Moving with the eagerness of a vampire who enjoyed his job, Spike grabbed the Andrax and pressed the dagger into his throat. "Any torture in particular?"

"I think you should start with cutting out his tongue," the clan chief suggested as Lector's screams echoed off the marble walls.

"An excellent choice," Spike approved.

"I'll let your imagination take you from there."

"Do you want him alive in the morning?"

"Not particularly."

"No," Lector managed to rasp despite the hole in his throat. "I'm your best fighter. You can't do this."

It turned out Spike could.

And did.

With remarkable ease.

In less than a heartbeat, the young vampire was dragging the struggling demon down the hall, leaving Jaelyn alone to face the clan chief of Chicago.

"Such an unpleasant creature," Viper said with a grimace.

"Then why do you keep him around?"

The dark eyes turned to study her with an unreadable expression.

"He wasn't boasting when he claimed to be my best fighter. Or rather . . ." The vampire gave a dismissive wave of his hand. "He was."

"Will you really let your guard kill him?"

"Yes, I really will." His smile revealed his complete lack of regret at the loss. Damn. Jaelyn had thought she was cold-hearted. "Now tell me what brings a Hunter to my humble establishment?"

She thrust aside all thought of the soon-to-be-dead demon and focused on her reason for coming to the Viper Pit.

"I need to speak with the Anasso, but I'm not sure how to contact him."

The dark eyes narrowed at her abrupt request. "Your Ruah . . ."

"This isn't Addonexus business," she interrupted. "I'm working on behalf of the Oracles."

"And they sent you?"

She deliberately ignored his question. "Will you take me to him?"

"I see the Addonexus haven't spent much time training their recruits that they can catch more flies with honey," he said dryly.

She resisted the urge to point out the Addonexus didn't run a freaking charm school.

See? She did have at least a little tact.

"I'm sorry, but it's urgent that I speak with him," she managed to say between clenched teeth. "Please."

He studied her grim expression for a long moment. "Very well, but it will take a day or two to set up a meeting."

A day or two?

She stepped forward, shaking her head. "No, this can't wait." She held up her hand as his lips parted. "Not unless you actually want the return of the Dark Lord?"

"Thank you, Viper." A hard, commanding voice filled the hallway. "I'll take it from here."

Chapter 17

Jaelyn had mistakenly assumed that no vampire could match the strength and power of her Ruah.

Weren't the members of the Addonexus supposed to be the elite of the elite of the vampire world?

That's what she'd been taught.

But slowly turning to discover the six-foot-five Aztec warrior towering over her, she realized that her teachers had grossly overestimated their own worth.

Styx, the current Anasso, maintained the bronzed skin and proud angular features of his ancestors as well as the dark, silky hair that fell in a braid to the back of his knees. And while his muscular form was currently covered by a green silk shirt and dark dress pants, it was all too easy to picture him striding through the jungles of South America.

There was something not quite civilized about the vampire.

Turning from Jaelyn, Viper regarded the King of Vampires with more curiosity than fear.

She'd heard rumors that the clan chief and Anasso were acquainted, which was why she'd sought out the Viper Pit, but now she suspected that they were actually friends.

Odd.

Two such alpha males rarely bonded.

"Do you want me to stay?" Viper was asking.

A rueful smile touched the ancient vampire's lips. "I think I can manage."

"You can use my office." Viper glanced toward the silent Jaelyn. "I think I'd better make sure there aren't any other surprises roaming my club."

The clan chief slid into the shadows and swiftly disappeared as the Anasso waved a hand toward the nearby staircase.

"This way."

Jaelyn hesitated, impatient to say what needed to be said so she could be on her way.

Thankfully she was impatient, not mental.

If the six-foot-five Anasso with massive fangs and enough power to destroy Chicago wanted her to go upstairs, then by God she'd go upstairs.

It didn't, however, mean she'd be happy about it.

Climbing the steps Jaelyn allowed herself to be led into a well-appointed office with recessed shelves that were lined with leather-bound books and a stone fireplace on the far wall.

Styx pointed toward one of the wing chairs sitting near the heavy walnut desk, waiting for her to take a seat before heading toward the carved side table and opening the built-in fridge to pull out a bag of blood. With surprising expertise, the vampire poured the blood into a crystal cut glass and popped it into the microwave.

Almost as if he was . . . domesticated.

Her inane thoughts were brought to a sharp end as the vampire crossed the dark wood of the floor to press the glass into her hand.

Instinctively she gave a shake of her head, attempting to thrust the glass away.

The dark eyes flared with warning. "Drink."

"No. I can't."

He muttered something beneath his breath about Addonexus and stubborn relics.

"It's clean and you're about to collapse." His voice slid over her with a promise of pain. "I can make it an order if you want."

"No," she muttered, gulping down the blood.

He was right. She was dangerously weak after the energy she'd used to survive her brush with dawn and if the Anasso wanted her dead he wouldn't need to use tainted blood to do it.

Even when his power was leashed it was like a pulsing threat that filled the room.

Removing her empty glass, Styx moved to lean against the corner of the desk, studying her with an unnerving intensity.

"You're the Hunter who helped Tane and Laylah," he finally broke the thick silence.

She shrugged. "Our paths crossed."

"Did you manage to capture the Sylvermyst?"

Jaelyn's fingers tightened on the arm of the chair, but her training allowed her to meet the dark gaze without flinching.

"My mission has been changed."

"I see." He folded his arms over his massive chest. "Well, I don't actually see, but I presume that it has something to do with the return of the Dark Lord?"

There was just enough of a bite in his voice to warn that he didn't like the thought that he might be out of the loop.

Control freak?

Naaaaw.

"The child is in the hands of Tearloch and his pet wizard," she abruptly admitted.

"Yes, Tane told us the child was stolen by the Sylvermyst and Sergei in the Russian caves. A pity, but at least we rescued Maluhia."

Maluhia?

She assumed that must be the twin to the baby held by Tearloch.

"The wizard isn't Sergei," she corrected, her heart contracting at the reminder that the mage was even now with Ariyal. Somewhere. "I'm not sure what happened to him."

"Then who?"

"Tearloch summoned a spirit that goes by the name Rafael," she informed him. "I think you know him."

The Anasso abruptly straightened, a scowl marring his brow.

"Rafael? You're certain?"

"Yes."

"Shit."

Shoving his hand into the front pocket of his slacks, Styx pulled out a slim cellphone and jabbed in a series of numbers.

Jaelyn rose to her feet, feeling her strength returning from the blood her king had forced her to drink.

"What are you doing?"

"Dante will want to hear this," he told her, turning away to speak softly into the phone.

Once done he returned the phone to his pocket and turned back to meet her questioning gaze.

"Dante?"

"The vampire who killed Rafael the first time around." He smiled with cruel anticipation. "He'll be pissed if he gets left out on a second chance. He's on his way."

"Fine, but I don't have time to wait for him."

Power prickled over her skin, and Jaelyn silently cursed her uncharacteristic lack of control.

Dammit, the King of Vampires wasn't a benevolent leader who ruled with a gentle democracy. He was a powerful demon, perhaps the most powerful in the entire world, and he was well within his rights to crush her if she offended him.

Thankfully the brief punishment was the extent of his reprimand.

"Tell me what you need from me."

Relieved to have gotten off relatively unscathed, Jaelyn swiftly outlined their pursuit of Tearloch since leaving the Russian caves, carefully editing the more private details. Not that she was fooling anyone.

Styx could no doubt sense her inner turmoil when she spoke of the Sylvermyst who was supposed to be her enemy.

The Anasso listened in silence, his expression hard as she revealed the wizard's attempt to fry her with the morning sun.

"The child must be rescued," she at last concluded her tale, her hand unwittingly clutching the stock of her gun.

"I agree," the king said without hesitation. "How many are in the caves?"

"Tearloch and a half-dozen Sylvermyst as well as the wizard." She held up a warning hand. "But there could be others."

"Others? You suspect the Sylvermyst has allies?"

"I doubt that Sergei has given up his ambitions to rule the world."

The Anasso grimaced, obviously familiar with the Russian magic-user.

"He's a tenacious bastard," he readily agreed, his piercing gaze never wavering from her face. "But I sense he isn't your primary concern."

"No. While we were searching for Tearloch, I had a run-in with a cur."

"A very stupid or very brave cur," the king murmured. "I assume he's dead?"

"No."

A dark brow arched in surprise. "No?"

"He was a magic-user."

Styx tensed. "Damn, I wonder if Salvatore knows? He won't be pleased."

"Neither was I," she said dryly.

He frowned, as if debating some inner quandary. "The Were called a meeting for tomorrow night. I suppose the information can wait until then." With a shake of his head, the vampire returned his attention to her. "Is the cur connected to Tearloch?"

"I can't say for sure, but I'm not a big believer in coincidences."

"Me either." Styx lifted a hand to brush a finger over the amulet that was hung around his neck. Jaelyn knew from her studies that Aztec people believed that they could tap in to the power of their ancestors with such talismans. Yeah, like this man needed any secret weapons. "Was the cur alone?"

"No, he was traveling with another cur and a human witch. And . . ." She gave a lift of her hands. "I don't know."

"A demon?"

She considered her words, disliking her lack of concise facts. Vague speculation too often led to poor decisions.

"My guess would be a vampire, but it was able to disguise its scent." She regarded him with a frown. "Is that possible?"

"If he's traveling with a witch he could have an amulet to mask his presence," he suggested.

She shook her head. "I don't think that was it. I could sense him, but it was muted, as if he was blocking my powers."

An odd expression tightened the bronzed features, almost as if Styx had been struck by an unpleasant suspicion. But before she could question him, he was pacing to study the row of monitors that revealed the crowds filling the club below.

"He must have considerable skill if he was able to shroud himself from a Hunter."

She narrowed her gaze. He was hiding something.

"Does it ring any bells?"

"None that I'm will to comment on without further information," he said, revealing he hadn't been deceived by her delicate attempt to probe. "Where are they now?"

She didn't even consider pressing for an answer. Actually, she wasn't sure she wanted to know.

She had quite enough on her plate, thank you very much.

"The last I knew Levet was trying to track them."

Styx shuddered as he turned back to face her. "Good God."

Jaelyn smiled. The tiny gargoyle seemed to have a genuine knack for irritating males, no matter what their species.

Then, as the thought of Levet reminded her that he was currently with Ariyal, and that they both might be in danger, she headed toward the door.

"I must go."

"Wait." With a speed that shocking even for a vampire, Styx was standing directly before her, his expression forbidding. "I need you here."

"I've already told you all I know."

"You've recently been in the caves." He took a deliberate step forward, towering over her. "We'll need you to lead us to the child."

"I can draw you a map."

"You have someplace more important to be?"

She met the dark gaze, refusing to be intimidated. "I'm still under contract to the Oracles."

His jaw clenched. "I'm sure they'll understand if you take a short detour."

Understand?

Clearly this vampire had never had to deal with the Commission.

"I've already detoured more than I should have," she informed him, her tone edged with the impatience she could no longer control. "Now I need to go."

Grudgingly he stepped aside, but as she pulled open the door he called out.

"Hunter."

She glanced over her shoulder. "What?"

"I intend to gather my most trusted warriors and enter the caves tomorrow night, just before midnight," he informed her. "Your presence might very well mean the difference between success and failure."

"But no pressure, right?"

He smiled without apology. "All's fair in love and war."

"Yes." A smile touched her own lips as she turned and hurried from the demon club. She had been playing by the rules since she'd been turned into a vampire, but the world was hurtling toward Armageddon and she intended to snatch whatever happiness she could discover before it was too late. "All's fair in love and war."

Ariyal slammed the treacherous mage into the wall of the abandoned warehouse. At the same time, his power filled the late-night air with enough heat to make the candle sitting on a broken crate melt into a puddle of wax.

"You son of a bitch, I'm going to kill you," he growled.

"No . . ." Sergei struggled to breathe. "Wait."

"For what?" Ariyal demanded. "More lies?"

He had no doubt been a fool to trust the mage. But he hadn't had much choice.

Not if he wanted to get out of the lead-lined cavern.

And more importantly, to gain the information the magic-user had dangled like the proverbial carrot.

Predictably Sergei hadn't been satisfied when Ariyal's initial portal had taken them just a few feet from the caves.

He'd been convinced that the shadows were crawling with the Dark Lord's minions. And since he refused to reveal his information until they were on the outskirts of Chicago, Ariyal had little choice but to bring them to this empty warehouse.

Now, however, he was done. The bastard was going to be very, very sorry if he had tried to play games with a Sylvermyst.

The mage turned a pasty shade of gray. "I didn't lie."

"You told me you had information about Jaelyn."

"And I do."

Ariyal's fingers tightened around the neck he could crush with pathetic ease.

"Telling me she can cloak herself in shadows is not information," he hissed.

"If you would allow me to finish?"

There was a tug on his jeans, and he impatiently glanced down at the gargoyle standing beside him.

"What?"

"I think we should hear what he has to say."

"Fine," Ariyal rasped, returning his attention to Sergei. "But I warn you, mage, don't screw with me."

"Release me and I'll . . . arrg." The mage's eyes nearly popped from their sockets as Ariyal tightened his grip. "Okay. From what I managed to learn from Marika, a Hunter's primary skill is the ability to shroud themselves in shadows so thick they're virtually invisible." Sergei held up a pleading hand as Ariyal's fingers threatened to finish the job of crushing his throat. "Those same shadows also protect them from the sun for short periods of time."

Her shadows . . .

Of course.

"How short?" he breathed.

"A few minutes."

"Long enough for her to have escaped," Levet said, a

grin spreading over his ugly face. "I told you she was still alive. Ariyal?"

Ariyal was already at the door, hesitating only long enough to point a finger at the mage, who was now crumpled on the floor, gasping like a fish out of water.

"Keep an eye on Sergei."

"But . . ."

He vaguely heard the gargoyle call out, but Ariyal was already crossing the crumbling parking lot and headed back toward the caves.

Jaelyn.

The desperate hope that had kept him from raving insanity became a raw, throbbing need.

He had to find her.

He had to hold her in his arms until there was no doubt left inside him that she was alive and well.

And then he was going shake her until her fangs rattled for putting him through hell.

Intent on returning to the caves, Ariyal very nearly missed the sharp chill that edged the breeze. It was only when the familiar scent of power and pure woman teased at his senses that he came to an abrupt halt.

There was no mistaking the approaching vampire was Jaelyn.

But why was she coming from behind him?

Had she been near the warehouse? Or farther into the city?

And if so, why?

His confusion was forgotten as he turned to watch the shadows melt away and the female who had somehow become an essential part of his life was revealed in the moonlight.

An explosion of emotions nearly brought him to his knees as he greedily drank in the beauty of her pale face and the elegant strength of her body.

If he had lost her . . .

She took a step forward, and with a low growl he was reaching to yank her against his body, his arms wrapping around her so tightly it was a good thing she didn't need to breathe.

"Jaelyn," he murmured, reveling in the feel of her slender body pressed against him. "Gods. I thought . . ."

She framed his face in her hands, her eyes flashing with an indigo fire.

"Shut up and kiss me, fairy."

"Bossy leech," he muttered, even as he seized her lips in a kiss that revealed the terror he had endured. "Don't ever do that to me again."

She pulled back far enough to glare at him. "What about you?"

"Me?"

"All I could find was the spot of your portal mixed with the scent of Levet and Sergei," she accused. "I was afraid that you'd been taken hostage."

He stiffened, unable to believe he heard her correctly. "You believed I could be taken captive by a damned mage?"

Her lips twitched as she belatedly realized the depth of her insult.

"I wasn't thinking clearly."

He nipped her bottom lip. "Obviously not."

"So what were you doing with Sergei?"

Ariyal was in no mood to discuss the mage. Or their near-death experiences. Or the end of the world.

"Later," he promised, scooping Jaelyn off her feet and heading back to the abandoned farmhouse where they'd spent a few memorable hours. There he could be assured there was a cellar deep enough to keep Jaelyn safe from the approaching dawn.

Astonishingly, Jaelyn allowed herself to be carried through the darkness without hitting or biting or even complaining at his arrogant behavior.

Not that he was fooled by her momentary compliance.

Jaelyn was about as submissive as a rabid lion.

But busy nuzzling the tender skin of his throat and rubbing her hands down the clenched muscles of his back, she appeared suitably occupied as he at last reached the remote farm and charged into the empty house.

Just for a second he hesitated, torn between his overriding need to make certain that Jaelyn was safely tucked in the cellar and the urge to spend the next two hours that remained of the night making love to her in the comfort of a bed.

It was the light scrape of her fangs down his neck that sent him catapulting up the stairs and into the master bedroom, where a dusty, but thankfully sturdy, four-poster bed was waiting.

They would have the entire day to discover the numerous ways to make love in the cramped cellar. For now he wanted plenty of space.

And a soft mattress.

Gently laying Jaelyn on the quilt, he disposed of his sword and various daggers before kicking off his boots. He'd just managed to shuck off his jeans, when she gracefully slid off the bed and unbuckled her holster, setting aside the loaded shotgun.

But instead of getting rid of her few bits of clothing, she moved forward to place her hands against his naked chest.

"Ariyal, we need to talk. . . ."

No. No. No.

He wasn't an expert, but conversations that started with "We need to talk . . ." were never, ever good.

He pulled her into his arms and lowered his head.

"Shut up and kiss me, Jaelyn," he tossed her words back at her.

"Ariyal." She pulled away, her expression oddly uncertain. "There's something I need to say."

"It can't wait an hour?" Hoping for a distraction, he

pulled her stretchy top over her head and threw it toward the walnut dresser. He didn't notice when it instead caught on the edge of the hand-carved rocking chair. He had far better things to stare at, he readily acknowledged. The air was squeezed from his lungs as he reverently cupped the perfect globes tipped with rosy nipples. "Or two?"

She shivered, her eyes darkening with sharp arousal, but she gave a slow shake of her head.

"No."

Despite the driving instinct to press Jaelyn back onto the mattress and convince himself once and for all she was truly in his arms, Ariyal instead ran a comforting hand down her back.

The need to please her went far deeper than sexual.

And just how scary was that?

"Tell me," he urged in gentle tones.

Again he sensed her rare uncertainty.

No, he swiftly corrected himself. She might be uncertain at how to share her thoughts with him, but there was a fierce determination beneath her hesitant manner.

"You're going to return for the child, aren't you?" she at last demanded.

"Yes," he admitted without hesitation. It wasn't as if he could lie to her.

"And you know I'm not going to let you go alone."

Dammit. His brows snapped together as his hand curved her tight against his lower body.

"Jaelyn . . ."

She pressed a finger to his mouth. "Hear me out."

Like he had a choice? Ariyal heaved a frustrated sigh. "Fine."

"I'm a Hunter."

"Yeah, you've made that painfully clear."

She again hesitated, as if searching for the right words.

"We work on the barter system." Her finger shifted to

outline his lips in a light caress. "If I'm going to risk my neck to save the world then I intend to get something out of it."

Ariyal instantly hardened, finding it more and more difficult to concentrate on her words.

"Something?"

"You."

Oh . . . thank the gods.

He shuddered with need as he swooped down to press his lips to the curve of her neck.

"That's precisely what I'm attempting to give you, poppet," he said huskily, "if only you would cooperate."

"I want you." There was a long, dramatic pause. "As my mate."

Chapter 18

As showstoppers went, this one was a doozy.

As her shocking words sliced through the air, Ariyal instantly went into mannequin routine, remaining frozen in place for what seemed to be an eternity.

Not that she'd expected him to break into song and do cartwheels, she wryly assured herself. Still, she had thought he might be . . .

Pleased?

Excited?

Delirious with joy?

At last he pulled back to regard her with a wary expression.

"Mate?" His voice was thick with an emotion she found difficult to read, his hands holding on to her hips with a bruising grip. "You said that Hunters aren't allowed a mate."

"They aren't."

He muttered something beneath his breath. "Then what am I missing?"

She lifted a hand to brush it over the satin heat of his cheek.

"I had no choice about becoming a Hunter, just as you had no choice about becoming prince of your people," she said, wrinkling her nose at her awkward bumbling. Who knew it was so difficult to ask a man to become her mate?

It was a damned good thing she was a Hunter, not a diplomat. "We've both been trapped by duty."

His eyes smoldered with a bronze glow. "And now?"

"I want us to be trapped together."

Without warning he was spinning away from her, shoving his hands through his chestnut hair until it cascaded down his back in a ripple of satin.

"Dammit, poppet," he rasped. "You don't know what you're doing to me."

Jaelyn's fangs lengthened at the sight of Ariyal's body outlined by the moonlight streaming through the bedroom window. Oh, it would be so easy to be distracted by that chiseled, male perfection.

Wondrously, insanely easy.

With an effort she resisted the urge to close the short distance and explore every sexy inch of those muscles.

"I thought you wanted to be mated?" she accused, feeling unnervingly vulnerable.

It wasn't a sensation she was used to.

And it was making her downright edgy.

Perhaps sensing her unease, Ariyal turned back to stab her with a frustrated glare.

"Not if it puts you at risk from the Addonexus."

He worried about her?

Was that why he hesitated?

Relief jolted through her as she offered a slow smile, shimmying out of her tight pants. Obviously he needed to be convinced that she didn't give a damn about the dangers.

Walking forward she wrapped her arms around his neck and pressed herself against his fully aroused body.

"We both know that there's not much likelihood of us getting out of the caves alive." She deliberately rubbed against him. "We'll worry about the Addonexus if we manage to survive."

He sucked in a sharp breath, but his brow furrowed as if he had been struck by a sudden, unpleasant thought.

"Hold on."

"What?"

"What if we weren't facing certain death?"

It was her turn to frown. "I don't understand."

"If we weren't facing imminent death, would you still want to have me as your mate?"

Holding his accusing gaze, Jaelyn took his hand and placed it to her chest. Her heart might not beat, but it functioned just fine when it came to love.

And in this moment it was overflowing.

"Feel," she commanded softly.

A wicked smile softened his expression as his gaze skimmed over her bare breasts.

"With pleasure."

"No, I mean really feel." She lowered the last of her guards, releasing her too-long-restrained emotions. "You're my mate whether we exchange blood or not. I just want to make it official."

She didn't know what she expected.

Arguments.

Teasing.

Embarrassment.

It wasn't for Ariyal to slowly kneel before her, his face pressed against the bare skin of her stomach as his arms wrapped around her.

"I thought Morgana le Fay had destroyed all but my loyalty to my people." His voice was low, raw. "You have given me back my heart."

She tangled her fingers in the warm satin of his hair, her love for this man blasting through her.

It was nothing she had wanted, or expected, but now she couldn't imagine how she had ever survived without Ariyal in her life.

"Will you share it with me?"

He tilted back his head to regard her with a somber gaze. "My proud, beautiful Hunter."

"My stubborn, gorgeous fairy."

"You forgot sexy," he softly chided.

"Did I?" She deliberately licked her lips. Hey, it worked in the movies. "Maybe you should remind me."

On cue, Ariyal surged to his feet, locking his arms around her waist. Then, with gratifying speed he was tossing her onto the mattress and covering her with the welcome heat of his body.

"If you insist," he murmured.

She stroked her lips down the stubborn line of his jaw. "I do."

He shuddered in violent response to her teasing caress, turning his head to crush her lips in a kiss of pure demand, his hands lightly tracing up the curve of her waist to cup her breasts.

Jaelyn moaned in approval, arching her back as he teased the tips of her nipples into aching peaks. But it was the rich scent of herbs filling the air that made her fangs throb with need.

Wrapping her legs around his hips, she ran her hands up and down his back, urging him put an end to her torment.

"I want you," she moaned.

"It's too fast," he muttered, his mouth pressing frantic kisses over her face before he at last lowered his head to capture her nipple between his lips.

She scraped her nails over his hard ass, smiling as he hissed in pleasure.

"Slow and tender can be good," she assured him. "But there is a time for fast and hard."

He lifted his head to meet her hungry gaze, lingering a long moment on her exposed fangs.

"And this is the time for . . . ?"

She groaned at the sensation of his warm skin moving against her, heating places that she would have sworn couldn't get any hotter.

"Us."

The bronze eyes flared in agreement. "Yes."

The simple word was a solemn vow as Ariyal entered her with one smooth thrust.

They groaned in unison, Jaelyn's eyes squeezing shut at the feel of him buried deep inside her. Then, as he began a swift, steady rhythm that bordered on the right side of rough, she grabbed his face and brought it down to meet her lips in an explosive kiss.

This was no delicate dance of sensuality.

It was raw and needy and exactly what she desired.

She distantly heard the slam of the bed hitting the wall and the squeak of the mattress, but her concentration was focused solely on the delectable man and the urgent pace that was spiraling toward a blissful completion.

Ariyal threaded his fingers through her hair, his mouth shifting to nuzzle over her cheek to her ear.

"Now, Jaelyn," he whispered.

She hissed at the savage excitement that flooded through her.

"You're certain?"

He peered deep into her eyes. "You would know if I was lying."

"True. Something you should keep in mind if you decide to stray in the future."

He frowned at her hint of unease, which had nothing to do with being a vampire and everything with being a vulnerable woman at the mercy of her heart.

"Do you think this mating is any less binding to me?" he demanded.

It was, of course, the question that teased in the back of her mind.

"Do Sylvermyst mate?"

"You will discover later," he promised. "Bite me, Jaelyn."

A dark, primitive need swept aside any lingering question at the sanity of what she was about to do. Why hesitate? This moment had surely been fated since the beginning of time.

Lifting her head, she aimed with lethal accuracy, sliding her fangs into the throat he willingly offered.

And promptly stiffened in amazement.

She hadn't been prepared for the potent power as his blood hit her tongue. Or the rich, addictive flavor.

Or the fact that it would prove to be the finest aphrodisiac.

She groaned. Her entire body felt as if it were on fire, her hips lifting off the mattress to meet his deep thrusts with growing desperation. Then, as the blood slid down her throat, she experienced the first sense of the mating.

"Ariyal," she breathed in wonderment.

There had been an imprint of this male upon her heart from the very beginning. Something she'd done her best to ignore, despite the danger. But now . . .

Even prepared, she was staggered by the sheer intimacy of their connection.

She could actually feel what he was feeling. The pleasure of their lovemaking, the possessive male need to protect her, and, overriding everything, the fierce love that beat in his heart.

A shimmering, golden love for her alone.

Dazzled by the glorious sensations, Jaelyn carefully withdrew her fangs and licked shut the pinprick wounds on his neck.

Ariyal growled softly, shifting so he could run his lips down the length of my throat.

"My turn," he muttered, abruptly biting her hard enough to break through her skin.

There was a momentary pain, but Jaelyn barely noticed as she felt him suck at the wound, causing her orgasm to crash through her with dizzying force.

"Holy . . . shit," she muttered, feeling as he thrust to his own climax.

She wrapped her arms tightly around his shoulders, clinging to him as the last of the powerful convulsions wracked her body. Sex with Ariyal had always been a combustible event.

But this went beyond all fantasies.

Ariyal was hers.

Completely, utterly, and for all eternity.

Slowly relaxing beneath him, Jaelyn was floating on a warm sea of contentment when Ariyal slowly slid off her, ignoring her sleepy protests as he regarded her with a mysterious smile.

"We're not done yet."

She lifted her brows. Again? Well, hell, why not?

"If you insist," she murmured with a small smile of invitation.

"I do." Without warning he was off the bed and holding out a commanding hand. "Come with me."

She frowned. "Come where?"

He arched a brow. "Do you trust me?"

She did, of course. This was the one person in the entire world who would never, ever hurt or betray her.

Placing her fingers in his hand, she allowed herself to be pulled out of the bed and coaxed out of the farmhouse to stand in the center of the backyard.

Ariyal turned to face her, his expression somber, but before she could ask why they were standing buck naked in the middle of nowhere, a shimmering mist began to form around them.

Jaelyn's eyes widened as the mist thickened, the color

flickering from the palest silver to the deepest crimson as it surrounded them.

"What is it?" she asked, her voice low with reverent wonder.

He lifted her hand to the center of his chest, his eyes reflecting the various colors of the mist.

"The Sylvermyst mating ceremony."

"It's beautiful." Almost as beautiful as the man standing before her, she silently acknowledged. "What will it do?"

"The sharing of our blood has united our souls," he explained softly. "The aurora will unite our hearts."

She trembled as the mists brushed her bare skin, bringing with it the scent of herbs.

Suddenly she could sense the beats of Ariyal's heart. And more than that . . . the basic essence that made him the man that she loved.

His ruthless loyalty, his strength, and his ability to love without conditions or judgment.

"Yes," she said, pressing against him as the mist wrapped them in a shimmer of light. "Mine."

He wrapped his arms around her, his face buried in her hair.

"Mine."

Behind the Veil

It was like a building out of ancient Greece.

Lots of fluted columns, arched windows, and carved friezes.

Not that Santiago was in the mood to appreciate the vaulted marble chamber that surrounded him, or the mosaic tiled floors, or even the thick hush that filled the ancient air, stirred only by rush of scurrying servants.

His entire body quivered from the unpleasant experience of being pulled through the Veil.

Dios.

For a few seconds he'd feared he might actually be ripped in two as he'd briefly hovered between two separate worlds. And then there had been the painful prickles of electricity that had nearly flayed the skin from his body.

It had lasted less than a few seconds, but it had been enough to convince him that it couldn't be the normal passage. Who the hell would ever travel to this place if it threatened to eviscerate them?

Pushing away from the gold-veined marble wall that had been keeping him upright, he glared at the female who stood in the center of the corridor.

"You did that on purpose," he growled, as annoyed by the sight of her perfection as by the lingering weakness in his knees.

The raven hair flowed smoothly down her back, framing her exquisite, icily composed face. Her robes were unwrinkled, without a speck of dust. And her slender hand was infuriatingly steady as it stroked over the large medallion lying just over her unbeating heart.

Worse, he suspected there was a hint of amusement in the dark eyes as she regarded him with a faux air of innocence.

"Did what?"

"Yanking me through the Veil like I was a barnacle you were hoping to scrape off," he snapped, his hand instinctively reaching to make sure his sword was safely stowed in the scabbard angled down his back.

She shrugged. "You were in no danger, I assure you."

"No danger? I was nearly fried."

Her dark brows lifted as his words bounced eerily among the forest of columns.

"Is anything hurt beyond your pride?"

"Do you care?"

"I will take that as a no."

With a faint smile she crossed toward the nearest doorway, moving down the long corridor. Still seething, Santiago followed in her wake, barely noticing the occasional glimpses of vampires moving through the columns, or the doorways leading to libraries, antechambers, and a dozen other rooms, which they passed at a rapid pace.

He'd heard rumors of what was beyond the Veil.

Glorious buildings constructed by the finest artists all shrouded by constant night. An endless countryside that remained untainted by humans. Or even demons. Gardens that bloomed with flowers that had no need of the sun.

And no doubt the roads were made of gold and the rivers ran with honey, he silently mocked.

A regular Garden of Eden.

Without the serpent.

Or was it?

The same rumors he'd heard regarding the beauty of this world also hinted that while the vampires lived in peace, they had maintained ancient powers that had been lost to his brothers.

Shape-shifting, mist walking . . . mind control over lesser vampires.

And now one of them might be determined to unleash hell on his world.

"You are being frighteningly quiet." Nefri at last broke the silence, halting to study him with blatant suspicion.

A humorless smile curved his lips. "Just taking in the magnificent sight of Shangri-la."

"This is my home, not a fabled paradise."

He grimaced. Home? It felt like a mausoleum.

"You have a real thing for marble, don't you?"

She tilted her chin to a proud angle. "I enjoy beauty."

Santiago stepped toward her, oddly annoyed by the sight

of her standing there, so aloof and untouchable she didn't appear quite real.

"Cold perfection?" he taunted.

"I beg your pardon?"

He was moving before his brain could remind him just how stupid it was to provoke a vampire who was not only stronger than him, but whose own territory he was standing in.

While he was very much the outsider.

"True beauty should be untamed, even flawed," he growled, one hand grasping her upper arm as the other lightly circled her slender neck, his thumb stroking the cool satin of her skin. "It should entice and entangle the senses."

The dark eyes widened. "What are you doing?"

Now that was a good question.

A fan-fucking-tastic question.

"You had your fun" was his lame comeback.

He felt the cool rush of her power, but she made no move to pull away from his touch.

"What fun?" she inquired.

"You made the journey through the Veil as unpleasant as possible."

There wasn't the smallest hint of apology on her pale, lovely face.

"I am unaccustomed to having a passenger."

He snorted, not fooled for a minute.

"And you didn't enjoy watching me squirm?"

"I told you . . ."

Deciding to be hung for a sheep as for a lamb, or whatever the hell the saying might be, Santiago tossed away the last of his common sense and leaned forward to halt her words through the simple process of kissing her.

"I know what you told me," he whispered against her lips.

"Santiago."

She pulled her head back, but not before Santiago tasted her fleeting response.

And was struck by lightning.

Perhaps not physical lightning that came from the sky. But it was just as potent and seared through him with far more damage than the traditional bolt.

Dios. She tasted of exotic woman and forbidden pleasure.

His brooding gaze lingered on her parted lips, a heady desire pulsing through his body as his fingers continued to caress the bare skin of her throat.

"I like my name on your lips," he said, his voice harsh in the still air.

"Halt this at once," she commanded.

"Halt what?" He moved closer. "Touching you?"

"Yes."

"Why? Like you, I appreciate beauty."

The dark eyes flared with an indefinable emotion. "Does that mean you consider me flawed?"

He chuckled, his fingers drifting to trace the line of her jaw.

"Clever women are always the most dangerous." He dipped his head down to nuzzle the corner of her surprisingly sensuous mouth. "And the most exciting."

"Enough of this nonsense." With an ease that scraped against Santiago's pride, she pushed him away, turning to resume her trek down the corridor. "I must speak with the Elders."

With fluid speed he moved to block her path. "Do they know that we're here?"

She halted, her expression smoothed to an unreadable mask.

A certain sign she had something to hide.

"They would have sensed my return," she admitted. "Even now they are gathering in the Great Hall."

Santiago went rigid as he was struck by a nasty suspicion. "You can sense them as well?"

She was silent so long he thought she might refuse to answer. Then at last she gave a dip of her head.

"Yes."

"Are they all accounted for?"

"What do you mean?"

"It's simple," he rasped. "Have all the Elders gathered?"

"Not yet." She waved a dismissive hand. "But there could be any number of reasons for their absence."

He stepped toward her, his barely leashed anger making the torches that were set in shallow alcoves flare in reaction.

"What reason?"

She stood firm, even as her hair stirred from his swirling powers.

"You are here as my guest, Santiago," she warned, the words coated in frost. "Do not make me regret having allowed you to travel with me."

"Why are you avoiding my question?"

"I do not discuss our clan business with outsiders."

"Outsider?" he hissed.

"Yes."

Why did he find that word so insulting?

He sure the hell didn't want to be included in a clan of vampires who cared more for their precious desire to find a higher purpose than their own brothers.

"Have you forgotten that one of your clan might be a traitor?" he snarled. "That makes it very much my business."

Her lips tightened, but her composure remained intact as she moved to brush past him.

"I think it is best if you wait here for me."

His hand shot out to grasp her upper arm, the sickening foreboding making him blind to the danger.

"Nefri."

"Not now, Santiago."

"What are you hiding from me?"

"I have told you." She grudgingly turned to meet his hard gaze. "It is clan business."

"It's Gaius, isn't it?" he charged, knowing that if he hadn't been watching her so closely he would have missed the slight flicker of her lashes. "He's the missing Elder."

Naturally she refused to admit the truth.

Most vampires were talented in the art of deception and this was one seemed more skilled than most.

"Your bitterness toward your sire has made you incapable of thinking clearly."

Santiago refused to be bluffed. "I'm thinking clearly enough to know that I'm right. Can you deny it?"

She averted her face, her profile revealing precisely nothing.

"Remain here."

"So you can try and hide the truth?"

"Nothing will be hidden," she attempted to assure him.

Did she really think he would just take her word for it?

He might not be an ancient, but he hadn't been turned yesterday.

"If you don't have anything to hide then there's no reason I can't come with you."

"By all the gods." The ice momentarily melted as she turned to stab him with a blazing gaze. "You truly are the most stubborn vampire."

Chapter 19

Ariyal pulled his damp hair into a long braid as he stepped out of the upstairs bathroom of the farmhouse. Despite the lack of hot water, the shower had at least washed away the dirt from the caves. Not to mention his more recent activities in the cellar.

Wicked, decadent, extraordinary activities.

A smile curved his lips at the delicious memories of the day spent in the arms of his mate.

The past few hours had been a revelation.

After centuries of being trapped in a harem he would have sworn there was nothing that could shock him when it came to sex.

There wasn't anything he hadn't done.

A thousand times.

But being with Jaelyn wasn't just sex.

It was a connection so intimate that there had been moments when it felt as if they had truly discovered paradise.

Unfortunately, the day had eventually disappeared. Along with their excuse to linger in the cellar.

The wizard still held the child, and now Ariyal had to worry about the leeches that his mate had warned would be gathering for a full-out assault at midnight.

He understood, even applauded, her desire to rescue the child, but he intended to make sure that his people were protected from the approaching vampires.

Entering the bedroom, Ariyal pulled on his jeans and boots before tucking a dagger into a holster attached to his ankle. He was reaching for his sword when he sensed Jaelyn approaching the door.

She'd been oddly adamant when she'd announced she intended to search the house in hopes of finding a shirt for him to wear, muttering something about covering his bare chest. As if she wasn't strutting around half naked.

Watching as she stepped over the threshold, Ariyal was briefly distracted by her sheer beauty.

From the top of her glossy raven hair that had been pulled in a tight ponytail, to the tips of her bare toes, she was lethal elegance that made his heart race and his knees weak.

And, of course, there were the predictable manly parts that hardened in ready approval.

Lost in his silent appreciation, it took a moment to realize that she was holding up a gaudy yellow Hawaiian shirt with huge pink orchids splashed across the silk fabric.

His smile faded as folded his arms over his chest and scowled at the amusement that shimmered in her indigo eyes.

"Are you kidding me?"

"Hey, it was that or this." She pulled her other hand from behind her back to reveal a frilly apron with the phrase KISS THE COOK splashed across the bib. "Take your pick."

He snorted. "You did this on purpose."

"Do you think I actually want my mate to look like an overgrown orchid?"

His irritation melted like dew beneath the summer sun. "Mate," he murmured, moving to wrap her slender body in his arms. "I like the sound of that."

She shivered as his lips found a tender spot just below

her ear, but, dropping the offensive shirt and apron, she pressed her hands to his chest.

"So do I, but you're not going to distract me."

"You mean distract you with this?" He stroked his lips down her throat. "Or this?" His hands gripped her hips to pull her against his growing erection.

She groaned, but arching back she stabbed him with a warning glare.

"Ariyal, you promised after your shower you would finish our discussion."

"Discussion? Is that what you call it?"

"I was attempting to get you to listen to my perfectly logical suggestions."

He nipped the lobe of her ear before grudgingly dropping his arms and stepping back.

He couldn't afford to be distracted. Not if he intended to win this particular argument.

"They sounded more like orders than suggestions, poppet," he said dryly.

She folded her arms, her chin tilting to that familiar angle.

"Only because you refuse to be reasonable."

"I don't call asking a Sylvermyst to sashay into a herd of waiting vampires reasonable," he countered. "In fact, I would call it downright suicidal."

"Sashay?" Her brows lifted. "Really?"

He held her gaze, his expression somber. "Jaelyn, I trust you with my very life, but don't expect me to extend that trust to your brothers. They've been my enemies for a very long time."

She wasn't foolish enough to try and convince him that her fellow leeches were prepared to accept him into the family just because they were mated. He was more likely to believe they were plotting the quickest means to dispose of his body.

"You're a warrior," she said with a shrug. "You know

that there are times when you have to join forces for the greater good."

"The enemy of my enemy is my friend?"

"Maybe not friend, but . . ."

"Jaelyn, those Sylvermyst in the caves are my brothers," he interrupted, his tone suddenly harsh.

Her expression softened. "I haven't forgotten."

"Then you should understand why I'm not overly anxious to allow them to become dispensable fodder for the leeches."

She moved forward, running her hands down his arms, her touch comforting as he was battered by the memory of his brothers being forced into slavery by the loathsome wizard.

"Styx is not a savage, Ariyal, although he is . . ." She searched for the appropriate word. "Intimidating. He has no more desire than you do for a bloodbath."

He didn't doubt the truth of her words. It was well known that the current Anasso was attempting to civilize his people. But he also knew that vampires were predators at heart and no command from their king was going to leash their natural impulses.

"Perhaps no desire, but once a battle has started all bets are off."

Her fingers tightened on his arm. "We can't allow the child to remain with Tearloch. Eventually they're going to dig out the altar and resurrect the Dark Lord."

"I know."

She made a sound of impatience. "Talk to me, fairy. What are you plotting?"

"I want the opportunity to go into the caves before the vampires start their massacre."

"No." Her nails dug into his arm as she shook her head in denial. "It's too dangerous."

Gently he extricated himself from her painful grip. He didn't want to lose an arm when he confessed his plan.

"I want to give my brothers the option to surrender."

There was a hint of fang as Jaelyn regarded him with a growing frustration. She better than anyone understood his uncompromising need to protect his tribe.

"You think they will?" she slowly demanded.

"Yes, if I can speak with them," he said, recalling the conversation he'd overheard. "They've lost their belief in Tearloch's cause, but they're terrified of the wizard. They'll join me if I can promise them a chance to escape as long as they aren't being threatened by vampires."

"It's still too dangerous," she muttered.

"They're my tribe, my family." He knew she could feel his grim determination. "I can't abandon them to certain death."

Her hands clenched, as if she was considering the possibility of locking him in the cellar. Then, bending down, she snatched the silk shirt off the floor and shoved it into his hand.

"I'll speak with Styx."

He tugged on the shirt, more pissed by her words than the ridiculous garment.

As if he needed to ask permission from a damned bloodsucker.

"This is not his decision to make."

"Yeah, yeah." She rolled her eyes. "Look, we can all work together if no one tries to turn this into a pissing match."

"Tell that to your Anasso."

"I intend to."

He halted his attempt to button the shirt, lifting his head to meet her steady gaze.

"You do?"

"Of course."

Hmmm. His instincts prickled in warning.

That had been way too easy.

"And you aren't going to fight me on my decision?"

She averted her gaze, adjusting the shotgun strapped around her tiny waist.

"I try not to ram my head into brick walls."

"Good."

"But . . ."

"Shit." He shook his head. "I knew there was going to be a 'but.'"

"But, I doubt I can earn us more than a few minutes' head start." She ignored his complaint, her head lifting to meet his resigned gaze. "So you'd better locate your tribesmen and convince them quick."

His eyes narrowed in warning. "Us?"

"I'm your mate." She lifted her hand to poke him in the center of his chest. "My place is at your side. No matter where you go."

"You were just pointing out that it's too dangerous," he said between clenched teeth.

"I also mentioned something about the futility of ramming your head into a brick wall."

"Dammit, Jaelyn."

"Come on, mate." Turning, she headed out the door, ignoring Ariyal, who stomped behind her, blistering the air with his foul curses. "We don't want to be late."

Jaelyn had always suspected that males were lacking the DNA sequence necessary for rational thought. Why else would they be so eager to thump their chests and flash their fangs instead of calmly discussing a problem?

Now there was no doubt left.

What the opposite sex needed was a good thumping, she acknowledged, watching as the six vampires deliberately circled Ariyal, their expressions ranging from mocking derision to outright hatred.

She hadn't expected the meeting to be pleasant.

Or even polite.

But did they have to start off by being as obnoxious as possible?

The question had barely skimmed through her mind when Styx stepped forward, looking like a walking nightmare in black leather pants and black T-shirt that was stretched across his massive torso.

"Nice shirt," he drawled to Ariyal, fondling the hilt of his huge sword.

Yep. As obnoxious as possible.

"Styx," she hissed, moving to stand at the side of her mate, who was already holding his bow and wooden arrows notched and ready to fire. "All we're asking is a chance to convince Ariyal's tribesmen to leave the caves before you enter."

The power of the Anasso was like a heavy throb in the air. "Why should I trust him?"

"Because I said you could." She stood her ground, acutely aware of Ariyal's smoldering fury. *Gods, please don't let him do anything stupid.* "Do you trust me?"

Styx lifted a broad shoulder. "He's your mate."

Her lips twisted. The vampires had sensed her mating with Ariyal the moment they'd approached the caves.

Which had only added to the tension.

"Yes, I know."

The large vampire shifted his attention back to the silent Ariyal.

"Your loyalty now lies with the dark fairies."

"You son of a bitch."

She barely had time to place herself between her mate and certain death, slamming her hands against his chest to hold him in place.

"Ariyal, please."

"He can say whatever he wants about me."

"Thank you," Styx drawled.

Annoying SOB.

"Shut up, leech," Ariyal snarled, his gaze never leaving Jaelyn's pleading expression. "But he's not allowed to insult your honor."

Her heart melted, even as she wanted to slug him for his stubbornness.

No one had ever defended her honor before.

No one.

"There's no insult in wanting to know if I'm about to be led into a trap," Styx said without apology.

Ariyal placed his arm around Jaelyn's shoulders and tucked her close to his side.

"If you thought it was a trap then why the hell did you come?"

"When the Hunter approached me she hadn't yet bound herself to our enemy."

"Oh, for Christ's sake," Jaelyn snapped. "He's not our enemy. We all want the same thing."

"Do we?" Styx demanded, his power brushing over her as if seeking the truth of her heart.

"Yes."

There was a short, tense silence as the Anasso continued to study her; then with a smooth lift of his hand he gestured for his vampires to step back.

"You have fifteen minutes."

Jaelyn's rush of relief was cut short by Ariyal's typical male reaction.

"You may be King of the Vampires, but you're—"

"Ariyal." She stepped directly in front of her mate, framing his face in her hands. "If we haven't convinced them to join us in fifteen minutes then we'll already be captured or dead."

Simple and straight to the point.

For once, it worked.

Hallelujah.

Clenching his jaw, he forced himself to draw in a calming breath and speak to the Anasso in a voice that wasn't deliberately intended to provoke the vampire.

"What's your plan?"

Styx slid his sword into the scabbard that ran the length of his back, his own expression altering to one of commanding efficiency.

"I have three Ravens performing sweeps through a five-mile perimeter to make sure nothing is allowed to sneak up on us."

Ariyal tilted back his head, testing the air. "I smell Were."

Styx lifted a brow, as if caught off guard by Ariyal's ability to detect the distant scent.

"Salvatore is in the area searching for the curs who attacked you," he admitted.

Ariyal wasn't pleased. "Will he be joining us in the caves?"

"Not unless absolutely necessary." Styx smiled without humor. "He was trapped down there not long ago. He's in no hurry to repeat the performance."

Jaelyn briefly wondered if the Were was responsible for the damage in the lower levels. Well, the initial damage. Ariyal had done his own share.

Then she was struck by a sudden thought.

"Did you warn him that the cur is a magic-user?"

Styx nodded. "Yes, as well as the fact he's traveling with what we suspect is a vampire that has unusual talents."

Jaelyn very much wondered about the strange vampire and exactly what Styx was hiding, but before she could press for an answer Ariyal was speaking.

"You might also warn him that Sergei is still lurking around, along with that damned gargoyle."

There was a rustle from the trees that lined the nearby graveyard before the unmistakable scent of granite wafted on the air.

"Hey," Levet protested, waddling forward with a wounded expression. "I just rescued you from a fate worse than death."

"You rescued me?" Ariyal made a sound of disgust. "Don't you have that backwards?"

"Oh." Levet blinked, coming to a halt next to Jaelyn. "Do I?"

Ignoring the rueful amusement of the vampires, Ariyal glared at the tiny demon.

"Where's the mage?"

Levet cleared his throat, his tail twitching. "He might have escaped."

"*Might* have?"

"Very well, he escaped." Levet's wings fluttered in a shimmer of color. "Is that what you desired to hear?"

"No, it's damned well not what I wanted to hear." Ariyal looked as if he could happily have turned the gargoyle into a teeny pile of rubble. "I specifically told you to keep an eye on him."

"I could hardly keep an eye on him when it was daylight, could I? Gargoyles have needs." With an offended sniff, Levet turned to offer Jaelyn a charming smile. "Ah, *ma enfant*, I see that you are unharmed. I was so concerned."

"Not now, Levet," Styx growled.

Levet blew a raspberry toward the towering vampire, but with an impatient curse Ariyal leaned down to grab the gargoyle by the horn and turn him back to meet his fierce glare.

"Did you try to track the mage?"

"Of course I did."

"And?"

"And he must have an amulet to mask his scent."

Ariyal hissed in frustration. "So you have no idea where he went?"

Levet wisely stepped out of reach of the Sylvermyst, waving a hand toward the entrance to the caves.

"His footsteps led in this direction."

"Shit." Ariyal sprinted toward the caves. "The baby."

"Wait." Styx muttered a curse when Ariyal ignored his command. "Fifteen minutes, Sylvermyst."

Jaelyn was swiftly following Ariyal as he darted into the caverns and headed down the nearest tunnel. She understood his concern. If the mage actually managed to get his greedy hands on the child and escape they might never track him down.

At least not until it was too late.

And if he screwed up and got caught then the wizard and Tearloch would be on guard, making it almost impossible to locate Ariyal's tribesmen without attracting unwanted attention.

They had reached the lower levels of the caverns when Ariyal came to a sudden halt, turning to face her.

Jaelyn frowned, her senses on full alert. "What is it? Do you sense something?"

The bronze eyes shimmered with an emotion that seared her to the tip of her toes.

"You're my heart and my soul," he breathed.

"As you are mine." She lifted herself on tiptoe to press a tender kiss to his lips. "We'll face whatever comes together."

He wrapped her in his fragrant heat. "Together."

Chapter 20

Tearloch leaned over the pool of water where Rafael had scryed the image of a half-dozen vampires currently hovering near the entrance to the caverns.

No, not just vampires, he silently corrected, a sick sensation twisting his gut into knots. It didn't take a genius to recognize the towering Aztec and the lethal predators that stood at his side.

The Anasso and his Ravens.

"God dammit," he breathed. "I told you that you were wasting too much time."

The wizard ignored Tearloch's complaints, waving his hand over the water to zoom in on a vampire with dark hair and silver eyes who looked like a pirate with a bad attitude.

"Dante, how exquisitely appropriate," Rafael murmured, a disturbing smile curving his lips.

"You know the vampire?"

"He was responsible for my death." An eerie chuckle filled the cavern. "Now I intend to return the favor."

Tearloch clenched his hands, the sharp burst of fear slicing through the cobwebs in his mind.

"Are you insane?" he demanded. "We have to get out of here before we're trapped."

Rafael clicked his tongue in resigned disappointment. "You are always in such a hurry to run, Tearloch."

"Being intelligent enough to realize when I'm outnumbered has kept me alive," Tearloch pointed out, his hands clenching at the sneer curving the wizard's lips. "Obviously it's a lesson you failed to learn."

The red flames flared in the spirit's eyes, the stench of the grave filling the cavern.

"Our master has no place at his side for cowards."

Tearloch pointed toward the images reflected in the water. "You truly think you can defeat a half-dozen vampires?"

"We will be invincible once we have resurrected the Dark Lord."

It was a promise that had been whispering in the back of Tearloch's mind since leaving Avalon. Now, however, the seductive promise was more than a little tarnished.

"Then why didn't you perform the ceremony when you had the chance?" he accused the worthless wizard. "Now it's too late."

"It's never too late."

"No? Your precious altar is buried deeper than ever thanks to Ariyal."

Rafael's gaunt face tightened with remembered fury. "Yes, he will pay for that, but for now we shall have to create a new altar."

Tearloch scowled at the smooth words. A new altar? After they'd wasted days trying to unblock the destroyed tunnels?

"If that was one of our options then why the hell did you waste our time trying to dig out the old one?"

"Because I assumed you would disapprove of my methods."

"Why would I disapprove?"

Rafael waved a bony hand. "You seem to be rather attached to your tribesmen."

Was that supposed to be a joke?

"What do my tribesmen have to do with your altar?"

"You are not stupid, Tearloch." Without warning the spirit moved to stand next to the child, who was cradled on a flat rock in the center of the cavern. The dark robes flowed around his skeletal frame as he bent down to study the babe, who remained locked in a deep sleep. "The Dark Lord demands a sacrifice. The altar must flow with blood."

Shock blasted through Tearloch at the unemotional pronouncement that he would have to watch his brothers being slaughtered like helpless lambs.

But why?

He'd known from the moment he'd conjured Rafael that he was an immoral bastard who would willingly destroy the world to sate his lust for power.

What was a little thing like murdering an entire tribe?

The knotted muscle of his jaw made it almost impossible to speak.

"No."

"Yes." Rafael stabbed him with a ruthless glare. "There is no other means."

"You treacherous snake." Tearloch instinctively backed away, having a dim recollection of Ariyal's warnings. Why hadn't he listened to his prince instead of allowing himself to be swayed by the voices that filled his mind with confusion? "This has been your plan all along, hasn't it?"

The wizard straightened, his hand toying with the pendant around his neck.

"Plan?"

Tearloch bumped into the far wall, his stomach cramping with horror.

"Gods, I've been so blind. You deliberately lured me and my brothers to these caves."

"Do not be an idiot," Rafael snapped.

"You're right to fear the wizard," a voice assured him

and Tearloch turned to watch as Sergei stepped into the cavern looking considerably worse for the wear with his silver hair tangled and his once-exquisite suit torn and filthy. But there was an arrogant confidence on his slender face as he moved to stand at Tearloch's side. "I did warn you, if you will recall."

"Mage." Rafael made the word sound like a curse. "I should have known you would turn up like the proverbial bad penny."

Sergei never allowed his attention to waver from Tearloch, a frantic gleam in his pale eyes.

"Listen to me, Sylvermyst. The spirit can't be trusted."

"And I suppose you are prepared to swear that your motives are purely honorable?" Rafael mocked.

The mage shrugged, still keeping his attention locked on Tearloch.

"I've never hidden my ambitions, but my plans to resurrect the master have never included slaughtering my allies."

There was a low hiss from the wizard, his power swirling through the air and seeping through Tearloch's mind, trying to confuse him with that terrifying fog.

"That is because you do not possess the skills or the power needed for the ceremony," Rafael said in a low, singsong voice that sought to entrap the listener. "You may be capable of bluffing the gullible, but I am not so easily fooled. Nor is Tearloch."

Sergei grasped Tearloch's arm, sending a prickle of magic over his skin, no doubt in an attempt to counter Rafael's spell.

"You know nothing, wizard." Sergei's fingers dug into Tearloch's arm. "My powers are greater than you could ever imagine."

Rafael's derisive laughter bounced off the smooth walls. "No, you are the one who must imagine them because they do not exist except in your fantasies."

The mage whirled toward the taunting wizard, his face red with fury.

"Shall I prove how wrong you are?"

Tearloch shook his head, wondering if he was the one who was insane.

"We're about to be massacred by vampires and you two want to waste time measuring your magical dicks?" he rasped.

Rafael waved his too-thin hand, something that might have been frustration burning in his pitiless eyes.

"I want you to realize that the mage cannot fulfill the promises he made to you."

Tearloch snorted. "Right now all I care about is getting the hell out of here."

"A wise choice," Sergei murmured.

The wise choice would have been to remain loyal to Ariyal as all his instincts had urged, he silently told himself. A damned shame he was only realizing the truth when it was too late.

"Get the child," he commanded the mage.

"Of course."

Sergei warily moved forward, his gaze on the wizard, who was frowning at Tearloch in disbelief. Clearly he couldn't believe that his sway over Tearloch wasn't as great as he'd thought.

"Do not be hasty, my friend."

"Hasty?" Tearloch's laughter held an edge of hysteria. "Like an idiot I've allowed both of you to manipulate and use me to gain the best advantage for your own glory. But no more. I'm done with this game."

"I have promised to perform the ceremony," the wizard reminded him in that captivating voice.

Tearloch pressed his hands to the wall behind him, concentrating on the smooth stone beneath his palm in an effort to block out the wizard's voice.

"And yet, you always have an excuse why it must be delayed."

Rafael glanced toward Sergei, who continued his tentative approach toward the babe before he was smiling with malevolent anticipation.

"Very well."

With a dramatic lift of his hands, Rafael shook back the sleeves of his robe and began to weave his fingers in a complicated pattern. It couldn't have looked more clichéd. The scary-ass-looking wizard in satin robes. A dark, spooky cavern. A horde of vampires about to attack.

Tearloch might have laughed if it hadn't been so achingly sad.

Then those waggling fingers began to glow with an eerie light that spread through the air, shimmering like a portal.

"What are you doing?"

"Thinning the veils between our world and the Dark Lord."

He might have thought it was just another trick if it weren't for the distinct change in air pressure as the shimmer widened until it was the size of a typical doorway.

"That's the ceremony?" he asked, a strange dread pooling in the pit of his gut. "A wiggle of your fingers?"

"It is the beginning." Moving with a startling speed, he was standing at the base of the flat rock, blocking the child from Sergei. "We will use this as a temporary altar. Of course it must be sanctified."

Tearloch stepped forward, reaching over his shoulder to pull his sword from its leather scabbard.

"I told you I will not sacrifice my brothers."

Rafael merely smiled, his hands shifting toward the mage. "Then it is fortunate that we have Sergei's blood to offer."

"No." Sergei tried to back away, only to discover that he'd been caught in the wizard's spell.

Rafael chuckled as he made a sharp gesture with his hand. "Come to me, mage."

The mage gave a strangled groan, his hands clawing at his throat, as if he was being choked by an unseen force.

"Tearloch, help me," he pleaded.

Rafael moved to stand directly before the mage. "Do you refuse to be of service to our beloved master, Sergei?"

Tearloch licked his lips, watching the two magic-users with a swelling sense of regret.

This was what he had so desperately wanted, and yet now that the moment was here, he would have done everything in his power to turn back the clock.

"That's all you need to resurrect the Dark Lord?"

"Of course it isn't," Sergei managed to spit out, falling to his knees as his face turned a peculiar shade of puce. "He merely needs my blood to part the shroud between worlds enough that the Dark Lord can slaughter you and your brothers. Only then will the master share his spirit with the chosen child."

"Shut up," Rafael snarled, moving to knock the mage to the ground before shifting his attention to Tearloch. "He seeks to betray you, Master."

"No." Tearloch shook his head, his thinking clear for the first time in weeks. He pointed the sword at the creature he had so foolishly called from the grave. "You're the one who has betrayed me. Now I'm going to banish you back to the hell you crawled out of."

"You leave me no choice, Sylvermyst," the wizard growled, releasing his magical hold on Sergei to point his hand toward Tearloch.

In the process of severing his connection to the spirit that kept Rafael anchored in this world, Tearloch was unaware of just how dangerously exposed he left himself.

Not until a blinding light filled his mind, scouring away all thought and bringing a brutal end to his brief taste of independence.

Tearloch was lost.
Crushed beneath the will of the wizard.

Ariyal sensed his tribesmen shadowing them as they entered the lower tunnels.

Impatience gnawed at him as he continued to jog forward.

Dammit. Time was slipping away. He had to convince
his brothers to leave before the vampires attacked.

A little difficult when they were making it clear he was
an unwelcome intruder.

But he wasn't stupid enough to try and pull rank on them.

Commanding them to stand and talk was likely to earn
him an arrow in the back.

Or worse.

Acutely aware of Jaelyn's barely leashed frustration as
she followed behind him, he deliberately turned into one of
the larger caverns. It had reached the point of now or never.

Thankfully, it was now as the Sylvermysts at last took
the bait and, leaving the shadows, surrounded him and
Jaelyn in a tight circle.

"That's far enough."

Ariyal stood motionless as the tall, slender Sylvermyst
with long amber hair pulled into a queue at the nape of his
neck and pewter eyes moved to stand directly before him.

Their gazes locked in a silent battle of wills before Ariyal
acknowledged his brother with a faint dip of his head.

"Elwin."

"Just slumming or has the mighty prince decided to join
with the riffraff?" the older Sylvermyst mocked.

"I don't join with traitors."

Elwin's lips tightened, clearly annoyed by the sharp

rebuff. But Ariyal didn't miss the fact the man didn't call for his bow or pull the sword holstered around his narrow waist.

"Then why the hell are you here?"

With a low hiss Toras shifted to stand next to Elwin, his pale gold eyes perfectly matching his hair, which had been cut to shoulder length.

"Can't you guess?" he growled.

Elwin paused; then his eyes narrowed as his gaze shifted from Ariyal to the silent Jaelyn.

"Mated," he spat out. "To a leech?"

Toras pointed a finger of condemnation at Ariyal. "He's here to turn us over to the bloodsuckers."

"And you call us the traitors?" Elwin sneered.

Ariyal leashed his burst of anger. Later he would teach his brothers the penalty of showing anything less than respect for his mate.

For now nothing mattered but getting them safely out of the caverns.

"I'm here as your prince to offer you safe passage out of these caves."

"Straight into the arms of the vampires?" Elwin's hands fisted, a jaded distrust smoldering in his eyes. And who could blame him? He'd first been convinced to trust Morgana le Fey, and now he was trapped in the caves with a leader who verged on madness. Why wouldn't he assume that Ariyal intended to betray him? "You can't lie to us—we know they're up there."

"Yes." There was no point in trying to lie. The vampires had made no effort to hide their presence. "They're preparing to rescue the child and to send the wizard back to hell. I requested they hold off their attack until I could speak with you."

Toras snorted. "So now you're allies with the leeches?"

Ariyal shrugged. "For as long as it takes to halt the return of the Dark Lord."

"Have you forgotten that he's our master?" Elwin demanded.

Ariyal didn't miss the edge in his brother's voice. Elwin might mouth the right words, but he was no longer drinking the Kool-Aid.

"I've forgotten nothing, which is why I intend to do whatever necessary to keep him banished from this world." He paused to turn slowly, capturing each of his brothers' gazes until returning to Elwin. "I have no intention of bowing to another master ever again."

A tense silence swelled through the cavern, the future hanging in balance.

Ariyal barely dared to breathe as he absorbed the mishmash of emotions that battered against him. The wariness, the fear, and the fragile hope that could be so easily destroyed. And running beneath it all, the steady comfort of Jaelyn's presence. Without saying a word she was assuring him that she had his back.

Always.

At long last Elwin cleared his throat. "Say that we're stupid enough to trust you, what happens to us?"

He waved a hand. "You're free."

"Free?" The pewter eyes narrowed. "We can just walk away?"

"Yes."

"What of our duty to you?" Toras demanded.

Ariyal arched a brow, every inch the prince they'd forced him to become.

"You have revealed yourself to be unworthy of my trust." His voice held pinpricks of magic that reminded his brothers of his power. He hadn't become the leader of his tribe because of his winning personality. "If you wish to return to my tribe, then you must earn your place."

The Sylvermyst shifted behind him, wise enough to realize that his words were hardly designed to lure them into a false sense of security.

Not that they were ready to jump on the bandwagon. Even if any of them knew what the hell a bandwagon was.

"This is a trick," Toras muttered, proving his point.

Ariyal stepped toward the golden-haired Sylvermyst. "Have I ever lied to you?"

"No, but—shit!"

There was a sudden burst of magic that made the Sylvermysts gasp in pain and Jaelyn scowl in confusion.

"Ariyal," she rasped, "what's happening?"

There was only one explanation.

"They've found the mage," he muttered, grimly accepting that they'd run out of time. Things were about to go bad in a hurry. All he could do was salvage what he could. "Elwin."

The Sylvermyst snapped to attention at Ariyal's commanding tone. Some things were just instinct.

"Yes, sire?"

"Take the men and get the hell out of here."

The man wavered, concern etched on his slender face. "What about the vampires?"

He reached to grab his brother's arm, holding his gaze. "You have my word they won't harm you so long as you don't do anything to provoke them. Will you trust me?"

Elwin paused, then gave a slow nod of agreement. "Yes."

"Good."

There was a collective surge of relief from the gathered Sylvermyst, as well as a barely leashed yearning to rush from the dark caves to breathe the fresh air. But Elwin didn't immediately leave the cavern. Instead he regarded Ariyal with a frown.

"What of you?"

"I have to get Tearloch and the child."

Elwin gave a shake of his head. "He won't listen to you. He's under the thrall of the wizard."

Ariyal shrugged. "No one gets left behind."

Something shimmered in the pewter eyes before Elwin was abruptly dropping to his knees, his head bent in regret. In less than a heartbeat the rest of the tribe were also kneeling, their swords being drawn and tossed onto the stone floor in a gesture of surrender.

"My lord," Toras breathed. "Forgive us."

"We have all made mistakes," Ariyal assured them. "Now we must hope that we can learn from them."

Elwin lifted his head. "If we survive this, I pledge that I will do whatever you ask of me to return to our tribe."

Reaching out, Ariyal firmly pulled the Sylvermyst to his feet, his expression somber.

"All I ask is that you take care of our brothers."

"You have my word."

Elwin placed a hand on Ariyal's shoulder in a silent pledge. Then with a sharp whistle he had the rest of the tribe on their feet and racing silently from the cavern.

With a silent prayer that they would make it out safely, Ariyal turned toward his mate, knowing better than to even suggest she join his tribesmen in their flight from the darkness.

He might not be Einstein, but he wasn't stupid.

"Are you ready?"

She held her sword in her hand, her fangs fully exposed. "Let's do this thing."

Chapter 21

Jaelyn bit back her protests as Ariyal led them through the increasingly narrow tunnels that reeked of ambush.

A fighter never allowed herself to be cornered in cramped spaces. It was too difficult to maneuver for even the best trained warrior.

Unfortunately, while she couldn't sense the magical battle that must be happening ahead of them, she could feel Ariyal's pulsing urgency, which meant that haste had to overcome caution for now.

Not that it had to make her happy.

Concentrating on her duty to make certain nothing approached them from behind, Jaelyn was unprepared for Ariyal's abrupt halt.

Ramming into his hard back, she swiftly regained her balance, rubbing her nose as he turned to face her with a tense frown.

"What's wrong?"

"Listen," he said softly.

Distantly she could hear the sound of Sergei and Rafael in a heated argument, the occasional shake of the tunnel warning her that they were doing far worse than merely throwing punches at one another.

If they weren't careful they would bring several tons of rock plummeting onto their heads.

Not the most pleasant thought.

But even as the image of being buried alive flashed through her mind, Ariyal's eyes were widening with a fear that had nothing to do with a cave-in.

"Ariyal?"

"The wizard," he managed to rasp between clenched teeth.

"What about him?"

"He's started the ceremony."

"Shit. We have to stop him."

Ariyal shook his head. "It's too late."

"No, it can't be."

She moved to dart around him, only to be stymied as he caught her in his arms and began pushing her back down the tunnel.

"We have to get the hell out of here."

"But . . ."

"Dammit, Jaelyn, those idiots have created a rift between dimensions."

"What does that mean?"

The question had barely tumbled from her lips when she caught sight of the white mist that was boiling through the tunnel, heading directly toward them.

"Hold on," Ariyal commanded, pressing her head against his chest as the mist surrounded them, seeming to suck them forward with a ruthless force.

She focused on the feel of her mate's hard body pressed against her as the world melted away. It would be terrifyingly easy to become lost and disoriented in the thick fog.

After what might have been a few minutes or an eternity, the sense of movement came to a halt. Tentatively, Jaelyn pushed away from Ariyal, studying the walls of mist that appeared to go on forever.

"This isn't good." She pointed out the obvious.

"No."

Ariyal pulled his sword as Jaelyn sent out her senses to probe the fog.

She wasn't an expert on alien dimensions. Her varied training had included many things, but vampires weren't intended to travel from world to world. Not unless they happened to be ancient Immortal Ones.

But she did know enough to realize that this wasn't typical.

In fact, she would guess that they were standing in the strange place between dimensions, not actually in one or the other.

Not the most comforting thought.

And it was becoming even less comforting as she caught the distinct scent of the wizard in the distance.

"We aren't alone," she breathed softly, uncertain how sound would travel in the mists.

Everything seemed . . . muffled, but she wasn't going to take unnecessary risks.

"Where?" Ariyal demanded, his voice equally low.

She hesitated, struggling to get her bearings before at last pointing to a spot over his shoulder.

"That way."

Ariyal didn't hesitate, turning to flow through the mists in the direction she'd indicated. Following in his wake, Jaelyn felt warmth spread through her heart at his absolute faith in her abilities.

That trust was as precious to her as his unconditional love.

They moved in silence, the strange mist swirling around them.

Or at least she assumed they were moving, she acknowledged with a grimace.

Their feet were stepping forward.

And there was a faint breeze she could see stirring the loose fabric of Ariyal's shirt.

But the landscape remained shrouded behind a fog that

made it impossible to determine if they were making progress or running in place.

Refusing to consider the horrifying thought that they might be eternally trapped in the smothering mist, Jaelyn forced herself to latch on to her strengthening awareness of Rafael. Moving or not, they were growing ever closer to the wizard.

Which had to be a good sign, didn't it?

"He's near," she warned softly.

Ariyal slowed, his sword held ready. "Can you tell if he has the child?"

She shook her head. "No. If the babe is here it's still wrapped in the spell that prevents me from being able to track it."

Ariyal's lips parted, but before he could speak, a form abruptly appeared out of the fog, standing directly in their path.

Tearloch.

No, not Tearloch, she silently corrected, catching sight of the Sylvermyst's eyes.

The beautiful silver had been consumed by a crimson that smoldered like the fiery pits of hell. A sure sign that he had become a mere puppet to a powerful being.

Her nose wrinkled. Even his scent had been over-whelmed by the acrid stench of brimstone that made Jaelyn's stomach churn in revulsion.

Without expression he held up his hand in warning. "Stop."

Ariyal studied his tribesman with a wary frown. "Tear-loch?"

"You may go no farther."

"Tearloch, can you hear me?" Ariyal took a step forward. "Brother?"

The Sylvermyst didn't respond. Hell, he might as well have been a lamppost for all the reaction he gave to Ariyal's plea.

Not that he it made him any less dangerous.

Jaelyn reached to lightly touch her mate's arm. "He's completely enthralled. Could the wizard do this?"

"Not without help. Only the Dark Lord could so completely crush his mind."

It was the answer she'd expected, but that didn't prevent the sharp stab of unease.

Who wouldn't be a little antsy at the thought of the ultimate evil creeping around in the fog?

"Great." She swallowed a curse as she sensed the wizard moving deeper into the mists. She couldn't allow him to escape. Who knew if she'd ever be able to track him in the damned fog if she lost his scent? "Can you keep him distracted?"

The bronzed eyes shimmered with frustration as he glanced in her direction.

"Jaelyn."

She sent him a warning frown. They didn't have time to squabble over whether she was going to put herself in danger or not.

"Can you do it or not?"

"Yes," he grudgingly conceded. "Just don't . . ."

"Do anything stupid." She finished for him, reaching up to steal a swift, possessive kiss. "Ditto."

"Ditto?"

Stepping back, Jaelyn pointed toward the motionless Tearloch.

"Right now he's your enemy, not your brother," she reminded him. "Don't let yourself be fooled into feeling pity for him."

Ariyal grimaced, but there was a grim determination etched onto his beautiful face.

"I'll do what I have to do."

She felt his bleak regret as he leaped forward, his sword slashing through the air directly at Tearloch's vulnerable throat.

Mindlessly Tearloch met the strike with his own sword, fighting back with an obvious skill.

Jaelyn forced herself to ignore the instinct to join in the battle and plunged into the surrounding fog. She demanded that Ariyal trust her ability to take care of herself. How could she offer him any less?

Even if leaving did suck.

Big time.

The ringing of steel on steel began to dim behind her as she moved steadily through the white landscape. Dammit. Where was the bastard?

She continued on for what felt like miles before a sudden prickle of energy rippled through the mists and she came to a sharp halt, her senses on full alert.

"Who's there?" she demanded, her feet spread in a fighting stance. "Wizard? Show yourself."

On cue Rafael stepped out of the fog, his robes flowing around his thin body and his bald head shimmering in the odd light.

"Welcome, vampire." A sneer twisted the gaunt face. "I was hoping that it was Dante approaching, but I suppose you will suffice."

"He's already put you in your grave once," she mocked, her tongue stroking down a massive fang. "It's my turn."

His thin lip twisted with a hatred that burned in his crimson eyes.

"I do not know what I dislike more, the sheer conceit of vampires, or females who do not know their proper place."

Jaelyn made a sound of disgust.

A male chauvinistic pig.

Why wasn't she surprised?

"Come closer and I'll show you the proper place of my foot," she promised sweetly. "A hint . . . it's up your ass."

His spiderlike fingers stroked the pendant hung around his skinny neck.

"You cannot defeat me. Not here."

The suspicion that he wasn't just blowing air out of his ass curdled in the pit of her stomach.

She could actually feel the force of his power throbbing in the air around him.

"And why is that?" she demanded, more in an effort to gain some time than any true interest.

If she couldn't find some Achilles' heel then she was in a shitload of trouble.

"In this place the power of the Dark Lord pumps through my veins."

With a demented smile the wizard pulled back the sleeve of his robe and used a fingernail to slice through his brittle skin. Instantly a thick, gray sludge filled the wound; then slowly it dripped down his arm.

Jaelyn stepped back before she could halt the revealing movement.

She'd seen a lot of *ewww* things in her life, but that vile slime was right at the top of this list.

"God almighty," she breathed. "You do know you're insanely creepy, don't you?"

His smile widened as he lifted his arm and licked the sludge off his skin, smacking his lips as she shuddered in horror.

"I shall enjoy making you scream."

The jackass no doubt intended the taunt to rattle her further. Thankfully the familiar words only jerked her out of her mesmerized sense of horror.

She'd promised herself a long time ago that when she met her death it wouldn't be with a damned whimper.

"Yeah, I get that a lot."

"I am not at all surprised." The wizard gave a casual flick of his hand. "The Sylvermyst must be desperate for a mate to have chosen you."

Unable to sense the magical attack, Jaelyn was unprepared as the sensation of a fist slamming into her chin sent her flying backward.

"Damn," she muttered, flowing to her feet and glaring at her opponent.

"Not quite so confident now, my dear?" he mocked.

She managed a grin despite her shattered jaw. She wasn't going to give the bastard the satisfaction of seeing her pain.

"We can chitchat or we can fight." She shrugged. "Your call."

Anger rippled over his face as he lifted his hand once again, but this time Jaelyn was prepared. Even as he sent a blast of magic in her direction she was flowing to the side, kicking out to crack his ribs.

He hissed in shock, but with a movement faster than she would have believed possible he was turning to hit her with another explosion of power.

Jaelyn's teeth rattled as she struggled to stay on her feet, the magic slicing a hundred tiny cuts in her skin as it blew past her.

The smile returned to the wizard's lips. "Obviously the rumors of the near-mystical powers of the Hunter were grossly exaggerated."

"You think?"

She flowed with blinding speed behind him, her claws raking deep wounds through his robes and into the flesh of his back.

"Bitch," he snapped, barely seeming to notice the nasty gray sludge that oozed down his back. "This is my favorite robe."

"Surely you must know that all vampires like to play with their prey before striking the killing blow?" she taunted.

He muttered a low word, and Jaelyn suddenly felt bands of air wrapping around her, holding her prisoner as surely as if they'd been made of steel.

"An odd way to play," Rafael rasped, moving forward to wrap his fingers around her neck. "Unless you enjoy pain?"

Oh . . . shit.

This wasn't going nearly as well as she'd hoped.

Actually, she was pretty sure that it couldn't be going any worse.

"Even if you defeat me the vampires are gathered to halt you," she ground out. "They will destroy the child rather than allow the return of the Dark Lord."

"You mean that child?" With a smile the wizard glanced to the side, clearly capable of parting the mists with a mere thought. Not that she had time to admire his talent. Instead her last hope died as she caught sight of the baby nestled in the fog, its eyes wide open and watching her with an unnerving awareness. "If they stand in the Dark Lord's path they will be destroyed," he assured her, his nails digging in to her throat. "Just as you will be."

A small voice in the back of her mind urged her to keep her mouth shut. It didn't take a genius to know that her death would be a lot less painful if she didn't keep provoking the wizard.

It was a voice that was easy to squash, along with any common sense.

"You truly believe your master will be strong enough to battle a half-dozen vampires and a pack of Weres?" she scorned his cocky confidence.

"He will once I have offered him the blood he needs." The crimson eyes flared with a disturbing hunger. "Your blood." His smile widened. "And then the Sylvermyst."

Fury boiled through her, searing away the fear that was clouding her mind.

At the same time she became sharply aware of her connection to Ariyal.

He had been in the back of her mind, a bundle of fury and regret. But, as if the mention of him suddenly brought him into focus, she was conscious of the sensation of pain, as if he'd just taken a vicious blow to the shoulder. And then, an overwhelming grief that brought tears to her eyes.

Dear gods . . . Ariyal.

The intensity of her sorrow was so deep that for a hideous second she actually thought she was mourning the loss of her mate. Then as the sense of him remained firmly settled in her heart, she at last realized that it was Ariyal who was consumed by his feelings of brutal sadness.

Relief blazed through her, nearly drowning out the more subtle changes that swelled through the fog.

In fact she almost missed the sensation of emptiness as Tearloch's soul slipped away, and the iron tang of blood that scented the air.

Human blood.

Momentarily confused, her gaze searched the mists for some sign of the intruder. It didn't make sense. How could a human manage to cross the magical boundary between dimensions?

At last, she accepted there were no unpleasant surprises creeping through the fog and returned her attention to the wizard. Only then did she catch sight of the red stains that marred the sleeve of his robe.

Red?

As in blood?

Mortal blood?

She dismissed the pain from her injuries as she rapidly sorted through the various explanations for the odd transformation from gray goo that had been leaking from the wizard's wounds to plain, old-fashioned blood.

At last she accepted that it had to be connected to Tearloch's passing.

Somehow his death had made the wizard mortal.

At least in this moment.

A slow smile of anticipation curled her lips. "You will

never get your filthy hands on my mate," she warned in frigid tones. "Never."

His eyes, which were now a pale shade of blue, flickered with unease, although the creature didn't seem to realize what had happened.

Or how vulnerable he'd become.

"Such brave words for a woman about to die," he rasped.

With a covert movement she shifted her hand to grasp the smooth stock of her gun, her finger resting on the trigger.

"Don't be so certain."

"But I am."

His whispering beneath his breath reminded her that even if he were temporarily mortal, he was still a powerful mage who could turn her into something nasty.

Or worse.

She had been given a miracle; she wasn't about to waste it.

"And I'm about to prove the mystic reputation of Hunters hasn't been exaggerated," she informed him, lifting her hand to press the muzzle of the gun against his temple.

Then, before he could react, she pulled the trigger.

At the last minute he managed to jerk to the side, but the bullet still managed to rip through his skull, sending a spray of blood and gore flying through the mist.

His hand released its hold on Jaelyn as he fell to his knees, his face unrecognizable. But even as she felt his life draining away he reached out to grasp her leg, his touch causing an agonizing pain to jolt though her body.

"You will pay for this," he warned despite his mangled lips.

"Really?" She kicked him away, shuddering at the tiny tremors of pain that continued to torment her. "Where's your Dark Lord now, wizard?"

His eerie laugh was swallowed by the fog. "I will serve him even in death."

"Yeah, yeah . . ." Struggling against the urge to collapse,

Jaelyn shoved the gun back into its holster and waited while the wizard slowly died. *Serve him in death.* What a load of . . . "Crap," she hissed, belatedly realizing that the human blood she'd just minutes ago considered a miracle was now flowing in small rivulets directly toward the child.

Like an idiot she leaped forward, trying to halt the flow of blood, or at least to divert it away from the babe.

A wasted effort.

The blood continued its unwavering path, as if directly being controlled by the child.

And perhaps it was, she was forced to accept, meeting the steady blue gaze that held a disturbing cunning.

Damn.

What to do, what to do.

The thought of leaving the baby behind was unthinkable. If the Dark Lord managed to resurrect himself then none of the worlds would be safe from the hell he would unleash.

But even as she moved to pick up the child the fog began to thicken around the tiny body, obscuring it from her view.

She tried to battle her way past the flimsy barrier, but it was like treading water, a lot of flailing around without getting anywhere. Muttering in frustration she circled the spot, the hair on the nape of her neck standing on end at the electric pulses of energy she could feel coming from the fog.

Something was happening.

Something very, very big.

And with the way her luck was running, it was also very, very bad.

Which meant that it was time to go.

Backing away, she kept her gaze trained on the wall of mist, nearly stumbling over the swiftly rotting carcass of the wizard. With a shiver she leaped to the side, her attention briefly distracted.

As she skirted around the body a silvery laugh danced

on the air and Jaelyn snapped her head up to discover a slender young woman standing just a few feet away.

She was a beautiful creature with long, dark hair that spilled over her naked skin, which was tinted a rich honey. Jaelyn guessed she was seventeen in human years with a pair of disarming dimples and wide blue eyes that were alarmingly familiar.

Eyes that she'd seen mere minutes ago in the face of a baby.

The Dark Lord.

In the flesh.

Quite literally.

Seemingly pleased by Jaelyn's gaping horror, the female held out her hand in a coaxing gesture.

"Jaelyn," she purred, her voice a potent weapon that nearly sent Jaelyn to her knees. "Sweet vampire, join with me and I will fulfill your every desire."

The urge to move forward and clutch that offered hand beat through her with merciless insistence. Her foot had even taken a treacherous step forward as she frantically fought for the strength to break free of the Dark Lord's compulsion.

It was at last her bond with Ariyal that saved her from certain enslavement.

Clinging with a fierce desperation to the feel of his presence buried in her heart, she conjured the image of his lean face and stunningly beautiful bronze eyes to distract her mind.

Suddenly she was filled with his essence, the scent of warm herbs almost tangible in the air.

A faint frown touched the creature's exquisite face as she sensed her hold on Jaelyn slipping away.

"Vampire, I command you to come to me."

"No." She shook her head. "Hell no."

Spinning on her heel, Jaelyn took off through the fog as if the devil was nipping at her heels.

And she was.

Behind the Veil

If Santiago was foolish enough to believe he had won the battle, Nefri swiftly disabused him of the fantasy.

While she willingly led him to the hallowed halls of the Great Council room, she had refused to allow him to enter.

He grimaced, pacing the marble hallway with a growing impatience.

It had been worse than a refusal.

She had walked into the massive room, with its glowing chandeliers and long ebony table surrounded by a dozen pompous-looking pricks he assumed were the Elders, and rudely slammed the door in his face.

Locked out, Santiago had been left to twiddle his thumbs.

And to curse the powerful female vampire who was rapidly becoming his personal nemesis.

A most beautiful nemesis, a renegade voice whispered in the back of his mind.

And sexy as hell despite her aloof, can't-touch-me demeanor.

Or perhaps that's what he found so enticing.

What predator didn't like the thought of hunting his prey? The more elusive the better.

Passing the time with images of the perfectly groomed Nefri lying rumpled and sated with pleasure in his bed, Santiago was able to resist the urge to beat something or someone to a bloody pulp.

Almost as if he was actually civilized.

Ha.

At last the heavy double doors of the Great Council were thrust open and Nefri stepped into the hallway, her perfect composure unable to disguise the concern that burned in her dark eyes.

Moving forward, he deliberately blocked her path with

his larger body. She might be more powerful, but he wasn't above fighting dirty.

She wasn't getting away until he was satisfied that she'd revealed every word that had been exchanged behind closed doors.

"Well?" he prompted.

Her lips thinned, but she didn't bother to pretend she didn't know what he wanted.

"Gaius is no longer behind the Veil."

Even expecting the words, Santiago stiffened in shock.

For centuries he'd refused to think of his sire, or to wonder what his life might be like with his new clan. But somewhere in the back of his mind had lurked the knowledge that Gaius was alive and well behind the Veil.

So why, after sacrificing his relationship with Santiago, not to mention all the others who depended on him, would he leave?

And why now?

Aware of Nefri's piercing gaze, Santiago managed a humorless smile.

"I won't tell you I told you so."

"So kind," she said dryly.

He folded his arms over his chest, barely noticing the hushed echo of footsteps as the remaining vampires spilled from the room and disappeared through the various passageways.

If they were truly as wise as was claimed, then they would know better than to interfere in his private conversation.

"Where is he?"

Her hands smoothed over her dark robes. "No one knows for certain."

"Convenient."

"Our people are not prisoners, Santiago." There was a bite to her smooth words. Had he touched a nerve? "They are free to come and go as they please. That does not make him guilty."

"When was he last seen?"

"Nearly a month ago."

"A month?" he growled, his brows snapping together.

"Yes."

"And no one thought it was weird that he just disappeared?"

"Our people are dedicated to their studies." Her chin tilted. "It is not uncommon for us to seclude ourselves for weeks or even years."

Freaking perfect.

If it was Gaius who had attacked Caine and Cassandra in Salvatore's cellar and later kidnapped them from Caine's home, then he had plenty of time to prepare a hidden lair where they would never find him.

Their only hope now was figuring out what the hell had prompted the vampire, who had been legendary for his brilliant intelligence and complete lack of political ambitions, to commit treason.

"Where's his lair?"

Nefri's eyes narrowed with suspicion. "Why?"

He made a sound of impatience. He wasn't used to explaining himself. And he most certainly wasn't used to asking for permission.

Even his clan chief, Viper, understood his need to be in charge.

Which no doubt explained why he sent him out of Chicago to run one of his numerous nightclubs.

"Because there might be some clue that can reveal his connection to the Dark Lord."

Of course that couldn't be the end of the matter.

He was beginning to suspect that the female would argue with him if he said the sun rose in the east.

"We have no proof there is any connection."

"Hence the search."

"Do you have no respect for personal boundaries?"

With a wicked smile he stepped forward, his head lowering until his lips were brushing softly against hers as he spoke.

"None."

Electric currents of pleasure jolted through him, his body clenching with a primitive need to haul her against the nearest wall and sate the hunger that was becoming an insistent, all-consuming ache.

She froze beneath his light touch, as if she was battling her own demons of need. Then with a deliberate motion, she pressed her hands against his chest and shoved him away.

"If you will follow me I will take you to Gaius's lair."

With precise movements she had stepped around him and was leading him past the marble columns to a wide marble staircase at the end of the hallway.

Santiago scowled as he followed behind. Her spine might be stiff beneath that long, silky curtain of dark hair and her muscles clenched beneath the flowing robes, but he hadn't missed the pure feminine desire that had flared through her eyes before she had pushed him away.

Dios.

Nefri, the freaking Queen of the Immortal Ones, was a complication he didn't need.

Especially not now.

But when had lust ever struck when it was convenient?

And that's what this was, he assured himself as they moved swiftly down the staircase. Lust with a capital L.

Anything else would be . . . nuts.

Reaching the bottom of the staircase, Nefri led him through the vaulted chamber with Greek gods painted on the ceiling and a fountain with a black marble statue of Poseidon in the center. He caught the musty scent of ancient books from a nearby library and the tantalizing perfume of orchids from the bathhouse, but Nefri moved toward a corridor that led away from the public rooms to what he assumed must be the living quarters.

And still she continued forward, turning into hallways that grew progressively more barren and dangerously narrow.

At last she came to a halt in front of a door, pausing with obvious reluctance before shoving it open and allowing him to step over the threshold.

Not burdened with pesky scruples, Santiago moved to the center of the room, inspecting the narrow cot and plain wooden trunk shoved in one corner with a growing sense of puzzlement.

Mierda.

It was like a monk's cell with its unadorned stone walls and stark lack of personal possessions. There wasn't even a rug to warm the marble floor.

"Bleak," he muttered.

"Gaius has never revealed a desire for material possessions," Nefri pointed out, although he sensed she was as startled as he was by their stark surroundings.

"No, he always preferred function over fashion," Santiago agreed. The older vampire had often teased Santiago on his love for luxury, claiming that Santiago's lair was more suitable for a pampered human than a dangerous predator. Grimly he shoved away the memory, reminding himself that the vampire he had once loved and respected had been nothing more than a figment of his imagination. "But he used to enjoy the basic comforts," he continued through gritted teeth.

"We all change over the years."

He snorted at soft words. "Evolve to higher beings, you mean?"

Her lips tightened, but predictably she refused to rise to the bait.

"For a rare few. Most of us merely do the best we can to survive."

"Very deep, *dulcita*," he muttered, moving to pull open the closet door.

"Some truths are simple."

"If you say . . ." Flicking through the dozen robes hung in a neat row, Santiago's words were forgotten as he caught sight of a small box set on the narrow shelf at the back.

With a hand that wasn't quite steady, he grabbed the ornately carved object, an emotion he refused to acknowledge clenching his heart.

There was a wash of cool power and the scent of exotic woman as Nefri moved to stand at his side, her serene presence offering a surprising balm to the tumultuous feelings that threatened to consume him.

"What is it?"

He held up the wooden box that was well worn from fingers that had lovingly traced the intricate patterns over the years.

"I carved this for Gaius just days before he left," he said, his voice thick.

He didn't add that sculpting the box had his been his means to mourn the brutal loss of Gaius's mate. He had poured his grief into each tiny engraving, attempting to capture the beauty she had added to his life.

"He obviously has treasured it," she said gently.

Why?

Why would Gaius have taken such care of this gift and at the same time dismiss the son who had created it for him?

With a shake of his head, Santiago opened the box, his brows lifting at the sight of a heavy, old-fashioned key that was hidden inside.

"Now I wonder what this might open."

"I haven't the least notion."

Tossing the box onto the cot, Santiago began searching

for a hidden door. If there was a key, there had to be a lock, didn't there?

Finding nothing in the closet, he searched the floor and then moved to the walls, his hands skimming over the smooth marble.

At last forced to accept he was at a stalemate, he turned his attention to the beautiful woman standing near the door, watching him with obvious displeasure.

So what was new?

"A little help?"

Her lips thinned. "I do not approve of invading another's privacy."

"No?" He shifted to stand directly before her, his expression hard with warning. "Do you approve of the end of the world?"

Their gazes clashed in a silent battle of wills before Nefri hissed in resignation.

"I should never have allowed you through the Veil," she muttered.

"Too late." He stroked a hand over her alabaster cheek, relishing the feel of her satin skin. "Now you will never get rid of me."

"Is that a threat?"

She met his burning gaze with cool indifference, but she couldn't hide her tiny shiver of pleasure at his touch.

"A promise," he said huskily.

There it was again.

That small, tantalizing shiver.

Then she was brushing past him to wave a slender hand through the air.

"There."

Fully aroused, it took Santiago a second to realize that she was pointing toward a door that had seemingly appeared like magic in the wall beside the cot.

He studied her with a suspicious frown. She'd done the

same voodoo magic in Salvatore's wine cellar to reveal Cassandra's presence there. At the time he'd been too busy making sure they didn't get eaten by the King of Weres and his sidekick to question her unexpected powers.

Not this time.

"What did you do?"

She shrugged. "I nullified any magic in the room."

Her tone was offhand. As if it was perfectly normal for a vampire to be capable of destroying a magical illusion.

Hell, most of his brothers would kill for such a gift.

"*Dios*," he growled. "A nice trick."

"It only works for the space directly around me," she qualified. "And only if the magic-user is not actively casting the spell."

"Can all of your clan do that?"

"No." She shook her head. "Only me."

He prowled forward, holding her dark gaze. "Because you're special?"

She stepped back, then hastily tried to cover the revealing movement by moving toward the cot.

"Shall we continue?"

Normally Santiago would have pounced on the hint of weakness.

Hey, it was a vampire-eat-vampire kind of world.

But, while Nefri might aggravate the hell out of him, and he couldn't resist attempting to crack through that cool composure, he never wanted her to feel anything but strong and proud when she was with him.

Grabbing the end of the cot, he pulled it out of the way, his gaze on the wooden door.

"Why do suppose Gaius would want to keep this door hidden?"

"No doubt you intend to open it and find out," she said dryly.

He flashed her a wicked smile as he stepped forward and pushed the key into the brass lock.

"You're beginning to know me so well."

"Unfortunately."

Turning the key, Santiago was unprepared for the door to swing open with surprising force, revealing the hidden room beyond.

"Stand back," he commanded, instinctively shifting to protect his companion.

Who knew what might lurk in the darkness?

Then, when nothing leaped out to attack them, he cautiously stepped through the narrow doorway and promptly came to an incredulous halt.

He was . . . speechless.

The room was barely larger than the closet and built of the same marble as everything else. But there was nothing barren in the life-size mural of a beautiful Egyptian female with long, ebony hair and dark, oblong eyes who was painted standing in front of the Great Pyramids.

It was so lifelike that Santiago half expected her to step off the wall and pull him into her welcoming embrace.

His gaze shifted to the wide shelf where a line of candles burned before moving on to the ivory satin gown that was neatly folded on top of a pair of gold embroidered pumps. Next to them were several wide gold bracelets and a matching necklace that glowed in the flickering candlelight.

Entering behind him, Nefri made a soft sound of shock. "Oh my."

"Dara," he said, an age-old sorrow twisting his heart.

"You recognize her?"

He gave a slow nod. "She was Gaius's mate."

"Was?"

"She and Gaius were captured by a rogue vampire clan." His gaze returned to the lovely face that was filled with a rare kindness among vampires. There wasn't a day that passed that he didn't regret having traveled away from the lair the night it was attacked. "He was forced to watch as she was burned to ash in front of him."

"How ghastly." Nefri's fingers lightly brushed his shoulder, as if she sensed his own pain at the loss of Dara. "It is no wonder he sought the solace to be found here."

Solace?

Santiago frowned, putting aside his grief as a vague warning that something wasn't right niggled at the back of his mind.

Once again his gaze made a slow circuit of the room, from the picture to the clothing that was clearly chosen with Dara's modest taste in mind.

It was, at last, the scent of detergent and the realization that the gown had been recently washed that made him stiffen in horror.

"You believe that he came through the Veil seeking solace?" he demanded, a chill inching down his spine.

"Of course." Nefri lightly touched the portrait. "Where better to grieve? He would have been allowed the solitude he needed to recover from his dreadful loss."

"Or the solitude necessary to disguise his hidden agenda," he added.

Her hand dropped as she regarded him with confusion. "Agenda?"

"Look around you, Nefri," he urged softly. "This isn't a shrine to loss."

"What are you talking about?"

"It's a symbol of hope." Plucking the gown off the shelf, he shook it beneath her nose. A dead wife didn't need a new gown and her favorite shoes. "He wasn't saying good-bye, he was preparing to be reunited with the woman he adores."

"Impossible," she denied, even as her eyes darkened with a growing dismay.

He understood her reluctance to consider the thought

that her clansman might be a raving lunatic beneath his careful façade.

Hell, Santiago didn't want to believe it.

Even after Gaius had abandoned him.

But they didn't have the option of sticking their heads in the sand.

"Perhaps, but if the Dark Lord was able to convince Gaius he could return Dara, do you think there's anything he wouldn't do to make it happen?" he asked, waving a hand toward Dara's portrait. "Including betray his own people?"

Without warning she was out of the cramped chamber and crossing to the open doorway.

"We must tell the Elders what we have discovered."

Rushing forward, Santiago grasped her upper arm and pulled her around to meet his stubborn glare.

"And then we go to Styx and warn him."

"Yes."

He blinked, wondering if he'd been whisked into some bizzaro land.

"No arguments?"

The pale, perfect face was impossible to read. "No arguments."

"*Dios*. I suppose there truly are miracles."

Chapter 22

Kneeling in the swirling mists, Ariyal cradled Tearloch's motionless body in his arms.

A part of him understood that he was surrounded by danger. And that he should be searching the fog for his missing mate so they could get the hell out of there. But a greater part was lost in the searing pain of taking the life of his brother.

It didn't matter that Tearloch had betrayed his tribe. Or that he'd led his fellow tribesmen into the vile hands of the wizard.

Or even that he'd spent the last few seconds of his life trying to take off Ariyal's head.

For countless centuries they'd been brothers, standing side by side in battle and offering each other comfort after spending time in Morgana's bed.

Their ties went too deep to be destroyed by a few weeks of madness.

Lost in his grief, Ariyal was barely aware of Jaelyn's silent approach. Not until she lightly touched his shoulder.

"Ariyal."

"I couldn't reach him." His gaze never left the lifeless silver eyes. They had once shimmered with amusement or flashed with fury. Now they were empty. A reminder of what had been stolen. "I had no choice."

She bent down beside him, her expression filled with sympathy.

"I'm sorry."

He gave a slow nod. "Is the wizard dead?"

"Yes."

"Good." A fierce stab of satisfaction pierced his heart. "He's the first to pay for twisting Tearloch's mind and nearly destroying my tribe. But he won't be the last."

She squeezed his shoulder, offering a comfort that helped to blunt the sharp edges of his pain.

"Ariyal, I feel your grief, but we have to get out of here."

He frowned at the throbbing urgency in her voice. "You said the wizard was dead."

"He is, but when he died his blood was . . ." She grimaced, searching for the word she wanted. "Absorbed by the child."

"Absorbed?"

"There's no other way to say it."

He didn't fully understand what she was talking about, but he could feel the fear that beat through her. Gently laying aside his brother, he rose to his feet, watching as she straightened.

If Jaelyn was scared, then something really bad was going on.

"Where's the child now?"

"It's no longer a child."

"The Dark Lord?"

"Yes."

"Damn."

After everything they'd been through, everything they'd sacrificed, they were still too late.

"What happened?"

"After Tearloch's death, the wizard became mortal. I

didn't even consider the consequences when I put a bullet through his brain."

"Jaelyn." He grasped her face, attempting to ease her rising panic. "It's going to be okay."

"No, it's not." She shook her head. "He's resurrected. Or I guess she is. Or whatever."

Still trying to sort through her flustered explanation, Ariyal froze at the wash of electricity that suddenly danced over his skin.

"Jaelyn," a female voice cooed, slicing easily through the fog.

Suddenly he understood his mate's panic. That voice alone was enough to crush his will to leave.

Jaelyn dug her fingers into his arms, her eyes wide. "Can you get us out of here?"

"Not in this spot," he admitted. "We need to get back to where we entered."

"What difference does it make?"

"The barrier was thinner there." He shrugged, hoping she didn't realize that he was flying on a wing and a prayer. "I might be able to use a portal to get us out."

It said a lot about her faith in him that she didn't hesitate, grabbing his hand to pull him through the fog.

"Let's go."

Or maybe it wasn't faith, he wryly conceded, struggling to keep up with her impressive speed. Maybe it was the fact she was scared spitless and desperate to get away from the monster in the mist.

He didn't blame her.

His skin felt as if it were being flayed from his body as the Dark Lord's power spread outward, the air so dense he could barely breathe.

Jaelyn didn't hesitate as she continued through the disorienting mists, almost as if she knew exactly where she was going.

A relief considering he didn't have a damned clue.

The constantly shifting landscape was screwing with his sense of direction.

He could only hope his ability to open a portal wasn't similarly affected.

After running what felt like miles, Jaelyn at last began to slow her relentless pace. Then without warning she came to a complete halt.

Not that Ariyal was about to celebrate.

The frown marring her brow warned that she wasn't stopping because they'd reached their point of entry, and they were about to escape the endless hell of white mist. But because something was troubling her.

Glancing over her shoulder she rubbed her arms, as if struck by a sudden chill.

"Is it my imagination or is the fog getting thicker?"

He studied their surroundings, his heart sinking. "It's not your imagination."

She growled in frustration; then they both stiffened as they caught the faintest scent weave through the air.

"Do you smell that?" she whispered.

"Were. Two purebloods." He drew in a deep breath, trying to capture the elusive scents as they disappeared as swiftly as they appeared. "And they're vaguely familiar," he admitted, unable to pinpoint where he would have met with the purebloods, although he suspected it had something to do with his time spent with Tane and Laylah. "As if I crossed their paths before."

"This just keeps getting stranger and stranger," she muttered.

Ariyal stiffened as the purebloods' scent was replaced by two others.

"And stranger," he said, bending down to whisper directly in her ear.

He felt her tension as she tilted back her head to meet his warning gaze.

"The magic-using cur." Her voice was equally low, her fangs visible in the eerie light.

Her memories of the cur weren't warm and fuzzy.

"And a vampire."

"Shit." Her anger shimmered through him as he confirmed her earlier suspicions. "How the hell did they get in here?"

"A question to ponder later."

"Yeah."

Clenching his hand in a grip that would have crushed the bones of a lesser man, Jaelyn resumed their trek through the seemingly eternal whiteness.

Well, not exactly a trek.

Her pace had slowed until a snail could give her a run for her money and her path zigzagged like a drunken sailor. He wisely held his tongue. Now didn't seem like the best time to question her ability to lead.

At last she came to a halt, giving up any pretense she knew where they were going.

"The fog is too thick," she growled. "There's no way to tell which direction we're headed. We could spend the rest of eternity stumbling through this damned stuff."

He shifted to pull her into his arms, resting his head on top of her head.

"We'll wait here. At least for a while. The fog is bound to thin out eventually."

She snuggled against him, seeking comfort even as she gave a snort of disbelief.

"I doubt we'll last that long."

"Well, aren't you just a bundle of sunshine?" he asked dryly.

"I'm allergic to sunshine."

Despite his grief and the acute fear that they were well and truly trapped, Ariyal managed a faint smile.

It didn't matter what was happening so long as he was holding Jaelyn in his arms.

They stood in silence for several minutes, each drawing comfort from the other. Then the moment was destroyed as the pungent odor of dog intruded into their fragile sense of peace.

"The cur," he whispered. "And close."

Expecting her to take off through the mist, Ariyal was caught off guard when she instead wrapped her arms tightly around his waist.

"Don't move."

He glanced down in surprise. "I approve of your enthusiasm, poppet, but now is not really the time or place."

Ignoring his protest, she pressed even closer and without warning, Ariyal felt her cold power wrap around him.

What the hell was she doing?

The cur was only a few feet away. And right behind him was the vampire.

Moving directly toward them.

They had only seconds to escape.

Instead the frigid air continued to wrap around him and, trying to halt his shivering long enough to prepare for battle, he belatedly realized that the mists had grown darker.

No.

It wasn't the mists.

Jaelyn was wrapping them in her shadows.

Shadows that could hide them from even the most highly trained hunter.

Gritting his teeth against the bone-deep cold, Ariyal held on to Jaelyn, amazed as the darkness thickened to the point he could barely see beyond the barrier. Damn. He hoped that Jaelyn's superior eyesight was better suited to see through the shadows.

His hearing, however, was as acute as ever, and he had no trouble overhearing the conversation between the cur and the vampire.

"You have made certain that the prophet can't escape?" the vampire demanded, his speech oddly formal, as if he hadn't spent much time mixing in the world.

Not that unusual.

There were many vampires who would disappear into their lairs for decades, even centuries at a time. It took a while to stop sounding like someone out of a time capsule.

Besides, Ariyal was more concerned with *what* he was saying than *how* he was saying it.

The prophet.

They had captured the pureblood Were who Jaelyn had informed him was a true seer. Along with the information that it had been Cassandra's timely foreseeing that had warned Tane not to kill Ariyal.

He owed her one.

Always assuming he was given the opportunity to repay the debt.

"She and the Were are being held in stasis until the master has fully regained his powers," he heard the cur reassure the vampire.

"A wise choice, no doubt," the vampire approved. "We do not wish to risk our prisoners escaping."

"No." There was a short, revealing pause. "But still it is a pity to waste the talents of a true seer."

Ariyal and Jaelyn exchanged a knowing glance.

The cur had ambition.

Something that could be used to their advantage.

"Knowledge of the future is power," the vampire retorted, his cold voice edged with warning. "And power is something our master does not share."

Either too oblivious or too stupid to heed the admonition, the cur pressed his point.

"Especially if the future doesn't please him." There was a humorless laugh. "As he's proven in the past. How many prophets did he have killed before he was banished?"

Ariyal sensed the vampire coming to a halt, as if irritated with his companion.

"Is there something troubling you, Dolf?"

"It was one thing to perform the duties of our beloved prince when we were hidden in the shadows," the cur complained, "but now that we've come out of the closet things are about to become a whole lot more dangerous."

"It was inevitable."

The cur made a sound, as if he hadn't actually thought through the fact they would eventually be exposed.

"But the danger would be considerably lessened if we had an early warning system. Who knows what the seer could tell us?"

There was a tense pause and Ariyal wondered if the vampire intended to kill the cur.

It wouldn't be a bad choice considering that the Dark Lord might very well destroy anyone near the cur if he learned of his traitorous thoughts.

"How long have you served the master?" the vampire at last demanded.

"What does it matter?"

"Because the stupid rarely survive more than a few decades," the vampire explained in smooth tones.

The cur growled. "Are you calling me stupid?"

"It is either that or suicidal if you believe you can double-cross the Prince of all Darkness."

"Christ, I didn't say I wanted to double-cross him," the cur protested, an edge of fear in his voice as he belatedly realized the danger. "I merely wondered why we're not allowed to use such a powerful weapon when our enemies are quite literally at our doorstep."

"And wondering if he is hiding a foretelling that speaks of our ultimate failure?"

"You said that, not me."

The vampire's humorless laugh sliced through the air. "Perhaps you are not so stupid as I feared."

That was still up in the air as far as Ariyal was concerned.

He understood caution, but the cur was right to question why he wasn't being allowed to use the services of such a potent weapon.

Could it be that the Dark Lord was indeed afraid of what the future might show?

Or did he simply refuse to allow his minions any power that he didn't give them directly?

"How long have you served the Dark Lord?" the cur abruptly demanded, perhaps needing reassurance that he hadn't made a colossal mistake in joining forces with the dark side.

"Several centuries."

There was something in the vampire's silken tone. Something that echoed the grief that still gripped Ariyal's heart.

"A long time to wait for your rewards," the cur muttered.

"Ah, but some rewards are worth waiting for."

"I suppose." The cur didn't sound entirely convinced. "What were you offered? Riches?"

The vampire made a sound of disgust. "What is money to an immortal?"

"It's pretty damned sweet if you ask me."

"So young."

"If it's not money then what?" the cur demanded. "Power?"

"We both know I have no need to barter for power." There was enough of a bite in the air to reveal the vampire was offended by the question. "I have possessed rare abilities since I was a mere foundling. And I only gained in strength after traveling through the Veil."

Ariyal's brows snapped together.

The Veil?

What the hell did that mean?

And what rare powers did he have?

Meeting Jaelyn's wide gaze, he wasn't reassured. She obviously understood what the vampire was talking about and wasn't happy.

Which meant that he wasn't happy.

"What's left after money and power?" the cur mocked.

"Love."

There was an awkward silence before the cur at last managed a sharp laugh.

"Are you shitting me?"

"There is nothing more treasured by vampires than their mates," the vampire informed the cur in frigid tones. "They would give their lives to protect them."

"Yeah, but . . ." The cur cleared his throat. "You want our master to give you a mate?"

"Don't be an idiot," the vampire snapped. "I want him to return the mate I lost."

"Ah." Another awkward pause. "Just to be clear. When you say 'lost' you mean . . ."

"She was killed when our lair was attacked by a rival clan and their pet witch." The sheer lack of emotion in the vampire's voice revealed the depth of his grief.

"Damn, I'm sorry."

"As I watched her being burned on a stake our mighty prince came to me. He promised me in that moment that my mate would be returned to me if I pledged my loyalty to him."

He felt Jaelyn's shiver as they shared a glance of compassion.

Before he'd taken a mate he would never have understood what could drive a man to make a deal with the devil.

Now it was all too easy to imagine.

Of course, that didn't mean he wasn't going to kill the vampire if given the chance.

"What was her name?" the cur asked.

"Dara."

"Pretty."

"She was exquisite," the vampire corrected. "And she will be again."

Ariyal sent Jaelyn a questioning gaze.

So far as he knew the Dark Lord could give the power to reanimate the dead as a zombie. Or call on spirits like the Sylvermysts.

But he'd never heard of bringing someone back from the dead and returning her to her former life.

Jaelyn gave a small shake of her head, revealing that she was equally confused.

"I don't mean to be a downer, but are you certain that the master can make good on his promise?" The cur readily voiced their suspicion.

Ariyal shook his head.

Right now he wasn't sure what was puzzling him more.

How a seemingly rational vampire could believe his mate was going to be returned from the dead. Or how a cur who couldn't open his mouth without sticking his foot into it managed to survive for so long.

The vampire hissed. "What are you implying?"

"Bringing back the dead . . . I mean, it seems . . . iffy."

Ariyal swallowed a sudden shout of alarm as pain lashed over him, tearing at his skin and threatening to crush his bones into powder.

"Do you doubt my power, or my willingness to fulfill my pledge, Dolf?" a soft female voice asked.

Ariyal didn't need to see the two men falling to their knees with their heads pressed to the ground at the approach of the Dark Lord.

It's what he would be doing if he weren't holding so tightly to Jaelyn.

"My prince," the cur breathed, his voice ragged. As if he was bearing the brunt of the Dark Lord's displeasure.

"Hmm. Intriguing. It would seem as if I will need a new title." The tinkling laugh was like shards of glass shooting through Ariyal. He clutched Jaelyn tighter, sensing her own distress. Just being near the Dark Lord was punishment. "What do you think, Dolf?"

The cur whimpered. "Yes, my . . . master."

"We will discuss this later," the Dark Lord assured the cur. "In private."

"Yes, master. Thank you, master."

Ariyal had to give the cur kudos for effort. He managed to say the right words. Unfortunately, he couldn't entirely hide his lack of enthusiasm for his private tête-à-tête with his master.

Lucky for him the monster of all monsters had other things on her mind.

"For now, I have a small task for you to perform."

It was the vampire who answered. "What would you have us do?"

"Ah, my faithful Gaius." There was a hint of mockery in that crushing voice. "So pure of heart."

Gaius.

He met Jaelyn's gaze to see if she recognized the name. She shook her head.

"I am yours to command," the vampire readily offered.

"Yes, you are." A new wave of pain rippled through the air, nearly bursting his inner organs. Holy hell. If they didn't get away, the damned Dark Lord was going to kill them without even trying. "You will search for the intruders who killed my precious Rafael."

Jaelyn stiffened, but she was a trained Hunter. Thank the

gods. The bone-chilling shadows that hid them from detection never wavered.

"The wizard is dead?" the cur demanded in shock.

"Yes, and I want those responsible sacrificed on my altar within the hour." There was a muffled sound of agony from the two servants as the Dark Lord reminded them of the price of failure. "Understood?"

"At once," Gaius choked out.

Jaelyn and Ariyal remained locked in each other's arms as the cur and vampire scurried away, followed more slowly by the Dark Lord.

Only when the last prickles of pain had faded did Ariyal take a breath and Jaelyn allow the shadows to dissipate.

"That was way too close," Jaelyn muttered.

"No shit."

"Let's get out of here."

Chapter 23

Styx paced through the cavern that looked as if it had been through World War III.

Piles of rubble littered the floor, while huge cracks ran through the once-smooth walls and a choking cloud of dust continued to fill the air.

Not that he bothered to notice his surroundings.

His attention was firmly locked on the handful of Sylvermysts who knelt beside a slab of stone that was charred from the recent rip between dimensions.

When the evil fey had first charged out of the caves, Styx had commanded his Ravens to stand aside. As much pleasure as it might give him to drain a few of the rare creatures, he had given his word to Ariyal.

But astonishingly, the bedraggled fairies hadn't bolted for safety as he'd been expecting. Instead they had informed Styx that the mage was already in the caves, and that Ariyal and Jaelyn had been determined to rescue Tearloch as well as the babe.

They'd also insisted on returning to the caverns after the massive explosion had revealed something bad was happening below.

Styx had grudgingly given in to their demands, only because he was incapable of detecting magic.

There was every likelihood that he would need their talent.

And if they hoped to lead him into a trap . . . well, there was still the option of draining them.

His decision turned out to be a sound one as they reached the lower cavern to discover it empty.

It had been Elwin who'd discovered the markings on the rock and had been able to sense that there had been a temporary opening through the barrier to another dimension.

He'd also offered the services of his men to try and reach through the barrier to return Ariyal and Jaelyn.

Not that they'd managed anything more than a shimmer in the air that led to precisely nowhere.

Pacing the floor, Styx's mood took a dip toward foul.

He didn't like feeling helpless.

Especially when the entire world was hanging in the balance.

At last he gestured toward the Sylvermyst with long amber hair and pewter eyes.

"Elwin."

With a grimace of impatience the Sylvermyst rose to his feet and moved to stand in front of Styx.

"Yes?"

"How much longer?"

"It's impossible to say." The fey gave a lift of his hands. "None of us have ever tried to use a portal to reach through dimensions."

Styx scowled. "Can it be done?"

"We can only pray."

Pray? That wasn't what Styx wanted to hear.

He was a vampire who expected results, not vague promises.

And he didn't give a damn whether or not he was being fair.

"Not good enough."

The Sylvermyst clenched his hands, his eyes flashing with fury.

"No one wants to rescue our prince more than I do."

Styx folded his arms over his massive chest. It was a gesture that he had discovered could make many demons piss their pants on the spot.

"You'll forgive me if I find that a little hard to believe," he drawled. "You did, after all, choose to betray him."

Clearly made of sterner stuff than most fairies, Elwin met Styx's condemning stare with a grim expression.

"We were fools to have been swayed by Tearloch's promises, but I intend to devote the rest of my life to earning Ariyal's forgiveness."

"Or to taking his place."

Elwin hissed at the low words. "What the hell does that mean?"

"Tell me, Elwin, who becomes prince if Ariyal doesn't return?" Styx asked, his gaze shifting to the Sylvermysts who remained kneeling beside the stone, their hands held toward the shimmer in the air as they chanted in low tones.

Elwin's anger tinted the air with a warm scent of herbs, but it was no match for the brutal chill of Styx's power.

"You son of a bitch," the Sylvermyst muttered.

A low chuckle announced the arrival of Salvatore, who managed to look *GQ* ready in his black Armani suit and pale blue shirt with a yellow silk tie.

Styx shook his head.

How did the damned dog manage to remain pristine when climbing through the rubble? There wasn't so much as a speck of dirt on the handmade Italian leather shoes.

It was . . . unnatural.

"Trouble in paradise?" the dog mocked.

Styx shrugged, biting back his sarcastic comment.

Behind Salvatore's taunting smile was a haunting memory

of his near-death experience in the caves. He understood the toll it was taking on the Were to help in the search for the child, and of course, Jaelyn.

And while he might never admit his gratitude (it just wasn't done between natural enemies) it wouldn't be forgotten.

Instead he nodded toward the glowering Elwin.

"Just trying to make certain that the Sylvermysts are giving a hundred percent to the effort to reach Jaelyn."

"Vampires," Elwin cursed.

Salvatore raised his hands. "Hey, you have my full sympathy."

The fey pointed a finger in Styx's face. "Don't interrupt our efforts again."

With his warning delivered, Elwin turned on his heel and returned to kneel next to his brothers, completely indifferent to the fact that Styx could rip off his head with one hand.

"I miss the days when I could just kill those people who pissed me off," Styx snarled.

"Being king is a bitch, isn't it?"

Never had truer words been spoken.

"What about you?" Styx turned his attention from the fey. Even if they were doing everything possible it was obvious their efforts weren't going to pay off anytime soon. He needed a plan B. "Any luck?"

"None." The Were grimaced, his hand smoothing over the dark hair that was pulled into a tail at his nape. Styx hid a wry smile at the dog's vanity. "I spoke with the local coven and they denied knowing any spell that could open the barrier between dimensions."

"I don't believe it," he said bluntly. "The wizard obviously used magic to take the child through."

Salvatore shrugged. "The wizard practiced dark magic."

"Then we need a magic-user who practices the dark arts."

"Easier said than done," the Were confessed. "They tend to remain hidden in the shadows."

Well, of course they did.

"Dammit."

Salvatore regarded him with a questioning expression. "What about Laylah?"

Styx arched a brow. "What about her?"

"Jinn can travel between worlds."

"She's a half Jinn," he reminded his companion. "Which means she can only shadow walk."

"Shadow walk?"

"She can enter the mists between dimensions."

Not surprisingly Salvatore appeared confused by his reluctance to call for the half Jinn. But while it had been one of his first thoughts after discovering that Jaelyn and the child were missing, he'd quickly dismissed it.

"It would be a start," Salvatore pointed out.

"I can't expose her to the Dark Lord," he refused. "And more to the point, Tane would never allow her to take such a risk."

The Were snorted. "And she actually listens to her mate? He's a lucky vampire."

"No, Laylah has a mind of her own, but she has devoted years to protecting her child from the Dark Lord." He shook his head. "She can't take the chance of being used to get to Maluhia."

Salvatore gave a grudging nod of agreement at the mention of the child that had once been wrapped in the same stasis spell with the missing baby. The twins had been created by the Dark Lord centuries ago and hidden in the mists, only to be found by Laylah.

It was bad enough to have lost one child.

They couldn't risk the other.

"Then I guess we have to hope the Sylvermysts can reach them."

Styx's fangs ached with the need to sink them into Elwin's throat, but he couldn't deny the truth of Salvatore's words.

A rock and a hard place.

Dammit.

"Yes."

Resuming his pacing, Styx was futilely attempting to remind himself of the virtues of patience when he detected the familiar scent of his brother, along with a less familiar odor.

Mage.

With a new flare of hope, Styx turned to watch as Dante strolled into the cavern.

The younger vampire's resemblance to a pirate was emphasized by the dark hair that was left free to frame his lean, handsome face and the silver eyes that danced with humor. Oh, and the wiggling prisoner he had slung over his shoulder.

Crossing the cavern, the vampire tossed the mage on the floor at Styx's feet.

"Dante, so good of you to join us," he murmured.

"And I come bearing gifts."

"So I see."

He lowered his gaze to watch Sergei struggle to a kneeling position.

His lip curled. The mage looked distinctly worse for the wear with his silver hair tangled and his suit covered in a thick layer of dust.

"The weasel was trying to hide beneath the rubble," Dante revealed.

"Typical," Styx said, his voice thick with disgust. "A coward to the bitter end, eh, mage?"

"I wasn't hiding," the man ridiculously protested. "I was knocked unconscious after my battle with the wizard."

"Yeah right," Dante scoffed.

The mage sniffed, trying to gather the tattered remains of his pride.

"You can believe what you want."

"I don't give a shit why you were cowering beneath the rocks," Styx snapped, glaring down at the lean face that had lost a considerable amount of its arrogance. "All I want to know is how long it will take you to open the barrier."

The mage blinked, as if Styx were speaking a foreign language.

"I can't."

Salvatore shifted to stand at his side. "He's lying."

The mage lifted pleading hands. "No, I'm telling you that I don't have the power."

With one smooth movement Styx was reaching down to wrap his fingers around Sergei's throat and jerking him upright. Holding him so they were eye to eye, Styx ignored the mage's feet that dangled off the ground and even his struggle to breathe.

He wanted answers.

And he wanted them now.

"Everyone knows that you've been preparing to resurrect the Dark Lord for centuries," he growled. "Obviously you have a spell that will reach through the barrier."

Grasping Styx's wrist, Sergei turned an interesting shade of purple.

"I'll admit that I have prepared for the ceremony," he gasped.

"Then do it."

The pale eyes flared with annoyance. "First of all, I can't just 'do it.'"

Styx gave him a violent shake. "Mage."

"Wait," the man pleaded. "I need an altar and a sacrifice and . . ."

"You're starting to piss me off," Styx growled.

"Trust me, you don't want him pissed off, Sergei," Salvatore informed the mage.

Sergei didn't seem to need the warning as he shivered in terror.

"I'm telling you the truth," he pleaded. "Such a massive spell takes a lot of time and effort to perform."

"Ah, he has performance anxiety," Salvatore mocked.

"It's not that," Sergei denied.

Styx gave him another shake. Just because he liked seeing the mage flop around like a bobblehead doll.

"Then what is it?" he demanded.

Sergei grimaced, clearly reluctant to admit the truth. "I'm not really sure that it will work."

Styx's fingers tightened in frustration. Did the mage think he was stupid?

"Lying bastard."

"No," Sergei squeaked. "Please, you must listen to me."

Styx allowed his grip to lessen enough that the idiot could explain.

"Speak quickly."

"And as if your life depends on it," Salvatore added, his eyes glowing with a dangerous golden light.

The King of Weres was always a threat. But if he actually turned wolfy he would devour the mage in one bite.

"When Marika approached me I was a hack mystic in the Russian Court," Sergei admitted.

Styx narrowed his gaze. He'd already gotten the background information on Sergei when he threatened Tane and Laylah.

"This is quickly?"

"She promised me eternal life and power beyond my deepest fantasy if I would join with her." He licked his dusty lips. "All I had to do was discover a spell that would resurrect the Dark Lord."

"Marika wasn't an easy mark," Styx said. He hadn't personally known the female vampire, but from all he'd heard she had been as cunning as she was ambitious. "She would never have taken your word that you could satisfy her needs."

"No, I swiftly found a spell that should work." Sergei grimaced. "At least in theory."

Styx ground his teeth. He already knew he wasn't going to like what the bastard had to say.

"But?"

"But I don't know if I have the necessary power to complete it," the mage confessed in a rush.

Styx fleetingly considered the pleasure of simply throttling the worthless ass and leaving him for the worms. Then sanity thankfully returned and he leashed his more primitive urges.

With enough force to make the mage grunt in pain, Styx returned him to his feet and released his hold on his neck.

For now the mage was their best shot at opening a rift in the dimensions.

God help them all.

"We're about to find out," he informed the mage.

Sergei shook his head, his fingers messaging his bruised neck.

"I told you, even if I wanted to do the ceremony I need an altar, as well as a sacrifice, not to mention days to prepare myself," he complained. "It's a very complicated and dangerous spell."

Styx gestured toward the silent vampire standing behind the mage.

"Dante?"

Dante grinned. "With pleasure."

Sergei scowled as he watched the younger vampire move to lift the massive slab of rock from the center of the cavern and shift it directly before him.

"What are you doing?"

"Here's your altar," Dante said with an evil smile.

"I can't use that."

"Make do," Styx growled.

"But . . ."

The mage forgot what he was about to say as Dante grabbed him and, using a dagger, sliced a gaping wound into his inner forearm.

Sergei screamed in pain as Dante yanked him forward, holding his arm over the stone so the flow of blood fell on the flat surface.

"And here's your sacrifice," Dante announced.

"Are you insane?" Sergei shrilly demanded, futilely attempting to break free of Dante's grip. "I'm going to bleed to death."

Styx shrugged. "Then I suggest that you work quickly."

"I can't."

Styx had his sword out of its scabbard and pointed at the mage's throat in one graceful motion.

"You have until the count of ten."

The mage made one last attempt to avoid his inevitable fate.

"No. please."

"One. Two. Three . . ."

Chapter 24

Jaelyn decided she hated white.

And fog.

And the constantly shifting landscape that made it impossible to know if they were traveling in circles.

At the point of concentrating on simply putting one foot in front of the other, Jaelyn nearly moaned in relief when she felt Ariyal slide an arm around her waist, tugging her to a halt.

"Stop, poppet," he commanded softly. "You're about to collapse."

She didn't try to argue.

Not only could Ariyal tangibly feel her weariness, but she was beyond trying to put on a brave face.

They were lost, alone, with no way of escaping the mists.

Turning, she pressed herself against Ariyal's welcome warmth, laying her head over the steady beat of his heart.

"We failed."

His hands ran a comforting path down the curve of her spine.

"Not yet."

She made a sound of resignation at his determined

optimism. "In case you missed the memo, the Dark Lord has already used the child to resurrect himself. Or herself."

"Yes, but he . . . I mean she, isn't at her full strength."

Jaelyn shuddered. Considering the power of the Dark Lord was one thing. Actually being close enough to feel the grinding pain was another.

"God help us when she is."

"I don't think we can count on any celestial help." Ariyal's arms tightened around her. "We're on our own."

Jaelyn stilled, concentrating on her bond with Ariyal.

She could sense his stark fear for her safety, his regret that he hadn't found a way to escape from the fog, and a growing determination that made her heart twist with dread.

Tilting back her head, she made no effort to hide her suspicious frown.

"Ariyal, what are you scheming?"

He lifted one shoulder. "This is the last chance to stop the Dark Lord from entering our dimension."

She should have been prepared for the blunt confession.

Hadn't Ariyal been trying to halt the Dark Lord's return from the moment they'd crossed paths?

He had been willing to sacrifice everything, including his own life, to protect his people from the fury of their former master.

Nothing had changed except the fact they were now mated.

"And you want to play hero?" she snapped, infuriated by the thought of him putting himself in danger.

He gave a slow shake of his head, his expression somber. "It's not a matter of what I want."

She grimaced.

It wasn't, of course.

They might not have asked to be put into the position of being the last thing standing between the Dark Lord and the world, but fate had chosen for them.

Now there was nothing left to do, but try and do their best.

"I know. I just . . ."

"What?"

She returned her head to his chest, savoring the scent of herbs.

"Wish that things could have been different."

He gave a light tug on her ponytail. "The future isn't written yet."

"True." Her lips twisted in a humorless smile. "Of course, if we do survive I want your promise that this is the very last time we have to save the world."

She felt his muscles clench at her teasing words. "Jaelyn."

Already sensing his protest, Jaelyn abruptly shoved her way out of his embrace, her chin jutted to a stubborn angle.

This was one argument he wasn't going to win.

Not ever.

"Don't even go there," she warned.

He held up his hands, no doubt shifting through his mind for the best way to pacify the little woman and keep her out of danger.

"I need you to find a way out of here." He at last hit on inspiration. "There's no point in defeating the Dark Lord if we're stuck here."

She planted her fists on her hips. "What you need and what you get are obviously two different things, Sylvermyst."

The gazes clashed as the heat of his frustration brushed over her with a physical force.

"Does it have to be a fight every time?"

"I'm not the one who is fighting."

"Jaelyn."

Whatever he was about to say was lost as Ariyal went rigid in shock, his attention turning to a point just beyond her shoulder.

She spun around, not sure what to expect.

Vampires, magical curs, resurrected Dark Lords.

What she found was more of the damned fog.

"Do you sense something coming?" she whispered softly.

He frowned. "Didn't you feel that?"

"Feel what?"

He took a minute to answer. "Magic."

Okay, that was nice and vague.

"The Dark Lord?"

"No."

"The cur?"

"No."

She threw her hands up in defeat. It was annoying as hell she couldn't feel whatever magic was in the air.

It was like stumbling around blind.

"We're running out of options," she muttered, then gave a shiver as she considered the various possibilities. "Or at least I hope we are. I don't want to think about what else might be lurking in the fog."

He moved past her, holding out his hand as if searching for a precise point.

"It's coming from the other side."

The other side?

She frowned. It seemed remarkably convenient that he would sense the magic just when he was losing their argument.

"You're just saying that to try and distract me," she accused.

He glanced over his shoulder. "Jaelyn, you would know if I was lying to you, wouldn't you?"

Oh. He had a point.

She certainly didn't sense any deceit. In fact, there was a growing sense of relief that was flooding through their bond.

"That doesn't necessarily mean good news," she warned, not wanting him to get his hopes up too high. Prepare for the worst, and expect the worst. That was her motto. And it had stood her in good stead over the past decades. "There are thousands of the Dark Lord's minions," she reminded him. "It could be one of them trying to break through."

"I don't care who it is," he retorted. "Anything or anyone that can get you out of here is good news."

Muttering at the stubborn stupidity of Sylvermysts, Jaelyn circled to stand directly in front of him.

"There's no 'you.' It's 'us,'" she informed him, stabbing her finger into the center of his chest. "We'll go through any opening together or neither of us will go."

"Poppet."

"Don't poppet me," she interrupted, her voice revealing she wasn't going to tolerate any excuses. "We'll go through and prepare for the Dark Lord. If we can unite the vampires and Sylvermysts, not to mention the Weres, there's no way he can defeat us. We'll at least have a better shot than trying to do it on our own."

His lips parted to argue, only to snap shut as he realized the sense of her words.

"You do have a point," he reluctantly conceded.

"Thank you," she said dryly.

She didn't have any time to congratulate herself on her small victory. Or even to feel relief that they might actually escape the nerve-racking fog.

Not when a vicious pain sliced through the air, along with a female voice that made Jaelyn's skin crawl.

"Jaelyn."

She sent Ariyal a resigned glance. Whoever might be trying to enter the mists was too late.

"Shit," she muttered.

He brushed his fingers over her cheek, his gaze skimming over her upturned face with an aching regret.

"It looks like the decision has been made for us."

"Looks like." She palmed her shotgun, pulling it free of the holster. "Do you have any suggestions?"

Holding out his arm, Ariyal called for his bow and arrow,

his gaze searching the mists. A good warrior wasn't so distracted by the lion that he failed to notice the cobra hiding in the grass.

"She's not yet at her full strength, which means there's the potential that her body can be injured."

She swiftly followed his logic. "So if we can destroy it . . ."

"Then the Dark Lord will be back to where he started," he completed. "Unable to enter our world." He grimaced. "Or at least that's the hope."

Hope.

She might have laughed if the Dark Lord hadn't chosen that moment to part the mists and appear in front of them.

Jaelyn shuddered, struck by the horrifying irony of such evil being hidden inside a young female who might have been the poster child of innocence.

It was just . . . wrong.

"Sweet Jaelyn, why do you run from me?" the creature taunted, a whimsical smile making her dimples dance. Then, as if caught by surprise, the Dark Lord widened her china-blue eyes. "Oh look, a Sylvermyst." She released a giggle that battered against Jaelyn like shards of glass. "Yummy."

The fear that threatened to crush her was abruptly pierced by a savage fury as the female drifted toward Ariyal.

"And mine," she gritted, pulling the trigger of the shotgun.

The Dark Lord brushed aside the pellets with a wave of her hand, but it at least had distracted her from Ariyal.

"Surely you don't mind sharing?"

"As a matter of fact I do."

With a blur of motion Jaelyn had her shotgun reloaded and was firing.

Again the Dark Lord brushed aside the projectiles, stepping toward Jaelyn with a smile of anticipation.

She was enjoying Jaelyn's fury. Perhaps even feeding off of it.

"But he's been such a bad, bad boy. He should never have tried to hide from me." The creature shook her head. "And to leave me for Morgana le Fey? He hurt my feelings."

"Somehow I doubt you have any feelings to hurt," Jaelyn muttered.

"Perhaps not. But I do get hungry. And Sylvermysts are so tasty good," she taunted, licking her lips.

Jaelyn lifted her gun, as if preparing to shoot; then hoping to catch her opponent by surprise, she leapt forward to slash her claws through the female's throat.

"Drop dead," she hissed, darting backward.

Briefly baffled, the girl lifted a hand to her neck, pulling it back to study the blood on her fingers.

"Now look what you've done."

"I intend to do far worse," Jaelyn warned, flashing her fangs.

She didn't actually think she could defeat the creature, but she had to admit she was shocked that she managed to draw blood.

Maybe Ariyal was right.

Until she'd gained her full strength her body was vulnerable to injury.

Clearly pissed off, the Dark Lord allowed the air to thicken with an excruciating heat, as if they were surrounded by the fiery pits of hell.

Jaelyn groaned in agony, afraid her bones might actually melt.

"How dare you strike me?" The sweet voice sent a thousand pinpricks of pain into Jaelyn's brain. "I am your master. You will bow before me."

Jaelyn was willing to bow if it would stop the unseen flames that were searing through her.

Hell, she'd crawl on her knees and kiss the creature's feet.

Before she was reduced to begging, however, Ariyal lifted his bow and with a blinding flurry he filled the girl's back with a dozen arrows.

The blue eyes widened as the creature stumbled forward, and Jaelyn groaned in relief as the heat was gone as swiftly as it arrived. Obviously the Dark Lord hadn't truly considered the idea that she might not be as immortal as she thought.

At least not yet.

With a frustrated curse she turned to concentrate her powers on Ariyal, her hand lifting to send the Sylvermyst flying through the air.

Jaelyn grimly ignored the audible crunch of broken bones and Ariyal's muffled shout of pain. She had to concentrate on the Dark Lord if she was to help her mate.

Not giving herself time to consider the wisdom of a direct attack, Jaelyn launched herself forward, wrapping her arms around the girl's shoulder and sinking her teeth into the side of her throat.

The blood hit her tongue like a punch, burning a path down her throat and making her stomach cramp in misery. Still she held on tight, fiercely draining the blood as the female clawed at her arm and face.

"You . . . bitch," the Dark Lord muttered. "I will make you suffer untold torment."

Jaelyn believed her.

Despite her numerous injuries the female remained as strong as ever. It wouldn't take long for Jaelyn and Ariyal to run out of tricks.

Then they would be at her mercy.

A fate worse than death.

Still she continued her desperate attempt to drain the bitch, swallowing the poisonous blood until the Dark Lord reached up to grasp her by the ponytail, yanking her away despite the fangs that ripped through her flesh. Then, with a contemptuous motion, the Dark Lord was tossing Jaelyn through the air.

She landed next to Ariyal, who was making a heroic effort to rise to his feet, a sharp pain drilling through her heart as the Dark Lord pointed a finger directly at her.

Oh . . . gods.

Lifting a hand, Jaelyn pressed it to her chest. It felt like someone had reached inside her and was attempting to rip her unbeating heart in half.

She couldn't bear it.

Lost in the searing pain, Jaelyn dismissed the faint sound of her name being called. It seemed reasonable that she would be going mad.

No one could survive such torture with their sanity intact.

Then it came again. This time with all the arrogant command of the King of Vampires.

"Jaelyn." There was the sound of muted curses. "Dammit, hurry up, mage. Jaelyn, can you hear me?"

At her side, Ariyal went rigid in shock. "What the hell?"

"Styx," she choked out, barely able to speak past the sensation of her heart being slowly shredded. "Hold on."

Wrapping her arms around her, Ariyal angled his body to shield her from the Dark Lord just as the mists behind them thinned.

There was the strange sensation of the world melting around her before there was a female shriek of fury and the feel of a hand reaching to grasp her arm.

"No. You'll never escape me."

Ariyal cursed, reaching for his sword and swinging it to slice deep into the slender arm. Jaelyn wasn't sure if the Dark Lord could feel the wound, but the fingers digging into her arm abruptly released and they were tumbling backward.

For a disorienting moment it felt as though they were

falling through the air, the pain in her heart thankfully easing, although there remained enough pressure to warn they weren't completely free of the psycho bitch.

Then a prickle of electricity raced over her skin and she was landing on a hard surface with jarring force.

She had a vague impression of Styx leaning over her as well as a silver-eyed vampire. More distant was the scent of Were and Sylvermyst and . . . mage.

Sergei.

She turned her head to discover him lying on the ground next to her and Ariyal, as if they'd knocked him down during their abrupt return to the caves. But oddly he appeared almost oblivious to her presence, his horrified gaze focused on the air directly above her.

She didn't want to look.

It was going to be bad. And she was tired of bad.

But of course she did.

Not knowing what was coming was the only thing worse than knowing what was coming.

Slowly she shifted to follow the mage's gaze, her entire body clenching with fear as she watched the outline of a slender young female becoming visible in the shimmering mist.

Oh . . . no. Not again.

Ariyal cursed, pulling her tightly against his chest, but there seemed nothing that could be done to halt the Dark Lord from passing through the barrier.

Then, astonishingly, the shimmering air began to thicken.

Something that might have been shock widened the china-blue eyes and the pretty young female lifted a hand to bang it against a seemingly impenetrable barrier.

The mage whimpered beside her, and Jaelyn might have done a bit of whimpering of her own as the air became so heavy it threatened to crush them all. Suddenly she wondered if she'd escaped the endless white fog only to die on the stone floor of the caverns.

But even as she rolled onto her side to say a final farewell to her mate, the pressure was abruptly gone. Along with the shimmering mist.

She held herself perfectly still, terrified if she moved that the air would split open and the Dark Lord would reappear.

Not that far-fetched a fear considering the past few days.

Only after she had counted to a hundred did she cautiously sit up, her body aching from head to toe. She groaned, but didn't protest when Ariyal wrapped an arm around her waist and assisted her to her feet.

The mage remained on the floor, passed out cold and still bleeding from a wound to his arm. Beyond him stood the King of Weres and a handful of vampires. Farther back the Sylvermysts hurried to get closer to their prince. But her attention was commanded by the six-foot-five vampire who stood with his hands on his hips.

"What the hell was that?" he demanded, his dark eyes revealing a rare disquiet.

Very few things scared the Anasso.

"The Dark Lord," she said, leaning heavily against Ariyal.

Salvatore made a sound of choked disbelief. "That . . . girl?"

"He was resurrected in the child." She grimaced at the memory. "One minute he was a babe and the next he stepped out of the mist looking like a young girl. It was creepy as hell."

"Yeah, understatement of the century," the Were muttered.

Ariyal tugged her even closer, his cheek resting on the top of her head.

"Can we do this later?" he growled. "Jaelyn's been through enough."

"In a minute." Styx pointed a finger toward the spot where the Dark Lord had appeared. "If he was resurrected then why didn't he . . . or she . . . come through the barrier?"

Jaelyn parted her lips to admit she didn't have a clue when Ariyal beat her to the punch.

"Because Jaelyn took her blood."

"Blood?" Styx regarded her as with a hint of wonder. "From the Dark Lord?"

Jaelyn shuddered, only now realizing that she could still feel the echoes of power from the blood.

"Trust me, it was an act of desperation."

"An act of incredible courage," the Anasso corrected with a faint dip of his head.

"So why would taking her blood keep the Dark Lord from passing into this world?" Salvatore asked the question on everyone's lips.

Including Jaelyn's.

"The child was created to hold the soul of the Dark Lord, but to have a unique enough essence so that the Phoenix wouldn't recognize it when it moved through the barrier." He shrugged. "After all, that's what keeps the Dark Lord on the other side. So long as the Chalice holds the goddess of light, the darkness remains banished."

Styx furrowed his brow. "So when Jaelyn drained her of blood?" he prompted.

"She stole the life of the symbiont."

"No." Salvatore shook his head. "From what I could see it was very much alive and very pissed off."

"The Dark Lord survives," Ariyal agreed, "but now he has no more than an empty shell that is incapable of travel from world to world."

Styx studied Ariyal with a searching gaze. "So that's the end?"

Ariyal shrugged. "For now."

Jaelyn studied him in amazement.

Gorgeous, lethal, and now brilliant.

Suddenly her aching desire for a hot bath and a soft bed evaporated.

All she wanted was to get this Sylvermyst alone so she could ravish him in private.

"We'll finish this later," she announced, sending her mate a smile that had him scooping her off her feet and heading toward the nearest exit.

Styx growled in annoyance. "But . . ."

"Later," Ariyal snapped. "Much, much later."

A week later
In a lair south of Chicago

The two-story brick farmhouse with white shutters and a wraparound porch was as picturesque as it was isolated.

Perched on a bluff that overlooked the Mississippi River, it was surrounded by acres of meadows filled with wild-flowers and patches of woods that were as necessary to fey as plenty of fresh air to breathe. And far enough from the main road to prevent all but the most determined tres-passers.

Inside, the house had been modified to please the most demanding vampire. The tinted windows allowed the sun-challenged to move around the house no matter what time of day or night. The rooms were large and the furniture a charming mixture of antiques and modern that was chosen for comfort rather than fashion. And of course reinforced to withstand the love play between a newly mated vampire and Sylvermyst.

It was, as far as Ariyal and Jaelyn were concerned, a little slice of heaven.

Unfortunately, they couldn't entirely ignore the world outside their secluded lair.

Ariyal's tribe was settled throughout the countryside, often bringing their squabbles to Ariyal to settle or just stopping by to request his opinion on various decisions they were about to make.

Jaelyn never complained. Not even when they interrupted a romantic evening she'd planned, down to his favorite dinner . . . a pair of edible undies.

His people were slowly healing beneath his patient leadership, and for the first time since Jaelyn had met Ariyal, he wasn't burdened by the guilt that had been slowly destroying him.

And then there had been the visits from Styx and Salvatore.

The two kings had been impervious to Ariyal's distinct lack of welcome as they had grilled him and Jaelyn on their time in the mists, as if telling the story over and over would somehow reveal what the Dark Lord might be plotting.

Not that she blamed them.

She was as anxious as anyone to find a way to rescue Cassandra and Caine from the mists. Not just because she wouldn't leave anyone to the tender mercies of the Dark Lord, even if they were Weres. But because it was too dangerous to leave a true prophet in the hands of their enemy.

And of course, there had been the disturbing news that Gaius, the vampire who'd given his loyalty to the Dark Lord, was an Immortal One who was able to travel through the veils separating worlds.

Which meant that even if the Dark Lord was prevented from entering this dimension for now, he was able to send his minion to do his bidding.

Not the most comforting thought.

It all combined to keep them from having the private honeymoon that they had once hoped to enjoy.

A damned shame, she acknowledged, wanting nothing more than to spend the rest of the night in bed with her delectable fey.

Instead she was forced to pull on a pair of jeans and a

dark T-shirt as she watched Ariyal finish buttoning the loud red Hawaiian shirt with yellow flowers. In the past few days they'd come to a hard-fought agreement that when they were in mixed company she would put aside her stretchy pants and sports bra, while he would cover that magnificent chest.

Mating, she was swiftly discovering, was all about compromise.

They braided each other's hair. Then as his hands began to roam in a manner that warned his thoughts weren't on their impending meeting with Styx and Salvatore, she firmly took his arm and steered him out of their private bedroom.

"We can play later, Sylvermyst," she promised, leading him down the carved oak staircase that glowed in the light from the small crystal chandelier hanging from the open beamed ceiling. "Styx and Salvatore are already here."

He grimaced, his hand flexing as if he was considering the comfort of calling for his bow and arrow.

The truce between the three powerful leaders was uneasy, at best.

"What if I tell them to go?"

"They'll just come back later," she warned, a smile curving her lips at the large bouquet of wildflowers that was arranged on a table in the small foyer.

Ariyal's love for nature could be seen in crystal vases all over the house, perfuming the air and adding splashes of color that Jaelyn was rapidly becoming addicted to.

She'd had no idea how bleak her life had been until it was filled with Ariyal's vibrant warmth.

He tugged on her braid, his expression rueful. "Didn't you make me promise that if we survived we were done saving the world?"

"All we're doing is meeting with Styx and Salvatore."

He grimaced. "I'd rather meet with the Dark Lord."

"Ssh." She pressed a finger to his lips. "That's still a possibility, you know."

He heaved a sigh. Although he was convinced that the Dark Lord couldn't use his new body to travel into the world, there was no doubt that the bastard was on the other side plotting a means to return.

So long as he existed, there would be danger.

"Fine," he said, "but spending time with the Royal Highnesses gives me a rash."

She chuckled, studying the elegant beauty of her mate's face. "I thought you blue bloods like to hang together, Prince Ariyal?"

He swooped his head down, pressing a possessive kiss to her mouth.

"I prefer to hang with my princess," he murmured against her lips.

She pulled back with a snort.

Princess.

It might be true that she was becoming fond of Ariyal's people. Excessively fond. And that she would kill anyone or anything that tried to harm them.

But she'd be damned if she'd be called princess.

It was just so . . . pansy-ass.

"Watch it," she muttered. "I already told Elwin that if he ever called me that again I would slice off his tongue."

He arched a teasing brow. "But whether you like the title or not, you are their princess."

She shook her head as they moved to the large room at the front of the house that had once been the formal parlor.

When they'd first arrived it had been stuffed full of the former housewife's finest possessions. Sofas, chairs, china cabinets, and a grandfather clock that Ariyal had taken out back and burned within minutes of their arrival.

There was nothing quite so annoying to creatures with

super hearing than the constant tick tock of a clock. Add in a cuckoo bird and it was nothing short of hell.

Now it had been thinned to a few sturdy pieces of furniture and shelves that Ariyal had built to display their collection of . . . well, they hadn't exactly agreed what they would collect.

But whatever they chose, it would be theirs.

A display of their life together.

"Princess. That's going to take some getting used to," she admitted.

His eyes filled with a smoldering warmth as he deliberately ignored the large vampire and pureblooded Were who stood with unreadable expressions near the bay window.

A warmth that she felt down to the tips of her toes.

"We have an eternity," he promised.

"Do not be so certain, Sylvermyst."

The voice of Kostas echoed through the room a heartbeat before the Ruah dropped his shadows to reveal his large, muscular body that was attired in a black T-shirt, camouflage pants, and shit-kicker boots.

Decades of training sent Jaelyn to her knees, her head lowered as her leader approached.

In the back of her mind she'd known this confrontation was coming. You couldn't defy the Addonexus and expect to get away unscathed.

But she'd hoped that she would have time to discover some escape clause that would allow her to keep Ariyal without forfeiting her life.

Obviously, time had run out.

"On your feet, Hunter," the ultimate leader of the Hunters commanded.

Slowly she lifted herself upright, her gaze skimming over Kostas's finely hewed features and the slicked-back black hair before settling on his soulless eyes.

"Jaelyn." At her side, Ariyal shifted to wrap a protective arm around her shoulder.

"You will stay out of this, Sylvermyst," Kostas commanded, his gaze never wavering from Jaelyn. "I will deal with you later."

"Please, Ariyal," she pleaded softly, deliberately untangling herself and stepping away from her mate. If she was going to be sacrificed to sate Kostas's bloated pride, she didn't want Ariyal caught in the cross fire. "Hello, Kostas."

His lips thinned, as if he was annoyed by her response to his surprise visit.

What did he expect?

Wailing and pleading and serious ass-kissing?

It simply wasn't her style.

"Do you know, I had great expectations for you, Jaelyn?" he chided, speaking to her as if she were a disobedient child rather the vulnerable young woman he'd tortured and tormented for decades. "You had the potential to become the greatest Hunter in the past millennium. It was only your heart I questioned."

"And so you tried to destroy it." Her chin tilted. "I will never forgive you for that."

He shrugged. Emotionless.

"A Hunter cannot have a weakness."

She could feel Ariyal's growing fury, laced with fear, as it pulsed in the air. She sent him a warning glance not to interfere before turning her attention back to the man who had the right to destroy her.

"I happen to believe it's my greatest strength," she countered.

His lips curled into a sneer. "If that were true then it wouldn't have led you to betray your loyalty to the Addonexus."

"I never asked to become a Hunter."

"It was your destiny."

"Chosen by you."

"Chosen by fate," he insisted. "Do you have any notion how many vampires would quite literally kill to be in your position?"

She did.

Being a Hunter brought her the sort of awed respect her fellow vampires coveted.

It was bound to go to any female's head.

But the few benefits didn't come close to making up for the nearly soul-destroying price she'd paid.

"Then you shouldn't have any trouble filling it," she said.

Kostas's fury spilled through the room like icy needles. "Now is not the time for flippant remarks."

She shrugged. "Do you want me to beg?"

His eyes narrowed, assuring Jaelyn that even if she could manage to kiss this man's ass he wouldn't be satisfied.

"You could, but it would do no good," he drawled, proving her right. Not that he wouldn't enjoy seeing her on her knees begging. He might be missing a heart, but his ego was fully functioning. "You have committed the worst crimes known to the Addonexus."

"I thought attempting to kill the Ruah was the worst crime?"

He imperiously ignored her accusation. "Not only did you allow yourself to form a relationship with your prey, you actually mated with him." He cast a condemning glance toward the rigid Ariyal. "And if that were not bad enough, you have reneged on a contract with the Commission."

"Actually, I didn't renege," she swiftly denied. "The terms were altered by one of the Oracles."

Kostas stiffened, clearly caught off balance by her revelation. Siljar had told her to keep it secret, so that's what she'd tried to do.

In fact, she'd only confessed the truth to Ariyal a few nights before.

"It does not matter." The Ruah at last dismissed what he didn't want to hear. "Any one of those atrocities carries with it a death sentence."

"Why you . . ."

Ariyal charged forward, but as fast as he was, Styx was faster, moving to intercept the maddened Sylvermyst and wrapping him in his massive arms.

"Stop, Ariyal," the Anasso commanded, clamping his hand over Ariyal's mouth. "You're only making matters worse."

Jaelyn was relieved that the king had moved to keep Ariyal out of danger, but she couldn't deny the small pang of disappointment.

She hadn't assumed that she and Styx were suddenly buddy-buddy, but she hadn't expected him to actually help Kostas send her to the gallows.

"Either you get rid of him or I will." Ariyal's words were muffled, his anger a warm flood that battled against the chill in the air.

A humorless smile pulled at the Ruah's thin lips. "The Anasso is the King of Vampires, but the Hunters belong to me," he informed Ariyal, pride thick in his voice, although Jaelyn suspected he resented the fact that he wasn't the ultimate leader of vampires. Hideous thought. "It is my right to punish my people how I see fit."

She couldn't argue the truth of his words.

All she hoped was to convince him that it would somehow serve his purpose to keep her alive.

Yeah . . . fat chance.

"And what purpose will my death serve?" she demanded.

"It will remind other Hunters that our laws are meant to be obeyed."

"So you'll kill me just to make an example of me?"

The empty gaze moved slowly down her rigid body before returning to her face.

"You're like a cancer that must be destroyed for the good of the Addonexus."

He truly believed what he was saying. She could feel it to the very depths of her soul.

So this was the end.

No chance of escape, no last-minute pardon.

Squaring her shoulders, she held her chin high.

"You can do whatever you want to me, but I will never regret loving Ariyal," she announced loud enough that her voice bounced off the walls. "Never."

Kostas reached to grasp her chin in a brutal grip. "Such a pity," he murmured, studying her with a faux expression of regret.

She yanked away from his touch. "Don't pretend you're not getting off on this. You love when you get the opportunity to flex your muscles."

His jaw tightened, clearly annoyed. Not that she gave a shit.

He was going to kill her.

Who cared if she offended him?

"Come along, Jaelyn," he ordered in frigid tones. "The sooner we're done with this unpleasant business the sooner I can return to my duties."

She thought she heard Styx mutter a low curse, but before she could glance in his direction there was the sensation of the air pressure abruptly changing. Spinning around she watched as Siljar popped into view, along with her daughter, Yannah.

As always, the two tiny demons looked nearly identical, dressed in long white robes that were pristine despite the faint whiff of brimstone, with their black, oblong eyes and razor-sharp teeth.

Only a closer inspection revealed that Yannah's hair was

fair rather than silver and her eyes lacking the ancient wisdom of her mother.

Seemingly unaware of the shock her abrupt entrance had created, Siljar held up a tiny hand, her attention focused on Kostas.

"Wait."

Chapter 25

Ariyal was going to kill the King of Vampires.

And then he was going to kill Kostas. Slowly and as painfully as possible.

And then he just might kill Salvatore for standing there like a damned mannequin while Jaelyn was being hauled off to her certain death.

Not that he blamed them any more than he blamed himself.

Jaelyn had deftly sidestepped him when he'd tried to question her about the Addonexus and what was going to happen when they discovered she'd taken a mate.

She'd claimed she would find some means to get out of her duty as a Hunter. She'd even assured him that she was certain there was some obscure law that would allow her to escape punishment, but he'd known deep in his heart that she wasn't being entirely honest.

If Jaelyn died, he would have no one to blame but himself.

Fighting against the arms that held him prisoner, Ariyal nearly missed the sudden appearance of two small female demons. In fact, it wasn't until he felt the deluge of power that could only belong to an Oracle that he turned his head to catch sight of the intruders.

He stopped his struggles. Gods, was that Yannah? Warily he watched as the elder of the demons stepped toward Jaelyn, her dark gaze keeping track of Kostas as he performed a stiff bow.

"Siljar," the vampire murmured, obviously familiar with the Oracle.

Ariyal didn't know if that was a good or bad sign.

"What is going on here?" Siljar demanded, her voice soft but powerful enough to make the conceited jackass pale to a pasty white.

Still, he was nothing if not arrogant, and with a smile he managed to flash his massive fangs.

"Nothing that need concern the Commission, I assure you."

"I beg to disagree." Siljar pointed a finger in Jaelyn's direction. "This Hunter is under contract to me."

Ah. So this was the Oracle who had put a contract out on him. Not that she seemed particularly interested in him now. Actually, she appeared far more concerned with Kostas than anyone else.

Thank the gods.

"She was," the Ruah agreed, pressing a hand to his chest in a gesture of regret. "But, I fear that she has betrayed us both."

Siljar didn't blink. "Betrayed?"

"She has mated with the Sylvermyst." The vampire's voice dripped with disgust. *Nasty worm.* "Most unfortunate. However, I fully intend to see her punished and your contract completed."

"By you?"

"Of course."

The female tilted her head to the side, looking like an inquisitive bird.

If a bird could topple a city with a thought.

"But I don't want you," she at last announced. "I want Jaelyn."

A stunned silence filled the room, and Ariyal's heart remembered how to beat for the first time since Kostas made his over-the-top appearance.

Was it possible that the Oracle was actually here to help Jaelyn?

Dammit. They were due some luck.

"I . . ." Kostas halted to consider his words. "I do not understand."

Siljar moved forward, her robes brushing the wood floor that he had sanded and polished on Jaelyn's orders.

"I was the one who insisted that she remain close to the Sylvermyst," she informed the Ruah, not at all intimated by the vampire's brutish size or the hint of cruelty etched into his features. "There was a vision that revealed that it would take both of them to prevent the Dark Lord from entering this world."

Ariyal barely noticed when Styx released his bone-crushing hold and stepped back.

So that was why she'd ordered Jaelyn to remain at his side after she'd escaped from Avalon.

Not that he cared why. Her command had made sure that Jaelyn had stayed with him long enough for his charm to work its magic. In fact, if they survived this latest disaster he intended to send a bouquet of roses and a thank-you card to the magnificent Siljar.

Of course, he was less enthused about the vision of them being responsible for preventing the Dark Lord's return.

It had been sheer chance that Jaelyn had drained the blood of the Dark Lord's host body. And that her efforts had prevented him from following.

If the world had truly been depending on them . . .

It made him shudder just to think what could have happened.

Across the room Kostas frowned, not at all happy with the direction of the conversation. He had obviously come there to get his ya-yas by condemning Jaelyn to death.

He wasn't going to be pleased if he was forced to leave without her.

"Even so."

"Are you having difficulty hearing me, Kostas?"

He shifted beneath that relentless black gaze. "No, of course not."

"Then perhaps I am simply not making myself clear." She took another step forward, her head tilted back to reveal her grim expression. "The Hunter is still under contract to me."

Kostos was nothing if not determined.

"But she is mated." He shot the silent Jaelyn an accusing gaze.

Siljar shrugged. "So much the better."

"It is forbidden."

"By whom?"

"By tradition."

"Then perhaps you should reconsider your traditions," the female suggested.

The vampire jerked as if he'd taken a blow. "With all respect . . ."

A smile that sent a chill of alarm down Ariyal's spine curled Siljar's lips.

There was something unnerving about that sweet smile when it was combined with those razor-sharp teeth.

"Shall I have you brought before the Commission to discuss the issue?"

The air of superior confidence was at last shaken as Kostas took a hasty step back.

"No," he barked out before he was battling to conceal his rampant fear. "That will not be necessary."

"Good." Siljar waved a hand in dismissal. "Now I believe your work here is done."

"As you wish."

Walking like he had a stick shoved up his ass, Kostas managed to make it to the door before Siljar halted him.

"Kostas."

He glanced over his shoulder, his eyes cold with thwarted fury.

"Yes?"

"I will not be pleased if I learn Jaelyn has been harmed," she warned softly. "Indeed, I shall take it quite personally."

For a crazed minute, Ariyal thought that the vampire might do something incredibly stupid. Then, gripping his hands into tight fists, he gave a nod of his head.

"I understand."

The Ruah disappeared from the room, and unable to deny his overwhelming instinct another second, Ariyal crossed the floor to pull Jaelyn into his arms, his gaze never leaving the Oracle.

Siljar might have protected Jaelyn from Kostas and the rest of the Addonexus, but that didn't mean she wasn't going to do something even worse.

If he'd learned nothing else in his long life it was *If something seemed too good to be true . . .*

Wiping her hands down her robe, the Oracle gave a tiny shudder.

"Such a ghastly demon."

Styx stepped forward, offering her a deep bow. It might have been strange to see the massive vampire showing such respect for the tiny demon. At least until you looked into Siljar's dark eyes.

Her power simmered like a nuclear explosion just waiting to happen.

"You cut that a little close, Siljar," he said. Gently.

Ariyal felt Jaelyn stiffen in his arms, her gaze shifting to the Anasso.

"You knew Siljar was coming?" she demanded.

It was the Oracle who answered.

"Styx approached me when he discovered the Ruah intended to seek you out."

Styx shrugged. "I couldn't by law keep him from returning you to the Addonexus and putting you to death," he admitted, his eyes narrowing. "Something that I obviously need to correct in the near future. Only an Oracle could prevent the inevitable."

"I'm deeply grateful."

Ariyal frowned, studying his mate's pale face. He knew that voice. And it usually meant danger.

"We're both in your debt," he added.

Without warning, Jaelyn was out of his arms and flying across the room to slam her fist into Styx's arm with enough force to make him stumble to the side.

"Damn you."

"Ouch." Styx grabbed his arm, his expression more bemused than angry. "Is that any way to treat your king? A king, I might remind you, who just saved your pretty neck."

"I was scared shitless." Jaelyn planted her fists on her hips. "You could have given me a little heads-up."

Ariyal folded his arms over his chest, in full agreement with his mate.

Although he wasn't foolish enough to take a swing at the King of Vampires.

"Kostas has his position as Ruah for a reason," Styx reminded the glaring Jaelyn. "He would have sensed deceit the moment you entered the room."

Her jaw remained clenched, but it was obvious from her expression that Styx had a point.

"So is it over?" he demanded, moving to pull Jaelyn back

into his arms. He was fairly certain he was never going to let her go again. "Is she free of the Addonexus?"

Siljar turned the dark, disturbing gaze in his direction. "She is still under contract to me."

His brows snapped together. "What does that mean?"

Jaelyn jabbed him in the side with her elbow, nearly cracking a rib.

"Ariyal."

"I would prefer to know if someone is going to try and take you away from me," he growled.

"I have no intention of taking away your mate, Sylvermyst," Siljar assured him. "But I do reserve the right to call her to service should the need arise."

"Of course," Jaelyn hastily answered, as if fearing Ariyal might say something stupid.

Thankfully he was too overwhelmed with relief to say a word.

It was Styx who asked the question running through all their minds.

"Do you see the need arising anytime soon?"

Siljar gave a vague wave of her hands. "Without the prophet it is impossible to say, but we must assume that the Dark Lord will not abandon his attempts to destroy the barriers between worlds."

With an abrupt motion the King of Weres stepped forward, his expression troubled.

"We can't forget that in meantime two of my people are being held captive," he growled.

"Caine and Cassandra have not been forgotten." Something that might have been frustration touched the Oracle's face. "Unfortunately we have not yet found a way to reach them."

Salvatore scowled. "Or anyone willing to try?"

"As you say." The tiny demon heaved a sigh. "We will not give up."

Salvatore's attention shifted from the Oracle to the door, his eyes flashing gold.

"What is that stench?" he muttered; then he growled as he shot Ariyal a disgruntled frown. "You really need to be a bit more discriminating in who you invite into your home."

Ariyal rolled his eyes as he caught the unmistakable scent of granite. Hell, if he had his way, he wouldn't let any of them into his house. It was only to please Jaelyn that he'd let the vampire and Were over the threshold.

"My thoughts exactly."

Grandly indifferent to the fact he was intruding into a private lair, the tiny gargoyle breezed into the room, his wings flapping as he moved to take Jaelyn's hand and lift it to his lips.

"Bon soir, ma enfant."

Jaelyn smiled, not nearly as annoyed as she should be by the trespasser.

"Hello, Levet."

"It was very naughty of you to have a party and not tell me," he gently chastised, glancing toward Styx and Salvatore, who scowled at him with equal displeasure. "Unless of course my invitation was lost in the mail?"

"Something like that," Jaelyn hastily assured the ridiculous creature.

"I thought that must be the case. After all . . ."

His words trailed away and his tail suddenly stood out straight, making him look as if he'd been hit by lightning. Then slowly he turned, his gaze narrowing at the sight of the tiny demon who had remained in the shadows at the back of the room.

"You," he breathed, his expression stunned.

Siljar lifted her hand and the demon stepped forward. Ariyal blinked in surprise, belatedly realizing the gargoyle was looking like a lovesick sap at the sight of Yannah.

Jaelyn had mentioned the ridiculous gargoyle was

jonesing for the mysterious demon, but this went beyond the hope for a drink at the local bar followed by a quickie.

The poor bastard had it bad.

At any other time he might have been amused.

Now he just wanted them gone.

"Yannah," Siljar said in the stern voice only a mother could achieve. "Is there something I should know?"

The girl tilted her head in the exactly same manner as her mother.

"Not yet."

In a besotted daze, Levet moved toward her, his hands held out in pleading.

"Why do you run from me?" Levet demanded, his French accent thicker than usual.

She giggled. "Because I like to be chased."

"But I have much I want to say to you."

Yannah leaned forward, landing a kiss squarely on the gargoyle's mouth, her fingers running a teasing path over his quivering wings. Only when the gargoyle was ready to melt into a puddle at her feet did she pull back, her dark eyes shimmering with amusement.

"Then catch me."

With a pat on Levet's cheek the demon disappeared.

Really and truly disappeared.

Like there one second and gone the next.

Blistering French curses filled the air as Levet stomped his way to the door, his wings fluttering in a blur of shimmering color.

"Leaving so soon?" Ariyal demanded.

"Do not fear, I will return," the gargoyle promised, leaving the house in obvious pursuit of Yannah.

Ariyal wrinkled his nose. "That's my fear."

Seemingly indifferent to her daughter's peculiar taste in demons, Siljar pressed her hands together.

"I must leave as well." She allowed her gaze to sweep the

room. "But know this. The days of evil are not ended. The Dark Lord remains a constant threat, as well as his minions, who grow in number with every passing day. We must be prepared."

Her warning was still echoing through the air when she vanished into thin air.

"Cheery," Salvatore said with a shiver.

Ariyal didn't blame him.

He felt like doing a little shivering of his own.

"And right," Styx grimly pointed out. "We all know that the Dark Lord is still poised just on the other side of the barrier, waiting for the opportunity to escape."

"While his minions are infesting the world like a plague," Salvatore added.

Styx lifted a hand to stroke the tiny amulet hung around his neck.

"You know, I have a sudden need to be with my mate."

Salvatore abruptly grimaced. "Oh . . . there's something I forgot to mention."

Styx narrowed his eyes. "Why do I suspect I'm not going to like what you have to mention?"

"Because it has to do with our dearly beloved mother-in-law."

"Sophia?"

Ariyal lifted his brows at the edge of fear in the massive vampire's voice.

Or was it horror?

Salvatore looked equally disturbed by the talk of their mutual mother-in-law.

"Yeah," the King of Weres muttered. "Harley talked with her yesterday and it seems the bitch from hell, I mean . . . Sophia, has decided she wants to spend more time with her daughters."

"What do you mean, *more* time?"

A sudden smile curled Salvatore's lips. "She bought a new home just a few blocks from you."

Styx shuddered. "Oh no. Hell, no."

"Oh wait, it gets better," Salvatore promised. "She's opening a new strip club featuring vampires and pure-blooded Weres."

"A strip club." Styx threw his hands in the air. "I need something to drink. Preferably something that fights back."

Salvatore slapped the huge vampire on the back. "Me too."

"Then by all means, don't let the door hit you on the way out," Ariyal urged, more than eager to have some alone time with his mate.

Styx pulled back his lips to reveal his humongous fangs, going eyeball to eyeball with Ariyal before he gave a sharp laugh and glanced toward Salvatore.

"He's going to fit in just fine."

Salvatore smoothed a hand down his silk tie. "Always assuming we don't kill him."

"True enough."

"Out," Jaelyn snapped, pointing her finger toward the door.

Still smiling, the two most powerful demons in the world strolled out of the room, putting aside the heavy burden of their leadership to enjoy their fleeting moment of camaraderie.

Ariyal understood.

Completely.

The day of reckoning hadn't been avoided, merely postponed, and soon he might very well have to lead his people into war. For now he intended to grasp at any happiness the fates were willing to offer.

In fact, he intended to grasp a whole lot of happiness.

With a wicked smile he scooped his mate off her feet, his blood heating as her arms instinctively looped around his neck and her indigo eyes darkened with arousal.

"I thought they would never leave," he growled.

Running her tongue along her fully exposed fang, she snuggled against him.

"Now that we have this big old house all to ourselves, what on earth are we going to do?"

The mere thought of those fangs sinking into his throat had Ariyal rock hard and moving toward the sofa.

There was no way in hell he was making it to the bedroom.

And if that gargoyle waltzed through the door he was going to mount him over the mantle.

"Allow me to demonstrate, poppet," he murmured, laying her on the cushions. He forgot how to breathe as he took in the pale beauty of her perfect features and the river of raven hair that spilled free of her braid.

His exquisite Hunter.

His mate.

"You know, Sylvermyst, if you play your cards right I might allow you to demonstrate more than once," she promised, reaching up to rip open his shirt.

He chuckled as he tossed aside the hideous garment, leaning down until their lips were pressed together.

"I never could resist a challenge."

Dear Reader,

I hope you're enjoying the Guardians of Eternity series. I'll admit that I fell in love with the characters from the moment I sat down to write Dante's story in *When Darkness Comes*. And my passion has only deepened with every new installment. It's been a magical journey as the stories have unfolded and I've spent my days surrounded by a clan of beautifully lethal vampires, hot-blooded sexy Weres, and now the lost tribe of Sylvermysts. Oh, and one very charming gargoyle. What could be more fun?

Next up will be Caine and Cassandra's story, scheduled to be released in September 2012. I know many of you have been anxiously waiting for their book and I assure you that I'm having a fabulous time trying to tame Caine into a reluctant hero. I hope you'll take as much pleasure in his transformation as I am!

In the meantime I have several novellas that you might want to check out. They're all a part of the Guardians series with many characters you'll recognize, along with a few new ones I hope you'll welcome into your hearts.

In *Yours for Eternity*, coming in September 2011, my novella "Taken by Darkness" introduces Juliet Lawrence, a half witch/half imp who is resigned to being sought after for her ability to detect magical objects. But Victor, the clan chief of London, desires much more than her talent. He wants her in his bed—and the powerful vampire is accustomed to getting what he wants.

In *Supernatural*, also available in September 2011, my novella "Darkness Eternal" follows the vampire Uriel as he goes in search of Laylah's mother, Kata. He intends it to be a simple "snag and bag," but after being held captive by one vampire for four centuries, Kata has no intention of trusting a blood-sucking leech, even if he awakens an intoxicating desire.

In *The Real Werewives of Vampire County*, being published in November 2011, my novella "Where Darkness Lives" returns to Sophia, the mother of Darcy, Regan, Harley, and Cassandra as she settles in an elegant gated community in Chicago. Not surprisingly, it doesn't take long for one of her neighbors to want her dead, but she learns the true meaning of danger when her bodyguard, Luc, the wickedly delectable pureblooded Were, moves in to protect her.

And as a special bonus, Kensington will be repackaging and republishing my Immortal Rogues trilogy. Many of you may not be aware that I began my career writing Regency romances under the pseudonym Debbie Raleigh, or that the trilogy that included *My Lord Vampire* (coming in March 2012), *My Lord Eternity* (coming in December 2012), and *My Lord Immortality* (coming in 2013) were my first paranormals. They tell the stories of three heroic vampires who travel from their home beyond the Veil to Regency London to protect the women they love. You'll recognize Nefri from *Bound by Darkness* long before she meets the aggravating Santiago!

I also want to take this opportunity to thank all of my wonderful readers who have not only enjoyed the Guardians of Eternity, but also shared word of the series with all of their friends. It's because of you that I can continue this amazing journey, and I never forget that without you the Guardians would never exist. Thank you from the very bottom of my heart!

Best,
Alexandra Ivy

Books by Bestselling Author
Fern Michaels

___The Jury	0-8217-7878-1	$6.99US/$9.99CAN
___Sweet Revenge	0-8217-7879-X	$6.99US/$9.99CAN
___Lethal Justice	0-8217-7880-3	$6.99US/$9.99CAN
___Free Fall	0-8217-7881-1	$6.99US/$9.99CAN
___Fool Me Once	0-8217-8071-9	$7.99US/$10.99CAN
___Vegas Rich	0-8217-8112-X	$7.99US/$10.99CAN
___Hide and Seek	1-4201-0184-6	$6.99US/$9.99CAN
___Hokus Pokus	1-4201-0185-4	$6.99US/$9.99CAN
___Fast Track	1-4201-0186-2	$6.99US/$9.99CAN
___Collateral Damage	1-4201-0187-0	$6.99US/$9.99CAN
___Final Justice	1-4201-0188-9	$6.99US/$9.99CAN
___Up Close and Personal	0-8217-7956-7	$7.99US/$9.99CAN
___Under the Radar	1-4201-0683-X	$6.99US/$9.99CAN
___Razor Sharp	1-4201-0684-8	$7.99US/$10.99CAN
___Yesterday	1-4201-1494-8	$5.99US/$6.99CAN
___Vanishing Act	1-4201-0685-6	$7.99US/$10.99CAN
___Sara's Song	1-4201-1493-X	$5.99US/$6.99CAN
___Deadly Deals	1-4201-0686-4	$7.99US/$10.99CAN
___Game Over	1-4201-0687-2	$7.99US/$10.99CAN
___Sins of Omission	1-4201-1153-1	$7.99US/$10.99CAN
___Sins of the Flesh	1-4201-1154-X	$7.99US/$10.99CAN
___Cross Roads	1-4201-1192-2	$7.99US/$10.99CAN

Available Wherever Books Are Sold!
Check out our website at **www.kensingtonbooks.com**